PUBLISHED WORKS IN ENGLISH

"The Body of the Text." Translated by Catherine Duncan. *Polysexuality*, Semiotext(e) no 10 (1981; repr. 1995): 14–21.

Wanted Female. In collaboration with Sam Francis. Los Angeles: The Lapis Press, 1993.

Eden, Eden, Eden. Translated by Graham Fox. London: Creation Books, 1995.

Prostitution: An Excerpt. Translated by Bruce Benderson. New York: Red Dust, 1995.

Tomb for 500,000 Soldiers. Translated by Romain Slocomb. London: Creation Books, 2003,

Coma. Translated by Noura Wedell with an introduction by Gary Indiana. Los Angeles: Semiotext(e), 2010.

Independence. Translated by Noura Wedell. Los Angeles: Semiotext(e), 2011.

IN THE DEEP

SEMIOTEXT(E) NATIVE AGENTS SERIES

This edition Semiotext(e) © 2014
© 2010. Originally published by Éditions Gallimard in Paris, France under the title *Arrière-Fond*.

Published by Semiotext(e)
PO BOX 629, South Pasadena, CA 91031
www.semiotexte.com

Cet ouvrage publié dans le cadre du programme d'aide à la publication bénéficie du soutien du Ministère des Affaires Etrangères et du Service Culturel de l'Ambassade de France représenté aux Etats-Unis.

This work received support from the French Ministry of Foreign Affairs and the Cultural Services of the French Embassy in the United States through their publishing assistance program.

Special thanks to Mary Kallem and Marc Lowenthal.

Cover Photography: Pierre Guyotat in Joubert, Fall 1952. Bibliothèque Nationale de France—Manuscript department.

Page 1: Pierre Guyotat, in the waves in Raguenès, France, 1947.

Back Cover Photography: Catherine Hélie
Design: Hedi El Kholti

ISBN: 978-1-58435-161-0
Distributed by The MIT Press, Cambridge, Mass. and London, England
Printed in the United States of America

PIERRE GUYOTAT

IN THE DEEP

Translated by Noura Wedell

Preface

After *Formation* (untranslated, 2007), which was not a memoir of childhood but rather the narrative of the formative years of a child who would give his life to creation, I wanted to concentrate my powers of memory, empathy, and poetry on my fifteenth year.

Among other "facts"—a Creator God, a Redemptive God, Virgins, paternal conflict, maternal friendship before my mother would disappear three years after this narrative, the Cosmos, History, girls, women, boys, girls again, Nature, animals, the ruins of war, the circus, and especially, through Poetry, the sex organs of women—we will encounter here the history, the description, and the explanation of a practice called the "beat-sheet." Since the sketched description I made of it in 1972 in "The Body of the Text" where I signaled that I'd already given it up, it has elicited and continues to elicit, both abroad and in France, erroneous interpretations, distortions, not to mention the gossip of a memorialist with a crude and impounded memory.[1]

Rather than follow chronology, as I'd done for *Formation*, I proceeded here with days, often long, followed by their nights, which occurred between the end of June and the end of August of the year 1955.

I could make mine today the troubles, torments, impulses, wisdom, logic, and the attraction of the Absolute, as they are expressed and set to music here—in each scene all the themes announced at the overture are taken up, and delved into (the gestures of the scene make them come out)—with greater wisdom, greater knowledge, and perhaps greater pain and hope—but with less Faith?

You will also see that the language that I use, as classical as it may appear, is no less mine for that (from *Tomb for Five Hundred Thousand Soldiers* to *Progeny* [*Progénitures*, untranslated]).

In this text, where I have tried to do justice to the intensity of the internal and external events of an adolescence that was distressed, a distress further abetted by my parents, and by the belief that I only half-lived these events, or lived them

---

1. Guyotat read the original "Langage du Corps" at the 1972 Artaud-Bataille conference at Cerisy. A shortened English version by Catherine Duncan was published in *Polysexuality* (New York: Semiotext(e), 1981).

very little, the rift is raw between the open act of poetic creation and the clandestine act of the "beat-sheet"—before it grows resolved into a single text in *Tomb for Five Hundred Thousand Soldiers*.

That clandestine act slowly produced an imagery, a decor, a people, and an idea that was impossible to confess at the time and that I here name the "deep."

Since then, I have acknowledged that world quite well.

—Pierre Guyotat

From where did I enter the high room? Through the door or through the window after a gliding descent from the summer sky and the blue summits down toward the earth that is ready for harvest? Am I standing or lying on my stomach, pockets closed on my clandestine objects—and by what?

This, in the ancestral home, is the bedroom of the main engenderers: a tiled, pre-Revolutionary floor rises up from the door to beneath the window where I am recovering from my flight.

Nothing remains of the First French Empire furniture and décor, above the white marble chimney and in the alabaster lintel of the trumeau mirror, but the naked adolescent, a robe—a *chiton*?—draped over his arm, who offers, or offers himself, small member erect, to a seated hirsute satyr and to a standing goddess: the scene drops into the mirror in which I also see part of my mother's face embedded, with her ancient, very dark, young Polish girl hair.

Will the house, three quarters of which have been destroyed, last long enough for her to speak to me?

I squat on the tile floor below the central beam along which the taut lacing of Jocaste's black rope stretches out. At fifteen and growing rapidly, am I as tall as I am today, or am I still my old height?

Before me is the large *lit bateau* with the rounded waves of its headboard and its gilded medallions where they used to take me between them as a small child: is it her, alone, wheezing, collapsed inside the sheets? I'd like to straighten my back and position my ear to be able to detect the small bursts of bone from the illness she is dying of, but her voice rises ever so soft and limpid from the mass of light and sheets: I don't hear the words and sentences, all I hear is a questioning music in which I understand that she's worried about what she'll have to pronounce to her Judge in the afterworld to be admitted.

Why does she ask me, her son, the fourth of their six children, for the words she needs to wholly justify her before a God who is Completely Whole?

Of the several poems I had already written—the first of which now feels so distant—and that she read over my shoulder, I had just barely finished the second-to-last line.

Having risen to my feet I leave the room; what wakes me? Is it the clinking of disjointed tiles beneath my feet on the second-floor landing?

Asleep again, my feet leaving the same red tiles, I walk down the stone staircase, its walls adorned with historical engravings, in the direction against the flow of Time; at the top of the highest steps, Modern Times, at the bottom, Antiquity. In the entrance, through the double doors opening onto the dining room where portraits of ancestors lean down from the high flowered walls toward the large table, I see the family carve and eat a large, bloody roast: death makes you hungry.

I wake again, but to the extinguished lighting of the dormitory on this morning at the end of June 1955: should I fall asleep again so that, dreaming, I can appease the palpitations and the weeping that I can only emit in dreams because I sleep in the dormitory?

What is this dream of agony? How can I return to it, to examine the faces, the face of that woman who was collapsed upstairs, in the large bed of generations, more beautiful than she was when she stood amongst us, the face of those sitting at the table around the meat, and the face of my father whose tears are being diluted in blood?

Awake now, I head to the shared sink: my thick hair reaches down to my cheeks; I dip my head under the faucet; the tears brimming at my eyelids are now streaming down to the porcelain drain; no sob no shaking shoulder: I keep them back, like in the dream not knowing Who is before me!

Washed and dressed, in the stairs where we are exempt from standing in linc on Sundays, I hold her last letter tight in my fist and in the pocket of my shorts—from which I strip for Mass, to slip into the pants uniform.

On the landing, I pull it out, open it, and read it again: having written it three days ago, how could she have been already preparing herself for death? Yet, on my father's prescription paper, these lines in her calm handwriting, the ink slightly bleeding into the sweat of our games and our daily exertion: "…Your father is tired and we live day to day; and so, my darling, take patience, accept that you must work on subjects that you don't like; after the baccalaureate, you can realize your dream, poetry…" The palpitations come on again, grow stronger until I reach the golden bronze doors of the big chapel, and only abate with the Latin words of the Transubstantiation, the descent of the Holy Ghost onto the earthly species.

After the small communion Mass, in the dining hall, Eric, sitting across from me, his long blond hair hiding the bowl where he laps his *café-au-lait*, juts his foot into my knee.

If only he were a girl, with her breasts on the table!

We go outside to walk in the playgrounds, in the courts where the little ones still rub at their eye sockets, in ours, the junior courts, and in the senior courts, where some children of Algerian Pieds-Noirs, darker than we are—and sent to Metropolitan France by their parents to escape the "events"—take out their knives and flip them open.

Alongside the Middle School, with their perfume, the trees in bloom, the grass gone to seed, and the high flowered stems encroach on the stench of sulfur that rises from the Gier valley, from the factories, the affluent rivers, and the bodies of workers.

In the vast drawing room, beneath the central attic of the school, Eric, several other students, and I take out our charcoal sketches. On the desks and easels are our unfinished drawings of sculpture "in the round"; in front of us, busts, Athena with a helmet, Ceres with her hair pulled back, Titus and Nero's frizzy and curly heads, or Cicero, bald.

Through the low windows level with the floor, we watch the city, its smoke uninterrupted in the Sun beneath which our same-age brothers are already living and working, pale-skinned children who fuck well and speak with a lewd tongue.

Once we've finished the chin of Athena, the bangs of Titus, that destructive "darling of the human race," the butcher of Jerusalem and a trader of Jewish slaves, or the matricidal mouth of Nero, we walk down to the High Mass in golden tunics: some parents are taking communion. They have come to get their children for the afternoon, children who, after having fasted since sundown, are eating a better breakfast than usual in a small dining hall separate from ours.

Finally, during study, I can continue my work on the reverie of *Saül*: after a *Moses* that I wrote under the spell of a poem by Alfred de Vigny about the solitude of the one who thinks for others, now, because I am tormented by my growing body and my shrinking Faith, it is Saül, the first king of Israel, into whom I enter to understand him and make him speak.

After lunch, we run to our courtyard with a few close friends for a game of soccer.

Are *bad thoughts* more fertile than good ones?

Between passes, I compose my first stanza: my lips, mouthing the first alexandrine verses, open for the call-outs of the game.

Our sweat is still warm, the back of our shirts is black with it, and our calves are tight when Eric and I run to the angle of the white fence that seals the school off to the east. On the other side of the communal byroad leading to the foot of the Paraque-ue Cross, the only daughter of the teacher of pagan rhetoric, who teaches the upper classes and whom we'll have next year, sometimes appears on the terrace of a millstone house blackened by charcoal soot but surrounded by flowering ivy.

Our members erect in our shorts against the concrete of the railing, we see her pass behind a wide-open window wearing a flowered dress; some ivy, then another window, and then we see her cleavage as she parts the dress open to the side with one hand on the shoulder strap. My left hand and his right hand brush against each other along the concrete, his slips into my left pocket, mine into his right; both pockets have holes—each of us has ripped his own: our members bare in the shorts; do we look into each other's eyes, when the hand of one caresses and grasps the member of the other? Mine is circumcised; his is uncut.

But it's from her, from the pink silk hugging her sides which, arms raised, underarms open, hands joined above a red pony tail, she swings to the sound of a ballet dance, from her and from us looking at her and desiring her each in his own way, he already for her *sex*, I for her breasts, that our members jut through our fists.

When vacation comes, as we sort through the dirty laundry, I wonder how I can explain this hole, this torn pocket to my mother?

Already, in the back of the attic to the side of my room at home, where I return two days a month, on the opposite, southern side of the Mont Pilat, under a heap of wood and rags so dusty they seem the ashes of death, I hide a pad of paper on which I've flattened an old cloth made of a shredded bathing suit with side laces on which some sperm has dried— and, during school breaks and on vacation, I slip this aggregate mass between the box spring and the mattress of my bed: for me, it's both paper that has been written on and carnal remains, my Attila's meat.

I don't want pleasure from it, but desire: to go further, to *sow* fear.

Even if this Eric, who is completely blond with nearly purple lips, and whose ass rises beneath his palms between the passes of the soccer ball, whispers to me that we love each other, I refuse to believe that no girl will love what I have become: instead of the head and body that were formed as I grew in the torment of poetry, I would rather have the head of Jean, from the film *Before the Deluge*, the only son of an abusive mother, but who, as an adolescent, still had the head that nature could have kept for me from childhood, classic features, a straight nose, a fleshy pout, common charm pleasing to all and easy to produce even at the top of a naked body. Do I dare prefer myself in him, who is an accomplice to two murders, the worst of which is the murder of a Jewish friend?

After the evening study, where, several desks away from Eric, I pull from my fresh innards and the dinner which has filled them something that might provoke Saül's more ripened guts against his God who has turned away, we race back to our courtyard awash in red dusk. Friends, back from Lyon by train, drag us under the covered playground into the dark angle of the storehouse where the richest among us take a supplement of sugar.

The sand combined with dirt on the floor lifts when they pry open the girlie magazines for us: what are those red entrails, agape, gleaming, viscous, venomous, that shake our shoulders into a strangled laugh?

* * *

Near the end of July of the same Summer 1955, from Bourg-Argental where I was born on January 9, 1940, beneath the great chestnut tree with its large buds that turn clammy in springtime like a jerked member, in the afternoon, my backpack on my shoulders, I take the Garampazzi bus for Châteaucreux, the train station in Saint-Étienne: I have three days to get to Belford in northern Northumberland, England, below the Scottish border.

Dorothy B., an English friend of my two paternal aunts, Suzanne and Lily, who was a nurse with them on English and

French Asian-bound ocean liners, is waiting to bring me to the cottage she shares with her husband Norman and her father, a retired gardener for the Queen, at Bamburgh-on-the-Sea, their yearlong residence.

My father, who loved me as a child yet has been scoffing for a year, sneering, jolting, and even insulting my fast-growing body, judging me in private and in public as incapable of any logical action, and furiously pointing out my clumsiness, lets me leave alone on a long and complicated voyage: ferry, borders, change.

Is my ticket from Saint-Étienne to Belford or do I just have the ticket from Saint-Étienne to London, which includes the ferry? I have enough to eat for the first night and the first day.

I settle into the train for Paris-Gare de Lyon but I have to change trains during the night at Saint-Germain-des-Fossés.

At Saint-Germain-des-Fossés, two policemen enter an empty compartment at the end of the car, one of them handcuffed to a man in a beret.

In the newspapers and in our region I have come to know the faces of collaborators, targets of public hate: faces gaunt with silent brooding—remorse? or sunken in the assertion of their crime?—with worry in the crowd, diverted stares, and maybe the grimace of those who made no mistake and whom future events will vindicate.

With my heart, my faith, and my reason I side with the reprobate: what more can I give him, passing through the hallway, than my smile through the glass? How can I make him understand that I am smiling at the reprobate, not at the informant and assassin? A policeman immediately pulls down the blinds.

And what if he were a rapist, a child murderer…?

Leaving Nevers, half asleep, a big bird hits against the side of the compartment: is it an owl—Tawny Owl or Little Owl—the kind with lice? Should I wait for the train to slow down between the ruins of La Charité, and push it toward the open window and freedom? Or should I capture it—but in what box or cage? I only have my bag—and bring it along to England, as companion, eye, and eyelid of Wisdom to my shameful torment?

Having arrived at the Gare de Lyon in the morning, I go down into the subway toward the Saint-Lazare station. The first time I rode the subway was last year, when I took it twice with my aunt Suzanne: changing trains in Bastille, a destitute man in the corridor stops me and I give him five francs, a third of my pocket money for the trip.

The train for Dieppe leaves in the middle of the afternoon. I have time to see the train station and its glass roof painted by Monet, to walk around the neighborhood of *Europe* and the *rue de Liège*. I know that Georges Duhamel lives here. He is a wartime friend of Charles Viannay, our maternal great-uncle to whom Duhamel dedicated *Civilization*, and in whose family home in Brittany the writer spends his summer vacations, with us, whom he has to quiet down at dinner.

The train runs along the valley of the Seine, passes through Rouen, repeatedly destroyed between 1940 and 1944, and, in the afternoon, reaches the city of Dieppe that is in the midst of reconstruction after the bombings and dynamiting of the war.

It takes the entire summer night to cross over to Newhaven. In Newhaven, the train for London waits in the fog; the subway is complicated, the tube flashy, from Victoria Station to King's Cross Station, where the trains leave for northern England: I don't take the subway until the end of my journey: and so I walk through Westminster, visiting funeral monuments to William Shakespeare, the Brontë sisters, and Charles Dickens, along the banks of the Parliament, in Saint James Park, Trafalgar Square, Piccadilly, and Soho where I take the tube again.

In King's Cross, I buy my ticket, in two parts, for Belford via Newcastle-upon-Tyne. In the train toward the romantic North, map in hand, I move from the corridor window to the compartment window to see as much landscape as possible, as many hills, streams, rivers, woods, forests, villages, and towns, as many places and place names for sites of battles, treaties, plots, loves, and lost power. After Nottingham, the railway runs alongside the border of the Black Country, Sheffield. It's only when we get to York that green encroaches on the black. Nature opens up more and more: the velvety green of the hills, sharp sinuous valleys, the smell of the sea through the open window and in an empty car; in Newcastle, the stationmaster rushes me through the quick change of trains and the railway gains on the sea and the Sun lowering onto it, partly hidden by the train smoke hugging the ground.

In the nearly emptied car, the ticket controller sits across from me and tells me, slowly so that I can understand, how tonight he will go home, find his ailing wife, sick with an incurable disease, and his children, one of whom is my age— I hear the wheels of the wheelchair digging into the gravel of the courtyard and the feet of happy children around it. He lowers his cap over eyes bright with held-back tears. May I caress the empty hand on his knee?

In Belford it is night. On the platform, Dorothy, whom I've only seen as a child upon the return of her friend Suzanne, our father's sister, from the Nazi camps in 1945, hugs me with her long arms: "How you look like your father!" I frown. With Susan, her younger sister, beautiful in a light, flowered dress, we head to a small inn—with a library and a piano—to drink hot chocolate. On the way, on a illumined vacant lot near a circus tent that shirtless boys are securing against the wind, I catch a glimpse of a girl in an acrobat or horse rider leotard, her left buttock bare and pale and sunken like her cheek, bare-foot in the low grass where the sea mist is pulling back toward the wheat fields.

Susan's black sedan is driving toward the North Sea. Between Seahouses and Bamburgh, along the dunes at the entrance of Bamburgh whose fortress appears blacker than the black sky, the cottage is open and lit up.

They sit me down at a guéridon to eat a black stew. All of them are sitting or standing to watch me eat: Mr. Praundlock,

Dorothy's father, with his gray vest, his red face and his gray-red hair, Susan, Dorothy, Norman her husband who works for the British Railways, and their two children, Alison and Anthony, a blond and troubled boy.

They set me up in a room adjoining the veranda open onto a garden at the back of which a palm tree waves its palms. After a warm water bath, I lie on the bed, and on my stomach, my notebook on the bolster pillow, I transcribe the notes I've numbered in my memory—more than thirty since the bus in France, and shaken by the trip, how many do I recall?

I turn off the light: in the human silence and the sound of the sea I feel my *growth* growing in my legs, in my hips, in my torso, shoulders, arms, wrists, and neck—is it growing in my brain? Have I grown by inching so far north?

Will I tomorrow, or after tomorrow, so close to Scotland, finally meet the young girl or young woman whom I want—and give her children?

On the day side of night, sleepy and dreaming, as a hand opens my pajamas and slides toward my erect member, I tip over to the right—what might the hand do to the ass?—but it renews its movement toward the dip of the thigh and with it a soapy warmth leans over me, toward my back, my shoulder, my neck and cheek; the hand lifts the testicles, grips the member along with them; a deep, hoarse voice, muffled with small sharp upturns, brushes against my left ear: "…your cock…," descends as breath to the left corner of my mouth, itch against itch. In the dream from whence I hear and feel this voice and this caress, there are only wheat fields, the edges of towns. No one speaks like this except in my imaginary when I'm awake, and on the sheets of paper of what I call "orgiastic writing," and where, a simultaneous masturbation leading me to a maximum of truth, confession, and poetry, I compose "brothel" scenes.

I reason in the dream: if what I hear and feel is not there, it must come from somewhere else; and I try in the dream to reach that place: to force my legs to move toward the hovel in front of which, on the sidewalk, a striped mattress slides under the thrusts—a dirty, naked foot settles there like a finger? Should I go back to the wheat fields where I think I've left my shoes, black in the blond? I forego the search to excavate and make an inventory of my backpack, and assemble my effects, which carries the dream to its climax and propels me out of it.

Anthony's face is above mine. But, my head lifted and knocking against his, with my natural vision, without corrective lenses, I can only see his blurry hand on my blurry sex: "It's not for you."

I can't see if he's naked or barely clothed, but I pull the sheet back over myself, and fall asleep again. Later, still asleep, on my left I see my brother's bed in our attic room in Bourg-Argental. I leave the attic, walk down the dark stone staircase toward the kitchen to drink some water—I drink a lot of it at the time—and I leave the cottage toward the moonlit road that runs along the dunes and sea. The honking of a red truck, carrying a heavy load, wakes me up at the side of the road, against the fence. The attic room of the cottage where Anthony and his family live is lit. I linger to watch the hares run and jump on the dune that has solidified in places. Are the sea swallows already leaving their caves, face to the open sea, toward our African lands in insurrection?

In the morning, early, breakfast—jelly, repulsive leftovers from the war—a run in the dunes toward the sea, a swim, and a visit to the village, the huge castle of the ancient kings of Northumbria. Anthony takes a while to join us, but with his eyes locked on mine, he licks some jelly from his pink lips.

In the afternoon, I go for a walk alone with Dorothy in the partly wooded hills to the west of the village. The smell of wheat wafts up toward the green slopes and the flowering undergrowth. Alternating between English and French, Dorothy tells me how much she loves the two sisters, my paternal aunts, the eldest Lily lost to the horror of generalized cancer two years ago, Suzon heroic under torture on Avenue Foch and surviving Ravensbrück; heroes as well, brothers and sisters of my mother whom she knew in Paris before the war, Hubert, the youngest, dead of hunger and beatings during deportation, on the human pyre of Sachsenhausen-Oranienburg.

Bees, bumblebees, birds and horses accompany with their lisping, their cries and neighing, her tale of crossings: Suez, the Red Sea, the Horn of Africa, the Indian Ocean, and the China Sea. In his small tower with windows of stained glass, a Major in the Indian army, in a whisper fluted through the edge of his very ancient lips, tells me about the 1919 Amritsar massacre in Punjab: I can't understand whether or not he was among the officers of General Dyer who abandoned the people in agony, without any medical help. But since he claims to have known Rudyard Kipling and maybe the original Mowgli—but there were so many of them running naked in the jungle—I decide to see him again.

The whole family congregates for tea, and during the evening, once they've prepared my dinner, which I eat on the guéridon among them in the living room, everyone reads, knits, plays on the floor, soft-voiced dialogues occur. I've heard this is what happens in the English home: tolerance, freedom for all, and self-mastery.

In the early evening, I settle into an armchair beneath a shelf with what I take to be a radio, with a screen; my legs are spread wide, I'm wearing gold corduroy shorts with wide cuffs, I'm dreaming—about what I'll paint tomorrow, about poetry, parallel to the *Saül* that I started before my trip, about Nature and water. A hand, that same night hand, inches up my thigh, creeps beneath my shorts; I cross my legs: the hand is caught; the wrist and forearm with its large silver watch pry the thighs apart, and Anthony, crouching before me, gazes at me with his blue eyes: "…your cock, Pierre…" From the far end of the living-room, Susan, with a soft, amused tone: "Don't wear Pierre out, Anthony, he's tired from his travels. You'll be together tomorrow." The grandfather coughs, raises his arm and lowers it, then rises, walks toward us, and loosens the bind. "Pierre, will you come see the pea plant I've created for Her Majesty the Queen?" Dorothy comes down from upstairs: "Father, will you leave our Pierre alone, you can show him tomorrow."

I settle next to them opposite the screen: an image appears: a speaker announces, with pursed lips, that the French government has created a new faraway entity: the French Southern and Antarctic Lands—including the Clipperton Island—from territory taken from the British.

After the news, a live concert from Edinburgh, the pianist Solomon performing Beethoven's Fifth Concerto, *The Emperor,* sound's conquest of space: isn't the expression of power, of powers—even in Art—wrong after what the World and its humans have suffered? Shouldn't that be left to Nature, to the Cosmos?

One day, I'll make words penetrate space…

As I start on the stew at the guéridon, I learn that we are going hiking in the Cheviot Hills in three days, and that we'll spend a day in Edinburgh the week after, but that I'll have to learn to play cricket before that.

Tomorrow, Sunday, Norman and Dorothy will take me to the Catholic Mass in Belford, then join the family in Bamburgh for the Anglican service, and return to Belford afterward to pick me up.

I say I just want to go to Saint Aidan: Dorothy reminds me that a letter from my mother recommends that I attend Catholic Mass. I answer that since I want to become English, I should begin with religion—here, Anglican. Dorothy has announced that we'll have lunch with the reverend and his children. I can already imagine two or three of them, girls and boys, bending their blond, tormented heads behind the colored windows of the Parsonage over large notebooks heavy with precocious writing, as if imbibed for life with the humors of inspiration and a juvenile passion.

I go to bed. Discretely, Dorothy places a key on the table on which I've set my limited gouache and watercolor supplies, a sketchbook, and mid-sized sheets of paper; I keep my notebook, the sheets of poetry and the rest locked in one of my backpack pockets with buckles, at the bottom of the bag.

With her gone and back upstairs, I take the key and insert it into the lock to the door of my room: it fits. I lock the door securely.

Lying down, I take my poetry notebook from the bag against the bed, and touch the tattered rag in which I'd folded the current "orgiastic pad," four days ago, at the door of my attic room, deep in the bottom of the right pocket of my golf pants, and which, in the bus from Saint-Étienne, with my heart already racing with the turns of the road, I'd pulled from that pocket to stuff deep into the bottom of my backpack. Touching this ball of secrets makes me hard, and even more the rushed feeling of what I'll write in it, later, at midnight, in the hour of immunity, of suspended social time—no evictions—or tomorrow.

Lying on my back, I leaf through the notebook, look at the uninterrupted poetry—with the other writings, it's already the memory of my life, a certainty of existence, the proof of my will and reason against my father and against myself and against all the models that I read or hear about; it's also a way for me to be united with the world. Turning on my stomach, I sketch a few more lines, a bit greener. I take out the sheets of numbered notes; now, having put it all back in the bag, will I prepare myself for the midnight operation?

First, lower the beating of my heart: is there a pillow in the dresser? (I didn't hang my clothes there yet, wanting to keep their mass to shield my ball of secrets at the bottom of the backpack.) Could I make a jizz cloth with side straps by tearing the rag? But isn't that raggedy swimsuit sometimes a piece of family linen used for the scrubbing brush? It's too private: I need something public, municipal dregs, without any indication of origin, rags from a garage, from a dumpsite; wait for tomorrow then to find and take some without being caught. I turn off the light. After a short rap on the door, Anthony, his new French breaking along with his voice: "Pierre, Pierre, open up… I want to get in bed with you."

I don't want him: my erection is for my ball of secrets, for what will be added there tonight or tomorrow; my erection is for the *whorehouse*, for the slightly defiled *pin-up* that appears there—hip-hugging the doorjamb—and for other hounded forms—not for a private body, almost familial, a schoolboy. Once again, "Open up, Pierre… I'm bored in my own body…

open up... please..." He who is usually so light, restless, unpredictable, a teaser, why is he so tenacious and mopey? What does he want from me? There are plenty of boy members along the entire shore, during the day on beaches and in the dunes, at night in cottages and camps; that boldness that has him rummaging through my shorts could make him jump fences, climb over walls.

It's not a boy I want to lie next to me, but a girl, a woman; not a member unsheathing as red as a dog's, but breasts.

Now his fingers are rubbing against the door, slowly at first, then fast, as if he were giving a handjob, his other fist churning the porcelain doorknob. In his voice I can hear the beating of his heart placated by the suspension of night, with the little squeals of its teenage cracking—do voices break earlier in England?—and on his breath is a question in English, words I don't yet know but which I guess are asking if I'm "spraying" yet—as we say "your cock sprays" in France. Will I tell him yes, but that it's not for him, whom I imagine growing tame around seventeen and thickening when time comes for the wedding? What would I do with his pretty, athletic body in the hazy depths of my "whorehouse": maybe I could use his voice, with its melodious York accent, slackening and thick in the work of the deep, with bursts of shrill sound?

But I'm already done with sex: I'm elsewhere now, and look and listen and feel and touch the deep.

I hear him go back upstairs; I want to fall asleep immediately instead of a repeated drop into the pit, but the thought of the whorehouse is stronger than my fatigue: I must push on through that place, have the figures come up, have sex, and speak.

Steps in the stairway, on the living room floor, in the short hallway leading to my room and to the veranda. I listen: breath against my door, the noise of joints moving: a sheet of paper slips beneath the door near the bed. Once the light is on again, on the left of the sheet of paper, I see a drawing of a member with its testicles. And at the bottom of the left side of the paper, the sentence: "Draw me yours." Although I could play the game for the fun of it, follow it and amplify it, I'm bored: what does he promise that could compare to what I penetrate at night? What gesture would my need *to write at the risk of desolation* be reduced to? In what pleasure would he annihilate my words? Even if it's only brief, I am already imagining and writing public, paid sex, public sexual submission. What kind of sex could two young vacationers have, in a family bed, even if they do speak different languages…?

I take the sheet of paper: later or tomorrow, in the shadow of the somewhat greasy palm print on the bottom of the page, I might transcribe parts of my "orgiastic writing," the insults of the "whorehouse," draw a speech bubble, like in a comic strip, with a sketch of lips along the filthy contour of the print, and write the narrative on clean checkered lines, pillars of schoolboy innocence.

But the trip from sea to land, and the shift from nation to nation, language to language, body to body has disrupted my *feeling* of the "whorehouse." Is the act of the beat-sheet now ridiculous? What, indeed, is this small personal ritual compared to the cosmic distance, the phantom of civilizations, and the abundance and strength of other languages, among a people whose bodies still have the reputation of being vigorous and calm since they've built the Empire and won the war? Apart from translating into Greek, Latin and English, I can only write in my own language, so frail beneath my fingers.

I have to reestablish that feeling by tracing a few words on the right paper in this still "foreign" room, under the threat of a new family and careful to hide this from the friends who welcome me—with respect—and trust me. Should I open the door? Since I am still a child, to slow down the speed of my heart I have a dialogue with Christ.

Although I have no desire yet for boys, and even less for this boy who parades his own desire too much, a desire that I foresee will not last, I know that if I turn the key in the lock my life could change.

What would he do to me? If he ejaculated, would he crash—and then, how could I chase him from the bed? At this point, I don't think of sin as original sin, or at least I don't think it's the sin of Adam and Eve, but rather the sin of God who has created all the objects and conditions of sin: Adam, Eve, the apple, and the serpent; the dust of the path that leads them, punished already, toward life.

Why does he want me to draw my member when he's known by hand its contour, its thickness in repose since the end of the day?

Should I draw and slip him under the door the private form—my *own* member, mine?—of what it seems that in my dark inner chamber a greasy hand traces with a flint or with a ball of color on walls that resonate with ever bigger ones, the hand oily perhaps from a dismembered carcass, a human body spread wide, or the gaping woman from the girlie magazine under the covered playground in the courtyard? Would I even be able to draw that thing he wants, an erect member, since I've never seen one, except for Eric B's in the spring—but did he take it out for me? I never see my own, because my hand churns it to extract its juice along with the extreme text, and because I watch the page of writing to write on and cross things out.

All I see of him, *in myself,* are blue eyes that reveal their violet hue when he reopens them, blond hair, and a voice: the rest is vague; this morning I swam with the adults of the house and with his sister, not with him: Should I imagine his naked body according to the body of his sister in a two-piece bikini jumping in the waves that crash against it?

Because he woke up late, I imagine that his nights are filled with another action than sleep, and that after bed perhaps he'll take me away from the cottage into an adventure; that way I'd completely take advantage of my stay, doubling my day life here with a night life elsewhere; and sleep off my lack of sleep on the boat home.

Where, for the sake of time, I'd dream about it strongly.

He, blond, I, brown-haired, we'd bike, hitch-hike or walk to a small circus we'd noticed the night before last in Belford…

The key is lying on the papers on the table because of the meandering gusts of the sea breeze. Instead of continuing to breathe against the door, why doesn't he push his body through the high, wide-open window? At the time, already, there is no private property for me, simply an intimate right over the place where we each exercise our conscience. So why continue to lock a room that doesn't belong to me? Why bar his entry, the child of the house? But if he crosses the threshold, if he enters the bed, if he takes my member, handles it, pulls from it what he wants to pull, I'll be like a female with her brood and no longer recognize him as mine.

But if I were to open the door to him, wouldn't I have to remember his entire body? As shortsighted as I am, I often imagine what I can't see: from the bed, thirteen feet away from the door, I wouldn't even see him clearly in the open door frame, and even in full light, or I'd have to shine light upon that body as if it were in a theater or in a movie shot; and even that wouldn't be enough, since I require sharp contours, a kind of linear absolute, symmetrical absolute, and an absolute enclosure: my eyes, my hands, my heart, my feet and sexual organs are already full of the desire and will to have reality explode and disappear from too much light. And to have me disappear along with it, for there is such violence against community in living and existing; and to make beauty disappear because it can't exactly be explained, because it is relative, contingent on civilizations, north or south, west or east, because if beauty exists there must be ugliness and ugliness is suffering and injustice; because at least for me, after climaxing I shift from one beauty to another in seconds, and the previous beauty takes on the mask of ugliness; because, since my eleventh year, what follows my climax has shown me the relativity of the beautiful and mostly its undreamed-of depth, its double nature, from that I understand that the religion of the beautiful is often the refuge of hypocrites, and that the beautiful cannot be separated from the rest, cannot be isolated, cannot be served as one would serve a deity when the world is burning all around.

Whereas my father, who foresees the permanence of my sexual indecision, persuades himself that all the rest of me has been struck by the same indecision, and ignores how thoroughly I think my poetry before I write it, how I labor over its lexicon, its rhythm, and even its layout on the page, I progress with method in the discovery of my art, starting from the beginning. Sometimes, in a single hour of study, I read French poetry from the Middle Ages to Symbolism so that I can undergo its evolution physiologically; then, in the space of a week, I read all of it again with other texts, retrace that same path but multiplied; and I do the same for painting with the few illustrated books that are around.

Perhaps because he thinks I'm only after my own pleasure, and that I'm disorganized even in that, and although he'd probably like poetry, my father can't imagine that I work to know it like a musician learns music; and he can't imagine how this body, mine, whose clumsiness and insufficiency he is always sure to notice, withstands and fosters a decided, extra*curricular* activity by exercising all of its senses, senses uprooted and enlarged by the growth of body and brain: an adult activity; and he doesn't even know that this open act that produces poetry is doubled by a clandestine one whose production ruins the first: the "whorehouse" ignores poetry, and the world does without; what I write there destroys all the moral and social foundations of art, culture, and poetry; and after I've written the "whorehouse" text with its ejaculation, the violent tear between both acts that I feel inside my guts only diminishes at the end of the following day, or even the next, according to the power and quantity of written text and ejaculated sperm.

I have no way of knowing if desire lasts longer with partners and without the production of text—in my own act, it takes three, four, five ejaculations before I crash—but from the novels I've read, the movies I've seen, or from what I've heard around, the very words "night of love" persuade me that the thing lasts a long time and that the partners wake up joyful; doesn't the text itself, and not ejaculation, produce the dreaded crash that is the starting point for my exclusion from the world: that tear seems to be the premise of future depressions.

I am always well composed; my face is always smiling, ready to break into laughter like my father's when he was young; especially here, I maintain the elegance of my origins; the lenses of my glasses cloud my stare, and despite the morass and idle daydreaming of adolescence, I am always on the move, running, swimming, watching, and laughing, and so that tear doesn't show—but can they hear it? Back at home in

France, my body tethered and my mind sluggish, constrained by the limits of an impossible dialogue, my heart re-enraged in the recomposed tribunal with our mother, already distant, as defense, what oozes through my own voice, what sound betrays the deep whose geography I conceal?

Back home, to hide the clandestine, in case our mother should ever discover the jizz wad, I think of writing the text, its interjections, in English—in German: in the language of the devil?—No, I want them in a sacred language, my mother's language. But where can I find the right words? If I asked Anthony, I wouldn't be bringing him into the shared secret of the act, but goading his desire; having him pronounce and search for the translation of my words would mean that we'd already be *making love*, and more deeply than the ordinary act of it: as if from behind the act, both of us puppeteers "pimping" an act committed by others.

Should I invent the words myself based on ordinary English terms for sexuality? Translation dictionaries don't handle such dangerous words yet; where can I find a medical dictionary here, so that once I've located the basic words, I can transform them? In Anthony's pronunciation, almost bored—even *professional*, as if he'd been repeating it for a long time—the word "cock" brings to my throat a kind of word—forgotten as soon as I think of it—that could only be pronounced in the deep, and would also take into account the echo of these widened vowels and consonants, and these respiratory market inflections.

I slip the paper back under the door; the hand pulls it toward the hallway. I turn off the light.

There is no longer any breathing against the door, but naked feet, their sweat clinging to the wax of the hallway floor. A draft flows from the outside door to mine. Lying in the dark on the folded sheet, I look at the full Moon: perhaps he'll pass into its rays, jump over the fence, and in other open cottages, slip the paper, my name crossed out and replaced by other names, under the door of boys he knows, whom he has already captivated or whom he desires—in order also to get close to their sisters and their sleeping *periods*.

What size is Mr. Praundlock's pea, lying in the veranda adjoining the bedroom?

During the Anglican service the next day in the village of Saint Aidan adorned with flags and banners, the choirs, young and old voices intertwined, revive the drama of the Eucharist.

Knowing that the reverend is married and that he fathered four children, when I see him walk up to the pulpit, lean his hands on the red velvet and tilt his beach-tanned face backward before speaking, with remnants of song still in my ears, I feel faint and nearly fall; although I don't know much, then, of the sexual act between man and woman, I imagine that these hands, this mouth, and this voice that is just now beginning to praise Christ, He who is so alone in his divine Ministry—there is such solitude in being a god among men!—have grown used to a woman, have satisfied her, have touched and handled forbidden parts, and secretions. Even as I glimpse his wife whom

Dorothy points out to me in the first row, a tall and somewhat gaunt woman with a mantilla under her hat, and remember that the Queen, who is still human despite her royalty, is the one who ordains priests and not, through the intermediary of the bishops, the Pope, Pierre's successor—although I accept the political justification of Anglicanism, I refuse the religious one—I am more tormented by the sacrilege and misfortune of prostitutes, bound by fate to pronounce the words of the human sacred, the words of motherly love, even those of ordinary charity and love with mouths and bodies soiled by paid tricks: in prostitution, it has never been the fact of giving one's body that torments me, as much as the imagined deprivation in which the same organs are used to do "evil" as to do good and say the beautiful; at night, with my then meager means, as I invent a free zone through which crowned shadows, skins—with no hair—pass and "expose" themselves, the sacrilege is in the ordinary, *household* usage of these organs, these desires, and these secretions whose existence seems to me at the time to depend on other creative instances than those of God: was it man himself who created them? I experience such extraordinary usage, in "prostitution," of these human creations as a return to God through excess, and my night text rises up against poetry as well as sermons against song!

For me, the prostitute is closer to God than the married priest: what distances one from God brings one closer to him.

My mother has written Dorothy that I sometimes quite suddenly leave places or assemblies, so when she sees me leave and

exit the church, she doesn't follow. I walk out into the cemetery around the church, very green with seagulls settling on
the gravestones; their cries are different than those of the
inland birds walking and running below the harvested wheat.

Beneath the smell of salt and heat I imagine a stench rising
from the tombs—English corpses, ghosts, and vampires; behind
me the door of the church opens onto the soft, sweet song which
precedes the Transubstantiation, the transformation of profane
species into divine, sacred ones, the body and blood of Christ:
why am I not inside to witness it? I wait for the chime of the
altar bells that accompanies the Transubstantiation, but how
can Christ resuscitate in the hands of someone who refuses
the filiation of Peter, a witness to Christ: what could be the
ideal music for such a vision—already at the time, the violin
solo known as the Transubstantiation from Beethoven's *Missa
solemnis* seems too profane and unworthy of the great remains?

…Having moved back to the porch, all I see is a single form
emerging from the shadows, a brown-haired girl in a light
dress with flowers and red flats walking toward me as I sit on
the granite wall on the perimeter of the churchyard; her eyes
are black. Through the door left ajar comes the noise of chairs;
is it time for communion? With both bread and wine?

She's from Brittany, and lives here at the edge of the row of
cottages near Seahouses. She's here on an "exchange": a boy
from the family with whom she's staying is now with her
family in Ille-et-Vilaine.

The large family is in the church.

She isn't "feeling well" and isn't very pious, so she left the church to get some air; a soft voice comes from under the very fine brown fuzz on her upper lip: "I've heard your family is very strait-laced."

I know the meaning of the term, but through the accelerated beating of my heart I think that she's referring to the lace collar Dorothy is wearing above her dark dress.

I get up to show her a pink marble tombstone: it belongs to a soldier who was in almost all of England's colonial campaigns in the second half of the nineteenth century; that this man's life sums up the entire history of England doesn't touch her at all; that her cheeks grow slightly pale, her eyes grow dark…; between the seemingly red-hot tombs, the imagined stench: she wants to sit again. Does that faint smell of rotting meat come from the red butcher shop below the churchyard on the other side of the street? Is it a cut of meat, or is it ground sausage filling? I am so used to smelling odors and perfumes even before entering the zone of their diffusion that I convince myself that seeing the red of the shop, with a faint trickle flowing out from a fissure in the corner of the building near the swollen tarmac, is what carries the stench to my nostrils from so far away. She turns toward me; the smell grows stronger as a crease forms on her dress near the top of her thighs, a crease that changes the beating of my heart into the beating of my member.

The stench persists after the families have said goodbye, as we return through the village to the parsonage: Anthony, walking between his father and mother, frowns when I look at him. If he asked me for a picture of my member now, I'd draw it erect; I have an urge to try my English with a question about the smell of rotten flesh that continues along the line of wrack, humid from the morning high tide; but my stutter stops me.

In the parsonage, with its long garden winding down to the edge of the dunes, the smell of roast rises up to the belvedere, three stories above the kitchen, where Anthony and I are looking out to sea through a golden copper telescope, guided by the reverend. Fishing boats with red sails and gray war boats move on the horizon; I'm searching for freighters from the commercial fleet that made the glory of England—are there any left?—toward the Baltic and Russia, from the time of the Merchant Adventurers, under Bloody Mary and Elizabeth the Great.

We see the waves, their troughs, and their foam. What do I see, immediately, before even observing anything? Mermaids and Oreads; is the lens amplifying the mermaids' songs and the frolicking of the Oreads? All I know of the Mediterranean I've learned through books and paintings, and with the midday sun hitting this northern Sea, which was tinted purple yesterday, I can imagine these beings frolicking at the foot of a Sicily that has jutted northward, and take a vertical, bluish cloud to be a cliff.

At lunch after Grace, the reverend's wife still wearing her hat, a young servant in a white apron carries in the roast, then a dish of boiled vegetables.

The reverend asks me what I think of the Pope, Pius XII. I answer that he likes and knows music: Wagner's *Forest Murmurs* and Mendelssohn's *Fingal's Cave*, written during a trip to nearby Scotland, and that perhaps the initial motion of its overture is a base for the mermaid's unknown song. He explains to me what I already know: that King Henry VIII broke with Rome because of a divorce that the pope refused. I see the hand of the reverend's wife advance along the tablecloth toward her husband's, his waist still fine yet his hair grey, like the hand of Anne Boleyn toward the king's: how can you break with a tradition that is nearly fifteen hundred years old, throw all your subjects into unrest and cause part of them to be persecuted for a "marriage problem"? I tell him that in France the Gallicanism of Louis XIV and others never led to a spiritual break. He reveals to me that a large part of the Anglican Church would be ready to renew with Rome, but I still see Anne Boleyn's head, three years after the marriage, roll from the scaffold into the basket: so much History for so little. Why want marriage when there is love: as king, he can love whom he pleases, and he can say and show it. Henry VIII, giant refined lover of pleasure, knows there will be others after Anne—I can list all of them; it's almost like the French trading posts in India. The king is above all representation and social pleasure.

The bloody roast, cut by the same hand that broke the sacred species, grows smaller with the appetite of the twelve guests sitting in the rays of sun coming in at a diagonal from the flowered bow window; it stands for the necks of all the king's favorites combined into one.

Under the table, Anthony brushes his leg against mine. I repeat my vision of the roast into his downy, salted ear—is the rest of his body as salty? He breaks into a laugh, as hoarse as a laugh from my *deep*: I start to think the deep has been diverted by the moving knees of the one who wants it next to him.

The servant brings the third dish: offal stuffing caught in small, smoking lamb-gut casings, with balls of lumpy mashed potatoes arranged around them. Anthony nudges me with his elbow and whispers English words which I hear in French: "They smoke and work a lot!"

The reverend announces that he'll lead the Vespers late in the afternoon. They'll sing a chorus by William Byrd and another, more modest chorus whose melody I'll recognize, he says, and if I wish, I can lend my voice to the voice of other children from the neighborhood. The mashed sand-grown potatoes are in the plate in front of me, encircling the stuffing freed from its casing, and the word *mash* comes to me, along with the mouth, surrounded by acne under the young fuzz, of a fellow student from Saint-Marie, our middle school, for whom it designates the lost sperm of the construction workers who are building the pool. As long as possible, I hold the mental and sensory vision of this friend among the workers, the sound of their cheery and brutal conversation in my ears among the soft, conventional babble of the table sanctified by ritual and by the active presence of the incumbent. Is the *deep* in fact joy?

Annick's silhouette behind the gothic panes of the bow window suddenly rises from among the smell of the lukewarm stuffing: will she come to Vespers? And will she then come into the sea with us, naked in a bathing suit (a one or two-piece suit?)—later, who knows, made of the same fabric as my jizz cloth…

In the garden, on the lawn between two rows of rosebushes, with their different smells, the conversation returns to the subject of Empire, the two Empires: although Dorothy regrets the crumbling of their Empire, the reverend asserts that all religions will find in it what they need. Mr. Praundlock, slightly dozing off in his red cheeks, mumbles that everything comes and goes, and Empires most of all: nature will live longer than humanity. Peas will perhaps grow the size of small lamb-gut casings, but they'll always taste like peas.

I hesitate between my desire and vision for an ultramodern humanity, wearing new materials, endowed with a universal language, common music, living in constructed dwellings with perfect architectural lines and full of automated objects, in a general nature, clean and geometric, with clearly signaled flora, fauna, earth, rocks, water, and my desire and vision for another humanity, naked or wearing loincloths, eating what its hands, feet, or mouths discover in a nature that is virginal and without machines, collective food, collective love. I hide those two extremes and also what I feel most strongly: the idea of a world where children and adolescents would choose other fathers than their life father, fathers of destiny—whorehouse fathers?—and so I say that the conquering powers, with their newly conquered territories still so young, should have invented, learned, and established a new political, administrative, and religious system that would be syncretic and artistic; that the West should have imported its social laws—although these laws were only nascent at the height of the colonial conquest—equality in the case of France, freedom in the case of England. I say that people today are demanding independence the way adolescents demand emancipation: both feel in their bones that their natural evolution is being repressed, and that authority is incessantly hovering over things that they know best. Am I not, myself, a colony of my earthly father?

The rose bushes shake, emit a more pungent smell, the blue of the sea turns to purple, shouts on the beach echo more sharply; at the bottom of the garden the sound of water falls on bushes and groves. Anthony and I head down there: his blue eyes open and close slowly; is it almost that time when he slips his hand into my shorts and grabs my member?

From the shadow of a palm tree a stout, sweating boy in light shorts, his white undershirt lying on the edge of the small window of the garden shed behind him, is using a thick black hose with a sparkling golden spigot to water bushes of red and pink hydrangea in front of blue borage plants resisting the flow of water.

Girlish shouts running along the wall: the boy, black hair in a bowl cut, stretches his neck toward the top of the wall, turns to us his smiling face, his mouth foaming slightly at the edges. Anthony, in a mix of English and French—did he learn some crude words last night in a room of vacationers?—and pointing with his finger, explains to me that the boy has a hard-on; Anthony wants me to stand in front of him, grab it and tell the boy that it's thicker than his jet of water, tell him that what is no longer in his head has moved down there; and all of this in French.

My heart beats in my ears: has he understood me? That this is the kind of thing that can be said in my deep: crude, cruel words in the smacking of bodies and in the friction of rubbing cloth: words of a supernatural tenderness that is prohibited to man? What can I do in this new place, under a foreign sky? How can I gather my wits as quickly as possible, and bring their parts back into my senses?

To hit him would mean to touch him, and he'd touch me in return.

As a child of the middle class—having no intention of text or art: nothing!—how can he show such social cruelty and make fun of such a beautiful *retard*?

The sound of a bike skidding on the tarmac: voices, fresh, before they've broken: Vespers already: how will I blend my voice, which has grown so deep, with their voices that are still so high? I climb alone to the house: did Anthony below grab the retard's member? The reverend, who has slept awhile, leads me to the fragrant church through the vestry with its Tudor furnishings.

The young choirboys fill the room, pulling on their white surplices. They have to practice the day's chants, then the

Magnificat and the *Nunc dimittis*; why would I sing when I've just refused to grab the young gardener's member? Why would I dare take out my voice, erect it, when I've just refused to *erect* the Word from my deep?

In the first motet, launched with a tenderness that is difficult for those growing bodies, I hear the two words *blessed virgin*. I remember: long ago, when I was ten, at Joubert, in the small clerical mountain school where I learned Latin and Greek, father Vallas, my beloved director, led his English class on the footpath to the Virgin, crushing a snake, and made us sing an English canticle to the Virgin: I knew that *blessed* meant *sanctified*, but I understood it as *hurt* [*blessée*]; hurt by what love? By what eighth sorrow? Pierced by what arrow? And in what flesh?

In France, I come from the diocese of Lyon, where, on December 8th, lights arranged in windows celebrate the dogma of the Immaculate Conception decreed by Pius IX in 1854: for all young Catholics who don't even know the act of copulation, all prayers enjoin and sing to them that there is no such act!

As a child, the flickering of the lantern flames against the windows on a winter's night seemed like the trembling of the spirit in the tempest of History: as many lanterns as there were windows, as many spirits in the house keeping watch over the world's salvation. Could the flame that cowered, rose, trembled, be virginity—the world's frailest fact—resisting the irritated injunction of God the Father, as a remainder from before Sin?

The Virgin gave birth to Christ, the son of God and the son of Man, "free from all stain of original sin." When I begin to understand, in a hazy vision of a man, leaning over a woman, in a nightshirt pierced where his member is at the groin, do I think that original sin means that Adam, father of all men, gives in to Eve, *mother of all women*, and disobeys God the Father, his own father—God who is Adam's father more than he is Eve's, because she is pulled from the rib of a sleeping Adam, put to sleep by God. Or do I think, because there is some *stain*, that Adam, a hole in the beast skin that he's wearing—He committed murder! He's become a man!—is leaning over Eve and committing the same act that animals are doing in the garden, in the street, in the fields?

The Virgin, alone amongst all women, escapes death through her assumption celebrated on August 15th, death being the separation of the body and the soul—thus the fear of death: no more body to conduct the soul, to warn, inform, or even hide it. Is this because she has also escaped its foundational act of copulation? But she carries the body of God for nine months. She is simultaneously the mother, daughter, and sister of this God. She exalts, worries and trembles before the "destiny" of the One who creates them all. He rises in her stomach, in her womb, a child before the Doctors, engaging them in debate— that is the image of Poetry. In her womb, having become a man and kneeling on the Mount of Olives, he sweats his blood-sweat. In her womb, only minutes shy of being *nothing but* God again, his human body suffers nails, asphyxiation on the cross. Afterward, the Resurrection, the rolling of the stone at the mouth of the cave, is outside her womb.

Does God the Father suffer through the agony of his son, as Abraham suffers because he has to kill his own?

Light and shadow one after the other, relief and tension. Does my mother pregnant with me know the destiny of the one she carries as the Virgin does?

God the Father, or the Greek Gods, do they decide in advance what is accomplished by the human puppet, Word produced only in order to reproduce myth? As a child or an adolescent, I watch that clothed belly—on vacation at the beach it is sometimes uncovered, and so beautiful. It contains and knows my future, or at least it carries inside the trace of the tension to foresee it.

I am still incapable of *realizing* the action my father's member does when entering my mother—I don't have enough of an eye yet for that! But the action of evacuating the fetus becomes familiar through what I see in animals—does it emerge through the same orifice or through the base? I'm still more inclined to think that the germ of all life is cast by God the Father into the mother's stomach who then makes it *rise*; and then to think that the father is the one who makes enough to feed the transformation of that germ till it becomes the small child emerging fully formed from the mother's thigh.

Redemption: what is there to redeem that could be worse than the act of copulation?

I see the erased act of the human birth of Christ as the most evil act, to be hidden to the point of negation. How would I not?

What else am I doing at night, when I call forth, expel and then project the semen seed for a few Words? And why each night this miming of original sin—at that age the mime is life itself—whose Word renews beauty before death comes to end it, a death called wordlessly through ejaculation and the crash that follows? After the cross, there is all that is left of that night, and one or two days of Redemption. Not remorse but desolation—and it's from this justification and defiance that desire is born again and with it the words that exalt it. If the act of using sex is the most condemned—damned—wash this stain with more stain, throw myself into it! *Deliver* myself to it! Deliver myself to men like a martyr to the circus beasts! As if to redeem all men's sexual weakness by *turning* these humans *on*, having them commit the reproved act on themselves. On the female reprobate? On the male reprobate? The condemned act made even worse with the loss of semen, discarded into her and him.

Here, on this pew, at fifteen, with the aid of masturbation and its text, I no longer believe in Adam and Eve, except as myth. I barely believe in a Creator God. Prehistory, Cosmic and biological space reduce Genesis to a small fire whose light dims with childhood. The story of Onan, the son of Judah in Genesis who is killed by Yaweh for "wasting his seed on the ground," is so short and merciless that it baffles me. What about me, wasting it into a rag! But Onan doesn't create text through his act. At the time, I don't know the word *onanism*. And I don't even know what to call what I am doing each night of freedom. What can I call a double act? I can only name what results from it: orgiastic writing. Is this what prisoners do, when they leave the prison with an overnight pass? I feel imprisoned by everything: society, nature, family, school, politics, the current state of democracy, the nation-state, my growth, my body, my being a minor, poetic impatience, the slow pace of evolution, and most of all my separation by birth from the "people," and by civilization from the naked peoples.

Orgiastic writing and sperm are the only visible, palpable productions of my freedom. And, at least after the first ejaculation—when the act is true: words or desire pulling out the juice until they draw blood?—I can touch them with my hand, filaments, lumps as fragile as life, fragments of brain, trails of trembling embryo, sentences, words interrupted or traced during orgasm when the self is freed from the self.

How can I reduce this self? Can I make it disappear, smash it the way the Virgin smashes the serpent? I circumscribe it within myself so many times during the day, chase it from my actions toward what I am forced to call "others" but through each of whom, by nature—"training" isn't everything—I am more than I am myself, and from whom I am separated only by skin and social mores. I always experience this self as a "defect," a venial, then mortal, sin, an offense, an infirmity that I should hide. This beat-sheet is like the prehistoric, rudimentary and pure fabrication of another self on which to prop the advent of a new world. I feel my limbs, my bones, my muscles, nerves, and neurons impatiently as if they were fated for a common, universal labor of salvation, of healing, and of gathering.

Often when I speak during the day, I stop myself when I hear the self speaking in my voice. How can I speak simply from universal reason and universal heart? Sometimes I don't even dare to speak, or the words break, crumble in my mouth, or language flees from me toward the inside like to a public dump.

The self, a family invention that would target and destroy an adolescent's individual will.

Can I not create an origin for myself, more pure, more rough than heredity, save in secret, in the secret of night or the secret of a place in nature, isolated yet burned by the Sun?

In a gymnasium—muscle for ideas?

Is my beat-sheet my father's inverted wish that I engage in violent sports?

In the manual labor that being a minor proscribes? But unless I flee to other regions of the world where the labor and the identity of children are not controlled, where in Europe would they hire me without my father's consent—hire me and make me depraved? And what father would accept to sign off his son's emancipation? Especially a father who demands that his sacrifice be endlessly acknowledged, the sacrifice of an entire life of hard labor with the human body so that he can pay for the education of his son? Since I write poetry, what would this education be? And with my mother being so weak, and her sanctity reinforced by my dream of her dying, how could I add to this weakness by disappearing, body and voice, into a world of sexual menace when I am still so fresh?

And my father: add to his solitude as well?

Voices that carry what is left of the effort it takes to pedal over the neighboring hills break into the song "Sing joyfully unto God our strength." Will I have to add my voice to theirs for the *Magnificat*? Will I have to sing a mother's joy at carrying a child of Destiny? Will I force my voice to sing its gratitude at being carried in a womb when the disavowal of my gratitude in the deep is what tortures me, when my destiny is that very hesitation between the whorehouse text and poetry, between Evil and Good, and when I carry that destiny in a body whose growth has almost deadened it to stupidity? The poetic gift that is just beginning is a source of joy. I am thankful to the world for it, thankful neither to a God nor to my ancestry, but maybe through Christ who delivers himself and wants to deliver us, thankful to the poets who come before me and are choosing me.

Since they are singing it in Latin, I join but without a surplice. The *Magnificat* begins, but I don't sing. I like the English accent and the childish tone as they sing the Latin song I know quite well. The difference in our way of singing gives me a hard-on; I shiver from my heels to my occiput. I hear the same fresh, resolute pitch, nearly hoarse, at night in my deep. I have to smother the sensation, stop it from rising, supplant their voice with mine in the softer verse that follows; and singing now, I take on the local intonation of the adolescents around me. Later, with "...*superbos*...," my voice has found its place. This God who has reduced the powerful and exalted the humble can only be Christ, stopping those who lapidate the adulteress, and pulling up from his feet the whore who is perfuming them. The gift of poetry—or any other gift—does not give any rights. It even weakens those who have received it, lowering them before society, before the "spirit," before philosophy, before intellectual authority. I claim no rights, no privilege from this gift, which I often try to hide, since I am so tormented by equality, disavowing it as Saint Peter disavows his Lord. Is it a treasure, a secret, a host of which I am the guardian? Is it the consecrated host of Tarcisius—refusal to deliver once again the real body of Christ—celebrated on August 15th, the day of the Assumption of the Virgin? Is it the baby fox that the young Spartan stole and hid under his cloak, and that devoured the boy's insides when he refused to reveal his theft? The gift imposes sacrifice, demands privation: only ten years since the end of the war, three years since our countries have stopped rationing.

Life emerges from constraint, beauty from regulation.

Writing precedes fact, just as the Trinity knows everything in advance.

After the *Nunc dimittis*, the reverend sets a new hymn for the end of Vespers on the lecterns. I look at my part, the title of the hymn *O Night*... Its first words remind me of a French chorus, "O Nuit, qu'il est profond ton silence," that we used to sing at Joubert during summer nights outside, "before falling asleep under the stars," the first line of our school song. Father Vallas himself, a musician, told us this eighteenth century hymn. I sing my part with fervent and impatient softness. When it's night here I can enter into even more freedom, live as much as possible at fading day, swim in the sea, run, climb, discover and capture animals from the sea, the earth, the air, interact with humans before I return to the underground space where I work at freeing my origin. No athletic feat, no stretching—blooming—of my limbs under the whistle of the gymnast will help me, but a discharge, an electric flash; the song is time that we are breathing; the more I sing, the more my song will swallow what time separates me from my deep. My part differs only slightly from what they are singing at my sides; one of them, thick chested, still smells of freshly cut barley fields, the other, whose twisted mouth gives a neat, rectilinear song, of solder.

When the rehearsal is over, as he prepares the liturgy, his wife setting up bouquets of tall flowers, the reverend tells me the origin of the song: it's the second act of Jean-Philippe Rameau's *Hippolyte et Aricie*, that the English are starting to want to play as the French are turning away from it.

Does he know that Hippolytus and Aricia are the young, endangered characters of *Phaedra*, Racine's last, pagan tragedy? My stomach grows warm: since I discovered the play, its characters follow me everywhere; its lines, addressed to the sea, to women... Sometimes our father mentions incest in backwoods farms. He cares for its results, only rarely monstrous and sometimes so beautiful, at least as children. For me, Phaedra could be any lusty woman from our family, or from our area, whose mores are known to be free, who speaks her mind, and loves as she desires, but she could also be any woman from that same area, sick or disabled, letting her incurable and forbidden wound, or maleficent monstrosity, be healed in tears and moaning.

Phaedra is in carnal and sexual love with her stepson Hippolytus.

Phaedra has had other lovers than her husband since he saved her from the confines of the Labyrinth. But being so consumed with love for Hippolytus, even dying of consumption, means that he must be beautiful and desirable. I see him afflicted by that passion too, wounded by it, carrying a wound in his chest or in his side from its exclusivity. Hippolytus is not penetrating Phaedra; Phaedra is penetrating him. The words of Hippolytus are always full of pain as well, like someone desired despite himself, whose gestures and whose youthful complaints and protestations of virginity only increase his appeal. Even by trying to get rid of his beauty, through mutilation, defacement, and castration, he reinforces it: the wound that Phaedra's passion has dug into his side is the same as mine—where is it on my body?—the wound made by the secret that *consumes* me.

From the pew, I look around for Annick in the congregation that is as full as it was this morning.

Outside, after Vespers, we meet her on the way to the beach. The tide is high but the sea is calm, the air still warm. Under the new dress wrapped around her body, which is darker than the one she wore this morning, has she slipped into a two-piece or a one-piece bathing suit? I have a hard time realizing what I know, which is that she is wearing one of those lace "panties." What could cover, *contain* what I have never really seen nor touched: "fine lingerie," embroidered on the sides, as useless as lace doilies in fairy tales to clothe this changeable, almost climactic organ, which has to do with the moon—and which never takes out what it has?

But what she shows me of herself is enough to make me want her with all my strength, and with all the strength of the Nature that surrounds and pressures us.

Under the ragged clothes worn by wild women or whores, isn't the female sex naked with Nature, beasts and man, habitual and magnificent like a naked heel, the sole of a foot?

More of the same musk from this morning in the powerful scent of the rising tide.

Should I place my hand on her naked shoulder, as she lifts the strap to her neck? Brush her hip with mine? Walk, as we always do, next to others, without being able to touch them, without being able to meet like Siamese twins… or fuse the two and more into one body possessed of a single self, fuse those ancient ones, possessed by the self, hounded like demons toward the Testament swine, toward the rats running here on the concrete down into the sewer!

The mermaids are going to sleep—but where? And do they sing as they fall asleep? Half-women, half-fish, do they have a sex organ, and where is it? Is it where their two natures join? Between Anthony's cavorting I almost hear the flapping of Annick the mermaid on the sand of the old coastal path, but it's just the sound of her red flats crushing small snails underfoot. Could Anthony, who visits bedrooms at night, explain the sex organs of girls to me? Could he also explain the musk that lingers, wafting from this petite brunette beauty in her uncertain walk toward a forbidden swim?

In the swollen sea—on the horizon, war ships again, and closer, waves with porpoises and seals, out where it's too deep to stand, the water at your neck, the self—head—is struck by the red ray of the setting sun that envelops it, transforms it into a ball, an object tossed about, the rest of the body as if weightless in historic waters; how is seawater replenished? The pressure of the water, the salt shrinking the sexual body like a primitive marine animal: a mermaid; annihilates it; only this flushed ball at the surface of the water can think and desire: the rest of the body has to grow accustomed, once again, to finding sensation in this element from which it comes.

At fifteen—before my legs, much later, will realize its real depth, and danger—I like deep water, whether seawater or freshwater. I like to cross the neck of lakes, of dams, rivers that I swim up or down under sun rays or shadows—and at times under the stare of great birds spying on the fish that my swimming has displaced. Anthony tells me that we can swim, tomorrow or after-tomorrow, from the coast to Holy Island, an island that houses the ruins of the Lindisfarne Monastery and that can be reached on foot at low tide through a long embankment of large stones.

But I can't dive. I judge almost all the actions of my life against that flaw, and perhaps, soon, this evening, tonight, I'll judge the act of "making love" or not, to this future seated woman, her head watching us over her knees, seated at the top of the beach shrunken by the rising tide between the water and the shadow of the castle.

My eyes close shut into the red: a slight kick of the heels to keep my head above water… going back to the beach, later, getting dressed, "going home," can I find the place where I can freely act and speak my desire, where all the desires of others and of oneself, gestures and speech free now, would compose a kind of musical society, soft or wild, sensible or lascivious, a paradise of endless desire and of its speech—and of its writing? Writing that must still be accomplished.

The Word precedes action: the real is only the future waiting to be named; even if a Creator God no longer exists—or almost, even if his mythological trace remains!—for me then—Christ does, inventing himself a father—the memory of his creative gesture remains in the gestures of men: the real is only the future waiting to be named again; but if I think too hard, my body in these abyssal waters, that the real doesn't exist, anxiety will rise in me and I will lose my footing: why persist in what does not exist?

Since I've been growing so fast the world doesn't seem so great and full, since I've seen it and made it move, through painting and poetry—like Time. Painting from nature, predicting the disappearance of the object, of color, of the cloud shadow reflection and going faster or slower, even sometimes painting a color from memory onto paper—red setting sun on the sea, red on the trees—before it appears and takes shape, in poetry, circumscribing a fact of Nature, of body, of feeling and committing it in a word or several means to leave the world of fixity and plenitude in which a child guarantees his move-ment in the world. Sometimes, my palm around the stone sphere at the bottom of a railing or a flight of steps, I feel it shrink to atom powder. Or, even further, seeing a badger rushing to his sett, its smell seems stronger more visible more real than its silhouette, its mass, almost like a full-fledged figure.

The wrack around my ankles, knees, and thighs: also some nearly nothing, albeit expelled from a more powerful milieu than what occurs on earth.

In the shadow of the castle grazing the water, receding now and advancing toward us as we swim to shore, above slabs of basalt, how can I revert to being a marine animal? I will not be reduced to a miserable animal like the wild dog restless at the corner of the butcher shop, in the ooze of the dregs of labored meats. Although I still eat meat, animals consumed in the vanity of table talk, I always feel that they are nobler than the human guests, some of whom are so certain of the superiority of their species, their metaphysical species; even to the point of criminality. The animal has already been killed, yes, but maybe some of its power—power that we've lost, we the most cowardly of animals—can lift us back up to its level!

The power of the sea, its swell and regularity provide those adolescent limbs, hidden beneath the surface from the gaze and from all human judgment, with a feeling of virginity and vigor that even the sweat of extreme exertion can't provide: he needs to return to the sea, live there within it and be nourished; his head and thinking also as if on the surface of the world, equal to all others, attentive to all sounds and without separation from the sky and stars.

Back to the beach, my knees treading the waves, my feet the undertow, I return to captivity.

Dry now, and dressed, we leave the chilled shadows of the Armstrong castle with its shining canons; we pass through the village, Anthony the retard, his sperm-coated hand cleaned by the bath, has to pick up a sewing basket that his aunt and a friend share with others from the parish.

They knit sweaters, socks, rompers, and mufflers for the poor.

Tea has been cleared from the table in the little house on Church Street, with its ancient windowpanes diffracting all the colors of the setting sun. In a back room, someone is playing a piece for piano that I know well, "The Girl with the Flaxen Hair," not because my sisters ever played it, since my mother rejected French music, but because I played it as a child, and in my head and on my lips I often hum this melody and others during the day. Every action in my life is preceded or accompanied by the hum or the mental unfolding of a melody or rhythm—I visualize the harmony—and I hummed this *girl with the flaxen hair* this morning as I left the church, before catching a whiff of the brunette's musky smell. In the early summer, painting outside with my mother on a fork of the river Déôme in France, I remembered reading somewhere that Claude Debussy had composed *reflections* like the painters of his time, so, keeping the sound internal, I'd hummed that melody, which my mother discovered with surprise, and, though she'd already heard and seen *Pelléas et Mélisande* and had disliked the song of Mélisande unwrapping her hair, she asked me to sing it to her softly.

Anthony and I knock on the door, and in the colored half-light, with the lingering aroma of tea and jam and toast, droplets still wet on our drying bodies, it seems it might be morning. We wonder who is in the back room playing the piano, on the black top of which we catch a glimpse of a vase of blue flowers. "The Girl with the Flaxen Hair." I'm not the one playing it haltingly, as I used to do, ten years before, in

France, in the house of Mrs. Teste, in the morning, window open onto a hanging wisteria.

Where am I? Quick, center myself on the axis of the Earth, collect myself in the Cosmos: origin, faith, action, body.

On the veranda, the sound of a chase, the door opens, with a cry a cockatoo bursts into the doorway open onto the sunset, and settles on its perch in the half-light. The melody in the darker depths of the house keeps its calm, its tempo, and its touch.

A very strong boy, with a bandage around his neck, crashes against the doorjamb, strikes it with both red fists. Among disheveled books and drawing pads, Anthony gropes for the sewing basket with his eyes and hands. A woman with long red hair and breasts slightly exposed throws herself on the back of the foaming boy, and pins him down. The boy lets himself piss abundantly. His mother pushes him into the veranda and the garden. Another young girl, from upstairs, grabs a rag from under the sink, mops the puddle, wrings out the rag and, kneeling, mops once more the concrete and wooden floor. Through the door and the veranda windows, I see a doghouse without a dog; there is barking, yapping, mewing in the surrounding gardens.

Once her hands are washed, the young girl goes into the garden, brings the boy back into the living room and upstairs to wash him and to have him lie down in bed. The circular gaze of the cockatoo starts up again. When my wits come back to me, I notice that my hand has grabbed Annick's plump elbow and is holding it, and that she leaves it there: If I want what is to be wanted for tonight, should I hold her elbow until then?

The beautiful redhead returns with the emptied serving tray and boiling, brewing tea. The melody continues, more and more confident. The veranda is all yellow and red. The telephone rings, Dorothy is worried because we're late. The jam they serve here is real jam, made with bramble blackberries and with a bigger kind of blackberry. We drink, Anthony's blue eyes gleam red; he lowers them to watch my hand letting go of Annick's elbow.

Half in French and half in English, the tall woman explains to me that she knows the south of France a bit, the mountainous backcountry around the Mediterranean, blackberry bushes, almond trees, that she paints there. How can I tell her I'd rather hear the secret of the boy's anger and the bandage around his neck? She works in a social services agency in Berwick-upon-Tweed; she has three children to take care of, her husband died very young at war.

Noise in the upstairs bedroom: the boy is upset again. His sister—do they have the same father?—rushes down the stairs but here he is, running down, without the bathrobe he was wearing in the doorway, now wearing only the bandage around his neck and his short bathing suit with side laces. His mouth is foaming, he is clasping his fists to his sides, his whole head contracts and reddens in the dimming light. Knives have been removed from the table, the scissors from the sewing basket. Anthony, sitting next to me, clasps the basket, wool yarn, needles, knitting, patterns, against his stomach. The cockatoo begins to coo. The boy, his piss stained bathing suit buttressed by what seems like a very large member, crosses the living room and the veranda, walks out into the garden, some of its flower bushes trampled to the ground. Everyone starts. The mother—the scent of what unborn child's milk on her breast, and from what father?—rises with her crown of hair and goes into the garden. The young girl angles her large chestnut eyes to us, rimmed with very dark eyelashes—and in halting, but melodious, French, announces: "We've hidden the collar and the chain."

Something stronger than my heart bolts in my chest. Before I'd even studied the anatomy and physiology of the human body in science class, I'd examined the colored plates and illustrations of flayed figures in my father's office: since then, in order to love or desire a body, I have to resist the vision of its insides. What makes a body lovable? Is it its surface, except for the bones, their size and jointing, the muscles and the nerves that animate from below what can sometimes move us to crime, a sheath that shines or not, hair well set, some internal flesh extraverted in the mouth, the lips, the tongue and eyes; is it the member, the vulva that we don't usually see…?

At the back of the garden, the boy is barking. The young girl goes on, slowly, Anthony struggling to translate the words she says and that I can't believe: "Douggie's worried we don't love him enough. That's why he goes to the doghouse. He says we love Doggy more than him, and that the dog's dead. He takes the dog's place, snapping its collar around his neck and yanking at the chain. Sometimes he drags himself on all fours, the chain around his neck, and will lift his leg against a bush to piss. That's how he hurt his neck. And now he's gotten used to pissing where he stands, not because he has to go, but because of some strong emotion. He doesn't think he's our father's son. He thinks he's the son of a dog that copulated with our mother. So we tell him that he has in his body none of the characteristics of a dog, but he says he'll be a dog when he grows up. He scares us. He breaks our hearts. But he's so much fun. We couldn't be faithful to our father without him, our father who died so that we could be free. We love him more than anything."

Why should this body and this life be normalized by a family's natural love? This body should be public, its imprisoned soul leaking as foam on its lips, piss through its member, blood visible in its young veins on tightened fists and bursting temples?

I see this body, this life, these humors. I hear and feel them hypertrophied in the Word, for comedy, and for greater sacrilege. What activity can I give him, what acts can I have him perform in that place that I still can't name? Shadow harboring shadow. I have words on the edge of my lips, on the edge of my will, concrete, abstract words to designate him to myself in the moving secret of my being: capture, abandon, jizz cloth, "whore," "streaker," "doorjamb," for life.

I have enough to populate the deep at the bottom of my brain, which I shove, as I recline, against the bolster pillow, the sand or the grass or concrete at the top end of the beach—and which at times I knock against the wall where I stand, a few bare seconds, to study the bearing and the gestures of those males or females that would stand *for show* against one of my "whorehouse" walls, and this in order to shake it and have it move to the fore of my brain into my full reason, or perhaps dislocate and destroy it.

Being captured by force or seduced, drugged and put down—what, besides violence, could return a being to that state where it would only accomplish such actions that even the word *lust* could not encapsulate, and that the Creator has yet to inscribe on his list of deadly sins?

The beings there need another reason than common reason, a closed reason in an open body.

They need a body, speech, moved as if by hunger, by "desire" alone: not really by the desire that ends in pleasure. They need bodies marked by the pleasure of another, of others, frictions, blows, insults, matter, remains of sound, money, a body, a Word, all virginal because of their asocial, "insane" nature. The morality outside of which they exist is what establishes virginity or profanation. I discover, as if a book or logical reasoning were open in front of me, that in my deep, which is managed by beings of ordinary reason and morality, *sex* only happens with the insane, with madness: but words coming from the morality of a prior life reinforce the voluptuousness of its discourse. What I know of the death camps, liberated just ten years before, what I know of the use of an oppressive morality by the executioners—common sense, hygiene—to justify and accompany the humiliation, torture, and profanation of the living body and of the dead, keeps me awake. I want to push far away from me the analogy with what my secret sets in motion. But slavery and the Nazi death camps, masters and executioners, the mysteries of their existence, their reasons and their capacity for action have so tormented me, and for so long, because I have the premonition, in what I'll write later that is most true, that I will make a small society act which is composed of those two extremes. Does that double torment, and others besides, make my mother dress me as a little man and take me, for an entire day, to Lyon by bus in early 1949 to consult with the youngest brother of my father, who is just starting his practice of psychiatry?

But here, six years later, now fifteen and far away—this is no longer home—in the sound of a language other than mine, boys and girls, all around, exuding the end of their overactive day, with the barking of real dogs in gardens and the sound of Douggie, that most beautiful of crazy brothers, with red darkening over the Western lands, and in the reek of juvenile piss, I can begin to conceive of masters and executioners from within, organizers but not executants, as each night the master—mistress?—of my deep takes the stand, or another master and a client handle a desired body, master and "executioner" combining their panting voices with that one, in the rustling of wads and cloth rags.

But the smell of tea, of toasts, of the mother coming back to the table, once the child is asleep on a deckchair on the lawn, the smell of oil paint and of wool bring me back to the world of good, of virtue—but in my deep, is that really regression at work? If it's not progress, then what is it? Some chimera, or a little bit of Man from the world I can begin to imagine after reading the title *Beyond Good and Evil* and the beginning paragraphs of the book over Guyot's shoulder, one of my classmates, who forgets his deficient body and face in books. At the time, my confidence in World and Man is still intact. But my nocturnal action—during the day in summer, on vacation, animals, trees, torrential water currents all around, what great desolation once the substance is sucked out to the point of drawing blood and the sheet of paper full—is what makes me doubt myself, doubt my virtue, doubt the sincerity of my speech and actions, or of my thoughts, even unsaid and unwritten. The World, even with its crimes, is more solid, more honest, more reliable than I am.

My only hope is the sap that I feel rise and course through my body—a body that I expect my father to love and to value rather than to depreciate as he does. His rejection is like being rejected by a buyer of bodies who would disclaim mine as too rebellious or imaginative, and would depreciate its appearance in the press or in the noise around the Dothan cisterns where

Joseph's brothers are selling Joseph, his father's favorite son. Is it from such rejection that I invent a deep where, even if I am not the one being sold or selling myself—since I haven't written enough, I don't yet know that once you start it's your self you put there—a sound like the paternal voice makes my creatures emerge from the dark and go back to it trailing sounds, gestures, "obscenities"—how I've dreamed about that word!

It's to my mother I return, to the good, to the beautiful, to progress, and to harmony, when, after I've crashed, I'd like to see the whole material portion of existence and of the world blasted away and scorched by the fire of God the Father, like in Sodom and Gomorrah, or softly brushed aside as if to "pass" through Christ—what a sorry name and figure, so used up—when, with another pencil or another pen, later, once the "indignity" has dissipated, I settle back to poetry. But if I can, after a while, show my blameless poetry to my mother—in which a future eye would still perceive a trace of the deep—I never dream of showing the "orgiastic writing" to my father—*with its material*—and tell him that of all my production at the time, this part is his due. A child's thought escapes the father's grasp, even before writing will annihilate him.

Sometimes, in the calm between two sessions, I see us, hear us, feel us, my father and I, driving endlessly from town to town, him at the wheel, my aching body on the seat, his arm and right hand around my shoulders and my neck, the open suitcase on the back seat sending out its stench of medicine and blood, revealing bulb syringes, tubes, and shining hoses; leaving me in "hovels" and taking me back to heal me and to cauterize—what wounds?—to sew back together the raw edges of my torn orifices; where is my mother, what does she do when we disappear? How does she hug me, when I come back, tight against her bosom? What does my father reveal of these outings and of their traces on my body and in my speech? Have I gone mute? Do I let a gesture learned in those "hovels" slip in when she is there, when she holds me close? Have I brought back words or accents to my poetry from copulations, which their pre-criminal fervor my father sometimes has to interrupt?

The most impassioned, the most violent, the loudest, the least sated among those he might lead me to would be the women, who'd want to tear me apart so that each could have that part of my flesh that excited them; my father, having stepped out of his car, would climb the stairs, suitcase in hand, four steps as a time, in order to drag me away from his furies by the feet and save the part belonging to my mother, the reason that I use for poetry—I haven't discovered yet that poetry comes from the heart, the guts and breath—although at night, for the deep, my heart, guts, breath, and chest are there.

The barking resumes, weakens to a yelp then to a plea; in the completely darkened room at the right end of the house, the melody starts up again as well, "The Girl with the Flaxen Hair." For my whole life, which I project will be short and full, will I always hesitate between what reason designates as good, as harmony—not yet love—and what I designate to myself as the beautiful—the musical friction of the animal in the human, its attraction precisely reinforced by a moral condemnation that I understand to be a hypocritical cloaking of our animal share?

Am I alone, at least here, living this double life? Do I begin to see this happen in music, this Double that forces Schubert to compose such wide splits between notes, with nothingness in between? Does nothingness stretch between me and me as well?

With this torn self—my heart and reason each account for the tear, and I pledge loyalty to both extremes because of the strength that lies in each—how will I approach the groups and populations whose naked poverty torments me? How can I give my self to others, when this self is not unified? How can I claim to help, protect, heal, search for and even clean those over which I can only spread this disjointed heart and reason?

The mist—which enters even the living room and the veranda—echoes with one, two, three hornpipes from around the castle, playing a melody in three voices. How is it possible that so many popular and classical musicians have composed so much new music from a mere twelve notes? I ask myself the same question about poetry. A beautiful popular song is just as deep, when you first listen to it, as the most beautiful of classical music. Even if we know that music is improvised by specialists, isn't it a mystery how one day a child or adolescent musician *finds* the note, the rhythm or the harmony that will spread from its setting at a party or around the fire into a melody that'll change the world?

This song that was already slow is now further delayed by the singing voices: what pain and solitude shaped it? What landscape did the shepherd, or shepherds, the same sadness between them—rage contained—look at as they played it through the bagpipes they'd just saved from the flames? Did he, did they, head to the mountains with what was left of their flock, while the British army, horses and infantrymen, withdrew in the valley below under the smoke of fires; bloody hands and swords, pasty, sticky sex organs.

But the music only lasts as long as its composition: the more beautiful the popular song, the faster we tire of it. We expect it to live, to spread its splendor wide and to blossom. Classical music is duration. The melody is announced, prepared, enunciated, repeated, developed, dislocated, varied, intensified through fugue variations, derided; other melodies confront it or blend in. A life is created: a single melody, even the most beautiful in the world, isn't enough. Just like the words of a lament or those of a little garden song, a prison song, a song of war or servitude—unless they are encased in the network of specialized music—can only carry emotion for the duration of the song, and its unchanged repetition—but should the blues extracted from bodies that are legally nonhuman, be made to last till the human state is found again…

I am only several hundred meters away from my backpack, which I've re-laced and re-strapped around my poetry note-book and my "ball of orgy." I see the stanza interrupted like a fire that is put out before leaving. My chest hurts from wanting to run there and start writing again, to finish the poem with all the new things I've learned, boat crossings, musky girl smells, cock lust.

In the next few days, how can I experience what I need to experience with Annick and also compose the series of poems that I'd outlined in France, in my bedroom the night before leaving: after *Moses, David, Samson, Judith*…? Or maybe *Saül*?

I imagine—where are we? Are we sitting?—my left arm around her breasts, showing under a deep cleavage and pungent, with the nipple growing hard under the top of the dress, my left hand moving up and down along her neck, behind her ear, my fingers inching up under her hair—who owns the hair owns the girl!—the tip of my finger touching her black eyebrow, while my right hand writes a live poem on the notebook leaning against my knee, not the overly violent *Judith* but several stanzas of what I feel of her shaking and of her spreading smell—pleasant this time—and the murmur of her high voice from her mouth, from her body bending and pressing up against mine.

The mother has grabbed the sewing basket from Anthony's hands and has resumed her knitting for the poor; as a child, the friction of the colored needles, the staggered crossing of the fingers under the yarn, the settling of the yarn around the needle and the progression of the knitting down past the wrists was for me, with the low steady striking of the hours, the half-hours, the quarter-hours of the Bourg-Argental bell-tower in the background, a measure of time that I could not imagine could be experienced without one's mother; later, and still now, it is a moving image of work, of what cannot be done in a day, like what is done by the Creator even before expressing any desire for it; the image of hope as well, Penelope; the image of a life lived only the time it takes to knit one's garment, one's shroud, one's tunic of Nessus; in the meantime, this woman, so plentiful and calm, was she perhaps knitting a garment for her son, yelping and whimpering outside, with wool that I imagined full of holes, mended, soiled, nabbed, thrown, exposed on the outside door leaf of the threshold to the deep.

But, above this, the radio which the young girl has turned on is airing a description and analysis of the latest Kenyan massacre, carried out by those among the Kikuyus who call themselves the Mau-Mau, rising up against the British: Anthony, his pink lips brushing my ears, repeats it to me slowly, pausing on the details of the sexual mutilations; I try to remove these knitted threads from my mind: what are they compared to those mutilated corpses that I imagine dogs are pulling from bloodied or seared clothes. But quickly, my mind, or some undetermined thing between mind and nether parts that takes its place, passes from the Mau-Mau to the Moi—a half-naked tribe from the high plateaus of Annam in the north of Indochina; their loincloths falling from their hips and their naked loins, the features of their fleshy faces—women, under turbans and ornaments—their frightened upright posture, naked thighs, naked feet in the mud before a blurred backdrop of huts and jungle, "these parts" that I imagine as large and heavy beneath the loincloth as the legs, endlessly laboring to beat down mud and small growth under-foot, fondled by those who rent them by the hour, the deep again is filled with bodies ranging from the naked Indians of the Amazon to their semi-naked brothers from ex-French Indochina. Or rather, they would stand there, still too noble to be touched, as tutelary images at the cavern's entrance and back wall, framing the "orgy" scene where only bodies I have created can act and can be acted upon.

But act what? And what mental image do I get when, during the day and especially tonight, I want to settle my interior gaze on the "orgy"; other images, ideas, abstract thoughts, rush toward it to erase or feed from it or feed it to excess and make it burst. Only writing and speech establish parts of our reality, only action can establish action. The only lasting mental image we can have is of what exists outside the real, set apart from our senses. Ideas, logical facts can only "stand" awhile in the mental image, that's what it's made for. Since I have started writing, and especially the secret text, I understand that nothing else exists outside my senses and outside the senses of other humans throughout the world, billions of humans, who create the real that rises against us as an obstacle or that charms us. Childhood is over—it remains elsewhere in adult man—that thinks there is a constructed world before us, that thinks that there is a self and the world…

Even after having written it, during the night or beneath the full Sun, I can only reconstitute this orgy in the form of an idea, a conflict, a knot of sentiments, the fight of clear, overly clear ideas. But in the impossible case that I had to give an account of their gestural and vocal acts—impossible because who could listen to such things except my creatures, or real creatures, also impossible, who would resemble mine and whose actions would occur in similar settings?—I could only do it by inventing the following scene, calls, exclamations and new orders, covering the older scene with a new, "wilder" one yet. And then *I* would be there, body and soul.

The veranda door slams loudly, the boy in the veranda trashes everything, the piano at the back of the house stops, the two girls join their mother; the radio announcer has changed, it's now a comedian but I don't understand what he's laughing about.

The Mau-Mau pull out of the living room, but it's a boy now, foaming and clasping his arms to his torso, trembling with rage and with the garden chill; these three women contain the worst in this small house: of those three, how can the mother paint peaceful landscapes with the same arm, the same hand she uses to contain the fury of the boy? How does she calm their trembling to secure her fingers on the pencil, on the brush?

The three of us are standing up; a movement that *she* makes toward me, as I'm still shaking slightly from the boat trip, the train, the two jostled nights, the church song, the swim and the rising chill, immerses me again in what I've just imagined: she leans against me, the both of us standing in this countryside full of the creaking and lisping of insects on the ground and in the air, and I, who've grown at least thirty centimeters since last year, clasp her under my armpit: why is it, as I hold her chest, that I feel my arm not long enough, my heart—although my father, afraid of the place I give him there, claims that my heart is bigger than the usual—my heart not big enough to hold all that I feel that she contains? Beneath my fingers moving from the nipples toward the stomach, what do I feel move and bulge like new breasts: could it be the toes of a restless baby on the inside?

Our five brains feel, diffuse their musky odor around the smell of this secret one; for me, more than the deepest sky or "nether parts," the forehead seems the mysterious point that is most fragile in the world: although I already conceive of the body with its interior, as mobile, colored, smelly, and slimy, and even if I've learned some details of the mass, the innervation and the workings of the brain, it also constitutes a mental image that is impossible to stabilize longer than the batting of an eyelid; wisdom, the harmony of the heart and of the mind, resides there in the forehead; the farther the forehead sticks out, the greater the hope is in the mind whose outpost it contains; but beneath the bar of the forehead, strewn with golden strands of hair, radiating at the top of this body as it shuffles between objects and furniture—perhaps between bushes, trees, and rocks outside—like the body of a naked beast, I wonder what more rugged, colored mind, racked with cruder palpitations, awaits?

If I could find some interest, some wisdom, some will in my brain and in my mind, I would gladly give it to him, because it contains hope; in return for his body, which I know I could use for more than the body—is this also a hope?—thus sparing him the hardening and reducing of his brain in a deadly institution; but there they are, he with no brain and I with no mind, my brain in his head rolling under the table and I without a head but with his body erect, and my old body as a ghost on the hardwood floor; and my dear father slipping his head in through the open door.

Until recently—although that seems already long ago—before I started writing for good—and already for "bad"—I could see no other goal for humanity than its complete conversion to Christianity, to Catholicism; no other impetus for being than the evangelization of all territories; the unity of Sky and Earth. With all peoples and all tribes filled with our God, fed by his Eucharist, with the embattled Muslims returned to the New Testament, the Buddhists embraced as brothers, the Animists more than brothers, we could convince our Orthodox and Protestant brothers to return to his authority whose dominion they reject. The only thing that undermines the utopia is the practice of the deep and its writings, which even after crashing I can't bring myself to tear up or to burn: but there are enough mysterious, scandalous enclaves in the Old Testament and in the New; there are so many spectacles in the passion of Christ, so many resolute moves toward redemptive indignity; in both, so much sex—the word "to know" for sex as the pathetic remains of the Tree of Knowledge and of one single stolen fruit!—so many perfumes, so many luxurious discharges, so many humans and animals possessed by the demon that one day, lifting my neck from the rock where it was lying after my beat-sheet session in the high grass, the sky above me rips open with a Voice that is familiar because I speak to him, even in this hidden act, and have done so wordlessly or in a soft voice since childhood, and the sky pours His speech out over this glistening south of France, and down into the hole where the hour strikes in my native village, its residents getting ready for mastication, and over my body that is relaxing in spurts, and starts to shiver from desolation; and as I hear this, rather than burn the paper on the rock—and have the rock and mountain burn along with me!—like an offering, of which the tenacious smell below would be unpleasant to His nostrils up above, I keep the fresh sheets of paper, splattered with the "seed" that runs through the Old Testament from generation to genera- tion—but do I know that what I've spread is seed, and that this seed ensures the population of the World—helped by what in women?—writing should not be destroyed, nor should the tables of the Law be broken; especially if, at his expense who doesn't know it yet, the writing feeds off what the child reads and learns and recites that is most sacred.

At the time, I believe in equality not through any moral, social, or political obligations, not through the accomplishment of my faith, but through logic and reason; the heart of that same reason is shattered by injustice and inequality.

What is this reason? It isn't the reason of philosophy. Is it maybe the reason that I wish that God the Creator had? But can you create all things equal, even if you are God? Is my "reason" simply utopian? Could it be Lucifer blaming God the Father for the inequalities of his creation?

For those who suffer from the inequalities of birth, of physical and mental constitution, and of chance, what is the fruit of this Tree of Knowledge eaten by the first couple? What knowledge? Seeing the other outside of oneself?

I don't want the Same to be everywhere: the self-same. But I want all beings of Evolution to have the same quantity of life that they can use as they will.

Even knowing what little I am, I always think of others as deprived of what I have or what I am. My reason seems such a privilege when I look at that beautiful being, where all movements, all shadows, all light make beauty, when I see his rage, *the possession* that brings foam to his lips—and what other humors besides that I don't see?—and the solitude that no woman's womb can surround and protect! Does he know inequality?—at least I am privileged to feel the inequality of the world, a privilege he doesn't have. Could this reason, which makes my heart reject it, be some fluid, some molecule circulating more abundantly in my body than in other bodies? Inequality again: in each of our brains' chemical constitution?

Solitude, isolation: every child and adolescent practices a secret, or at least believes it is a secret until a superior accuses him or her of that very thing: I keep a total silence around my beat-sheet—except for God in my own voice: maybe others don't have a word to name the act?

My act comes at such cost that I want to share part of its madness—I see the risks: a broken neck and member—the separation it creates between me and others, especially the people I love the most, who grow in numbers as I grow, makes a double desire rise that does not distribute my pleasure—by distributing it to my desiring figures—but that instead might leave me every time despairing on the edge of accomplishment: even as a child, I pull what I can out of myself to make myself in part like the retard, the criminal, the monster (Hitler even) at its source: I look for what suffers, moves, and reasons in myself like what I imagine is suffering, moving, and reasoning in that gestating monster—and what is "unscrupulously" opting for the greater misery of the world and of itself.

On the bagpipes, a jig transforms the last notes of the melody; then in the jig, an Italian circus song.

It's too late now to return to Kent Cottage: the adults will meet us at the circus.

They set up the circus tents in the afternoon, along the north-western side of the castle, beyond what we can see.

Douggie, who's been smelling the horses from the garden, waves his arms over his mother and sisters huddling around him. From his dilated mouth, a piece of golden *bubble-gum* bulges and grows.

Can we take him to the circus half-naked? Will they feed me stew after we're done? Will we be home early enough for Mr. Praundlock to show me his little pea, and explain it to me?

We leave the doors unlocked. We don't bring anything. The two young girls are the only ones carrying something, a heavy aviator coat that used to belong to their father, who burned in his plane, and they pass it between them as they walk; they'll use it for their brother, if he gets cold during the show.

The circus is in a depression surrounded by a paling fence, at the northwestern end of the large lawn that borders the fortress from the south to the north. I keep the money for the ticket in my bag next to the poetry notebook and the "ball of orgy," along with my mother's list of recommendations and my passport, signed by my father, which allows me to leave French territory; Dorothy is here, hugging me against her— I've been away from her for five hours, two of which were with the mother, her, and her three children... And what if I pressed my left side—what's best, to be on the left or on the right of one's mother?—against her right as we walk so that I can be inside her perfume—Annick leans against my right side with the strength of her purring muscles, that smell that has come back, and the fear of being seated on the circus bench for so long. Anthony's parents look for him; off to the side, near the road that is lit up by a few headlights in the rising mist, I see several blond heads moving restlessly around a donkey grazing near a truck with a long wooden bed: Anthony, with a few others, has pulled the long donkey penis from under the animal and churns it until the animal emits a coarse braying—a sinister echo to my secret act: is what I do as bestial?—and the field is showered with the strong, soft smell of life; I see him wipe his two hands on the donkey's sides, then on the grass. What power do his palms contain that they are able to obtain what the donkey keeps for the jenny? His parents have the same smile they had when he grabbed the member under my shorts in the living room; do I need to beat animals off if I beat myself off? From a donkey, what text can you expect but braying and defecation?

We settle onto the three-tier benches in the smell of oil lamps smoking in their globes and in their tubes at the entrance and inside the circus, under the patched tent, in the smell of the tide going out along the Lindisfarne causeway— the Viking sharpens his axe just like the Poilu soldier recharges his Lebel rifle.

Will I see the girl with the sunken cheek? Will her movements undress her, since the other girl is not? Will she ride horses, climb on hanging rigs? Will a ray of light reveal the dip of her cheek?

I wanted Anthony to sit between his two sisters, away from me, but while the seats were being filled, he squeezed in next to me. Even before the lights begin to dim, he tucks his hand

and fist into my shorts, pushing at the zipper. Since my member is almost permanently hard, he thinks this time it's for his fist, for him, for the night to come.

Leaning on the left against his mother's right side, I lift my left ass so that can I shift my rummaged hips toward Anthony, hoping to hide him from her gaze.

Douggie, his right side tightly squeezed against his mother's left, leans his head over, smiles with all his beautiful teeth beneath the stretched red line of his lips.

On the top bench, Anthony's father curves his head toward my ear. His breath, on which I recognize the almost unknown musk of the smell of the *five-o'clocks*, whispers: "He likes you, Pierre…" I remember immediately: three years earlier, during my first year in middle school, our English teacher, his belly very round under his gown, explained the difference between *loving* and *liking* as he read us *The Vicar of Wakefield* in the afternoon: in the gurgling that accompanied the sleepy rhythm of his voice, and through the whispers moving from bench to bench, from clear throats to raspy ones, I heard that the poor man, who had been unable to *love* during his life, now *liked* immensely. And now, the word chosen by the father to name and to give meaning to his son's act was proof that Anthony did not want me out of love or friendship but out of desire, flesh, body, and *feast*. In the growing darkness, among screaming children and parents, among so many bodies half-naked after the bath they took at sea or at home, encased in the stench of horses—and of what other exotic beasts?—in the clanking of the acrobats-jugglers-animal tamers-clowns clapping their hands as they enter the ring, Anthony's fist still sticky with donkey seed progresses along my erect member toward my testicles, implying that my body and flesh can be desirable here. Maybe some frictions, ointments and makeup might make them desirable to all those girls, women, boys, adults, and beasts fidgeting, becoming ecstatic, applauding, shaking their ass and tits, their dicks, trunks, fangs in the clouds of sand and sawdust.

Not moving, not thinking of my ass sweating against the bench, as this entire fantasmagoria accelerates the rhythm of my already deranged heart, I take his ear in my fist and latch my mouth against it: "If you have any balls, grab me by the dick and lead me down to the ring!"

His mother's hand grazes my left arm that shakes because of my poetry in action and because I've backed into the deep. It means that she has understood, and her hand now softly strokes my neck under my hair. Annick, sitting between the two sisters on the lower bench, turns around, her chest white under a ray of Moonlight that has slipped in between two unevenly joined pieces of tarp. Did she see Anthony's wrist pull back from between my shorts and my thighs? With the tip of my espadrille at the tip of my long leg, I wonder what part of her body I could touch during the show…? Douggie's mother's hand is on my neck; my foot, which I imagine is broken and in a cast extending from the groin to the toe, is lying on Annick's left arm; my center is now rid of Anthony's paw, and with that paw, I am also rid of what I do myself at night to produce the writing that condemns me and yet pushes me forward—from the deepest possible part of my self, thus from very deep in History; I force myself to forget the stench of donkey juice and lift my head beyond its reach, but Anthony's father, bothered by my height, readjusts me from behind with his sporty hands. Despite the drum and tap dancing of the clown announcing his act, I imagine and have the feeling that I've become an extra circus attraction, tied to a tether by the neck outside, naked and on all fours—or my hips covered in some torn rags—my member pulled, churned, emptied and still erect, grabbed again, churned and emptied again by paying hands; and before that, ever since my birth, I imagine that I've been beaten by blows of all kinds, abused by caresses of all kinds, bitten by horseflies of all kinds, the halter grinding at my neck; and that I am really what the donkey is not, a manual donkey, an intellectual donkey, a spiritual donkey, an absolute donkey—but with a purpose at least!

The clown is the head of the family; here comes his daughter, the ill-nourished beauty with the sunken ass-cheeks, who jumps on the bottom knot of the rope and climbs up into the dark heights—the naked woman from the magazine, a robe between her red legs! Tiny pink panties accentuate her pelvis. Everyone is staring at it, and way up on the top bench a man wearing a Scottish cap is even using a small set of theater binoculars. Maybe they're the same panties she wore during the day, and she's slipped them over her satin tights, runny and speckled with sawdust.

Douggie's mother spreads the coat over his thighs to cover his erect member. Is the trapeze girl far enough away for me to see her, in her truth, once I've removed my large-rimmed metal glasses? Is she far enough away to see as in a dream, through the eyes of a newborn, the way I dream of ancient men in caves after the hunt, noses up against the rock, men who use flint to etch into the first layer of rock the vague contours of the animal they'll kill in the morning, outside the cave and far away. I see that rawness through the honing light following the figure, through the color, the sound, and smell: give me back my sight and I'll give back my virginity. I'd rather bump into a girl and look at her up close with my bare eyes than go near her with glasses.

But with my eyes bare I have to squeeze my eyelids tight and strain my eyes to get a mediocre and temporary improvement: so instead of seeing the object precisely, its exact form and the space it occupies, I imagine it. Are we so important in the Universe that our Creator would have given us perfect vision so that we could see Him and see His work? So that we could see the One who barred us from eating the fruit of the Tree of Knowledge? When I'm outside in broad daylight, I get such pleasure walking bare-eyed through the light, the smells and sounds, hands gliding over the grass, the blond of the wheat rising into the blue sky, with only the sound of an automobile to signal the road that my eyes can't see! If I were a murderer, premeditating my act, would I hone in on my victim or my prey with more certainty in the glistening fog? Would I go toward as definitive a destiny in the "whorehouse" and those who would undress me there? Surrender to the living.

From this natural sight I wait and hope for a miracle, an apparition. With these raw eyes I see it all, the curvature of the world, from my temples to my ankles. This half-blindness holds the hope for revelation, conversion, and the transfiguration of my being that my corrected sight forbids. Through my glasses, society reorganizes itself, shutters me back in and silences me as its networks merge with my neurons.

Anthony's breath is on my right shoulder, his mother's palm on my left wrist, my foot in its espadrille submerged in Annick's warmth. I see the girl grab the trapeze: if she crashed to the ground, I would smother her dislocated body with such caresses and such care.

One boy, then two, then three, ages thirteen to eighteen, jump onto the sand and onto a stripped mattress, climb the rope together and let themselves glide all the way down, while the girl mimes her surprise from the top. Of both those sex organs, male and female, which one grows hot first against the rope? In males, where is the orifice that females have in front? You can ignite the end of a wooden tube if you roll it between your palms on a wooden base. That first small stream of smoke, rising from the ground where we are kneeling with my three brothers, is like the sperm that spurts in secret from my member…

The three boys are back up on the platform, near their oldest sister: how did they receive the gift that makes them move through space, what high speech did it come down from, like the Holy Spirit on the Apostles, filling them with all the languages of the Earth? And what bread could feed such Speech?

At the bottom, near the stage entrance with golden curtains, the father plays the drum in a clown dress and makeup.

I'm afflicted with delicate nerves, and I'm afraid I'll hear my eardrums burst as they hit the water when I dive… These children, brothers my age up there, girl and boys jumping, their skin so gray under the fragile tights, so sickly—yet so tempting—as if patched in places… maybe the power of their jumps, leaps, twists and holds will tear open their skin and let the loosened guts slip over the tear, break and fall and spill onto the mattress underneath; maybe the fetus of incest will pour down from the open girl, its umbilical cord torn apart?

Do they descend, as Dorothy has told me, from the people who were pushed back and uprooted during the English repression of the 1746 Scottish insurrection, a people who never returned to their land or to sharecropping but were fated to endless travel, and gleaned from their craft or music skills, which they possessed in addition to their farm labor, enough to survive in caravans with sculpted and colored sides, outside the social, sanitary, educational and political evolution of their fatherland?

I imagine them like Spartan Helots, a population robbed by cruel invaders—the People of the Sea—enslaved, jeered at, tortured, and inebriated to edify the young Spartans. Aren't they also like taciturn Tinkers, their movements both limited by the tight space of the caravans and spreading in the free space of the outside, even if limited by the Law, appearing before us, the still imperial English people, like those Helots repeating the same sideshows their entire life to edify our courage, our skill, and our nostalgia?

Applause for the last jump recedes, and I feel Douggie's heavy hand on my shoulder as he stretches his arm behind his mother's back: he's picked up the smell of animals entering the stage behind the curtains of the other entrance; the coat on his thighs lifts: for such a strong erection I wonder what kind of animal it will be? Will it be more naked than the most naked of animals? Will its attributes be larger and more powerful than those of the donkey outside who brays again—as other boys, tired of the circus, masturbate him?—the noise drowned out by a brass band opening the act.

It's just a monkey. Well-endowed in a skinny frame with short, ginger fur, but tall, and with an ass that looks like those cow joints you can find at the butcher shop, with some flesh still attached.

In the ring, the three young boys start to juggle; the monkey walks toward them, grabs their balls, climbs halfway up the rope, releases—farts—the balls that the boys retrieve; I see the father in the opening on the other side of the ring who totters in his clown getup and hangs onto the red curtains; a brown bear, on a leash pulled by the girl, emerges, wobbling, from the curtains; the monkey, from the rope, jumps onto its shoulders.

In the dimming light of the hanging kerosene lamp, the three boys speed up the movement of their nine colored balls;

behind them, under stronger light, bear and monkey shove the father whose fife falls to the floor; in the dimming light, a woman with very long, curly hair, her breasts full and pink, a half-naked baby in her arms, jumps out of the red opening, knocks over monkey and bear and kneels beside the man who is now lying on the ground with the motley red still palpitating on his chest. Dorothy gets up from the top bench and goes down, crosses the ring under the swinging aerial rig and drops her long haunches down onto the man with the painted face; the two women carry the body outside.

Artists and audience need to continue with the show; the oldest boy assembles a few lamps and lanterns around the group.

The rumor spreads that the county doctor is examining the father in the caravan he shares with his wife and newborn; the oldest daughter and the three boys live in the other caravan.

Surrounded by smoking lights, the three boys juggle at a slower rhythm, as if they wanted to make us cross into another world; no music, just the sound of falling balls in their palms, the clicking of lips and jaws, and the thrusting of their wrists and shoulders; as they crouch, thin waists and blond hair on pimply foreheads, demonic asses; are they playing for me alone the intervals between sex, passing the time—and our time—before they take their places again, their haunches on the orgy pallet—with woman on top of the source of the debauchery? What kinds of lovemaking, what blend of semen, laughter, blows, and bruising caresses made them? They are children of *love* returning back to love, love skins, love eyes, love fingers, love hips…: do the animals of the circus—donkey, monkey, bear, and snake—add some of their seed to this paste—and what else too?—paste which is the clay dust of a Creator God—paste from which they rise so beautiful, so uncertain, hardly of this world?

Their movements through empty space: what I imagine of my deep, the gestures, the mingling of members, and the discharge that hurls bodies against other bodies, where does it come from? Is it from a transformed reality, soiled and exasperated, or is it from myself, but where in me? Is it from an *idea* that I began to roll before me as a child the way a cattle herder rolls his expanding ball, increasing and consolidating it in front of myself and of my growing body? What I see, these acrobatics in the air… what I see, I know and see only because I know it; I knew these children of *love* even before they were born: *their formula* has been deep inside me even before, at age ten, during study hall in boarding school, I had to ease away my big need—so that I didn't have to raise my hand and ask for the right to satisfy a natural need—but they say God created us with this *infamy*: a member with double, opposite uses?—I started beating off.

As a child, the sacred—what isn't sacred for me then?—dazzles me so much that my small reason sees and suspects that there is excess there, and that behind the amazement—object, figure, notion—lies its opposite: behind the absolute of virtue, the absolute of its opposite. Even the images of the Nazi inversion of morality, which I see at the age of six in books on the camps, are already images of excess—carbonized, tortured bodies, naked like slaughterhouse piles—that are unusable in what is starting to be constituted as the deep at the bottom of myself: there is a possible inversion of the Good, but into Beauty.

From the circle of low and smoking lights a song grows, rising from the ground, from the languid legs, from the feet, from the three boys sitting down, almost reclining—what is still shining on the back of their knees? Gusts of wind from the sea makes the light quiver: eyes, mouths, deep cleavage, the song rises from the feet to the stomach, to the chest and throat as fast as food rushes down to the legs of those who haven't slept for one or two nights. What should I do with this magic circle of fire where fatherless children cling together in defense against a dreaded English audience, what should I do with these bodies that are capable of everything, of Paradise and of my deep—if the faithful have Paradise, Purgatory and Hell, I have a fourth element: the deep, not of this world, not of the other.

Douggie's nostrils flare out again, the red curtains shift, a naked girl's leg appears, caught in the coils of a thick snake's tail; she is now in the ring, a python hanging down the front part of her body, scales against tights and small pink panties, its sleepy head resting on the shoulder between the hair, she moves, the python tail trailing between her ankles, toward the circle of light where the three boys sing in very low voices in a language that Douggie's mother whispers to me is close to the Shelta of Irish Tinkers: the difficulty of love, the menace of the law, of famine, of infant mortality, and of camp sites they are not allowed to use.

From the audience, a whisper under the flapping tent, adults yell sentences repeated by the children who shout along the edges of the ring. I make out Biblical words. In my heart I start to see that the paying public has claimed the right to the substance of these bodies to whom they're crying out, and my desire grows to see those bodies, to hear and feel them drop out of their act and improvise: my compassion feeds on that desire and that desire on my compassion.

The heat of the circle wakes the python, its head nuzzles the girl's neck as she steps between two lanterns and penetrates the circle of her brothers; the boys rise, push aside the lamps and lanterns, whisper in each other's ears, wrinkle their brows, the youngest boy climbs on the shoulders of the middle boy, both of their arms outstretched, and together with their hands and arms they mime a tree, the youngest as the top with his tousle of blond hair that has been cut and washed at times but never untangled; I imagine them in this fresh and tender tree— sap as spinal cord—smelling of poorly-nourished flesh, raised outdoors on roadside food of wild berries and stolen fruit—as babies, carried away by eagles sometimes in the morning, and brought back to the tree at night after they've seen the Earth, and speaking about what they've seen before the thin soup boiling in the pot at the entrance of the public dump.

The girl unhooks the python, carries it in her two fists, edges its head between the thigh of the youngest boy and the neck of the middle one, places the rest of the reptile on the middle boy's right shoulder, its tail hanging down the front of the boy's body, then sides with the eldest and presses up against him. A voice lower than hers emerges from the eldest boy, his stomach becomes animated: the voice, accompanied by a movement of his raised finger, signifies, in the same dialect, what everybody knows; wind, of earth and sea, blowing in from under the tarp sheets and between the hooks, flattens the smoke onto the ring; the eldest boy—where has he come from?—throws colored balls into his brothers' hands, who juggle them: will the python's head follow the movement of the balls through the empty space? The balls speed up, the girl intercepts them and throws them back; from her stomach through her mouth a voice comes out that she collects from all the dumps and public pallets; the youngest boy, throwing back the balls, pinches the python's tail, and the python pushes his tongue out into the shaking light and the thickening smoke; a red ball flies around that the girl's mouth, drawn with pink lipstick, intercepts, rolls along the lines of her lips and pushes away, blowing it out in front of her into the darkness.

The children scream: at least they've learned the apple must be eaten; if not, what use would this ageless torment be? But couldn't we remain, waiting, in that game, and live according to that game? Before Sin that is like orgasm, there is this suspension of the World, and of human fate, and this quadrilogue between God, the Devil, Adam, and Eve.

The mother comes out of the red curtains with her baby, and another scene is possible, the name of which the children cry out: Christmas! But if there is no eaten apple, if there is no fall and no expulsion from the Garden of Eden, if Cain doesn't murder Abel, there's no redemption: thus no nativity.

The primal scene must end. The girl-Eve must swallow the red ball—without eating it. The middle boy tires under the combined weight of the python and of his younger brother; again, the girl pulls from her guts the tempting voice, which no other voice defies; the red ball returns from the darkness, settles on her lips, she parts them, and her jaw, and the ball lodges there in her young girl saliva that she's only just mingled with the saliva of her oldest brother.

The audience claps; they lower the python and set him on the sand under the renewed circling of the balls; the ball is swallowed and regurgitated in the shadows, caught again and thrown back by the others, then the elder brother's member, beneath his tights, rises under the silk, the pubic hairs crowd around it; red flows into his gray cheeks; the youngest and the middle boy turn their faces away into the dark.

In the rising wind, Douggie's mother pulls the coat from his thighs and wraps the shoulders, rear and chest of the shivering boy—strong flesh but a weak spirit. The python has coiled around a lamp; the girl, leaving her older brother, crosses the ring toward her mother; both exit through the red curtains; the girl returns to the ring, alone, the baby in her arms, joins the group speaking in soft voices crouching or lying on the ground; the youngest rises and leaves the tent through the entrance. The donkey's braying softens; the elder and the middle boy bring the monkey and the bear to center stage and into the light, usher them into what used to be the circle, away from the python, and whisper instructions in their ears.

The elder boy, crouching, forms a cavity in the sand. The girl hands him the baby, and stretches the length of her body across the hole; the elder blows out all the lights; a ray of Moonlight on his ass shows him placing the baby between his sister's thighs, and pushing it inside; the youngest, straddling the donkey, comes back in; the girl moans, convulses; the youngest climbs down from the well-endowed donkey, leads him to the edge of the circle where the middle boy is lighting tubes and globes; the elder, crouching, holds the girl in his arms while she clasps the baby to her breast; from behind, the bear leans his heavy brown fur over the small group.

The monkey in front starts joking around, making the baby laugh; farther back, the donkey begins to move: the youngest boy caresses its flank, kisses its cheeks and jaw, despite the boy's attempts, the donkey turns its ass toward the back of the girl and her brother, lets out a long fart, the youngest moves the lamps back slightly, the baby turns his head and laughs; the monkey jumps onto the donkey and stands on its ass.

Who is playing what sounds like a royal song on a trumpet backstage? The python wakes up, uncoils; the girl gets up, hides the baby in her arms, the youngest pulls the donkey on stage; the girl climbs onto the donkey with the baby. Leaving his mother's left side, Douggie stands up and goes down to the ring and to the girl who is bending with the baby over the donkey's neck as it walks, and he throws in his father's coat; the children around the semicircle shout, with the trumpets blasting and the python crawling head up, they flow out onto the ring and benches... the elder of the boys vents Herod's anguished order through his stomach: who will say it in my deep?

Dorothy does not come home; when we get back to Kent Cottage, Mr. Praundlock tells us that she's in the Berwick hospital, with the father from the circus; outside, on the road along the coast, groups are walking home from the show under the full Moon. Mr. Praundlock has pulled the stew out of the oven that I'll eat on the same small table as before: what dark liquids are making my body seethe and boil? This black stew in the hollow of the good china plate is a good rendering of it... my place, my fate, how I'll attain what forces I've conceded to myself, it's all over there, backstage in the circus, in the lurching of the caravan, the depths of its shaking bed, with the pain I have in my side, suspended like sexual offal in a net... but from time to time, in the evening I go back to sit at the table in the house with the piano playing, and lay my head on the mother's breast as she prepares, with her daughters, a bed for my tired body, weary of growing under all climates; but if an assassin were to walk by along the road outside, I'd tear the knife from him, rush in front of him and commit the crime in his place.

In my two years of writing, seeing how Time in me—the time of my poetry in process—transforms the real I wish to depict into an idea with a rhythm, I've grown so tormented about whether the facts the evangelists transcribed with nostalgia and the impulse to proselytize are real or not! I've spent so much of my childhood and adolescent time living the life of Christ with all the possible strength of heart, of mind, of knowledge and of the senses—touch, etc.—as an apostle, a passerby, a listener, a guest, possessed and dispossessed, sometimes as Himself—how hard it is to separate in myself His divine part from His human one! My reason could shatter against this, or be extinguished.

Often, when I am by myself in Nature, seized in fear by this need to live in Him, I breathe in deeply at the most intimate of the flower's calyx, in the interval of bark, closest to sand, or running or stagnant water, livestock under the full Sun—but in my native mountain, there are too few shared elements with ancient Palestinian mountains—what did He feel, what did He do with these sensations in his double mind, or rather, in his human mind and in the other, in the Holy Spirit—his Father's spirit blended with His?

Lying on the ground, during a rest with his companions, what did He see in the sky above them? What was missing in the Beatitudes?

Did his Divine part support the human one? Did his human part support the Divine one? Were they permanently linked, undifferentiated? When he began to preach, or eat, or sleep, did the Divine part take over? The remains of human speech, of human food, of human dreams must have seemed so bitter!

On the inside edges of His lips, did he keep the speech that was so overly Divine that no companion, king, sage, or philosopher could have understood it?

Did He pronounce a more human version, and when that wasn't understood, did He further simplify it in words and reasoning and, when he saw that the incomprehension still grew, did he reject it all in anger or in a parable?

Do we only believe according to what's real? Didn't his companions believe in "Him," little by little, with difficulty, rejecting, betraying, repenting according to something else than visible or audible reality, and didn't they die without any guarantee of "His" divinity?

Even in what is the most sacred of the Sacred, truth moves as the Earth turns on itself: this might be where the artist works, in the perpetually disjointed gap which is also maybe the demon's part, at least in the history of humanity. What scientists study with a patience unworthy of the act of Art, that is, the Cosmos or the human body, requires exactitude: is Nature as predictable as human nature?

Is the course of water, as it circumvents or erodes rock through what will become a valley and its river, as predictable as the motion of a passion in the heart of man, or of an idea in the mind of a thinker?

Maybe a shepherd, unaccounted for, and disappearing later into History, used the steel tip of his staff in anger to chip the friable rock that the water might have circumvented; but isn't this shepherd, ignored by science, found by poetry and artists who have him act on the material of science? Outside, inside, everything seems to tell me that Art is made by the infirm, the half- or third-witted—half- or third-hearted—like me, since I am only a half or a third of a man because I've yet to penetrate a woman; only philosophy and science, where my vision quickly blurs, are the work of complete adults.

I feel that, as much as I feel the attraction of beauty and the need to transform it: in order to create, you must lower your weapons before the real, step back from beauty, look at it in a daze, let it act in you and put you to sleep so that when you wake up it is standing, but yours now; the philosopher and the scientist inch forward, step by step, with so much cowardice; but when a civilization needs to defend itself against its own decline, the artists are the ones it offers up.

How can I express and organize my thoughts in front of an adult without revealing "the secret" that locks and bolts it: the deep—if not for my hope: poetry? At that point it's no longer expression that I need but an adult *word*, before me, as coherent and thorough as possible, its audacity on par with mine as I write in the rising orgasm; I need a friend and master to reshape my body and return what was captured by its ancestry like a quelling of the shimmering of contours, an abolishing of its perfume: its shine, its sexual attractiveness.

The plate of stew smokes on the guéridon; Mr. Praundlock has settled in his armchair, opposite me; I fold in my long, naked legs; after the swim, I'd rolled up my tawny velvet shorts in case I wanted to walk along the surf, and I have my strong thighs naked, there, with my spray imprinted on their backside like a wound at night, a scar that I fear people will notice during the day.

Anthony's grandfather—his lips slightly foaming with hunger: does he want the stew, or my member?—stirs in his big black leather armchair, his face already so red that I can't tell if he's blushing. My heart drops, and my fork along with, when I imagine my room with the *knock knock* of Anthony's hard knuckle on the door and him heaving "your cock" against the wood. Why doesn't he share the stew with me, and then leave me my member; his cheek next to mine, I whisper the deal to him in French: either the stew or the member!

He grabs a spoon from the china cabinet, sets a chair in front of the guéridon, sits down, shoves his spoon into the stew and eats; although I know he'll eat his share of stew and will still be at my door at midnight to have the member, as I see him wolf down the burning-hot brown mass, my heart suggests to me that for now he prefers the stew to the member… But he eats the food so avidly that he gets stew on his forehead, and I imagine he'd eat my cock like that as well… Pushing the plate toward him, I leave him everything to wolf down.

Mr. Praundlock, thinking that I don't like his daughter's cooking, tells me that he understands, that I can only reject their food since French cuisine is so beautiful and delicious— as a young soldier, he "lived" on the Somme front in 1916; Anthony turns around with his mouth full, and retorts in his strong Yorkshire voice and accent that if I'm not eating it's because we've made a deal, him and I, and that in France I come from a large family that eats inexpensive food, but food that's good for health, skin, members; his grandfather asks him to see if he can find something to replace the stew in the pantry: maybe cake?—with *jelly* on top... With the doors open onto the veranda, an owl cries in the garden, and wanting to be charming, I stammer the Shakespeare sonnet that I've known by heart since Father Vallas taught it to me—he's the only man today who could hear the secret of my deep without surprise or blame: *To whit! to-whoo! A merry note...*

Anthony's grandfather has retired to his room. Anthony slurps what's left of stew, I go out into the little garden in front of the cottage: the smell has dissipated; how can I keep the trace of his mouth against my cheek? How can I have it last at least till morning when we'll be reunited for a swim? I concentrate on this smell in the mist, and it reminds me of another one, a long time ago when I was waiting for my father for one more scolding. I'd gone to the back of his office near the sink to see his shiny instruments and flasks—poisons—and in the sink I'd smelled a cotton pad hard with dried blood that the maid would throw out later when she cleaned. In the noise of the waking village coming in from the window open behind closed shutters, in the honking of the bus for Saint-Étienne or Annonay or Le Puy or Lyon, I pinched it between my fingers: was it man's blood? Was it woman's blood? If woman's blood, from what crevice? Touching this plug of hardened blood was like touching the evidence of a crime.

Thinking that my father would come down by the wooden circular staircase leading from our kitchen to the waiting room with its spittoon, I didn't notice that he'd come down from the upstairs apartment by the common stairs of black stone outside, and had turned the key in the front door lock of the office, pushed the door, and found me stuffing the cotton tampon into the side pocket of my shorts; I saw him repress a gesture of anger, smooth his brow beneath the hat that he always wore in public; there were so many reasons for his anger that he glossed over this new dissimulation—I hid so much from him, was I even still visible to him?—and he settled at his desk—in a drawer of which lay the poems of his dear, dead friend—cleanly shaven for the general scolding; facing him, whose over-washed hands were always the color and smell of blood, I gathered up my embarrassed body on the patient's chair: what weak poems—yet behind which I saw the future poem shine—could I use to affirm myself and affirm my body, and defend my reason against his?

The wad of woman's blood softened under my tight shorts, flush against my private parts and my member, and that, in front of him, I no longer know whether they are men's parts and a man's member: can he smell that woman's blood is spreading along the slope of my thigh toward a wound below my parts, with the cotton ready to be used again?

From what crevice of Annick's body does her musky fluid trickle, ooze? Is there cotton to block the flow? Does the blood stop at that little valve when she is in the sea? Through what parthenogenesis do mermaids reproduce?

Is this slit bleeding because too many male members have penetrated it to the point of wounding it?

The night seems too long before I'll be able to run my entire arm behind her shoulders, with my thumb against her cheek, tip her head against mine and set out to purify and pacify her as I imagine the great numbers of penetrators she has, here and in France.

But if, later, back in my room under the vocal, resonant, and panting pressure of Anthony's desire, stretched out with my little package on my groin, what form will she take, with her numbers, as she emerges in the little world reborn at every minute under my hand on the paper soiled the night before?

And if this slit makes blood, it's because it's a true organ, not the place of surface games; depth with its own measure, its chemical reactions, another, autonomous life; it is no longer a game, nor even pleasure, but a technique, an effort; the adjusting of one world to another.

The street lights of Berwick-upon-Tweed to the northeast prefigure the dawn for me; since childhood, sleep has always seemed too long, even if my sleep is full of dreams where there are Romans, Greeks, and people from Antiquity, and where my "me" is finally reduced; we dream, we are crazy for a third of our life.

Hard, as a child, to understand why at night the body must rest from the day; in the X-ray image of the body of the day laborer asleep, I imagine the renewal, the reconstitution of his strength moving from the toes, progressing through the bones, in the muscles, in the nerves, the arteries, the veins, vessels, liquids, toward the legs, the groin, the chest and with some haste, into the skull to spread in the waking head.

The owl has brought its lice to a half-dead cedar tree behind the cottage; the tide is at its lowest. Through the crack of the door behind me I hear Mr. Praundlock snoring: was he already snoring like this as a young soldier in the trenches of the Somme in 1916?

We are now only three. Anthony rattles the empty plate and silverware in the sink. Desire stirs up in me again, between my thighs and between the two parts of my brain, not the desire for real bodies, the desire for Anthony or for Annick's kiss on my cheek, but for those shadows, those flashes of bodies and voices that I will animate, later, on my writing paper, as I tremble from the hand job. My spinal cord, my ass as it relaxes command me to stretch out.

If I go through the living room to get to my room, Anthony might enter with me. And so I head to the open window, climb up, and there I am inside locking my door. But after an entire day of companionship, spyglasses, bladder jokes, pissing contests, swimming, why wouldn't we heap our limbs onto the bed and fall asleep at once in a kind of joy that would continue in our dreams, as we used to do as children, brothers, cousins weary from running?

Or else, piqued by his father's absence, by his mother's, his sister's, his aunt's and uncle's, with his grandfather feeble beneath the quilt, he might, as host and one also responsible for a stranger, suddenly feel the urge to master, as he sees fit, his need to see and use a member that speaks a language other than his.

Are the monkey, the bear, and the python sleeping in their cages? The donkey, in the Moonlight, at the end of his tether in what's left of the meadow? The brothers and sister, tights off, in a pile on the family couch? In the caravan, with the baby rocking in its straw cradle, is the mother warming coffee so that she can stay up until the father returns—or until Dorothy comes to announce his death softly?

My new desire can hold its own before the sound of the rising sea, but it's nothing when faced with the real man, there, naked, from whose face they are wiping makeup, mascara and lipstick, whose red-haired skull they are retracting, whose artery they are rummaging through to unclog it, his ruined clothes rolling off the chair under the neon onto the nurses' shoes. Will this force the eldest son, old enough to take over the circus, to marry his mother?

When desire returns, all things converge there once again, and with this convergence comes the sensation and the certainty, despite this desire and its figures, that all human acts, all human thoughts are fated to their own end, to their inanity, and to the laughter from the sidelines that the devil cannot repress.

I need to satisfy that desire as fast as possible, through pleasure with text, so that when I'm sobered after the act, the life of humans can have meaning again, I can reinstate their actions, their passions, and their reasons in the correct light, the light that is endless and that will never end, the movement of divine reason!

And if I could instate this desire and the deep from which it sparks into that universal and infinite reason through the theological operation of an unknown Saint or group of Saints... if, like Him, child of man and woman, I could, with impossible sincerity and impossible purity of motive, explain to the Doctors of the Law the necessity beyond weakness of my secret act—may it fall on me alone!—I would find the words to charm old ears.

The desire that exalts and turns on my inner thighs like a castration, one day I'll find its "absolute" term! I know that crime is a desire that reduces the world around it to insignificance, to a laugh. The signature of crime is a murdered corpse. Once I crash, the signature of my desire and of my spurt is a nearly-dead body, and at the end of my hand as it opens, a few emphatic lines on the paper—and sometimes, the temptation to cover what little that is with a crime. But whom can I kill but myself?

The man who's moving with his back curved against the wind between the dunes, his face hooded, intermittently moonlit, he must have a knife.

And why are Anthony's father, mother, and sister still in the village? When too many human beings simultaneously fill my brain, I find an imaginary way out. Tonight, there's the agonizing father from the circus to the northeast and that man facing me to the east. Behind me to the west there's Anthony and his grandfather, to the south the lights from Seahouses with five to seven lives per light. Toward the north in front of me there are ships gleaming on the horizon with tens or hundreds of soldiers and sailors for each gleam of light. Above me, how many passengers per plane? And in the village, there's the mother, her three children, the reverend, the reverend's wife, the maid, the people from the circus, those thinking animals, and seven houses from ours at most, Annick sleeping in what's left of her blood. Sometimes what saves me is the narrow bed of a river carrying sunlit water over very luminous rocks—but soon enough those rocks transform into whitened bones and the river into the edge of a bloody battle, and my brain is peopled again with human beings running scattered between the razor edge of swords and the razor edge of tools. Widows, orphans, widowers, their guts, heads, vulvae on the burnt ground. At night, crows retreating to the trees with their red strips of flesh…

Dorothy returns from the emergency room where the father of the circus family is coming back to life, Anthony's mother, father, and sister are back from the village where they were planning a trip to Australia with some friends who want to move there, now we can finally sleep: tomorrow we'll visit Edinburgh, Holyrood Palace, Marie Stuart and a Paul Gauguin show.

Annick is still sick, will the family she is staying with let her come?

Will we take the coastal road, or the estuary? Will we go through the Cheviot Hills instead, where we've planned a day hike for the middle of the week? How can I sleep when the next day I'll breathe where Marie used to breathe, and where I'll see real Gauguins?

This keeps me up all night, more than Anthony's gentle stubbornness; I let him in before dawn, and in swimming trunks and T-shirts we take the coastal road to the cottage where Annick is sleeping; does he want me to get hard, as my body shivers from fatigue and from the sea breeze ruffling the curtains up there in the open window of the room where she is sleeping?

Does a boy, his sex erect in front, naturally go toward the sex of a girl?

Do sexes and organs recognize each other at a distance? Is my member down here, outside, hard for her organ that's now purified beneath the freshly laundered sheet? Is it hard for that mystery, that viscous unknown physiology? I've never seen any images or technical drawings of vaginas; do the crude, roughly colored photographs I saw in the late June porn magazines, of more or less gaping female sexes and ruddy ass cracks folding over the coils of thick, rigid ropes, place a veil of butchery over what is budding like a gift from God in reproductions of Rubens, Boucher, Ingres and Corot?

This time, the lack of sleep makes me go faster—what I can do that is most beautiful in dreams, that is, fly above the Earth, I can do here in the deepest part of me with this little girl, maybe curled into a ball, her delicate wrists between her knees.

In front of my bare eyes—I left my glasses on the table, so Anthony leads me in the dim twilight—her eyes palpitate in dream, and joy floods my entire brain at last—I let him take my member, now well erect and hard. It isn't "me" that makes love with myself during my beat-sheet sessions, but my member that makes love with itself when it leaves its phantom foreskin and goes back to it; it's the "orgiastic" text that makes love to that member, and "I," exalted brain and heart, am nothing but a carcass discarded behind the thing already in the darkness.

If I want to see him smile, and his lips foam a bit, I need to nudge my eyes, my face, to his: but I'd rather be close to Annick's eyes, up there, and with my lips follow the contour of her cheek until I reach the lips half-parted on the teeth; but my member blossoms, in that hand now full of mist or dew, the hand of that boy with the vigorous brain—have I seen anything of him, of his body, since I've arrived? Blond hair, blue eyes; have I seen his lower belly, seen between the thighs, have I even dared look at his ass, his waist, his back? Have I even seen the throat, the jaw out of which his heavy, breaking voice comes with crystalline tears and plaintive shreds?

Tonight, because he knows that I can only see him from up close, and maybe wishes to postpone that seeing, he gives me his voice to love. It trembles like the voices of my deep. Straining to remember Annick's voice as she spoke to me for the first time on the Churchyard wall, I lose myself in it while my member grows even harder in the fist as it warms.

Is it because of the boy's voice that I am hearing? Or is it because of the voice whose sound I search for in my memory?

The male body seems formless to me then: stick, club, bloc, column of an authority to come or one already established. Only women or girls attract me with their curves, the excess of their flesh, the widening of their waists into their hips, the mobility of their small warm masses, their unpredictable movements; the suspension of so much flesh and food in so little skin, the breasts; and the neck, the back of the neck where the hair starts—the *braid*: the back of the neck either very fresh or later when it resists the yoke of marriage; and the mystery of their thought: beings that everything, psalms, poetry, painting, sculpture, music, designates as the seat of ideal earthly beauty— and even in the beyond. Fra Angelico's *Coronation of the Virgin* in the changing light of the four seasons of the year 1947, hanging in my room during my first age of reason—thought can only conform to this celebration, the most pure, the one least charged with ulterior motives, the most learned and benevolent; the one closest to what should be ideal thought, the harmony of science and dreams. At the time, I cannot conceive the feminine brain as fated to the tasks of the male brain: the perpetual churning of an idea against its opposite, misery against joy, plotting against sincerity, darkness against innocence, lying against truth, or madness against reason.

What I've learned from life, mythologies, History, theater, painting, and opera about the duplicity of women, their cruelty, their absence of remorse, doesn't disturb the security of a private and public, specific and general, almost cosmic feminine brain that watches with indulgence and a smile over the human species troubled by males.

I've always questioned the girls and women around me to try to understand that luminous, liquid and sweet-scented mind. Then behind the high curved foreheads I've seen in paintings and in life, I've tried to probe how images and clear ideas, foreshadowings and resolutions are ordered. It's true that painters choose the forehead of women to represent the immensity and the silence of thinking, whereas they crease the brow of males, evangelists, philosophers, hermits or even God the Father.

When I was a child I believed that the forehead thought by itself, that it was something of a block, almost mineral, self-sufficient and as resistant as white, black, or another kind of marble: a thinking stone.

Later, seeing waste of an unknown color scattered under the summer heat on the melting asphalt, waste from the carcass of a dog dying of a shattered head, from which my mother pulls me away as if from the spectacle of human misery, I noticed in the shattered skull a shining lump larger than the rest, made of the same matter as this waste, and understood that the forehead was just a facade behind which lived a viscous, limp, and guilty mass and that this legless monster, without coils or fins, was a brain: the spirit of beast or man. The following night, I woke up afraid to move my head and the brain contained within it. And later, I'd see the brain, the spirit of those close to me, of those who leaned down toward me, or of those whose head was as high as mine as one would see someone speak, live, plead from the other side of a window pane thick enough to shut out the sound.

Then, and for a long time, I only saw spirit in women; and in men, only war. Only that fragile spirit above intrigued me, and not the spirit laboring here below by my side: how did that harmony function, in words at least, in the fluttering of eyelashes, or pouting? In France, I often watched my mother read and speak or paint or dream: was there room in that mind for disbelief, for resentment, for hatred or for deadly plots? Room for someone other than my father? What did she pull that was beyond us from all that she'd lived through, wars, bereavement, deportations, and the murder of her youngest brother, from all that she'd read, contra-marital passion, martyrdom, obscenities, atrocities, betrayals, from all of her encounters and her social vision, from the thickness of her dreams?

Did her activities as a mother, a wife, an assistant, a caretaker, and a confidante for village prostitutes form a *deep* within her? I am fairly certain of my father's, formed under the sway of bumps in the road between his day and night visits, and it's because I know this that I am speechless before him.

I know very little about the girl sleeping up there, her breath too weak to move the curtains. Does she even know where she comes from, as I do, at least here below? Do girls and women descend like me from their Creator, even if I always reassure myself and worry about that ascendance? In my eyes, every woman, every girl is the queen of the world, but man is endlessly unraveling her labor of peace, while she's watching and when she sleeps.

The front door is shut, a small dog barks—is it Marie Stuart's dog witness to her decapitation by axe in the great hall at Fotheringhay?

We see a ladder in the path leading to the garden behind the cottage. Anthony lets my member drop. We pull the ladder from its mesh of wild grasses, lift and lean it against the wall until it reaches the window on the top that is cracked open. Who will climb first? The window is narrow up there, we'll have to squeeze in and let ourselves slide down into the room. If I go first and enter an unknown room that Annick might not even be sleeping in, he could pull the ladder away and leave me alone with someone, sleeping, who might be scared by my body's form shining in the Moonlight coming in from the window. We decide he'll go up first to prepare our arrival. Seeing that my member is bothering me as it grows longer outside the swim suit—he didn't put it back—and that I have to let it go toward its natural home, free and autonomous—in my beat-sheet sessions I never grab it with my bare hands, but instead churn it through its cloth as it tightens around it—from the fifth rung of the ladder, fifth out of thirteen, in the twilight growing blue on the eastern horizon, his breaking voice filtered by snot says: "It's the member of truth… whatever you think… it moves, and becomes everything you're feeling."

The ladder is so close against the wall that at every rung I'm scared I'll have to push my member back against my stomach, and that I might fall off.

The little dog has fallen asleep on his bone. Up there, Anthony inches his head and shoulders in through the small curtains, his short-sleeved shirt slips down his back, I see his ass, then nothing.

I climb the ladder, my forehead low against the rungs; if I fell from up there I wouldn't see my fall; here I am now fumbling at the drapes. I push my head in, my shoulders, half of my body and then the rest. I scrape my knees against the ledge and slide into the room, falling onto Anthony's legs who is just starting to get up. What does he see in here? I put my member back into my trunks—I'll tighten the side laces later.

Sitting with our knees up and our backs to the window, we wait for the darkness to clear: what can Anthony's sharp blue eyes see? His weary breath wraps around my ear: "There are two girls in two beds. Annick is on the right, the one on the left is the girl who lives here. The dog woke her up but she's nearsighted like you so she doesn't see us."

On the left is the *odor*, and on the right, a smell in which the day's makeup mixed with deodorant dissolve into the light sweat of dreams.

The one on the left has gone back to sleep. Should we wait for both of them to wake before we do anything, or should we act immediately? With the sound of our voices, with our touch? Or maybe use our rugged, cool hands to pinch, like the prick of a needle, the joint of their arms and forearms where the small veins bulge as they spread out over the covers at the edge of the bed near the rug.

The blue rising in the sky lightens the room a bit, but I still can't make out the pattern of the rug under my feet;

Anthony tells me there are snakes, vines, tigers, and that near the back between the two headboards and bedside tables, there's an elephant with a group of hunters on its back, armed with bows and arrows, one of which has already pierced the tiger's flank.

Sweat covers my body: since we're half-naked, will they pierce us with arrows too? Everything that is naked must be shot, captured, ensnared, tortured, carved up, or burned…

How many millennia just to cover our bodies with skins, bark, grasses, and fabric…

We fell asleep.

In between fitful waking either my head is on his shoulder or his head on mine.

Now Sun loads the room entirely, I turn my head toward the window: outside and in my vision of the firmament as it shifts from right to left and from left to right so hazy that I barely see the solar disk in the middle of the back-and-forth of my eyes, it's as if all the gods of night were fleeing the day in their chariots, delayed by hunting and by love.

I look at Anthony, pull my shoulder out from under his head; his head drops but it doesn't wake him; will I squeeze back through the window and climb down the ladder? Or will I instead stay in the room, and with the haze before my eyes, create a space outside of social law, a space where I could push this member forward as it lifts again and edge it toward what lies awake in the body under the covers where mist is forming in the

Sunlight? The girl on the left wakes up: a red head emerges from beneath the covers. I think I see a Greek profile spotted with freckles. I've just learned that the canon of Greek beauty put under duress by Alexander's Federation is just a mask, and that beneath this political and philosophical mask of "perfection," even before Salamis wins against Xerxes and the West against the *Orient*, there are northern populations and especially the hated people from the east, there are freckles to the north— Cimmerians—and tan skin to the east and south. We are missing the paintings, with those face and eye colors, to restore the truth of what Greece reduced to the category of "metics."

As her eye flashes in the Sun, I see that she is watching me from behind a very red lock of hair—does my straining vision intensify the colors? She pulls the covers back, and I smell the *Odor* more than I see the girl as she straightens her body on the sheet, a body triply warm from the Sun, the covers and from those unknown dreams that fill the nights of girls. Will I walk to the edge of her bed, sit there—since I've been a child I've sat on the edge of so many beds, my sisters' beds, the beds of friends, and the bed of a friend's friend when I ran away— and, as she sits there with her fists in her eye sockets, see up close the waking of the girl or woman who begins to speak her day as soon as she's awake?

Mine, on the right, turns over on her back. I see her legs spreading under the covers, she pulls them back tightly to turn onto her side as soon as she sees me.

I crawl on all fours on the rug toward the left where she is laying her cheek maybe with her dark eye open straining to peek over the contours of her face. The less you see, the more you have to crouch, at least to see the ground along which you inch your way. I pass the foot of the bed and turn around. All I see of Anthony is his curly blond hair laying on the small radiator on the wall: if it were longer, and if it spread along the tubes, and if…, could I desire him?

Is he really sleeping? Or is he instead shutting his eyes and numbing his body, with the full light of the Sun shining on his dilemma and on the opposite objects of the choice he'll have to make, giving himself the lull of a brief sleep to prepare in his *darkened chamber* the clear-cut image of the object that he'll desire without himself being desired in return?

Maybe he wants to leave me alone before that being, its head now facing up and tense in the sunlight, and let me decide his desire and his life through what I'm able to make of this mess of Sun, wool, hair, yawns, sighs, and tiny bursts of laughter?

With my eyes on the ground and my head butting against the folding covers, I think I see to my left his blond hair move toward the other open bed and sink and lift toward the red-haired mass; sweat, that grows colder, runs down my back: I'm too far away now from his wall to know if he's still leaning against it.

Once again, the image of what I foresee, especially of what creates my pain, takes on real shape, whatever the space I'm in, inside or out. Thought abolishes reality in truth, in what I believe to be my truth: no one can convince me of its opposite. Crawling on all fours, it's not a member here that I carry beneath me, even a heavy one, but a beat-sheet pack that is devouring my liver.

Like doing a mundane task after someone has died: the ladder?

They won't see the ladder down below if *they* have the same bad vision as I do, and if they have good vision I won't see their anger.

I should forget what grows between my thighs and button the last button of my short-sleeved shirt over my trunks, move forward on palms and knees toward what I begin to see is spreading, covers, someone sitting up, face, breasts that turn to face the front, loosed from the unbuttoned collar of the nightgown with ruffles on the shoulder.

Is the bed so high that I'm invisible? Under the box spring, two or three stuffed animals: are we on the side of the snake? Of the wounded tiger in the extension of the window? What should I do with the edge of the bed? What should I do with this plump substance? There is no law against my touching it, but its nightgown wraps it with society. Is it for society that we must love? Does *this* member, one among a million members, look for its hole among a million holes to perpetuate society, make it grow, and pacify it? For whom and for what do we love? Is it for the good of society, for the State, for the continent, for civilization, or for humanity? Couldn't the Creator Himself have us be born or have our babies born from his hand or his forehead like he had his Son be born from a woman without seed? How can one desire ancestry, transformed into law and duty by society, with all the strength of a member, testicles and everything that flows into them?

A jolt of her brown hair and her fingers in its tousled mass to comb it momentarily makes my member stands up more in my trunks: it's because I see it in my deep of hair and fingers sullied and drained by their antisocial use. What shape, what color, what matter composes what she now hides with her two fists sinking in the flowered fabric between her thighs?

My heart, beating stronger than my member, leads me to her two breasts, which she's put back into the ruffled and now buttoned-up nightshirt. My sight is so short and blurry that I would not be able to see a trace of sweat there, or even milk…

I want to see the light fuzz on her upper lip behind a disheveled lock of hair. I could lay my palm on what I know is a woman's thigh but it's my lips that move forward as my body rises toward her speaking cheek, as if a hand were pushing my neck, my backbone beaten under impossible sexual labor: "So your straight-laced family let you out before breakfast?" My lips—scarred from a bike accident in the Col de Vars in the Southern Alps last July—their drab flesh made more pungent by the saltiness of the stew, open as they climb up the tiny tangled hairs along the ear: "Tell me if you're seeing Anthony?" But my jaw as it moves back closes down on the red pearl of her earlobe: what if I could decorate the ears of my shadows with small, fake jewels in my deep?

"He's here too? Where is he?"

I smell the bed at the end of the room, and from the changing light in front of what I imagine to be the door opening onto the stairs, I catch an odor of toast, fried eggs, and tea.

"Did the little redhead get out of bed?"

"You mean the red-haired girl, the girl of the house, Viva?"

She pronounces *reid* in her very soft young woman's voice and I restore it to the firm and open *red*. The word as she deforms it and in my restoration leaps from my testicles to my member and uncaps it from its phantom skin. For a few seconds I think that she's afflicted with the same bad vision as me, and that she can't see my loaded trunks trailing along the edge of the bed *beneath* the tucked-in sheet. Under the thin single-layered fabric of the trunks with their side laces—I used my mother's scissors and her needle and thread to make my beat-sheet jizz cloth out of one of those swim trunks, after having tricked my mother into buying two—my member hardens from that double, female and male sound. Now through the fabric my member touches the sheet on which a girl, a future woman, has exuded in her sleep those substances that everyone is so hush-hush about.

Back down the ladder, that we've laid back into its bed of grass, we run toward Kent Cottage as if we'd come back from the sea but didn't swim. Him upstairs and I below, we pull on our shorts and buckle our belts over our skin. After breakfast, we leave for Edinburgh in Norman B's overheated red Rover. I sit in front because I'm car sick, Dorothy and Anthony sit in the back with Anthony's mother and sister: their father has gone fly fishing.

Along the coast: rocks, forests, fields, meadows; Budle, Easington, Fenwick, Kyloe, Cheswick, Berwick, Cairncross,

Dunbar, Gullane, Cockenzie—Anthony touches my shoulder from behind—Prestonpans, Musselburgh, Scoughall where I say between two bouts of nausea that it's like an animal, part snake part cougar, Portobello.

As the Firth of Forth estuary grows narrow I sense that I will one day have to open what is still secret, take my soiled shadows out on the stage, in the places and the rhythmic space of my visible poetry. But since we're driving toward the narrowing of the estuary, and since nausea stops me from turning back to see my future as it recedes, I watch this narrowing as I would the coming need to concentrate my poetic powers into a tighter and tighter vision and a more and more cardiac beat—and toward the origin, the source of being and of song.

In front of the museum, the cold settles in after nausea, and my heartbeat skips in what I take to be a great mechanism in a red dusk. In a few seconds I review all the work accomplished during the first half of the year: uncovering of French poetry from André Chénier to André Breton, research on the "unknown," art and madness already.

Who am I? What have I become, standing in front of those paintings, real ones, that open up in front of me like a Garden of Eden?

Here hanging behind glass in real life is everything I thought about when I used to leaf through art books, what my father called "reverie," searching for the possible contours of a future poetry, nouns without any links between them except for meaning and sound. I try to see through my divergent lenses, foggy from the heat of the crowd; to isolate the details like I do in the albums, I take off my glasses and look at it raw, like at night or in the girls' room: bare-chested women with a vase of red flowers, boys on horseback, a yellow Christ from Nizon, that other village in Brittany where we go on vacation, the great triptych of Destiny, pigs and their small caretakers, the coast of Oceania, unruffled gazes, dreaming of what kind of intercourse?…

The origin, in all its forms, the artists' torment that pushes those who will last to simplify their art when they get close to dying, as if they could make it audible, visible, readable for those in the beyond: I now begin to doubt that it can be found in art, in life, except in those regions and populations of the world where we Westerners still believe that it acts naturally.

The progress of the text of the deep, its audacity for me at the time, and the power of the crashing that follows after I come, make me believe that I've found something of the origin with this paper, and in the bodies and sex that begin there; the clandestine nature of the operation, as if eggs were hatched under cover of the male and female and in the secret of nature, slowly proves to me that the origin is within me and under my hand.

But during the afternoon, the bloody spot on a Holyrood tile which marks the presumed assassination of Riccio, Marie Stuart's Italian poet, by her limp blond husband, brings me back to the indelible spot on Lady Macbeth's palm, and to the other blood secreted by the organ that I still have not touched; if it seems that temporary blood coming from a place that I don't know is matter that can be dissolved in other matter, the way water gets swallowed by sand or shit gets dissolved by water or sun, then the blood of crime is no longer matter; no other matter can absorb it, speech cannot abolish it; just as on the tiled floor in Blois the presumed blood of Scarface François de Guise, assassinated in 1588 by order of Henri III who was himself stabbed to death ten years later by Jacques Clément the monk, Riccio's presumed blood is not erased by the murder of Darnley in the plot concocted by Marie, a de Guise from Lorraine through her mother, and by Boswell, her destructive lover.

At the end of the afternoon seated in a large fish-and-chips shop on the port of Leith where old fishermen are smoking pipes and polishing their hornpipes, Anthony plays footsies between my thighs from across the table. At a back table I see a family, three or four boys, three or four girls, and a young father in a blue anorak, a girl next to him, his eldest daughter—or the mother of the family?—her long blond hair veering on white, a very white face with freckles, white arms on the table, voices, the heaving of voices distributing the newspaper-wrapped fish and chips, straightening her back then dropping her shoulders; I smell their odor from our table: dingy, piss-stained mattresses, leftovers for dogs, grease.

After eating, the children disappear into the courtyard in the back, led by one of their sisters, her blond braid lying against her black dress; alone on the bench, on the table heavy with the scraps of fish and crumpled newspaper, the father covers with his thick, hirsute hand, the arm and then the hand of his wife—or of his eldest daughter—and kisses her raised neck.

The floor shakes as ships pass—sirens, horns, collisions; later, when the children and their sister have returned to the bench, the girl gets up and disappears into the darkness, her high, skinny hips caught in short shorts and her bra strap visible on her back between the shoulders across the ribcage; the sister—the youngest?—entertains the children with a fairy tale in a gruff voice, the father steps over the bench and disappears into the darkness; still later, as a large boat shakes the pontoon, I get up to move onto firm ground, the court-yard in the back: a concrete alley with Turkish toilets at the end; the ground is stable but littered with fish bones, raw fish heads with the strong stench of fish guts.

At the back, across from me, a door swings and squeaks; as the darkness lifts I can see that the alley veers toward the right and toward the light; I walk through the trash to the Turkish toilet, its front step is covered in shit: the six or seven children have defecated at random and even in front of the door; I walk on, stepping between the turds; as I climb into the toilet, to the right at the end of a recess lit by a basement window open onto the light and noise of the elevated avenue outside, I see a couple, standing, having sex, and hear the noise of joints and suction beneath the rustling, the cracking and the lapping of the trash they are crushing under their feet; a few flies, black, blue, green—is there also rotten meat?—come and go from the coitus to the top, and from the two rubbing heads down to the trash and shit; the flies, as the condensation thickens, hide the details of the coitus now pivoting in small steps toward the tallest heap of trash.

I see the man's hips, and little by little, his large hirsute arms, sleeves rolled up to the elbows, grab with joined wrists the lower back of the girl-woman, his palms spread across the skinny ass, slide to the back thighs and lift them toward his hips: a sneaker falls from the girl's foot as she, arms and hands trembling in her curls, wraps the man's brown and red head with her nearly white hair. I can see over and under her lifted thighs. One of the man's hands, as the other holds the girl from below, rummages in the mess of folds at the lower stomach; will I finally see what I had started to see and what was so *contrary to reason* that I immediately forgot it? Will I see it for good this time: a man's member penetrate a woman's *sex*? Will the scattered trash, the stench of rot and death—even of animals—make the human act admissible this time? Suddenly, a cold sweat runs down my back like someone leaving me, the guardian angel of childhood peeling away—I crush it under my ass during my beat-sheet sessions—as a trickle of blood after a thrust from the man's ass leaks from beneath the mess and falls in very red drops onto the trash.

Woman: blood, always blood, more blood. Man is the one who spreads it, here and during wartime.

I've read stories of matrons coming in the morning after the wedding night to examine the sheets of noble children, or of peasant children. Although I didn't understand at first, and then didn't dare ask my mother to explain, I know that the betrothed is a virgin on the wedding night, that she climbs into bed a virgin and that at night the husband *takes her flower*.

As a child I try to understand what this flower is, and why this flower, when taken from the virgin, makes blood; but I've read in German fairy tales that the rose, although its thorns can make you bleed, also bleeds when cut and that from this blood a full-grown hero rises; what was that crown of thorns that wound tightly around the skull of a flagellated Christ? And if His side pierced by the soldier's spear secreted blood *and water* on the Cross, what more will come out of the gouged organ here? If blood is dripping from this organ now, was it blood from a virgin, earlier, when the trash was cracking under my shoes as I came in the alley? And since I must always think and understand what I am seeing, I stop moving and the couple starts its coitus again, but more intensely now, and their feet crack open the stench of trash.

Grunts.

From what I've seen of their faces in the shop, all of these children look alike, so does the girl, who is now a woman; she cannot be this man's young lover, and cannot be these children's mother. That means that she must be their eldest sister and, here in this alley, in this trash, near his own children's shit, near her own brother's and sister's shit, below the human life that strengthens at the close of day, her father is the one making her into a woman, his woman; and making me the witness of a crime, the double crime of penetration and incest.

The grunts turn into little laughs, the thrusts of the lower back turn into mouth and ear and neck and closed-eye kisses, but this only retracts part of the offense.

In my deep the figures do worse than this, but with no blood links and for pay, as an added insult.

The exasperation of family flesh spawns this first monster, so how can I resist immediately imagining other ones? The other sister, improvising fairy tales and monsters for her begrimed, shit-ridden siblings, is she only their sister? Has her father taken her flower yet? Does her deep voice prove that she's already his old lover? These boys and girls, aged four to fourteen, born of their father's come, do they return there with spurts and suction?

The mother—or the mothers—with another? With others simultaneously? In a hovel where she earns part of the children's food? Several mothers for one single child? The cries and twisted hair of the mothers tearing at their filthy corsets in a courtroom, with the rank newborn on a table? The wigged judge stepping down from his seat and unwrapping the baby with the help of his assistants to judge its full nudity?

Behind me a shadow inches forward: a high mast with a black sail moves behind the walls, fences, chimneys that separate us from the water, thick black smoke rises from the chimney of another boat sailing up the middle of the Firth.

In front on me, Anthony stands on the wall of the alley, holding himself stable with his outstretched arms: if he speaks, he falls. Does he have a better view of the coitus from above? Free, living in the city, doesn't he see such lustful combat daily in dead ends and doorways, under tunnels, in demolished houses, in the ruins of the war, and even from his bedroom window? When I am on spring break in France—I'm in town during the year, without any freedom of movement—in a fresh and virginal nature, although my father passes through it day and night and it's full of the tragedy, pain, and anger that increasingly unites us, all I see is the breeding of domestic animals, the cow with the bull, the mare with the horse, more rarely the jenny with the donkey and everywhere the bitch copulating with the dog, the dragonfly with the dragonfly, the difficulted operation from which the male head turns away, often to face us, drool dripping from its jaw, stupor, shame and suffering in its gaze? Nothing easy in an act that should be one of pleasure, unfolding in flowering glens, along clear streams, and in nourishing meadows: must the organs of the procreative duty be hidden from one another, almost inaccessible? Livestock, profits, slavery?

Dead? During a lull in the coitus I see a piece of black crêpe under the anorak: did the pain that brought the widower as he was crying to his eldest daughter's bedside—or to his favorite daughter's bedside—curb his head onto his daughter's breast? And did the girl feel that man's breath and sobs on her breasts as a woman, the man then, head under the sheets, feeling and catching a whiff of her desire?

Can they see me in the alley, my feet cold, shaking under the trash? Am I already dead, an invisible ghost, transparent to all gazes, especially to the gaze of girls, annihilated by the spectacle of the coitus of others? But this morning as I was sitting in the sedan, didn't Annick, on her way to the sea, drop her showered breasts, her beloved head, and her forehead onto my shoulder and kiss me on the cheek as I was pulling away? Through the open back window of the car, didn't she throw up her arms and fists against those of Anthony, who was pushing his face and mouth toward her across the back seat?

My father's sarcasm floods into my heart, the way he mimes the awkward movements and the sounds that my memory exacerbates into laughter and frenzy as if through a sound duct. Have I left behind the beauty of childhood so completely? Is it because I'm destined never to enter into beauty as an adult that this incestuous couple in front of me continues its offense unabashed?

I see the tip of her pink lips, between the almost white wisps of hair, searching for the man's ear, wet with foam: why does she acquiesce to being penetrated by the member of the one who made her in her mother? Is she old enough to acquiesce to what could make her into a mother herself? A father who gouges his little girl with his strong and short-lived urge… should at least want children!

Since childhood and since I started reading, regardless of age and condition and time, I've tried to be the other, to occupy the other's thought and heart; judging dishonors the judge along with those he judges; I have to be that heart, that failed hand! This couple is so distressed that no effusion of sexual matter can help, even if it is abundant and to the death. But from inside its crime, isn't it other than what it seems, a hero, a half-god, a god claiming his daughter back? Doesn't he take her back, at the end of childhood and adolescence? And doesn't she rediscover him with so much joy after that prolonged absence? Maybe they can't see that I am watching them, like Phaedra can't see the spectators to her tragedy as her heart burns for Hippolytus?

I turn around again. Anthony is now running, his arms spread wide, from one end of the wall to the other; he whistles softly, and as his run wavers to the right and to the left, his whistle loses its note. The trash weighs down on the top of my shoes, anchoring me to this alley. How will I make it out? He, up there and in real life, the contours of his body haloed in gold and red in the declining day, and me below, fascinated by the serpent, vermin crawling up my ankles. From behind my head, turned in his direction, a soft, enticing grunt: "Come on…"

Does Anthony hear the father's voice? Almost an order coming from an adult man, especially one who's doing the basic adult act? Will he come down from the wall—and how? What does the man want? Doesn't he have enough with his daughter, in his daughter?

My head is still turned. The grunting starts again: "Come on, boy." Anthony, from up there: "He has a big cock!"

Who? the man…

From what little I've seen of it, words blow it up until it's big enough to tear apart the girl.

"You…" The voice is so low that Anthony can't hear it from above. Who does the man want? It must be someone other than the two of us, someone that I can't see? Above them? But if so, the man would lift his head toward the high, windowless wall of blackened brick that shuts off the left side of the dead end. A head in the basement window? Can the man wait long enough for the body of that head to enter the shop, find the door to the alley and step in cautiously, over trash and shit?

Could it be the father asking the girl to return to him, through his guilty tenderness, abolishing her sex into that "*boy*"?

Could it be him turning her around against him like a boy? My head pivots again between the man's "Come on, boy" at my level, and the "He has a big cock" that Anthony repeats up there, his face reddened in the setting sun.

If I let my thoughts go free, then an indissoluble glue will hold my feet to the ground. My large heart is beating fast, and from beyond this heart…, an impulse… toward the desired body… and, since I left my *navaja* in France, toward the neck of the man I want to strangle? Between her thighs, what would I find of her gouged organ? Would it be enough, her father sleeping on the ground, that both our two mouths join with our tongues inside them? From what side should I start?

In the opening of her shorts, which her fingers and his combined have rolled all the way up to the fold of her ass and the edge of her pubes, will I find the same abomination that I saw last year in the nudie magazine our friends had brought back from Lyon, standing beneath the covered playground that June night in the dimming storehouse light: the red and black work of butchery, revealing those internal substances that only war, torture and crime can bring to light, but that all civilizations that come from faith and sacredness keep inside?

What we are taught is proof of God's existence must remain hidden, the tangle and infinitude of mechanisms, fluids, secretions of the human body, just as the fruit of the Tree of Knowledge must not be eaten: and this hidden substance, variegated with colors that are unknown to light, is full of movement and stinks like Satan; true microscopic Creation—neurons, genes—is invisible there; in the same way as an artist's thinking and words animate the backstage of a scene that would be human appearance, skin, gazes, touch, voice—but the smell… the horror of injured bodies. Shouldn't we just go back and forth between appearances and their origin, and abandon the horrible mechanics to surgeons, policemen, and medical examiners?

But a hand—viscous?—grabs hold of mine: "Come on, boy, don't be scared."

The couple wants to enlist me. Anthony repeats, "He has a big cock, He has a big cock," as he runs. In the man's grunt, I only hear, "is your cock hard enough?"

I see the girl-woman's face under her nearly white hair blush against the red face of her father.

My thoughts make one more turn, and here I am rushing into Evil and mingling spirit, heart, body, matter so that I'm in, and I don't have to suffer seeing it from outside.

But to mix with Evil here it's got to be *hard*. *Big*, yes, but is it *hard* enough for this *labor*? I've deduced from rumors and secrets that "to consume" the act of love or of desire means that man must *labor* woman: the strongest impulse between two bodies after the impulse toward God, the impulse that is most celebrated in poetry and in music, for which the most paintings and psalms have been composed, can be reduced to an artisanal, random mechanics; in the same way, in poetry—but I make the poem!—you have to guide the lines, predict the rhyme scheme, even sometimes alter the meaning because of it; poetry, music and the rest don't emerge fully formed from the hand of the creator like Earth emerges from God the Father's order; and yet in poetry, the hand grabs hold of genius.

But to mix with Evil here I'd have to abolish the desire for poetry from my memory, from my hand, my heart and my future: I'd rather die—I know Evil from my knowledge of servitude: I was born with it—at night, or under the full Sun, to do Evil without leaving poetry, and even to attach one to the other, I let the words flow out through my member, with its juice, that seals their pact.

I'm too much in it already to act from the outside as others do.

Am I too much of the father and too much of the daughter to stay, and act with my own member? Isn't my member too much already the man and woman's member? What sob in my breast does the man's fingers want to touch through the low neckline of my shirt?

The power in my shorts grows as the girl blinks her pale eye at me from beneath her hair, and as she pushes her mouth forward where all the blood of her head has congealed. The man's hand, heavy with the smell of what must be penetrated, and with the grease and salt of the chips, moves from my chest down to my belt and his palm grabs my member through the velvet. I catch the whiff of his daughter's saliva on his breath: "He has a big cock."

Coming from above toward my ears that are ringing and nearly blocked, I hear Anthony's faraway voice: "Come on, boy, don't be scared."

What beauty on the mother's forehead curves toward the tiny hands twitching in the crib?

After a few days of mourning, the brats are scummy and defecate outside the bounds.

A splash of wave hits against the dock, covers the top of the alley with the smell of sea: Anthony runs, yelling, on the shaking wall.

Will I hear his body tumble and hit the ground? Will there be enough trash to break his fall? When I dream, I use my heel to hit the tower floor and boost my body back over the void. Here, I kick the floor that has been cleared of trash as strongly as possible with my heel, almost hard enough to tear my tendon. At the same time, the alley door behind us opens and creaks. Maybe Anthony has taken an unknown path back down? The man's hand unclasps my shorts that are still shaking from the kick.

Slowly, since I am sensitive to turns, the sedan drives back to Kent Cottage through the interior coastal valleys, through Galashiels, and through the Cheviot Hills where tomorrow we'll go hiking. I stretch my arm into the night across the lowered window: my crotch seems dirtier from the man's fist than from the beat-sheet operation that I want to do tonight: what will I do with that real hand in my deep where bodies, members, mouths, hands, asses even, crotches that belong to males and females but with more or less lush folds only appear in flashes as ideas or as emotions—I learn the most about the difference between idea and reality when I think about that confusion.

That man, my father's age, could only grab my member two or three times through the shorts before I unloaded on his wrist and on his fake gold chain. What distress should have braced my courage? From what I've read, and from school bragging, I know that in real partners desire grows inflamed after the first thrust, and I start to see, to feel, and hear what I could have done with my erect member grown even harder in the girl who wanted it. What would I have lost if I'd used that prepared member in that primed sexual organ, and joined the camp of real men—for now, who cares if I am one, since I am one through poetry? A part of that member?

Does a substance still unknown to me but necessary to my mind, the girl's sexual organ, in its ooze, attracts it either to feed on it, or trash it, or destroy it with its sap?

Because everything grabs my heart and mind and settles in specific parts of my real body, I must be careful of everything; and in order to maintain the daily evolution of my poetry, I must not give over the body that envelops and protects it.

I am permanently delivered over to life, to others—others are myself, since I am each of them so intensely. So why and to what end should I reduce this universal innate nobility through a simple temporary desire, reduce this gift of God to a small earthly effusion? Others have designated it a gift of self: but what is it that transports, devastates and drenches Catherine and Heathcliff with tears?

And later, if I wish to love a woman as I should, when I drop my load in her, won't I see her under me lose her beauty and her confidence in me, as I lose my confidence in her?

The sinuous road is punctuated with sheep gates. We have to get out of the car to open and close them. In a deeper valley, Anthony and I go out into the night and push open the gate; on the hillside, under the Moonlight revealing the colors of the grass, the flowers, the earth, the peat, and the waking insects and birds, two big rams stand face to face at the bottom of the vale; the river burbles under the trees; some lingering remains of the alley scene pull both of us toward the animals: to purify ourselves of the taint of the day with an age-old act?

We run toward the rams, stinking sperm-throwers, crouch down on all fours, asses low, and squeeze under the hairy paunches; we turn on our backs, throws up our arms and hoist up our legs, suspending ourselves from our rams as if we could be reborn from them.

The adults, stepping out of the car, scream and laugh. Will the rams move and start their jerky race toward the top of the vale, or will it be the bottom, the female or the newborns? But with their vermin spreading to our bodies, they don't move; is the Moon in their big black eye and on their horns shining with the blood of their fight?

Far away, at the bottom near the mouth of the valley, shaking lights: the red sedan between the standing herds, branded in red; we'll have to throw our clothes into the washing machine, shower, and wash our hair; but we might need our stench with coarser girls, and even with girls that are not as coarse? With Annick? Or with the little redhead with the Greek profile?

And in my deep, as an idea to hang in the cave?

Natural noises grow dim; as we get closer, we can see that the lights are torches, lanterns, lamps: then a few stable lights in some farms that I recognize as meaning "tragedy has come knocking"; we get out of the car and move toward the moving lights: the torches are part of a celebration that began the night before; the lanterns and flashlights are covered with insects stuck to the glass; the people holding them, wearing tall muddy boots, are silent; but their jaws vibrate, they've spoken, yelled, foamed at the mouth a lot. From moans in which sobs are mingled, Dorothy learns but keeps it from me—and yet I know—that the body of a farm boy, gone missing since noon, has just been brought in from the river, forcefully drowned after being raped.

We move up a bit in the shadows. I see Anthony's small Adam's apple go up, down, and up again along his neck in between hair from the ram's belly. Some men are holding down another man, his shirt and fly torn, his face bloodied, against the edge of a waterway: with their fists against his neck, they lower the man's face, lit up by their torches, toward the surface of the water: "Look at yourself! Look at yourself before you die!"

In another man's fist is a thick rope: "Rape, rape."

Through the wide-open door, lit up inside and out, come sobs, cries, a woman's, maybe two, a man's as well, and something like the grinding of teeth. "Oh my boy, my sweet boy!"

Where is the child? Is he lying upstairs, like the child from the Montet farm back in 1947 whose throat was slit by the frame of the tool cabinet that toppled when he climbed it, and over whom my father held a wake, he who'd brought him into the world?

Dorothy enters slowly into the light in which she disappears; between the waterway and the riverbed, a patrol wagon, two police cars with flashing lights; other policemen, higher up, illuminate and comb through the crime scene; did they see, will they see the rope that is sliding through the fist of one of the men in high boots weighing down on the assassin?

A very young girl appears at the upstairs window, throws her arms to the edge of the beam of light, and with a sob, and a low complaint, emits a long, high cry, then low, then high; Anthony, who returns from the darkness, tells me that she's the dead boy's twin, and that a doctor from Wooler is up there certifying the boy's death, with a policeman holding her back.

Seeing the very young girl, whose age tells me her brother's age, thirteen, fourteen, emerge so entirely white—is it the color of her dress, or is it what I imagine to be her ghost since she's so pale?—diverts me from last year's vision, as they commemorated the massacre and burning at Oradour-sur-Glane, of the child who was shot with the adults, curled in a ball with his skull shattered. What does rape shatter that is as sacred as the brain? Even if I were to know it—and perhaps I do through school rumors and the deductions that go with them—I wouldn't know how to say or see it: what is necessary, how many rapes, before the fact can pass into my reason? Even if I were able to see the member and organ of the offense, the workings of rape, whether on film or in reality, and could repeat it and tell others, I wouldn't believe it: all my reason must settle exactly on the fact, the entire fact; my ordinary reason and memory must accommodate themselves to the fact, especially when that fact is beyond belief and beyond what is sacred; I would be able to tend the raped girl or boy, and even to extract the man's member from the organ of the girl or from that unnamed part of the boy; find the first, necessary words, while continuing to disbelieve.

For a fact to be completely a fact, I must believe in it as I still believe in God, then: with all the power of my mind, my heart, my soul, my memory.

Have I been making poetry for the last two years from this innate necessity? In secret, do I mix in equal parts the act, the product of the act, and the words that justify it because of this same obligation?

Didn't the apostle Saint Thomas himself need a few days and nights to believe in it completely, as his fisherman fingers thick from working with nets pushed into the new wounds of the resuscitated Christ—was there still blood? How did they stop its flow? Or were these wounds already scars through contracted Time?

The descent toward Wooler is slow and silent—coming from the opposite direction, new patrol wagons, hospital trucks, people returning from a day's outing or from the beach—I see Dorothy's arm and wrist shaking on the wheel; behind her, Norman, who must wake early in the morning, is already asleep.

Seen from above, a good portion of the sea is lit up by the Moon. We leave behind the blood zone that all this powerful water could not erase; at night, inside comfortable adopted family walls, should I stir and spread that blood above, and the sperm that would be waiting for me below if not for the crime, when back there they are stopping the blood in the twin boy's wound—sperm still in it, like water in the blood of Christ wounded on the cross!

Back in the plains, once the illuminated seascape will have disappeared and space will have been filled with people again, vacationers and locals walking and talking on roads, streets, back streets, and in gardens in the dwindling scent of sunscreen and of barbecues, with the door of the room closed on my impatient body, will I yield to my desire, reinforced by two nights without the *act*?

Will sleep take me fast enough so that my wrist will fall asleep on the open backpack before it can pull out the beat-sheet pack?

In the warm air, shortly clad girls and boys chase each other in the narrow flowering back streets: thighs, asses, breasts, arms, hollows of the knee, cheeks, tender and tan in the public light filtering through the swarms of bats; snippets of conversations in darkened gardens: life, good and beautiful and just, is there against which one must do and write what I assure myself— no one is there to confirm it yet—that I must do and write in secret—with the risk of losing my member just as the pianist- musician Robert Schumann, brother and father of my destiny, ligatures the ring finger of his right hand to reinforce his other fingers, and loses the public use of it for the piano.

We haven't eaten since the Leith fish and chips: Anthony is also watching all this twin flesh, the same age as we are, and does he lick his lips as I do in contemplation of the only stew that we imagine, just as his grandfather places the other in the oven to heat up?

Near Links Road, as the car slows, then on the small incline, with the motor off, I hear the sound of roller skates on the asphalt of the coastal road: Annick and the little redhead are coming and going behind the dunes, biting into candy. The little red-head, her hair untied, her cleavage bare, freckled breasts lit up by the Moon, a wool wrap sweater, short ruffled skirt, and high stockings…

Leaving the car, we run to kiss them through the intervals of traffic; in the beam from the car headlights, I kiss Viva above her smell that has grown stronger since morning: as I get older, I'll have more of such intercourse on alley trash and its stench of rotting bait, and "worse," until the stench of my own death—what did the Devil's camps exude! And I search behind her ear above for some perfume to cover the reeking of her *period* below—where and from whom did I learn that word, which disappears from me immediately?

We both stay silent about the rape up there, our bodies still reeling from it, its odor and taste of blood and burnt flesh slamming against the insides of our nostrils and our mouths.

Blood? Doesn't a boy also have a *hymen* where a man possesses him? A flower that the man comes to take, that he picks with the tip of his razor-sharpened member? All sexual operations must produce blood, but it's another kind of blood than what runs inside us; it's the blood of sacrifice, the signature of an act that should be sacred exception—against which I start to institute a blasphemous use of daily life by conjuring up a slave order in my secret writing.

Fire? Did it come from the rubbing, from the back and forth of the man's member in the boy's unnamed organ that produced sparks and smoke like a stick twisted or rubbed flat against a hole?

Did ancient man—whose survival I read about in tales of ethnographic expeditions, mostly in the Amazon—cull his idea of the production of fire from this act of penetration, from male to female or male to male, with burning discharge at the end?

Remains of hell? Signatures etched in burning blood—Faust's pact?

We return for the stew: the temporary term of my train of thought, since I'm so hungry, is the stew that we will both devour, and yet, stamping my soles against the asphalt I try to expel everything that later, around midnight and alone at last,

I might dare to draw out from what I saw above for my secret writing and with wresting of juice; but after that deadly rape and the pain around it, will I again be able to place figures around a scene the preliminaries of which are capture, "forcing," sale, and re-sale?

And who am I, my growing body awkward when it makes sound and is ridiculed by my father? What place would I have in this scene coming from the bottom of my brain?

My age puts me with the captives, those who are forced, sold, and serviced by the adults—but how old are the adults? Eighteen, twenty, twenty-two? At thirty you die.

I have poor eyesight, and corrective lenses are prohibited in those parts. So I could not look at myself in the mirror, head and body, to see my torment, to see those men or women clearly, or that single man or woman, who'd inch up to my body to choose it, or take it, and even see the price tag hanging from my neck.

Farther still: what was it in the boy's seductive appeal—I think I have none—that provoked the assassin's gaze, emotion and desire. In my memory, I look back on the recent history of England to find his penalty—death by hanging, his face covered in spit from the crowd.

Maybe the man worked the peat during the week? Did the fair make his blood boil, whores too expensive in Berwick-upon-Tweed? Did boredom, incomprehension, and melancholy pull the boy to the babbling river? Make him sit on the wall legs spread? Lift him up to stand with a leafless branch held in his fist? Immobilize him next to the current, one ass cheek raised? Or bend him over, crouching, ass fanning out, above the clear stream, pulling from his breaking voice a soft, proud hum? The solitary man for whom the fair was just more pain, the unloved one whose cabin chimney smoked at the end of the hamlet, what fear made his knees buckle now, knees that yesterday still bent on the church pew, as he watched through the leaves something that maybe he'd lost?

Now the girls are skating around the cottage, asphalt covered road, paved back streets; the Moon judges me up there. The clouds from a storm that is supposed to hit at dawn are rising on the horizon; they don't erase the gleam of her lucidity as they pass before her: there is no social law in my deep; the Moon can only judge the reasons that make me create: a desire I can't accept, whose nature and daily exercise is common to all? How boring to have *to court* a girl—is it boring? Isn't it instead a new game, where body and word mix? How boring to court a girl when there are hundreds and thousands of them? I refuse to be the seat of a desire with a limited orientation, since even as a child a horse's croup, male or female, would stir my member and make it rise?

Refusal to dive in? Fear of having to put all my body and my mind into an operation that is beneath them? And maybe I'm not strong enough for it?

Back in the cottage, Norman is asleep upstairs and Dorothy and her sister, distracted, are unfolding geologic maps on the sofa. Anthony and I start to eat the stew, sitting across from Anthony's grandfather who is falling asleep in his black armchair.

Are they eating in my deep?

Should I keep the deep as I still see it: without any objects of daily life, without signs of ordinary humanity? Maybe backstage helpers have come to prepare, to ready, and to push the bodies out and once the scene is done, they will repair, bandage, and heal the serviced bodies?

What should they eat that would be on the level of what is done to them?

In the scene, in between sex, as they sit on the knees of those who use them, some of the food that they receive in exchange for labor is fed directly into their mouth. Where did that device come from? From what little I've seen in town, in France, of public debauchery: maybe, during a windy heat wave, between the swinging doors of low-income housing, from the vision of a very young girl with a very short dress, bare thighs open on the hairy legs of someone whom I took to be her father laughing, the girl pulling with her jutting jaw the chain around the man's neck, he pulling hers to his own jaw as a heavy black lock of hair disappeared into her mouth? On the tabletop seen through the intermittent breeze, playing cards, a bottle of red wine three-quarters empty, glasses with flies; the wind slammed the door shut, then open; the man was making the girl drink; wine dripped from the bottom of her ear to her neck…

But as a child, how many times did my father sit me on his knee to help me finish the remains of food I didn't want?

I need a car to drive the captive, gagged child, or adolescent who will have to be "forced," whose knowledge, whose sweet memory of ancestry, and whose heart will have to be destroyed or perverted before they are pushed, naked or still holding the few clothes they've been left with, onto the scene where adult Desire blow just like the Holy Ghost sweeps through the place of Pentecost.

Am I there? This body no longer belongs to me or to my ancestry but to *another*. Is it still wearing the dirty clothes it wore back in the alley in Leith and under the rams in Cheviot?

My thoughts stay on course as I eat the stew, seasoned with the spices Dorothy brought back from the Far East before the war, despite my large appetite, despite Anthony's hurried chewing cheek-to-cheek with mine, despite the chunks that one of us begins and that the other finishes; neither are my thoughts moved as his hand slips between my thighs, so natural it is that in the same movement of the mouth and of the fist, the heart would want to grab with one the boiled flesh and with the other, the live flesh sitting down beside it; such thinking, this one in particular, is stronger than the immediate facts that resemble it and that might find their place within its course.

The natural needs created by foods, drink, excess of desire, crashing after a high and the fury that serviced bodies must quickly be pulled away from, where will they be relieved? I'll need toilets: *Turkish* toilets. For a long time I associate them with what's rehashed in folktales and in History: Ottomans kidnapping young Christians, training them for their harems or for their troops.

The door would be ajar and, under the harsh light, adults pressed by their urge, standing up after defecating, would make one or another of the available bodies come, approach them, open up…

And even as I stare into Anthony's lucid blue eyes, I continue to make those bodies shuffle back and forth, from tables and benches heavy with foreplay and sex to that toilet heavy with shit and construction site mud: the deeper I stare into his eyes, the more I know that he does not know where I am.

Such extreme power of thought, head to head against presumed normalcy, what a temptation that stiffens my member: it's like a ray of fire, targeting, striking, and burning down the thought of others!

Around the cottage, the two girls are still skating.

What comes to me so strongly from a body whose contours I no longer know since my mother stopped tracing my own contours with her hand during the bath?

And before another hand traces them again for me in love, on a bed, day or night?

A girl's hand? Or a woman's?

Could I share with a simple girl a passion that might crush to misery the exaltation of my deep?

I need a woman, maybe twenty years of age, to eat that part of my brain, and let me realize with her as compensation what strength is left of its passion for life.

What is this member with its hanging testicles in a body

that will only dive in dreams into the blue and gold emptiness of towns and mountains? Can it even perform the act of entry into the adult world, that act around which all thoughts collect and justify themselves?

Hot from the stew, Anthony gets up, opens a little window to the side; the purring of the skates draws nearer; but above it the shaking voice of the redhead explodes. The sound of her breaking voice projected from her rolling feet as she catches her breath, the passage of the two girls' bodies slightly staggered in the light, and my tearing apart begins again till I feel sick: the voice of the "brothel" on the one hand, harmony and the impetus of youth captured in painting on the other: must I already want to profane that beauty? Already?

But even before my first effusions, ten, eleven years old, Notre Dame de Joubert, I think beauty contains and hides its own corruption, its demon: beauty cannot simply contain itself; how it appears in paintings and in other places, here in the daughters of the Muses in Mategna's Parnassus, gives the illusion that it contributes to the Good; but if it's banned by certain true religions, it's because it *rises* like a rival of Creation, like the Serpent that wants to inject its venom into it, a substance created by God.

Does beauty demand strength in those who create it, a strength that they don't quite control, and whose nature they want to hide? As soon as we create, do we disturb, do we intervene, do we act on what He has created as perfect and immutable? Do we disturb the visual order; do we contract or retract time? Do we add sound to what His ear wanted for the world?

The two girls seen here from the side, beautiful, joyous, run toward their future. If I make them enter the darkness of my deep with that same impulse, then their future, or that of others, boys swept up in the same impulse, will be abolished in the desire and pleasure of adults...

Christ on the cross, Divinity itself profaned? The beauty that I labor to maintain in my deep disappears in too much blood, in too much torture: what is beauty for me, then— without which these depths are no longer justified or are transformed into what I loathe: an erotic exercise?

For that place, secret only to me but which I want to be open onto the still unformed world surrounding it in the darkness, I need a beauty that is predisposed to enter it in daily life, not an ideal beauty but one that is already touched by the prescience of prostitution: a particular swaying of the hips, a movement of the waist or on the face, the hollow of the cheek under an eye, vague already; the etching of wrinkles on the forehead, the opening of an ear to the sound of a new obscenity; and the mouth, the hands—swollen, deformed? The necks— scars of a botched teenage suicide? Signs, eyes, mouths, hips, of stupor, abandon before the inevitable: Greek destiny—vanquished queen, princess, young prince doomed to servitude, Amazonian Indians doomed to "extinction" in the modern age.

Slowly, I forget the young martyrs pulled apart by beasts who tear them open as if for an exasperated sexual act. I've forgotten them: they have a future, in the beyond, in Paradise; but what future could extend my figures, daughters of the Greeks and of pagan Indians, after use? In return for being created, they indicate to me that I have no beyond; they pull me out of my innate belief, at least in the time it takes to create them; what would Paradise do with such profaned bodies, enjoying the sad, nostalgic pleasure of shameful mourning, wanting to be profaned even more?

Do we go from Purgatory where we are living, to Hell where we are dead, so that we can "gain" Paradise, where we'd no longer be either one or the other?

Through the window, with the two girls now roller-skating along the other wall, I watch the night stretching to the north, its lights higher than those of the coastal plains. The food has settled quickly into Anthony's stomach. Behind me, he hits the stomach that it has reached: how could we let our inside body be filled with food from a dead animal when at the heart of that inside body lies the raped and murdered boy, and the endless pain of his family and his twin sister? Is the church closed, which we could open to wrap in prayer and light the raped child, and forget ourselves in a collective song with the children from yesterday's Vespers? Should I place him, dead, in me, and as I grow older and die, into what safe conscience could I transfer him? In mine the deep is there already, with its debauchery and its crime against freedom…

Is there something more, something purer, that I can do? Always this pain in me of the separation of the species into groups and individuals. How can we accept, since it must be accepted, that we are not entirely caught up in the destiny of others, that others don't live entirely in us and us in them? I cannot, in good faith and reason, get used to what is prescribed in ordinary morality as self-mastery, the balance of heart and reason, the impartial distribution of emotions, or the moderate use of will: we must live in passion, impulse and continuous and unlimited solidarity; we were not created for measure, but to join Him in His creative gesture.

The two girls pass by again, the one who smells, the other who does not: another night, a day and a night, and, isolating her from the other girl, I'll be able to walk with her along the beach in the surf and pull her in by her left shoulder away from a stronger wave, toward me standing to her left; and as she'd bend her left cheek on the right edge of my left shoulder, my cheek being too high for her, what would I tell her that might satisfy us both? Can love muster something from the back of my throat other than the "I love you" that would cause all of my deep to blush?

I watch her, immobile on her skates, as she and the other one watch Anthony and me licking our lips at the window.

The other one a girl still, she, now a woman: a darker dress than yesterday, tight fitting, a navy blue cotton jacket: did she borrow it from a brother? Blue and white sneakers to which the skates are strapped, one strap at the heel, another on the instep.

Where I come from, little girls quickly become girls and women: there is little time for adolescence, for girls or boys; farm labor requires bodies, members and assured minds. She is from Rennes, Brittany, a student, and her voice is already fixed; her gaze already sees society, wraps it in its wisdom; the light of sleep of what inside sleepers shines through her belly in the Moonlight?

The other one taps the pavement with the wheels of her skates, her cleavage gapes a bit; from behind me, Anthony breathes his need, and already the smell of sleep.

What makes my member move again and hit the windowsill? I feel my mind's real networks, already, so how can I desire someone else than the one that I am now beginning to *love*. Only God knows what my member wants, but how can I ask Him? Is there enough time? Before His answer, will my member have shrunken back?

How could I penetrate the one I *love*, and hurt her?

Novels, films, operas: not one extends coitus through the fusion of penetration; paintings of carnal love only show the separated objects of copulation, and sometimes the married couple, settled, procreative.

Not only do public, state, and religious morality exclude the act of carnal consumption from artistic representation, but isn't it always the shame and terror of the animal origins of the human? During carnivals, in Dutch paintings, men will sometimes throw themselves on women in isolated bushes, but their bodies and faces are closer to the bodies and faces of familiar animals, public copulators, than to human ones.

Anthony's breath on my neck is not what's tugging at my member, but, in his breath, the general breath of bodies huddling in sleep, the crossing, intermingling breathing of children, full of the breathlessness of the day of play that abates with sleep and with the mother's breath as she leans over them; for several years I've smelled the stench of sex, of the semen and secretions that blend in copulation, on the breath of others: forming, suspended, urgent, below the belly, their smell rises through the intestines up through the lungs to the esophagus; the bodies that emit this seasoned breath attract me, not for *love*—does love have its own smell?—but for the rumination of the deep.

Is my hard-on simply for the little redhead? There she is, turning her sanguine lips to us from behind the swarm of gnats that rise to the top of the street lamp; is it for the red nipple at the end of that beautiful white breast that I grab blindly with my fist, laid flat against the windowsill, and hold its skin, fabric, strap, buttons within my palm?

She falters on her skates. What else can I grab with my other fist without losing that breast? The other breast, the neck, the jaw?

My stomach against the windowsill cuts my breath in half, my heartbeat maddens in the other half; but I hold that breast—as if I'd never hold another in my life.

Under my growing palm, the skin, fresh and sweaty from exertion, slides over the warm globe of flesh; the nipple bumps and tickles the center of my palm, between the lifeline and the lines of love and chance; the odor of her lower parts rises through the sweat, but the breast's smell, reinforced by pressure from my fist, quells it: blood, future milk, salt from the sea and from exertion; the rest of the flowering wisteria hanging above diffuses its well-kept old lady perfume so appealing to children: as children, my brothers, sisters, and I play at discerning the smell of our grandmother who is so high and noble from the smell of the wisteria covering the exterior facade of her house; we bring her out to the back of the garden, far from the wisteria, to smell her, her perfumes and the smell of her clothes.

The girl, trembling slightly on her skates, with her hand along my wrist, lifts that organ of which I've read and heard that Roman persecutors took pleasure in having severed from live Christian virgins: I feel the blade of the dagger or sword or saw grazing the top of my hand.

That outgrowth of flesh, neither organ nor member, useless for the life of the one who carries it but receptacle of food for others, infants or old men—the Nazis had their SS feed at the breasts of Russian prisoners they'd shoot or hang immediately after the act—is glorified in painting, whether it is hidden or revealed entirely or in part, as the perfect human form, a slice of the human race.

If I can hold that breast, I can hold the rest, but the girl must move closer to the window: if I drop that breast, stand up and cross the living room to the door to the dunes, pass the gate running, skirt the facade toward the alley and the girls, will I still have enough heart, bypassing Annick, to grab that breast, take the other, and reach my hand farther down?

Before the scene ends the way almost everything ends at our age, in laughs, mockery, and for the boys at least in something to eat, I must advance in my knowledge of girl's bodies—as if I knew more about women's bodies—my future depends on it.

Because of school, I have no access to these bodies, parallel in age to me and in development: sisters, friends, study partners, or friends in summer camp; I almost forget them. Girls who are already women in body and in mind are what I dream about, and what I want; but women as well; sexually.

I feel that boarding school eclipses the moment at thirteen or fourteen when two ignorant children—away from families that watch and prohibit any life or thought beyond themselves, and even more so if done in the secret that offends them—a girl and boy discover one another through the other, and groping with the power of the—sexual—heart alone, discover how to love here below and till the end.

And so, tonight, on another body than the body I'm so delighted to *love*, and before her eyes, I want to contract that lost time into a hand, mine, heavy with part of my desire, digging, taking, pulling in that mass of flesh, of clothing, of short cries, smells, and foam, so as to at least touch the central organ—and it will let me know I've found it.

Since all my desire is for the future, why wouldn't I instead desire figures more advanced in age, in time, in their bodies and in their thoughts?

Annick is more developed than the little redhead; her voice, her eyes, and the way she holds herself announce it; and what age am I? Have I worked enough to push my poetry beyond my age? Have I thought enough? Did I study science, philosophy, law, instead of trying to impart rhythm to my lines, to fill them with a Nature that is too general, too landscaped, too full of feelings that are too general? Is the jolting of my deep text proof of my maturing, thought, heart, knowledge of the world and art?

My arm falters: from the lack of sleep and from this act that pulls me from the living; from behind, Anthony grabs my other hand and pulls it, pressing it tight in his, toward the inside where the adults, Dorothy and her sister fold the maps—through the open window above we hear Anthony's sister's doll-like babble before sleep. The two girls, skating in place, I, my arm folded back, then Anthony, what are we laughing about, under the Moon that the coming storm begins to veil?

Is it about what used to flower frankly, fresh and odorous deep within, and whose putrefaction reeks as it turns our breath lascivious, our speech embittered, only the breaking shards of which can restitute the new confidence, the new hope that's forming there?

The two girls skate backward toward the coastal road; after crossing the inside of the house, with its lights off, we join them on the wet asphalt.

As I kiss Annick on the cheek, the fuzz on her upper lip brushes against mine; because the hand that grabbed and held the other's breast, the little redhead Viva, stumbling on her skates, is flush against my ass, I can't caress Annick's back during the kiss; but my chest touches hers and I hear her rear twitch.

Once behind my bedroom door, can I extract enough from the rape back there, and this kiss here, to resist the need that is subduing me, cutting my legs from under me, here, outside, on either side of my member as it stirs, to return to my deep, text and beating off?

In the smell of the light shower before the rain, water coming down from the Sky, pure, as nourishing as manna and healing, Anthony's smell stands out, sports, shower, hygiene, the way of Goodness, Annick's smell from a perfume her mother and father in France gave their permission for and which one day I will have to disrupt in *love*—when will the time come when she buys that first perfume in secret? So many scents that dissuade me from abolishing them soon in the stench of my secret scene.

In the early morning we drive toward Wooler; from Wooler, a third into Harthope Valley. Our bags heavy with drinks, sand-wiches, and apples, we climb toward the peat bogs: Anthony's father leads the way. Our bodies, drowsy still, make Anthony and I pause in the babbling river. The beat-sheet pack is already tormenting me. I've left it in the drawer of the bedroom, locked with the key I'm holding at the bottom of my pocket under my closed fist, under the pounding of the pocketknife chained to my belt.

Flee this newly forming family?

I begin to feel, beneath the material sound of this river, that a voice is counting the time and space the water has run through, that all these shadows on its surface are the trace of that voice, and that from this aural and luminous space between that tiny world and us giants—ourselves tiny in relation to the trees that are less dense here—spirit-ideas rise where I could flee and live, adopted—by what element, one or the other?

To come [*jouir*] is then, and is still now, a word that doesn't resonate in my heart, my mind, or in my senses. I want more: pleasure without flesh, happiness. In *jouir* there is the *i* that encloses the word around the personal orgasm that is nothing.

Already I work in wheat fields, in the ocean, in gardens, to assemble around a self who dissolves in beauty all the reasons that I have and that I can still search for to live the happiness of an instant, and still do so for some time, once I've collected in my mind all the reasons others have for living that happiness, once all the sores are healed, once everyone is sated, stocked up, re-honored, and resuscitated, even the last dog.

How could I be content with the happiness of one, of a few? On what bed of blood, of tears, and of cries of hunger do we make our happiness?

From the minute he sat next to the path of black peat, Anthony leaned back on his bag and fell asleep; small insects whose name I do not know, *attached* to the peat, glean his upturned lips and frolic under his shorts with their folded cuffs above the thighs spreading and carried away by sleep.

Before what *orgy* have his manipulators abandoned him? Or have they rejected him as useless, and left him here as he is now, as if dead from not being able to serve, covered with a vermin that transforms him into a desirable body—not as if dead, but as if he came from common misery?

As I watch him sleep, turn slightly to the side, wiggle his ass cheek and stretch his leg, my upright flesh grows numb, my joints flinch: what use would I be in the *locale* of my deep?

Servant? Retainer? Of the flesh? Of "sperm"—the word that circulates in school comes to me, where from: *jism*?

Of voice? Of speech? Of hand? Of mouth?

We need to climb. I nudge Anthony's foot with mine, and walking alongside me on the path that grows darker and darker, with his very blue eyes, he searches for my eyes, blue as well but tarnished by my glasses: "You seem out of sorts, Pierre"—and, eye to eye, as he cleans his lips of insect bits and dusts his fly with his pink hand, through my stammering I say: "What were you dreaming?"

I don't need to dream to live in another world: my deep is such a world, and if I dream I go there, or I escape through flight; or, on a busy street, I lie on a bed with my price tag on the doctor's chart hanging on the bedpost or I can't find the *necessary* frock.

His cheek sinks in, his small apple rolls along his neck, his mouth stretches forward and his forehead creases:

"I was dreaming I'd lost my clothes."

"So you were naked?"

He blushes down to the neckline of his shirt: "And you were upstairs looking for something in the drawer."

"What was it?"

"A treasure, I guess."

Now it's my turn to blush, even further down than he does. My member stiffens; I hide it by turning my hip. Why blush? Since he wants my member, and even yesterday, designated it to others in the alley, could he reject its production and its preparatory rites?

Under the strong, mid-morning Sun, my head is drenched in sweat at the thought of this: yes, what does he want to do with my member—if he still wants it?

I saw him yesterday in the "fish and chips," back from the alley, exchanging coins and bills with the father and his eldest daughter: for what? Doesn't his athletic strength, and his taste for money, make him well suited to protect this member as a renewable good from which to profit?

We walk, fast, behind the adults: now in the heather and the very green grass on which small snails climb. Birds of prey lash downward, near the farms and lower still near the mouth of the valley, toward the harvested barley fields: so many stomachs palpitating between the stalks, so many mute breasts and throats that the beaks will pierce! the talons rent!

In a valley, under remnants of fog, a mound of black peat: Dorothy slows down and explains the uses of peat, up to its fiber for underwear fabric and bandages.

I shudder in the momentary coolness: listening to her speak as she tells about how the workers slice the peat in the valleys, cut it into bricks as construction and roofing material, nursery compost, and fuel to dry the barley for whiskey, I retire to my deep at the entrance of which her voice still echoes; what "wanking" and "orgy" frock can I extract from that fiber? I hear the fingers' hurried ripping—where can I find scissors?—of the cloth that should cover, wrap the bottom of the pelvis, the bottom of the hips, the ass, and the *shameful parts*.

In the darkness, what wounds, what bruises dressed by fabric of the same peat fiber mark the bodies removed from the center of the scene? From what factory pile can the scraps of cloth be taken?

In the darkness of the entrance, the peat workers don't take out money for their blackened losers: those whose work produced the heap that produced the fiber that created the textile don't pay to mix in with the *orgy*, to touch the underwear, laced up against both hips, heavy with the *shameful parts* of the adolescents delivered to the adults.

Dorothy's strong voice at the entrance calls me.

Dressed that way, circulating between the adult bodies in desire, the "sperm"—whose? ours or theirs?—drying in crusts on the crude fiber underwear, sitting on knees that jut forward, drinking from glasses, lapping the wine on the wax tablecloth of a table, laughing, wine on the lips, at what? at difficulted acts all around? Free—subversion makes one free—finally—but we are enslaved—for life? A short life: just as long as the beauty of the brothel lasts: the freshness before the rapt, the profaned freshness, the soured freshness—what remains of childhood beneath the wrinkles of those who've laughed too much, cum too much. Afterward, the "debauchery" will take care of the bodies: what use is a body deprived of its beauty? And so fiction doubles, by night, my day's poetry?

The girls with the breasts taut as if tightly drawing up the skin of the stomach, of the pubis—a rag on it would burn!—what an ass she has; but what I see in my deep is the front of bodies, crotches for boys and girls, breasts for girls, faces for both; and if I know with what the adult man penetrates the enslaved girl, I don't yet know what the adult man would use to make love to the enslaved boy: that desire is without penetration; it is impossible for me to imagine that the member of man could enter where one defecates, and so the organ of defecation remains an unformed place, without contours, without life, in the same way as I *struggle* to think that a mother's pure speech could come out of the public mouth of a whore.

From a big heap of forgotten peat heavy with insects and worms, and from the French word *tourbe* that I keep against the English *peat*, the adult bodies of my deep, whose stamping and laughing we hear at the entrance before they come in, are the "people" that we as children are not, my brothers and sisters and I, and where I see and feel— voice, gestures, odor—the remains of ancient enslavement to hard labor, earth, coal, steel, construction, roads, cattle herding, car mechanics.

Even before my first sexual discharge, I'd grown conscious that this new desire perpetrated and reinforced a separation that tormented me and would make me live, the separation of living and past humanity into the free and the enslaved, the submissive and the submitter. All sexuality is violence enacted on humanity: with the help of desire, we must reverse its terms.

Thus, in the deep, it is the enslaved, the people, manual laborers whose hands touch, take, shake, pull, lift, dig and rummage, flatter—the animals—form, transform, deform the *word* of material labor from which images and curses are made, who must subject the flower of freedom, the enslaved children of the dominators.

But if I see adolescents in this way it is because I see myself— or a more desirable double of myself—among them: through my family on both sides, I come from lineages that serve the State, the people, but that do not dominate them or possess them. I am not a child of the people; I am not of the same flesh: the brothel transforms me into its child and its flesh.

Among the "livestock" of the brothel, several adolescents seem more at ease, more approachable, because they belong to the people and because my desire is stronger, that night or that noon, and with it my desire to subvert the order imposed on it by my own social heart, and because it turns me on to further profane the beings and bodies that my heart, my education, and my convictions should protect from all new attempts at enslavement, by pimping them even to their dads and brothers—add-ons to the scene of subversion.

I am outside of society. Where and when have I felt free? I already feel the terror: I won't be free until I've penetrated a woman, and perpetrated the violence that confirms menstrual blood.

In the afternoon, with food and anxiety in my belly, we walk down the side of the valley through which we drove last night. From above, in the cries of the lambs, fear, hunger—birds of prey, more numerous now, swoop down to the summits—along the shining line of the river we see the hamlet which Dorothy tells us is where the child died.

From above, the hamlet seems empty, abandoned.

When the birds of prey swerve toward the bottom of the valley, I imagine—like everyone, even Anthony's father with his righteous thinking—that a corpse, or corpses, is attracting them to the hamlet from which we hear no sound; even the sound of the river is absent near the houses, taking up again farther downstream.

Dorothy, who used to comfort mothers who'd lost newborns or had small children die suddenly on intercontinental ocean liners before the war or under the bombs during the blitz, is sitting on a rock: did the mother and the twin commit suicide? Where was the father yesterday? Where is he today? Did they bring the child's body to a friend's house in Wooler to bury it there?

In the shadow of the trees, by the side of the barn with its gate open, we make out a black cattle truck with sheep inside behind the railing: should we go down to deliver them and return them to their field?

I search in the pure air for hints of the sea and the perfume of wild rhododendrons, for the smell of gas, then of powder, and then of poison. With my head to the side, I try to pick up the sound of the rope still swinging on its pulley, I try to smell the stench of the gyrating bodies, their bowels loosened and the birds of prey honing in on them: or is it a deer carcass that a hunter forgot beyond the houses?

Are the shutters of the room containing the boy's remains closed from the inside? Is the wood at the base of the farm door, at the base of the door that shuts off the first floor staircase, and of the door that closes up the room made of new, hard wood with no holes or teeth marks? Are the doors close enough to the ground to stop the rats from the barn, the stable, the cellar, or the drain from slipping underneath and jumping on the remains whose freshness is quickly decomposing?

In the barn, are they already jumping on the hanging bodies?

As the bodies cool, their smell is subdued: foundation, rice powder?

When I watch and smell my mother as she perfumes herself before dinner, or before she goes out to dinner in the village or nearby, or more rarely, in town, I dread that moment when she leans her head before the mirror, lightly taps the pink powder with a few fingers and applies it on her cheeks, the smell of the washing of the dead to prepare them for their wanderings; since my body has grown, my face is now at the level of her face, and seeing my distress reflected in the mirror, she quickly grabs the bottle of Guerlain, opens it, and with her eyes in mine that are happy again, she rubs the bottom of her temples and behind her ears with both hands. Maybe it's the same ear, next to my father's slight snores, that hears me at night from the marriage bedroom as I walk on the floor above among the furniture of my deep.

How can I extract the *I* from thought, for a thought without an I? How can I extract my self from my heart so as to love and help with the heart of everyone? Or at least interrupt this *I* an instant to be entirely without an *I*, and be given over to others without soiling the thought of their misery with my self? The hand that helps, that grooms, is heavy with ulterior motives.

There are no ulterior motives in my deep, at least in its nocturnal or diurnal invention; desire cleans everything out. *Bad thoughts* are operative there, and the search for the word abolishes everything, the way it is with joy.

The *I* returns when I crash.

Dorothy leads us along a path in the middle of the sloping hill. Facing the hamlet, we stop to watch as it extends in the air, now golden, where shadows jut forth before joining above the waterway.

The ring of tools on stone: two black shapes, one tall, one small, are moving around something that is shining in the lingering Sun, a manure heap, behind the waterway and in front of the low stable; the mother and the twin of the young rape victim, in mourning clothes, fork the manure.

Will the father finally leave the farm and climb into the cattle truck, start the motor and roll it toward the slaughterhouse?

At night, Anthony, his sister, his father, Dorothy, and Norman are asleep upstairs, and Mr. Praundlock is sleeping under the large portrait of his mother. As for me, my room is unlocked—the key is on the table next to the drawer key that I've taken out of my pocket—through the crack around the drawer, the smell of the beat-sheet pack intensified by my desire and my refusal to succumb to it spreads all the way to the bed where I am lying, sheets and covers pushed aside in the light of the sea Moon, I struggle not to take off my pajama pants, get up, naked below the waist, and spread the towel on the sheet, take the key, open the drawer, take out the pack, open it, remove the jizz cloth, crusty and sticking to the paper, slip it on between my thighs, lace it up along my hips, and lying back down, spread with my right hand the crumpled paper on the roll of sheets and covers, with my left hand grab my member, now erect in the strapped cloth—which curbs and restrains it—and with my right hand now beginning to write, the left beginning to caress, extract the member from its rag, slip it, hard now, into the fist, hoist the testicles that are wrapped tightly in the cloth to both sides of the root of the member, with the right hand write on the paper beneath the lines written four nights ago in France, the lead of the pencil digging for the word into the crust of sperm, advancing in the trail, still sticky from that secretion that I no longer care whether or not it is for procreation—will I get to the end of my sentence, even to the end of the line, before the sperm rises up too high into the member?—replace the circumcised member in the rag, being careful not to scrape its excessively taut skin on the razor sharp crusts, churn it again in the cloth, tightened as if to reduce it, cancel it out into an indeterminate or even a castrated sexual organ; touch it—as if I myself were other, others, the way I am so often in daily life—caress, flatter, grab it as if in passing or during a sale of human bodies, make that member public with all the power of my heart, my mind, my senses and my memory; extract all of myself from it—and even from the rest of my body; transform my left hand into a public hand, the hand of someone who chooses, rents, or buys, my right, the hand belonging to my clandestine self, into the one that subverts and records the fondling and the groping, and even stimulates them.

Behind this dislocation, the ordinary self, the moral, religious self whose inevitable biological end I try to forget, this self watches, but outside of me the way a mount waits for its rider, who is defecating in the bushes…

A few spurts before desire is exhausted. Where do the second and third spurts come from, the deepest, the most acute, their imminency producing the most beautiful and shameful text! The last spurts, fifth, sixth, seventh sometimes, pulled as if from a wounded or weakened body that can't relax, the most shredded, anxious, most sexual text as if to call desire back and make a link with the unwritten thought of my distress after the crash, with its rage and its distress.

After all this is done, remove the still-laced cloth full of this prolific seed, slowly, one leg after another—don't let the sperm touch the ankle or the foot!—with the left hand holding the cloth ball, the right cupping the droplets of sperm beneath the testicles, walk, door open, bare feet, to the clean sink beneath the Moon to quickly rinse the bottom of my genitals with water, and along the side of the butt crack, the dip beneath the thighs, the flat of the ass in case of abundant spurts; then rinse the cloth ball under the faucet, use the lingering remnants of desire or the stirring of foresight against the distress that's coming with its icy chill to decide whether to keep the cloth ball intact and let it dry for use this evening or the evening after tomorrow, or wash it here under a trickle of water that doesn't rattle the first-floor pipes too much and go back to my room, or roll the cloth between the sheets of paper and place the ball at the bottom of the bag, or hang it to dry on the lock of the open window, the cloth wrung between my fists; and then once I've returned to bed, watch it as it shakes in the night currents, and with the passing of war ships on the far horizon.

But tonight I think of this rape and the courage of both women—one already a woman, the other to become one fast—I've always believed that actions and thoughts are nothing if they don't confront a public (What kind of music can we present before the elements? Only the clandestine text, beyond humanity and morality!)—I wonder if I'd have the nerve to have a beat-sheet session in front of them? Neither children nor adolescents are killed in my theater, but their bodies are profaned by servitude and by the acts of desire and pleasure performed on them. Would I even dare begin the ritual of the deep in front of these mourning bodies, completely dressed in black except for hands and pale faces, and whose entire misery comes from the unveiling of a body, the laying bare of its appalling and tempting crevices; can I unveil in a *dive for juice* bodies that are as young as the little dead boy, even if those bodies are only low-level servants half-naked on the adult scene—where they will later come to mingle their uncertain bodies and their voices broken by teenage hoarseness?

Would the father show his threatening face at the window? Or tomorrow, recognizing me in the funeral crowd, would he point his finger at me, the finger of a good laborer and a real man wearing his mourning clothes and mourning hat, and designate me as an intellectual accomplice to the murder of his child?

Next to this father is my father, and his child. As my desire rises, desire that I will resist tonight, I feel so close to the child, so suddenly and with a vertigo I feel even if I'm lying down, that I could be him, in his place, coveted, accosted, spoken to, caressed, kissed, gripped—and penetrated? But if I'd given in to my desire, to the desire for text, in the chill of my crash afterward it would be in the murdered child that I'd rest and ponder my indignity.

Appearing at the window, pushed by desire, the father threatens me. With what? Why does he put his finger on his mouth? What has he seen of me and of my body as the Moon washes my sleep? Doesn't he have the same features as the man in the torch light? Are the women wearing black for another death?

Is it possible that he escaped as he was being transferred from Wooler to Newcastle-upon-Tyne? Or, with thoughts full of brute strength, did he clobber his jailers, jump over the prison wall, and ride a stolen motorcycle to the valley—and to the little raped boy's room, where he turned him over and had me commit his crime again because I am so repulsed.

What could I give him if he was hungry?

Should I steal food from my hosts?

But then I'd have to flee with him, sitting behind him, holding his waist, or rather, me in front, my back against his chest?

Would I give him part of my body if it were good to eat? The part that grows back the fastest?

Up early, I pull my shorts on, quickly wash up, go for a short run in the dunes and sit down in my room to write before everyone gets up. But Dorothy is up already. She inches open my door and seeing me at work, closes it softly; the masturbation ball is stuffed at the bottom of the bag, and I've sprayed it with cologne to lessen the odor of dried seed—do she and Norman still make love, having no children, and does she even remember the smell of seed? Poetry takes shape on the squared notebook; but I've left the notebook made of drawing-paper sewn down the middle, where I copy and calligraphy the finished poems, in France; will I work on the poem interrupted by my trip, the story of Saül who discovers he is sick and that his body is covered in boils?

I'd need a vaster solitude, more circumscribed than here, I'd have to be a master, assured, as if by a spell, of an impregnable interior or exterior space; I'd have to pull from deep within the adult pain that already exists there, pull it toward my throat, project it on my teeth, play with it, standing and turning my head one way or the other, discover boils on my body, on my shoulders, under my armpits, on my sides, in my crotch, on my stomach, on my thighs—and on my already shameful parts?—I'd have to grow rabid, foam at the mouth, then cry; can I do that here, in the smell of breakfast that's almost ready: bacon, eggs, fruit, toast, jam, tea? Why not? (What is most beautiful often emerges from contrast, from an opposing context, and I often find the most obscene writing when faced with the purest being.)

At breakfast, can I be so defiant as to think *superior* things in front of all of them, still half-asleep and in the wake of dreams, eating reality again, fried foods still oozing fat?

A poem that wouldn't make me look inside for my own guts? Or flee? Will I lose my desire to leave, to disappear to the other side of the world and make myself a new body there, a new self, if I interrupt the poem to eat—and eat what I'm hungry for this morning?

It is only possible to write, invent, dare, admit oneself to oneself, build, and compose a rhythm on an empty stomach.

Would this poem of flight and freedom betray these good, calm, and courageous people?

I must reach far inside my self and grab and hold my root to make Saül appear and sing, Saül, with his sin of pride, and his heart hidden from God. But since God knows everything, doesn't he also know our secrets, my secret, and their misery and splendor seen from the outside?

What will emerge, eventually, on my body, of all this expended sperm, all these bad thoughts—and more: speech—*lain* on paper, all these short sketches of twilight and debauchery— and mostly enslavement: the body God created in His image and that he meant to be free can't be bought or sold! Or, as announced by my stutter, will it instead be dryness of the mouth and ears into muteness and deafness; and even maybe dryness of the hand, the one that writes.

Putting myself into this *Saül*, which I will give my friends to read when I get back, would mean admitting to my secret practice, and I am still too young and fresh of brain to dare wear the cloak of a king of Israel.

A popular dance with girls and boys, which I'd begun in France, comes to me on the page.

And so I can take my place, happily, at the family table.

After the dishes are done, with Anthony in the lingering smell of bed pressing his hips against my lower back, it's hard to hold to the decision to write, alone in my room or outside, till lunchtime, especially when I've seen two bikes, ours for the month, shining in the lean-to?

But a boy with a strong head of brown hair calls up to the open window from the alley; it's Kenneth, whom I'd seen at the circus, hair slicked back with brilliantine—maybe some lard, as well, some bacon from breakfast on his fingers?—unbuttoned white shirt, loosened black tie, swimsuit showing against his body under the shirttail, towel swung over his shoulder; his mother leads a life of *ill repute* in Berwick, and he already has three fathers. Where does he come from, in the Sun, with sour cherries on his ears and wasps hovering? From his uncle's house, a wifeless reverend, here on vacation, who had given him a long warning during the night against the dangers and temptations of his coming life and had forced him to pray with him since dawn, both of them kneeling; his eyes flutter but his member is quite erect.

To swim, all three of us, in this green, still silent sea; to reduce the superabundance of our family and ties to his boundless nakedness, a destitution that both Anthony and I want, so that we can "conquer the world"; his mother's debauchery is already on his lips, and his speech, unpredictable.

With Anthony and Kenneth screaming and running along the beach, I return to the table and continue the dance: but a girl, and then another, enters on roller skates; how can I introduce those mechanics, that word into this academic form, and into this ancient rhythm? A periphrasis would be impossible. It would take too long to find as the laughter of both boys on the dune grows closer to my work; quick, "roller skates!"

But they recede and the dance beneath the ballpoint pen is now a stanza with longer lines, rocking words, the most tender words, where the raped and killed child whom I've only seen in the torn crotch of the one who raped and killed him reappears as a boy from Oradour with a shattered skull, my brother, my double.

In the returning noise, voices, cries, honking horns, motors, I discern Annick's voice, clearer, more free, pitched above the bicycle that jiggles her around—until the end of the month at least.

Hearing her, I walk to the window. We stare at each other and her voice weakens, her face, from far away, blushes, as does mine.

It's mid-morning: tightly wrapped in her pink dress, its neckline overflows with a white seam that I'm afraid belongs to a bra; if I have to—and it has to be today in this very light—how can I grab that breast and touch the edge of what is not fabric but is a *hard* object like some mechanical add-on?

The paper shakes on the table behind me: my hand must move from words and desecrated bodies to this flesh intact and near and living with a living soul inside it whose truth I will have to obtain with fear and joy—and by what means, my knees buckle already at the thought.

…I need to find the pathway to this soul, find the angle under which it becomes as desirable as the flesh that protects and diffuses it. Even in my deep, enslaved bodies in their servitude are endowed with a soul for play and blasphemy; but as opposed to the soul of free humans, it disappears from their cadavers after use.

But the soul of the girl twirling on the hot asphalt is natural, granted by the Invisible, as indestructible here on earth and in Heaven as is His name.

In women, in my mother, in Dorothy, in Douggie's mother whose breasts radiate forever in my eyes, it's there for eternity, it bends its light on us; where can I find it in a girl, through everything society uses to hide it? What is even my own soul? Who can see it in my eyes, hear it in my voice, and understand it in my words?

Can we love each other, she and I, untraceable soul to untraceable soul?

And what about society, the species, and our ancestry?

When we are just beginning to gain consciousness of our soul, so frail and impure, part beast part God, we lose it and interrupt its growth into a soul shared between two.

She and I, let's help the other find his or her soul!

Anthony and Kenneth watch her from the dunes as her ass leans down toward the handlebars; I retreat into the darkness of the room: both boys come back from the sea naked in their swim trunks, clothes and towels on their shoulders; my heart beats too fast for me to linger here to write: I could slow it down, go outside, run, caress that ass and the folds at the hips before they do, run my palm along the flowers at the top under the shoulders and down toward the bottom, hoping that my palm doesn't hit the elastic seam of *panties* under the dress.

Her breasts in the top of the dress, suspended without a bra, peek above the neckline. I deduce that maybe the central organ, the mount of Venus, is naked under the dress, and lies in two parts on the tip of the saddle with nothing but thin fabric underneath; but isn't that organ's nakedness reserved for women of ill repute, so it is easier to access?

What is she looking at on the ground to make her stay so long with her ass spread open? Will I get there in time, through the bedroom, the living room, the front door and the gate, to lay my palm on it before the others do? And what then, with the vacationers coming from the south, the north, the east, with their landing nets, balls, and iceboxes?

Her ass disappears into it.

I go out, enter into affluence; Anthony and Kenneth have left the dune; the smell of suntan lotion swells; so many half-naked bodies, breasts, asses, fresh or sagging; farther away, the sound of bats on balls, on wickets, the shouts of *cricketers*: I'm off.

Around the field, away from the beach, a line of spectators: along this line, their backs to me, Anthony, Kenneth, Annick holding her bike; Kenneth's hand on Annick's ass; Anthony's hand on Kenneth's shoulder, Anthony's fist against Kenneth's jaw.

The extent of what I reject at the time is limitless; what I've seen here since my arrival makes me nauseous; only the abandoned paper on the table of the bedroom, its window open—may she watch over it, Dorothy, our friend, our sister during hard times, and may she watch over my ball of orgy unbeknownst to her, she who used to watch over the survival of our beauty and our freedom!—I grab the knife at my hips.

Kenneth is leaning over Annick. On his forehead an oily mass of hair, broken loose from his slicked-back do, sticks to the pimples along the fresh wrinkles lining his forehead, hides his soft dark stare, and reaches down to the purulent zits on the corner of his mouth: if she wanted to kiss him on the mouth she'd kiss pus along with the boy. If she wanted to kiss his forehead in friendship, her lips, lathered with pink this morning, would take double the amount of pus!

With a shake of her ass, Annick nudges Kenneth's hand aside as it rises to touch and scratch his zits and bite his fingernails, unwashed from the night's spiritual sweat.

On the right, Anthony, his wrist on Kenneth's shoulder, spreads his fist open against Kenneth's jaw, his thumb moves up toward the cheek: his forefinger, which I don't see, is perhaps on the mouth, and is already pushing up against the teeth to penetrate the palate—will Kenneth bite that finger? From inside, will his tongue heavy with obscenities lick it?

The sound of the bats grows stronger; I must hear with my ears what it is that I must think now: in a spirit of secrecy, night or day, I am the one who pulls from the original darkness, as if from a canvas painted entirely in black, figures of prohibited desire and pleasure, and give them a form of speech that rebels against the speech of the Creator God and His Son. How can the "real, here below" that subverts this scene and that I still desire with all my strength, for sanity, be stolen in front of me by these three with their backs turned! Would they do it if they were facing me?

I take my glasses off, slip them into the case inside my pocket, run my palm over my face.

Did they learn from Anthony, who might himself have gotten it from his dreams, that I write blasphemies and "sex" in secret? And although they don't want to read it, perhaps they judge themselves, either as inferior, or free to have sex in front of me with their backs turned, leaving me to imagine what they are doing in front, since I know how to imagine, and do so much more than adults?

Will Annick turn around? What movement, what power of my eyes, what naked stare could make her turn?

Through the line of people, I see Anthony's father play, run, topple a wicket with his bat and with the ball: if he sees me I'll be recruited for the team! I'd have to put my glasses on and I could break them during the game, or play without them, and throw the ball into empty space, or hit the back of one of their players, or one of ours.

The paper on which *Saül* is written trembles on the table in the wind blowing from the sea; a vacationer could reach in and grab it with his landing net through the open window: who here could translate my poem into English from the French? Translated, although I do it mentally for all I write, even my secret writing, would it be firmer and more beautiful? Although as soon as it is written, I see it rewritten by me, later, better, and as an adult—but isn't a child or an adolescent who writes already an adult?

What should I choose? To go up to Annick, grab her ass and part of her left breast, and move away from the two friends? Or with my clothes on, to edge myself in forcefully between the two half-naked boys and wait there, my body charged with poetry and its smelly secret, on my right that normal body bound for the marriage bed, on my left, a body unloved by the one who should have loved it, bound for temptations, transactions, marked bodily in advance by the progress of debauchery, with its three fathers joined to make its yield increase beside its mother in hovels?

To go back to my room and resume the interrupted poetry, the most noble, my zits pulled from my face onto my back between my shoulders, the dagger of my guilt, the guilt of *Saül* and his purulent zits?

To go back? But I have my backpack between the foot of the table and the foot of the bed with the ball of orgy wound up tight at the bottom of the bag, and if I lean over slightly, with my right hand still holding the ballpoint pen over the text of Saül, I can touch and caress its shape with my left palm. Temptation to blend both texts?

Always choose what pushes toward the future. Even if this girl's body, this young girl's body is the future beneath my hand, flesh that will make flesh—and with what of me?—there is flesh and soul to be discovered in the other sex, in the opposite sex, even if these two half-naked bodies excited at the show of the game, whether in sand or straw, on sheets or otherwise, on the concrete floor of a garage, will not be the discovery of the flesh that I know from myself, but the prohibition and disgrace attached to consuming the act between males that would project them before all others in the policing light of Judgment.

The future is what doesn't yet exist; it's what I must create out of nothing: poetry and its double: the text of the deep—"beyond-creation."

Once my anger has subsided at seeing Kenneth's hand on Annick's ass, another desire rises from my heels up to my heart, stronger than the rest, as full a need as the need to eat: to make art, painting, poetry especially.

Of all the paths opening before me, I should choose the widest, where the gaze is lost.

Work: my father doesn't want to peek beneath the rock of sex with me, or can't, because he's scared of whatever swarms beneath it that would force him to define himself sexually, and use the word *sex*. So he resumes his continual fight against me with the word *work*—I've seen him work ever since my eyes could follow people's movements, going from one room to another, looking at him through the window from my mother's arms, the movement of him leaving the house and entering the car, which starts; ever since my ears could make out the word *work* in his voice speaking to my mother.

To resist him, to exist before his gaze, his speech, his smell, I must prove to myself that I am working: not so much in school, but like him and more than him in an exceptional resolute act that owes him nothing but part of the body that carries and will carry poetry.

Does he know that I feel pain when he relentlessly repeats a virtue with which I'm already familiar, as if it were an order: being conscious of time and space I'm conscious of a purpose: something must be done with this time and space; to work is to move forward and to produce mass.

She and the two others, desire and pleasure, with no other result than their same body in front of me; but poetry, its definitive image drawing near, is like a figure coming forward from the end of the park alley…

An act that takes everything from you, especially what you don't yet know of yourself.

I want to step back and leave, but how can I, visibly and invisibly—in my consciousness? They'd think I'm leaving them for a stronger and higher act. They'd think their hearts and minds can't perform such a willful act, and that they remain adolescents, with phantom bodies and intellectual appendages, adolescents in whom the member and the organ, shameful parts for lineage and for society, lead them with their growing power of attraction closer to all that will be barred from me.

All three are more assured of their bodies than I am: it's been a while since I've even seen mine; I flee from it in mirrors and reflective surfaces.

Eventually, not seeing your body can lead to death.

Since I can't see the movement of my thoughts, all I see of myself as I act, some nights, or every third day at noon during vacation, is my member erect in front of me, most often hidden in the cloth and under my fist. As for the soul, I glimpse my eyes through lenses that restrict their size, their radiance, and their color, between orgasms or very rarely through "scientific" observation in a shard of broken mirror after I've come.

A ball, thrown toward the line of spectators, falls just beyond Kenneth's bare foot. Anthony's hand drops from his back to pick it up behind them in the sand beyond the line of people, skims over the side laces of Kenneth's trunks, pulls them slightly down the thighs, uncovers a sliver of ass, white in the tanned copper body; his eye, bruised, the white squeezed tight, twisted along with his head between the cheek and the eye socket, sees me watching it: a smile draws the curve of his cheek nearer to the socket.

In the stronger beating at my temples: *Kenneth, tonight, I'll put your ass and the bruised white of your eye in my little hell, and you along with them.*

Did he feel his half-bared ass in the cool air? Does he have a boner in front? And why? The very hot Sun dries the small scabs and bruises around his eye socket. What will he do once he leaves Anthony and the rest of us? Once he'll have thrown on a few clothes, and let himself be called from the darkness of farms and workshops, in the village and in the inland farm lands, filling the afternoon with his genital stench, offering himself, opening himself, even if it wounds him, everywhere waking the sexes that were asleep?

Anthony throws the ball back into the game, his left hand doesn't return to Kenneth's shoulder but to his waist, and the trunks stay low; this body must be loved, but must be captured: captive, it would promptly gain some freedom— and be caught again. I inspect the shade of tan against the nearly white skin along the curve of the ass; Anthony's left hip against his right ass cheek hides the splaying of his ass toward the crotch, but a sort of vapor or smoke seems to rise from that hidden place, I can make out the sound of boiling.

His smile is now turned to face me: in the raw light, such a fresh and smelly shine! Its light is such that it should illuminate the path of his life, but others will lead him, other stares, other voices, other hands, other lips, other genitals; do I even have the right to imagine an immediate fate for him, before him as he watches me and even if he weren't watching, a fate so near, so definitive, decided at my convenience, for my own desire, for that single tickling of misery along the scars of circumcision, that influx of my blood that I take to be impure in the appendage that becomes meat as it floods?

Because "I" have a hard-on, can I will him to a destiny of debauchery, his body reduced to simple public remains?

It not because I desire it, that ass, that my dick is hard, but because it suddenly appears *useful* to me. He is desired more than he is loved, and so is opposed to my dignity and to the dignity of all human beings, which I defend, and even reinforce—especially through loss of useful substance!—in thought, and in my future writing, the precarity, the uncertainty, the disorder of his life—perhaps unwanted by his mother.

Anthony's wrist, its vein shining, climbs to the base of the shoulder blade, still so detached from the body at our age. Kenneth's chin rubs against the collarbone. His eyes stare into mine, but it's not my hand on his waist, it's not my vein bulging on that wrist from too much exercise, a vein and hand that could belong to a young worker if not for some plaster, earth, mud, or grease; mine, as I stand, still hangs below my hips, heavy, pulling on my shoulder: the ball of orgy weighs on it more than just its weight.

I sit on one of those cone-shaped pillars that mark the asphalt pathway to the beach; the heat of the cone burns my *fundament*—I've just learned the word—through my shorts and trunks.

How can *that* name a hole that you can't see, an organ that isn't one, that you don't touch, that stinks the most, that imprints on children's underclothes the Mark of the Beast, the sign of the animal origin of man and of the child of man who is late to admit that his parents also shit?

Fundament? It's more like the foundational hole into which you insert a pillar: the pillar is what founds, not the hole. Our Christian civilization was not founded by the slot at Golgotha, but by the cross; what does the male hole produce other than excrement? The female hole, in which I haven't yet slipped a hand, is an organ, hidden, yet active and productive; when birthing, it spreads, in *pain*, three, four, five times its width at rest.

Vacationers flow back from the beach toward the houses; my thinking proceeds in the direction contrary to their movement.

What should I do, here and once I'll have returned to France, with all these mutilated forms and sensations? As the couples walk back, hiding Kenneth's ass and Anthony's wrist on top of it, I see that beauty has seeped into their children, whether they are young or gone to seed; their shadows cover me: what kind of beauty to beauty love do they make in the slackening of summer? To make love you must be beautiful; both lovers must be.

Having watched and described bodies for a long time has taught me that beauty often hinges on very little: a few millimeters more, the curve of a cheek, a less protruding vein, a slightly longer neck, a perkier breast, one fold more, one fold less, pores that are more spread out; and so between two ripened bodies...

For the last two, three years I've been placing bodies that I see or that I compose from what I see against the buildings and in the shadows of my deep, and I know that even an unsightly body grows beautiful through the desire of others, in its abandon, naked or half-clothed with the hand of its owner resting on its shoulder.

I have created another place for beauty: beyond Nature, bodies, painting; a lair, which God knows and watches over, in which I throw a new captive nightly, and establish my own beauty: perhaps the demon Lucifer whispers in my ear but I can't tell whether it's him or some other whisperer of subversion: it's me, and I do what I want with beauty.

What I want? What *form* wants.

If desire, held back and contained by my hand on my member, is what pushes the figures and their speech onto the right hand page, thought, reason, and logic are what prepare them, all day, among those I love and who love me. Just as they say philosophers prepare their arguments and concepts while walking. Desire and craving accelerate the apparition of the desired figure, made in advance, its speech also composed beforehand.

I take from this permanent act enough to go on living, since everything I see, Good, beauty, Evil, or ugliness, plunges me into a distress that's equally as strong.

Adults who take pleasure in judging me think that those reflections and that wisdom, even if they are agonizing, are a vain and dangerous "reverie." But I discover in that reverie, in the simultaneity of thoughts, as the Good watches me with its transparent eyes, that in that stare I can reinforce a gestating interior scene that is contrary to it and negates it; looking at a display of social skill, without changing my gaze and with the naked eye, I discover that I can perfect within myself a scene of kidnapping and prostitutional defilement. And want both with the same intensity, while at the same time, acknowledging that I am being torn apart.

For the last two, three years, with a few sheets of papers, I've been tormented, I've complicated my life, decided my destiny! Even if I burned that stack of papers and cloth, both God and I have seen it; we've smelled its stench. Its words stick in my mind like a text of law. And that fire, in a dump, He who whispers in my ear blows on its embers, and it is now the burnt draft of a new text, a fresher, brighter, more tempting text whose figures speak with more assurance.

How can I destroy within myself this small construction, this encampment, theater, refuge propped up on the pillar of my member? If I cut it off, or had it cut, I know that another would grow on me somewhere; that this desire, which I think and lament as the desire for the other, an infirm desire, is the desire to create, the image rising with blood in my lungs and throat similar to the rise of blood and sperm into my member.

Did Kenneth place his hand on Annick's ass, or did he instead hover over it, and the hand's shadow made her twitch?

Most of the vacationers have reached the coastal road. Alone, a little girl tries out her bare feet on the hot asphalt: eleven, maybe twelve, three, four years younger than I, the right distance to start a family.

What is she naked from? Is her family Scandinavian, naturist? She cups her inner thighs with both hands, jumps, her wet heels steam slightly on the burning asphalt. What language is she counting in or humming in as she jumps? Drops of seawater run down her thick brown hair that swimming has flattened against her brown body; what do I possess that she might like that is not marked and deformed by my secret? My legs, I need time, I need to bike and swim to recover the use of them corresponding to my age; I need effort to clear from their nerves, muscles, bones and flesh all effects and traces of the tension, the clenching and the letting go of the beat-sheet.

Here these last four days and nights since I did *it*, even after a long trip, walks, bike rides, swimming, and hiding under rams... I can still feel the violence of what I carried out in my high room, in France, the day before I left: abundant discharge, blasphemous writing. Remnants of the sweat that pearled as I touched myself and wrote again after ejaculating my first load still line my forehead, nose, cheeks, chin, and neck.

Is that how she sees me? What does she see in my eyes seeing her look at me? Remains of what I've seen through them, the sketch of which is drying in the lump at the bottom of my bag?

Against her two arms, breasts that cover a wide area, but are still small: my gaze runs down both forearms joined at the wrist. But I see only one wrist, and a very long expert hand, and fingers with painted nails against the thigh. Where is the other wrist and hand? Has she stuffed them into her growing organ? What does she want to extract from there?

Pleasure, a shell, sanies?

A lump of firm lustrous flesh protrudes from the flat of her palm. My heart leaps from the stump seen on a young girl from my childhood, in our Dauphiné region: here, the right wrist is without a hand.

She removes her only hand from her inner thighs with such sudden joy, lifts her arm along her temples, and, standing tall, plays with her mutilated wrist with her complete hand, almost an adult limb, stretched high above her head.

I see nakedness as proper to Antiquity: the bodies that fight there are naked, or just barely clothed; and even in my long reflections on slavery, in which I try to understand how so many heroic and subtle minds have engaged in it, taken pleasure from it, or even admitted of it—ratiocination on the non-humanity of slaves—it is this nakedness, this permanent proximity of flesh and mass, its thermal and olfactory radiation that makes it possible: you can only sell and buy what you see, whose "qualities" and "defects" you can see and touch, whose voice and spirit you can hear emerging from a naked or partly naked body.

Clothes cover the body with humanity, civilization; that's why, in my theater of the deep, serviced bodies are pushed in, naked, or just barely dressed with rags or in the remains of "Christian" clothing.

The players pack their gear, trunks slam shut; after the rumbling of a few motors, human silence returns to the beach.

Far away down the coastal road, Anthony and Kenneth are walking to the village with Annick circling around them on her bike. Are they going to Douggie's mother's house before lunch to entertain the boy?

Seeing the monument to Grace Darling, the heroic savior of the shipwreck of the SS Forfarshire, in its gothic enclosure on its butte along the coast, I sense that this girl watching me with large blue-green eyes from under her raised arm, her slightly fuzzy armpit open wide, was saved from a shipwreck and from drowning by a hand that knew how to choose the right one.

Instead of asking her where she comes from, in a suitable language—great desire to "find" out how—I let myself imagine her origins: in front of the object, overly conscious of the excitement of my heart, I ponder, weigh it down and frame it with reason, with the networks of reason. I don't lift the secret; I let the enigma last before its object.

Does she understand what I am looking for, as she spins and twists on her heels, letting me look at all the profiles and facets of herself? Bodies are wild enough that mutilation or lack seems natural: blows, animal bites, snares, unnatural crossbreeding, mermaid mutilations.

My cheek starts to twitch from that tender stump—I can keep that at least.

As the body spins, spreading a twirling aroma of port rot, a swollen, violet and scabby wound on the top of the thigh momentarily hides the organ that I've imagined, and *seen*, as larger and more prominent than what I believe girls have.

Apart from humming, does she speak? How can I dissimulate from her eyes, as they get used to me, that my member is growing hard, pressed against my thigh, under the corduroy shorts?

I don't want to have a hard-on for a body, but for an image, an idea, a world in which I feel abandoned; to have only one body, only one organ that grows hard… that organ comes from elsewhere, and where does it go?

She's the kind of creature I've imagined since I was a child, and that I've been cautiously introducing in the early sketches of my deep, the wild girl of Peïra-Cava in *Farfadette*, or the Amazonian in *Journey to the Far Amazon*.

The desire swelling at the root of my being is for the hand of servitude resting on the shoulder of threatened virginity or freedom; my member rises for this friction of opposites; that shadow has to fall on any body I see and want to desire, or I must make it fall there; I'd have preferred myself to be otherwise.

The harder I get from her odor of freedom and filth, the more she veers her spinning toward me; a fraction of her short shadow—the Sun is straight above us—moves toward my feet.

Should I stand tall, throw the front of my body on hers as it spins?

Grab what is spinning? Is my belt buckled, unbuckled? Move toward her lips first, then grab her back, my arms under her raised arms, and spread my lips on hers? Probe her *nature* with my erect jumble of flesh and corduroy? What about that wound on the top of her thigh, a gash that is still open and that *watches* over it… if I rub my shorts and its folds against it, will I unhood its scab? Once I'm flush against her, it is no longer my self, or it's my self from the deep, here realized. Will I carry her into it then, but in real life? Under this full Sun, where can we both cross the trace on the ground of the threshold to the deep?

Of all the places that I now know, and that flash before me as I close my eyes, none of them have the darkness that we need: only the alleyway in Leith… but it's so far!

Under my eyelids, I still search for the ruins of a tunnel, of an underground passage. The more I search, myself in clothes pressed up against her naked, the harder I become: under my hands, in my arms, a free creature—but since when?—who agrees to follow me into servitude: up against her, I go from master of the ritual to the *herd*—shouldn't I take off my shirt? should I keep my shorts or take them off? or, better yet, tear them? or, once my shorts are off, should I just keep the small swim trunks with its side laces? and rub myself with them, lying on the roadside along the asphalt that is beginning to melt?— and in our state we must be off, walk, go inland to attract, in stables, garages, and factories, the greatest possible number of free men that might take us, enslaved? She, polishing her nature, her tits, so that they shine. And I, what do I do?

What would these robust, engaged or married men do with my member? Kenneth kept his ass partly uncovered because he knew it would attract a crowd: should I uncover mine a bit?

But where would I tell the men to meet us? In my brain? On the orgy pad? In my backpack?

Desire swells as I search for the place, or the place must exist, for eternity: in my hand, in my mind, and in my heart, created by the Everlasting, and for my eternity.

Her small shadow moves toward my ankle. Her smell swallows all the other smells, the small crackling of her dance, the very sound of the sea. So close one to the other, yet still one and the other!

Saül's delirium began when he violated the orders of his God, sparing and seeking out beauty as his own beauty was sought out to make him King. Only music returned him to sanity.

Reclaim my poetry from his anger, his delirium, or, as David plays the harp at the foot of the bed on which he despairs, reclaim it from his appeasement and his tears?

The state of my body and my heart to continue writing poetry depends on what I do to this girl.

But the stench of meat, driven toward us from the beach by the slight breeze from the rising tide, interrupts her rotation at her ass, and on the interior curve of an ass-cheek, maybe the right that is lit up most brightly by the sun, I see a trace of excrement.

At her age, is her *nature* already spreading into butcher's meat?

Standing against her, fingers on that lump swollen with the rush of blood, so close that it bloodies my palm, should I open my shorts in front according to the custom and let my member go toward what it must know, and let its naked extremity touch, even penetrate this wild flesh?

Can this urge and brutal back-and-forth be satisfied over and over as a supreme act upheld by the consideration of nations?

Our mother, whom we only ever see smiling at my father, who touches her so gently, would she have consented, the both of them crouching together, to forget herself—wails of pleasure—as the spasm builds? I *see* that we came out of her, and I even see us covered in blood and in the matter and smell of life, after she'd carried us, as we grew in size, sensation and understanding in her womb, but *before* that, I see nothing but the decision of the Everlasting to desire me and every one of us, each already different in his mind—and I imagine that moment as being outside of Time, neither dawn, nor noon, nor night, what vision, sound, odor, what reminiscence, as the Creator pulled me from the void like the painter placing his first mark against the black background of the canvas, knowing everything about me up until my death, and even beyond: my return to his creative brain or my damnation?

It wasn't to populate the Earth that he desired us, but to transform it.

What does the father do in this deposition of the idea of the Creator in the childbearer's womb? Instead of a father, isn't he a stepfather, a cruel man? Or, maybe a rapist?

The smoke thickens. The girl spins on the soles of her feet, her heels covered in filth; her ass and back disappear into the smoke through which she runs toward an outcrop of rock jutting out from the road into the sea. There in the distance, I can make out bodies dressed in black and with brown skin that move around a blaze bursting into flame, which they are trying to extinguish with armfuls of sea wrack. I see her blend into the group; they throw black rags onto her naked body. Near them, along the coastal road, I see a big, repainted red van, scratched and dented. Is it their mobile home?

I count six of them, two adults, four youth: she has the lightest skin of all; is she their daughter, their sister?

In the aftermath of war, did they snatch her as a small child from an institution for deficient children, first evacuated, and then in ruins? Was she born without a right hand? Or do they rent themselves out to circuses, either as a group, or only one or several among them, as backup acrobats, clowns, or animal trainers? Did she tear her right hand off during an acrobatic stunt or on a rope, or did a big cat catch it, rip it off, and eat it? Did she get the open sore on her thigh by sliding too fast down a rope, her skin heating up, burning, and then tearing?

The thing that I no longer want to see inside my head and that returns whenever I see a woman, the girl from the girlie magazine with her meat open against the rope of the striptease, here it is again in front of me with its smell of colored ink, teenage fingers, and maceration under mattresses.

I've gotten up from the cone and I'm walking, but the way they hit the fire with packs of seaweed and then disperse, and the half-clothed vacationers who've rushed up to help, makes my steps pause on the sand: the girl over there turns toward me, but they throw some black rags against the back of her head, and I see her hair, a thick brown mane, now dry, spread over her frail ass, like a child of the desert, pushed behind the cart where her ancestors are sitting with the utensils and the small treasures of their family line.

Does Saül dig his fingers covered in tears into David's mane of hair to encourage him to play and sing with more soul, or is it because he wants him to stop his singing and fingering for…?

I have to climb back, cross the road, the gate, the door, the small corridor on the left, the door to my room, and on the page, in the rhythm of the stanza's line, decide the poetry that I'll show my friends in France who accompany its development, and despite the stench of the bag against my feet—and the urge that sweeps over me—what will remain of that ass, that mane of hair, that wound on the thigh and that trace of excrement on the ass in my *Saül*?

Just the group's black rags, transformed into tattered clothes of mourning, behind Saül's bed as he mourns his reason.

Annick, Anthony, Kenneth, and I ride our bikes all afternoon in the backcountry.

I wanted to bring my own bike, but couldn't, and so riding this old, broken-down black bike that I quickly cleaned and oiled, I imagine I've got my own between my legs, with its red and chrome stripes.

For me, calves trained on mountain passes, this succession of small ups and downs of the road are an easy game where I continue to develop my *Saül*: what verses will he say to the sorceress of Endor?

On the first small hill between Bamburgh and Alnwick, the muscles of my calves grow tight from the last beat-sheet session five nights ago in France: should he ask her to conjure up some figures from his future? What are mine? What will I be in the future if I create my destiny from the scene of my deep, and if, against my God, I maintain, confirm and justify the strength that makes me create and speak that scene? In the poem, how can I dissimulate myself, me, in the first King of Israel, in the motives for God's anger against him, in the reasons for his melancholy?

What should I do with this secret text? What should I do with the strength and weakness that push me to produce it?

What I do not find in poetry and novels, and that I sometimes perceive in music and painting, abandon, the delivery of one's self to something stronger, the sale of flesh to those who desire it, I find in this Bible that my mother offered me at puberty: sin against God, use of flesh, stain, despair, madness.

I carry the Bible in my backpack on walks, bike rides, camping trips; here, I've got it in my room, with my bag, against my orgy pack; and even if it contains the New Testament, less laden with smells, portraying the innocent figure of Christ, and where the Acts of the Apostles figure, so pure and luminous, as well as Paul and Peter's harsh letters, and the monstrous and enchanting Apocalypse, I'm not scared of placing the stench of this ball against the stench of the Old Testament, impurity against impurity, sanies against sanies.

A line from his furious complaint to the sorceress—appearance of the judge who made him King—rises from my guts. Or does it come from somewhere deeper, from this member that duty turns into the root of a new lineage? But I don't feel it like that, then; so I refuse to believe that the line could come from there—in my lungs and through my esophagus into the throat and the palate of the mouth: the mouth produces the line, like the swollen cheek on the shepherd or angel's flute, or trumpet.

My right knee shakes on the pedal. The hardships of war have caused endemic rickets: what does he want the woman to conjure up?

Did I, myself, want poetry? Who wanted, who wants me to be an artist, a poet? Who forms its words in my mouth, both visible poetry and non-visible writing? What evil did I do, in my conscious life or before, that I was barred from the normal use of the brain? Will I have to live two lives in one? Am I even living? My leg grows cold: where is the proof that I exist? The friends fleeing on their bikes in front of me live with a single brain, and with members and an organ that they'll use for reproduction and for lineage, where they'll forget themselves. If I caught up with them, could they prove my existence to me?

Down the slope and along the flats, calm thoughts return with the acquired speed: but I must set to paper the uncertainties and questions of the uphill climb: since I have no paper in my pockets—the sketchpad and gouaches are strapped to the bicycle rack—I number my questions from one to five, seven, or nine, abstractions as well as images, I learn the order and numbering of that list, the numbers at the forefront of the list almost taking the place of the idea or the fact, progressively, in my visual memory: so for number 1 Saül disobeys the Everlasting; for number 3 he is disguised as a non-King; and I search for my indelible original sin for number 7.

As I memorize this list of notes, with its numbers and words, I know that once I pass the pond that I see shimmering in the distance, I'll be terrorized if I've lost one of them, even the most infinitesimal, only its number still upright in my immediate memory. My heart speeds up, and the blood drains from my legs and arms.

Should I also memorize the importance of each item of the list? Maybe establish a parallel numbering system? But in what order? Maybe in the opposite direction, with the 9 containing what's most important for the poem, and the 1 the idea that to lose everything would also be a way to renew my thinking and that I should rely on what I'll see during the afternoon, on what I'll read tonight, in bed, to discover it again?

The loss of an idea, an image, can take up one, two, even three days, can unhook me from the current of my life, even though I maintain a good front: finding it means that I'm tuned to the world again, to reality, to happiness.

But as I search for the lost idea, I encounter other ones, other detours, other arguments and *reliefs*, other forms of the music of reason and chance.

Ever since I left my childhood behind, objects, landscapes, ideas, feelings and sensations have grown thicker in time and space; my destiny, once so clear and joyous, even if filled with blood and tears, now takes on a shrunken obscurity.

Now I'm riding in front of my friends: I've passed them so that I can think of the poem's list in front of them. I have the itinerary to get to Alnwick in my head. A vast and heavy field of unharvested wheat reverberates in the asphalt, beyond a soft hill, its horizon enclosed by elms. I wait, afraid, as I cycle down the middle of the field, that its smell, the shifting of the shafts of wheat, the scurrying of small animals will add facts, ideas, and numbers to the afternoon's list that had started with the list of the poem to think through.

I slow down through a small village, where traces of thick earth deposited by the tires of farm equipment line the ground. Through the rays of an intermittent Sun, as a beginning storm lifts the hay of the manure heap in the courtyard, I see a woman from a three-quarter angle sitting on a chair, her breast out, feeding an infant, with a dog circling around them, snapping at flies as he goes.

Is she the mother? But her stomach is still so heavy.

Is she the sister? Is she a pregnant wet nurse? But how could she already produce milk?

We stop under the porch where we lean our bikes while the dog, stopping his rounds, comes up to lick our legs. We enter the yard with him.

Sated, careful not to impinge on the space of others, we inch toward that woman whose naked breast hangs from the top of her black dress. Why?

From the center of the courtyard, through my glasses that are foggy from the impending storm, I try to catch the milk on the baby's lips as he pulls them from the tit.

Annick, farther down the road, pink ass as if caught in the black cloud spreading on the left between the house and the stables, turns around, sets her raised index on her mouth. The dog sitting across from us on the concrete snarls and snaps his jaws.

His red member pierces through the dungy fur on his stomach: is he trying to protect what he desires?

The woman turns a white gaze toward us from inside her red face, the creases of her lips swell and dot with foam; the baby, his head extending beyond her hand—is that a milking glove lying on the ground?—shakes his legs in the recomposed swarm.

We move back to the shed. The intermittent Sun strikes tool blades, hooks, instruments laid out in front of the barn on our right.

The dog comes back across the yard and barks and growls at each of our legs as we climb back onto our bikes.

We leave quickly. When the rain hits, we stop in a shed down at the bottom of the line of wheat fields.

We can't fit in it with our four bikes: I unstrap my painting gear from mine, slip it between my shirt and skin; we run toward the shed, wood, cinder blocks and tar paper roof; a hint of smoke flattened by the shower of rain emerges from a stovepipe on the roof; Kenneth knocks at the door three times, opens it, and calls out: nothing but the growing noise of rain on the tarpaper and the stovepipe. We enter: once the door is shut and the obscurity lifts slightly, we sit on two side benches; the stove door opens onto a hearth, several bones smolder in the ashes, their smell is unfamiliar to us: smoke and ash hide their tips.

Set in a thick gap between cinderblocks in the wall across from us that opens onto the sloping wheat field, a white, blue, and gold Virgin, with a snake head beneath her feet, remains upright in the gusts of wind. The floor is very dark, beaten earth. Is it peat?

Is it the smell of the sweat of our three boy's bodies, or is it the lingering odor of a man who will return? Anthony, sitting beside me, fingers the knife hanging at my waist.

Amid the heightened noise of rain, and as we speak, more and more slowly, almost to the point of sleep, we try to come to terms with the woman and her fake breastfeeding: is she mourning a stillborn, and, pregnant with a third, does she want to feed the newborn that was birthed between the first born and the one to come?

Did she lose part of her sanity when the first one died? Or when she gave birth to the second?

Annick, as we look at her breasts, her wrists joined between her thighs, in that pink splay, lowers her eyes, her brown hair flattened by the rain lying against her cheeks and under her jaw against the top of her neck. Lighting flashes through all the openings, all the gaps in the shed; its cinderblocks grate against each other. Our speech leaves off at the dog and its member; Annick's cheeks blush; the lighting glimmers on the silver chain holding up a cross against her throat: are her shoulders and necklace shaking with cold? A deep cleavage, she's more naked that we are in our brute, curveless shapes; but her perfume, although modest, diluted by the rain, fills the entire shed. Can you smell it from outside?

As a child, I used to think a woman's perfume was her natural smell, along with the smell of milk.

The rain, as it flattens our clothes over the curves of our bodies, brightens our complexion, the color of our hair, the outward curve of our lips, our earlobes, even up to our bitten nails, and makes the four of us beautiful in this twilight: from inside, deep within the soul, we each strengthen the shining of our eyes.

I look at the bones in the hearth lit up by a flash of lightning; a clap of the thunder stops me from trying out a sentence about their origins. There is no trace of food or any utensils, on the ground, on the shelf littered with tool debris, or anywhere in the shed.

If I stopped seeing and observing everything, life would be easier for me: but these bones are smoldering. Are they fowl bones? Game? Air fowl? Water fowl? Farmyard poultry? Their size would seem to indicate a hen turkey. A large tom turkey? An ovine animal? Caprine? Cervidae? A large eagle? We'd looked down over the cemetery before the village from the top of our bikes: too uniformly green for human bones to have been recently unearthed there. The crematorium, which I used to stare at as a child, in a book, its carbonized human remains off to one side, I've always seen it since in the stoves in my lower and middle schools. How can I erase it from my thoughts under this clamor?

Through the opening, I see water, now mixed with mud, running in torrents through the very tall wheat; what do we want from each other? The smell of us three boys gets stronger with what we cannot say: of the three, Kenneth knows what he wants, and knows how to do it with Annick as he sees men doing it with his mother, but he'd just as easily start with one of us, Anthony or me, and if both Anthony and I still don't know how he'd do it, he certainly does; and what does Annick want with the two of us, as Kenneth's hand, to her side, inches closer on the bench toward the molded pink?

Did his reverend uncle obtain from him at dawn a promise of chastity for the week? He starts to hum and shake his knee; I see the blood pulsing in Annick's neck when she uncovers it, leaning her head to the other side as if moving away from a kiss she didn't want. Would Kenneth also demand that Anthony *pass* through me, and I through him; to limit his role as organizer and flouter of compulsory sex, I try to see and hear the slave, hiding his beauty so that the men of my deep desire it even more, in what he reveals of his curves and flesh, in the gleaming of his eyes, and in what he prepares in his throat, his cheeks, and mouth. And, turning him this way into a "whore" whose life was *purchased* along with his being, his duration and his past, whereas his mother only *rents* her body as it is, my growing erection is more for his imagined condition than for his real body. Does he see that?

Rain dries on our three bodies; our skin goes back to being oily with adolescent zits, hazy up to the eyes. But she, her face partly angled up, lights up the twilight; forehead, eyes, nostrils, lips, cheeks, throat; what will we make, later, of that soft fuzz on her upper lip, which is somewhat oriental today, reliable?

Is it possible to have a hard-on for two beings at once?

A double erection, which Kenneth will see: if he thinks I have a hard-on for him, he'll pull his hand away from the bench and the molded pink, leaving Annick to me. Being caught in forbidden desire will lend him frankness and modesty: and maybe words other than those of a manipulator of normal desires. Can he imagine that I desire him for his condition in the future of my deep, not for his body? All I see of it now are the remains of his perverse action.

I watch her wanting the rain to stop and our stares on her to stop, at least in this shed. Apart from inventing fairy tales, one after the other, there's nothing else to do here than touch each other, loosen our clothes and show some skin to comment on and so we can evaluate each other. Anthony's hip leans against mine, in the warmth of his chest, of my eyes behind my glasses, lenses foggy with our breath in the rest of smoke and smell of the hearth bones—should I remove them, and, steaming them with my own breath, take the crumpled handkerchief in my pocket, unfold it, even slightly, in front of her, clean my glasses in front of her, in front of him, in front of them, when at the time I am afraid of signaling myself in society by any object or any exterior fact, my soul alone being what should transpire in all of my body, all my gestures, what is unseen, impalpable, to be designated if need be? Anthony's eyelids grow low on half-vague eyes; he is getting heavy on the bench. I search for what could fit him into the diurnal motion where I prepare the nocturnal scene of my deep.

Would he take it as imposition or deliverance? I want the figures acting in that text to be entirely created by me: they are the creatures of my desire, and not those of reality, which are too common for the task: at most, once the creature is set up and already acting and acted upon, I *recognize* their doubles in reality, society, the street, the countryside, transportation systems, painting—allegories. I slip or hang cloth rags on souls—yet once they enter into servitude, they lose them.

Pruritus or tear at the corner of his mouth: a forced kiss morphing into a bite? Nostrils that flare for no reason: from smelling prohibited areas of the body? Cheeks: word and tongues. Wounded eye: belt tips quickly unfastened? Wrinkles on the forehead: tension during prohibited and repeated penetration?

Movement toward the seat of the mind: yet, like the soul, purchase has confiscated it forever.

Movement downward. In the open shirt, a prominent collarbone: from pressure exerted by the hand that chooses, grabs, and takes away?

But my mother so often grabs me that way—from higher and higher up, and with dwindling strength—her thumb on my collarbone, fingers on my nape, to obtain the truth from me as I stand, or to encourage me in my destiny.

Will I soil that gesture by remembering it in my own flesh, by bringing into focus that little secret world that is barred from her by my forehead?

What God sees, my human family cannot. Only Christ, who has suffered, and who offered himself naked to blows and nails, could read what even I don't dare to read before my desire returns—but sometimes I predict, speak, organize the scene of that discovery, dread, trembling—is there a punishment for such an act, such writing? Better to flee and never to return, if ever it was known and the material uncovered in broad day!

A secret between God—the Divine Trinity, the Creator Father, the Redeemer Son and the Holy Ghost—and me, their created, redeemed, and inspired one: no human gaze shall reduce it; the mind, the soul, the heart, only God and His Trinity can judge them. My senses and my desire, who created them? Was it through the body that my lineage made me, or through God's will? Through my soul, my mind, my heart, all divine creations? How could I trouble the ear and eyes of a priest, the all too human double of Christ on earth—who hears all and sees all—with something that is even worse than crime?

Christ and His divine nature can shine the necessary light on this writing. What about the Holy Ghost…?

I started to write for good when I was barely fourteen, this other text settled into my life, and I had to accept it when my poetry was still so frail, so fresh and so mimetic: was it also art? Poetry, as they'd tell me, was useless to society and to man. I must also be useless to God.

This secret writing is how He tests me, having me write what Lucifer could dictate. But I don't feel caught in the hand of Lucifer, if I even know of him with his attributes, his limbs, his flesh, and his vast mind.

Is it through my hand, my growing wrist that One and the Other vie for my soul?

How could a few words, a few small sentences that exceed the ordinary language of fiction, make them battle in me, an infirm in the Universe? The ejaculated sperm that interrupts them and leaves me mute, Which of Them turns away from it, and Which One looks at it as His property?

What do I know about freedom in Art, when the freedom of others has always directed my life? I've read about it in texts on modern painters; I feel it in front of my page of poetry as if I were in front of a space in which I was finally alone and responsible; for the secret text, in the darkness it produces in my vision as I concentrate all my powers of memory, novel writing, theater, descriptive practice, and my skill at setting servitude to voluptuousness—knowledge and senses—I have neither eyes nor time to wonder what part of human freedom I take there, except that the respect I have for my family and for my friends makes me hide this fiction from them, a fiction *torn* from desire, from a desire whose origin I do not know.

There are too many nervous, muscular, metaphysical, mythological, and other networks running through me for me to think that I am free: at best, maybe I can *go farther* than those before me, in life, in my civil emancipation, and in Art.

At the time, I don't see any political freedom for me, in a France whose Republic has given in to everyone, and where I have to wait six years for the right to vote: in the History that we learn in class, together or alone, in books, in what our family tells us, and in the History occurring before our eyes and in our name, where is the freedom? Only outside of History do we see it, do I see it.

Of the three friends seated before me, watching me rub, with my head down, the beaten earth with the sole of my shoe, I wonder what the English ones think of freedom? To place Kenneth, the son of a free England, in servitude is simply one more bind. I don't put any Eastern, Far-Eastern, African or Oceanic bodies into my secret text, not because I don't know them—although Gauguin's Tahitian figures, girls and boys, always beautiful even as they age, their light, the circles beneath their eyes, their languishing leave traces in my deep— but because they are already enslaved, through slavery or colonization.

But enslaving their masters, the children and descendants of their masters, enslaving the young Englishman Kenneth himself, his senses thought to be suppressed by Victorian morality, although, through his mother, he is already tearing that morality to shreds, fuels social blasphemy: that's what I want with all my might before the orgasm comes.

I look at him: if he smiles that means he understands what I'm thinking, what I'm looking for in him—could he do it through his mother, through the sights and sounds of her, the smell of clothes, of sheets, of wicker or couch fabric, what he sees disappear down the drain or the *lavatory*?—he under-stands that his perversity has returned and that I will banish him from my thoughts and from my deep; if he doesn't smile, but shows instead that he lets himself go, as a new adolescent, to the proud and quivering daydream of childhood, that means he can be captured, raped, and enslaved.

Downward. Under the slowly drying shirt, his nipple hard, like mine, with the renewed desire for some hand other than his to graze it. Wide fat hands: fit for the ass or for the mop. From his fly, with its center button missing, torn off in the effort of the ride—who sews the buttons back for him?—what is that source of light shining from his bathing suit, the laces of which he ties, with his shorts pulled down, before climbing back on his bike. It's because his member is hard: that's how it can appear, pulled from light to shadow; as I watch the artery visible even at his young age bulging in his neck under a spot of filth, from the word *fly*, which now designates that central section of our clothes, I imagine flies bursting—without shame—as if from a place of familiar food, from between his thighs and from what...

The knees, here, scraped—from the genuflected prayer that he and his uncle would have recited, at dawn, following the reprimands and the infernal visions?—knees that I see, and don't want to see, alongside other seated knees, larger, firmer ones; by what, then, scraped? Most of the time, I still see *my* enslaved bodies upright when they are to be bought or sold, or languid, hips tilted up, shoulders against a doorjamb or something else: what could scrape their knees? A kneeling position?

Who is there to adore or to beseech in my world? Neither God nor executioner.

What are the positions of an act that I still can't figure out? From what surrounds me here and in France, what could I possibly know of what is done beyond what I see in paintings? And even if I revived the pain of seeing that woman's meat in the girlie magazines from last fall, the details of the female sex secreting through its folds matter similar to what my father described about the digestive system when I asked him to explain my very frequent stomach aches, how could I imagine that piece of bloody butcher's meat, with its loud colors, in that place of half-darkness and abandon? Suspend it as a repulsive sign over the entrance of my interior hovel? Why do those men rush there, seating adolescent boys and girls down on their knees, and keeping them there? And these adult women who deliver these boys, subjugate them, use them, and give them over to languish, in the pleasure and sadness of their servitude to their human ancestry while they mourn its demise?

From several friends with a reputation for being free I've heard how men make love to women, through words, positions, the mechanics and the materials of the act. Yet I can't reproduce these in my secret texts: like other actions, other facts, I must invent them, *create* them myself, they have to pass through *form* (although still fragile) so that I can see and feel that they are real: I extract the reality of the world through my artistic logic. The world deploys its charms and terrors through my logic alone.

Is it a disorder of the senses, or of the mind? I know both separately, one because of images, the other through my hand, and can't conceive how both sexes could come into contact, penetrate each other, and do what needs to be done: here, too, I must invent another act.

And what do men and *boys* do beyond what it costs me so much to imagine? The French *garçon* doesn't disappear under the English *boy*, but keeps and strengthens its dangerous form. Is there even an English word for the *garçon* that I imagine? *Garçon* on man's knee, where could I even see such an image?

It is all abandon in laughter, fresh bodies borne by vigorous arms, throats spread wide, thighs splayed open, soiled skin and raggedy clothes—at the most extreme point: the corners of lips or where thighs join the groin?

No hole or penetration; nothing but surface and the sad stare of soiled adolescents whose enslavement has removed any consciousness of the beauty they were so attached to before their servitude.

As a newly grown adolescent, proud and educated, is pushed in tatters toward rugged men, why are there remains of a torn vest sewn with a piece of black mourning crêpe on the ground of the hovel?

The rain intensifies: the sound of water on the tar paper roof and around the foundations of the shed drown out our voices so we don't speak; what could I tell them of what I feel and see? Whom could I share this secret with, a secret reinforced, figures, gestures, sounds, by my shame to disclose it? If I had to disclose this secret, its figures, its contours, its architecture, and its traffic would take shape in my mouth, stimulated by the need to create: but this interior movement, this twilight that has been standing next to everything I see, feel, or think since I was thirteen, should not be transformed into fiction or a "literary genre"; it is a double, of me and of my life, beyond status: its very words must be invented from an intermediary language, between God and the Devil, comprehensible by Them alone, whose premises I can only trace today with a shaky hand building to an almost cursive speed with the rise of desire and orgasm, that same speed that my father has in writing his prescriptions, and for his preparatory notes for speeches for the General Council of the Loire *Département.*

What do my stare, my voice, even my smell betray of this world and of its sounds? There is no joy or pleasure in this double life, in the friction between these two realities within me: can I unify them into a single, free, transparent being?

Do any of those three harbor some secret thought that torments them, irresistible and painful: the seed of crime, common law or political? The seed of sanctity perhaps?

Would the sound covering our voices cover the sounds of these secrets?

At thirteen, on vacation, when the text comes to me as I beat off, and as I continue to think of it in secret during the day, in front of my family, my brothers, sisters, friends, people from the streets and from the fields, and when voices appear in this secret, what seem like sexual insults, I'm afraid they can

be heard outside of me and that my mind, behind my forehead, makes them resonate around my head toward other
people's ears, and so I try to reduce their power, or I stay away
from other bodies, and, keeping to myself, bedrooms or heaps,
dips, knolls, sheds, I try to let the tale with its interjections
construct itself within me, aided by what I am starting to
understand and to like of oratory, epic, and descriptive
rhetoric—fairytales and popular poetry can only intervene
later in the lulls in action.

Will a man come out from the wheat fields, and blinded by
the rain, push the door in with a bag of new bones in his fist?

A gust of wind rattles the roof, slams down the tar paper, and
through the stovepipe, spreads ash onto the bones in the open
hearth. The rain stops: the opening through the cinderblocks
grows light; we go outside, dry our seats and handlebars with
a handkerchief, I strap my gouache materials back onto the
rack, and we ride off to Alnwick with all the strength that we'd
contained for an hour in that shed; will there be time to draw
and paint the banks of the River Aln, filled the with deep and
stable reflections I remember Douggie's mother telling me
about the night of the circus? She and her children are joining
us there by car for the five o'clock.

Even if she did think my gouaches were good—she has
been painting for so long, with oil paints on large formats, and
shows and sells her paintings—the fate of this painting and
my own depends on my own judgment.

Rolling at the level of my seat along the small plain, I make the remnants of a rainbow on the small horizon between two dark woods into an infinite, softly sloping plain toward which I can disappear, dissolving into shouts, into what can't be assembled in an instant. I reject anything I do not finish, thought, sentiment, sensation, poetry, even secret writing, anything that does not connect with what I believe is the universal, in the same way as I reject my body. Rather than make a death for myself that would show me in my weakness, return to Who created me—may he never create me again!—how could I make Him forget He did!

But if the plain slopes upward, I must try, live, conquer.

With a movement of my thigh, one of the two laces holding my swimsuit tight under my shorts unravels: is it also that my member jumps up as I overtake Annick, her profile unchanged with exertion, but her breasts in the seething Sun slightly spilling out from the top of her dress? To *take* her, pink dress hitched above her naked *nature*, my member bound in cloth: beyond the deep, and beyond reality; only in the space of our love?

Will she unlace my jizz cloth, finally freeing the member it injures? But a woman's hand, a girl's hand on that member, the only member whose volume grows and shrinks before one's eyes, and even changes shape when it's uncircumcised? She can feel it without seeing or touching it. It can disappear in her, yes: but should she risk touching it with her hand, like white-hot iron? Touching what directs the scene of the deep under the cloth, and what beats its time, once freed, in the darkest twilight…

Should a hand other than the hand of the small creator who received the creative member from God violate its creative force by touching it?

With what languid hand does Adam touch his index to the index of God who created him entirely?

When we reach the banks of the Aln, we see Douggie's mother and her children settled on the other side; we cross downstream, over the rock bridge, Douggie paddling a ball against his face in the water; I set my gear down next to the mother seated on a blanket in the grass; we walk down to the river, the two girls in bikinis between Kenneth and me; Annick, standing near the blanket, pulls a large sheet around herself, and changes underneath; we are already swimming up the current when Annick enters the water in a red bikini; higher upstream, with Anthony and Kenneth diving in repeatedly from a small wooden pier on the other bank, she and I emerge out of the water at a small muddy bend in the river, and walk along the path leading beyond a coppice of alder trees to a dirt road lined with cottages taller than those on Links Road. Alone, has my heart ever beaten faster than this? In the slightly fading light of early August in the north, in the swarms of gnats that will flow back toward the alder trees at nightfall, how tender, gentle, and dependable she becomes when she is so close to me… Forget myself, forget my body, let it act through the heart that drives it… instead, in the tall and complicated stone and wood architecture towering above, I search, in details of sculptures, ornamentation, stained-glass, something to defer the stammering of confession; under an external canopy, I see a caryatid of shining wood, breasts extended: as I describe it, will I extend my palm toward hers? Should I remove my glasses, foggy with emotion, and perhaps already clouded with a tear at the corner of my eye, then inch closer and knock against her in my blindness? Her head stays down, but what does her brown eye, the one on the right for me who's trembling on her right, see of me who loves her entirely, her life, her heart, and now even the smell of her from two days ago? All of her, but her? My eyes, my hands, my voice, my heart that she doesn't see?

What about my limbs, their joints, my skin, hair, mouth? Everything that others seem endowed with, and in excess? As for *the* member—but I forget it, and what is it doing, *nearby?*— who could I fear?

One gesture and I lose everything, and hurt her.

Use language, and beneath it, make a move?

Hand, shoulder, cheek, below, her ass, but I can't touch her ass the way I've seen workers touch the ass of servants! Choose the noblest part of the body, the least physical; if I touch her left cheek with my palm, I'll have to skim the nape of her neck with my forearm; if it's her right cheek, I can only touch it with the back of my hand, but that gesture is not appropriate for my age, it's an adult touch to a child's cheek.

The nape of the neck: touch what is for me like a light shining behind women, and set my hand there like a yoke?

Lower my palm along her back, toward the dip before the ass: but won't I be tempted to lower it more, and touch the edge of her bikini with my pinky? Wait for her to speak, or act? From what I've read, I take it that the man should act first; but I try to think of her as a childhood friend, she, a young girl, and I, a young boy, bumping into each other as we play, intertwining our fingers to dig the earth or to look for a hidden object; each growing, nearly side by side; but boarding school would have interrupted all of it and now our two changed bodies, each far from the other, with organs that are almost new, are walking side by side.

What should we do with our half-naked bodies? I'm trying not to know whether I have an erection; has she ever seen a boy with an erection? Water is still running down our shoulders and along the dip of the groin: rays of Sun filtered through the alder trees hit the thin, red, crumpled, wet fabric of the bikini against her pubic bone; the bikini top covers more of her breasts than did the pink dress. I feel warmth near my hand at the bottom of my left arm as it dangles. Is it a ray of sun or is it her chubby hand moving closer to my left one, the one that masturbates?

How can I make her *feel good*, the way my family, prescribing it to me, has taught that me I should do to others? Do the same things make a boy and a girl feel good? And what pleasure is that? Of the flesh? But flesh awakened by desire immediately entails the act and its consequences, right here, on the ground, maybe with blood on the earth upturned by coitus: does her organ grab the member like two soft jaws? Does it alone do the *work* of extracting its substance—and is it the same as what my member discharges under my hand?

Can we defer the act, can we kiss, separate, meet again, kiss, separate, meet again; can we dream of each other, she seeing me in everyone and everything, and I seeing her in everyone and everything; can we hold hands, shoulders, perhaps even part of the ass in the excitement of the fairgrounds, although that's too close to seedy places… and can we postpone the act until the organ and the member grow full, and we possess the necessary mind and heart?

What does she see of me as her eye looks toward me?

With my glasses off, where would I put them? In the waistband of my swimsuit? In front? In back? Both arms of the glasses folded or a single arm slipped into the wet swimsuit? Wouldn't that point to where my member is, and scare or *scandalize* her?

Do we walk, or don't we? Lamps turn on in the lower parts, and under the sculpted awnings of the dwellings: does she even expect me to make her feel good? If she swims next to me, if she climbs onto the banks with me, crosses the coppice, and walks half-naked on the dirt along inhabited dwellings beside me, half-naked as well, by leaving Anthony and Kenneth to their water games, it means she thinks I'm capable of leading her where only a poet can lead a girl, and toward new pleasures; that the pages of poetry that Anthony told her he'd seen lined up on my desk give me the power to convince, to open doors, to speak with adults as an equal, and to transform the real before her eyes?

But do I have enough ass for her to place her hand on? Do I have as much as Anthony and Kenneth? Do girls consider asses a desirable attribute? But what have I ever heard about boys coming from the mouth of girls? On the beach and on walks, girls and boys go swimming, speak, and walk, but separately.

What is their favorite cut? Is flesh a delicacy? Beside the kiss on the mouth that seals the deal, and the act of procreation, can flesh be consumed?

Are we allowed to trace its forms and folds with the tip of the fingers or the edge of the lips, to lick them, bite them, dive our face in? And even if the shape, the smoothness, the odor of the flesh are beautiful and good, if the mouth goes farther and deeper and into those infamous zones, wouldn't that be acting like dogs who whiff and lick to evaluate the availability of bitches?

She should be grabbed, taken, clasped against me here, on this open road, visible by all who scurry beneath the lamps, rather than in a closed space, or under the cover of leaves.

Should I grab her ass and breast at the same time? How can I make her turn to face me? Could I resist her first refusal?

Does she see me? Does she think of me as an eater or as a penetrator?

How can I act through this confusion, hers, mine, the confusion of the day as it dies off in shouts, song, and noise?

As she lifts her head, with her brown eye still on me, I see a lock of hair settle under that eye and point toward the nostril;

I wait for her hand to follow, and grab mine on the way, but I confusedly sense that she lowers it to the dip of her back to join her other hand, arching and pushing her breasts up as she does so: is it because she wants us to continue our walk, and to talk like two friends stepping over dirt and rocks? If so, it means that she doesn't want me to want her, that she doesn't desire me: but can a girl not desire a boy? I need to hurry; pushing my face up to look at her, and sending my hand to bump against her temple: "What pretty hair!"

To mention a single lock of hair, the one falling under the eye, would be to point to a specific attribute, and most of all, to imply that it's the eye that's really beautiful and that I desire—that would be going too far—when with the tip of my finger I detect the slight pulse of vessels on her temple. Even if I think hair is a carnal attribute, the highest, noblest of both nakedness and prostitution, it's simply hair, which can be cut and which grows back, inedible; it's with what disappears in the sound of scissors—and what burns in the oven—with this attribute that mixes with dust in shops, that I declare my love!

But from this lock of hair can come the long, curly, mangled mane of Marie-Madeleine the prostitute, or of the wild girl of the wood; as her right hand rises to her shoulder, against which she is leaning her temple where my fingers are, I say, with water dripping from my long hair drying on my forehead and my eyelids: "We're gonna live like savages!"

From the contact of our two half-naked bodies, if we wanted to love each other every minute of our lives, how could we not want to stay fixed in that state, reject the other life with our clothes lying back there on the bank of the Aln, and live that new life in what is appropriate to naked flesh: Nature, its natural shelter, its fruit, its water, beyond human dwellings, and human laws.

But rather than inch her mouth to mine, she shivers and squeezes her elbows, arms, and hands against her chest, and her fingers cover her cheeks up to her temples; on the right temple they bump my fingers that pull away. My shoulders sink, is the water that is still dripping from our heads that same dirty water that fell on Adam and Eve after being chased from Eden, and are her hands against her temples, and her thumb on her ear there to block the sound of her Creator's condemnation?

Her first refusal, and my weakness, is what chased us from that Eden where I'd seen us live, and love each other without end; I feel how hard I was—could she see it in my swimsuit— and how soft I have become.

Should I lift my arm to her back, open my hand on her left cheek, press her head against mine, grab the mouth between her cheeks with my own… but from an open, sunlit window, on the first floor of a brick house, music wafts down, "Daybreak," from *Daphnis et Chloé.*

Unless she is also moved to tears by the music, everything disappears for me, at least all images, because the sounds of Nature lead this music to us, to my ears, and soon these sounds will hush, because the music, this music, is more beautiful than they are.

But she: "We have to go. If you recognize this music, it means you already know it. So let's go."

I could get hard again from this childlike logic, where she seems fresher, or from her joking that makes her closer to me than I had thought, more committed to our bond; but it's the music now, instead of her, that lives through me as she pivots on herself in the reddening rays of sun—how beautiful she'd be to take if only there was no music!

If I obey her, and return to the riverbank, I am unfaithful to the music that grows softer behind me. If I don't follow her, and let her go back by herself—from here, could I hear the patter of her arms on the current?—I lose my life.

Nature, feeling, flesh, idea, what can resist that heavenly shimmer under which I hear, in the low notes, something like the voice of the Creator of Day, heavy with tears?

Would she understand that I come from There?

I sit down on a crumbling, ivy-covered wall on the border of the coppice; I hope they don't shut off the sound, up there, that dims sometimes when bodies move in front of the speakers! Or is it children who run on the wood floors or on the tiles, adults, standing up, glass in hand?

Could I follow this music back to its source?

My poetry, *Saül*, in the closed notebook on the table back there facing the sea; there is nothing in this music that I could use for the King's pride and his anxiety, but everything to fuel my desire to continue poetry: and to make other poems, longer, more vast, constructing their columns on the page.

If this cutie who pivots on herself and begins to pout decided to grab these hands, these arms, these shoulders, this back that I must reinforce in order to produce, then part of my strength would flow out in her caresses; part of my strength would leave me in the customary words I'd have to say to love her.

Since I've stopped talking, the water I still have in my ears stays there, and the music reaches through filtered by that water…

"You're not going to stay here naked listening to classical music!"

With that word "naked" in the same sentence as the word "you" as she points to me, does it mean she desires both? Turning my head to the side, I see her bellybutton whose light reinforces the shadow of the dip.

From between the voices and the instruments of the orchestra, the sentence rises in my throat and passes through my lips:

"How beautiful it is…" Does she hear me? I see her place her hand in front of her bellybutton and blush: but it's maybe the rays of the Sun.

I said "beautiful" in front of her, with my head down and my eyes on the road before me, and pronounced "beautiful" louder than the rest.

Is she blushing because I said it about the music, or because, after we will both be further along in love, as I watch her come and go with our children, I could murmur it in our intimacy, in the secret of a heart she'd *completely* know?

Is she hurt or charmed?

On my left hip, the laces of my swimsuit have come undone; what if, bending toward me as I manage despite such indecisiveness not to hunch my back, she laced them back up with her chubby fingers against my shivering hip? What unloosed them? Was it the discreet pressure of the member, or was it her, a while ago... the heat that skimmed my hand and that I thought was hers?

Everything in me goes black; if I were standing, I'd fall.

As my breath heaves, will she place her hand on the nape of my neck?

Should I stand up? But then I'd have to lace the swimsuit, and the blood is rushing out of my fingers.

What figure could I summon before my eyes to appease and reason with my heart, a heart that is too large in me, according to my father whom I try not to anger at the time, a heart that is a fourth larger than what is normal?...

...That of the now seventy-seven year old friend from Notre Dame de Joubert in France, and of the clear and joyous English that he sings to us in class with the room opened onto the fresh-cut hay or closed against the snow packed up to one-third of the windowpane? Is it because, one late morning at the end of winter 1950 when I am ten, coming out of the latrines where the ice is still freezing excrement in the pit, wandering around during recess with blood on my nostrils, he calls me, by my first name, from the window of his office, and after running with all my strength and my galoshes to meet him, he treats my nosebleed at the infirmary and, in his bedroom-office, after pushing me into a tall armchair and scanning me from head to toe, from the galoshes that I shake out above the hardwood floor to the curls of my hair, gives me a large book of paintings and sculptures of Virgins that I flip through with assurance, my fresh fingers—poorly rinsed of excrement at the re-opened faucet of the covered playground— against his dry ones, until we reach the series of Virgins trampling the rising Serpent, seeing the vagueness in my eyes as they pull back, and from above me in the rustling of his freshly ironed frock: "I take it women don't really interest you?"

What do "women" mean for me, a ten-year-old boy on that deserted plateau who has been deprived of his mother for three long months?

For him, are "women" what could be desired, flesh desiring flesh? For me, isn't flesh an ogre instead? And love: light?

Is my flesh already destined to the fangs of wild beasts, or to the blade of pagan executioners? Or maybe I do not possess the flesh I need for what he calls "women"?

Is my flesh exclusively for God, and for the Word? And is he reassured and happy to see me thus closer to him—I'd heard at home that he had liked women, or at least that he had known some women before his ordination and had remained *very attached* to them.

What is it in my eyes that he is staring at with joy?

And what do I need to hide from him? Can he see that I've just *pleasured myself*, crouching above the latrines, not to defecate or piss, but to milk another, more discontinuous substance from this little member that piss runs through, and that I must already quell the anxiety of the first jet by provoking another?

On my return from Christmas vacation two months before, how was I able to find a way to appease the natural *need* to take a shit, in class or during study hall, or postpone it at least till recess? To raise my arm and hand would have been to designate to others a body in disgrace: as the producer of despicable and smelly matter.

By wiggling my hips on the bench, and kneading my needy little member with my hand in my pocket, my work interrupted, my hearing capacity reduced, I sense that if I tense my leg muscles a bit I can send a feeling of relaxation accompanied by shivers spreading between my thighs, and for the duration of this feeling the need to shit diminishes, and if I renew the pressure, feelings that I take to be purely internal at the time help me hold out until the end of class or the end of study hall.

But once delivered, flying through the courtyard, locked into the tall latrines, having stripped the bottom half of my body to piss and defecate over the icy hole, and repeating, whether in play or as a test, the gesture that produces the *thing*, I feel a substance come out of my member: and the pleasure is such that it lessens any surprise or fear.

A few days later, I repeat the gesture, and this time I collect part of that substance in my hand, which I've slipped under my member, and I examine it later in the hollow of my palm, although I don't dare to touch it with the fingers of my other hand: it isn't piss; is it some evil leaking out? Is it a dangerous substance, a poison?

Will I see the palm of my hand corrode, burn, smoke, as if my palm were pierced by a white-hot nail?

The following day I dare to touch the substance freshly secreted from my member; I notice when I touch my member that it is longer and harder than when I pee. So now what? Will the size and width of my member grow? Will I be able to put it back into my underwear and knickers? How can I hide it from everyone, from the Fathers? And on vacation, from my father and my mother?

Here, in the icy cold, where are my Creator God and His Son?

Caught in the ice up there as well?

Should I run back quickly into the poorly heated study hall, and find Them?

The drop and filament stick to my fingers, and the color dying out before my eyes is like milk cut with water. So the same member produces two contrary substances; one comes out naturally; the other needs to be gotten out; one, irrepressible, only relieves me while it's coming out, the other, you need to want it, and then pleasure spreads in the whole pelvis like a luminous and warm caress: it's so rare here; is it like the hand of my absent mother that passes over me from so far away?

Is it a useless substance, and if not, what could it be for?

Since I've never seen an erect adult member, I don't know if the member I have at ten, even if it swells in pleasure, will grow with me; from Adam's tiny member on his huge thigh, I infer the member doesn't grow unless the appearance of his Creator in front of Adam's eyes as he woke up to life made it retract; but why don't we see the same member resting on God the Father's reclining thigh, as He is veiled in his suspension of archangels and cherubs?

Who could tell me the nature of this discharge, whose contact grows sweeter day by day? Do others produce the same? Wouldn't older children, the most violent and most talkative, show it to us if they had it? But if they have it—and maybe they're already pulling it from their members, together in fields or lingering in the woods—are they ashamed or proud of it, and therefore keep it secret?

What, except for the will of the Creator, My Father in Heaven, led me down into my mother's womb to live there before I was delivered? Through the open door of my father's office and of the farmer's bedroom above the barn, the gestures that I witness on the very full stomachs of women, which put an end to the violence and the cries, make me understand that there are children in these stomachs, one, two, sometimes three as in the V. family, and that they have enough to sleep, eat, and drink there—but if they eat and drink, where does their waste go?

Do they lower into that stomach preformed? Or, like animals…?

If they are preformed, who puts them there? Does the surgeon cut out their contours, put them into that repository, and sew it up? Does the little haloed and radiant being descend into the stomach like the Holy Spirit, piercing it with its light, as it did for the birth of my youngest brother; when we entered the bedroom to find him clothed, the room filled with such a strong winter light that it erased objects and bodies?

With that semblance of a member and such meager production, how could I imagine that generations would emerge from that slightly rigid thing at the base of the young being, frigid in the cold and under whom, along the edge of the hole to the pit, runs a substance that a bird wouldn't even see and wish to pick at, and that mixes with fresh excrement?

What is left of this act, which I perform without effort, in my face and in my eyes when he looks at me?

In the book on the camps, I've seen rotting or charred corpses strewn across the muddy expanses or the barbed wire enclosures, and so I want to maintain the dignity of this face and body, mine. Are they already deformed by pleasure?

If blood has come out of my nostrils, it must be coming from my throat, and maybe even from below. Is it a consequence of pleasure? Does the Father know this? Why did he lend me this book of ideal women, and why would "women not *interest* me"?

A boy must go with a girl, a grown-up with a woman. Once I am grown-up, how could I go with someone who did not "interest" me? Is it because that kind of beauty does not affect me? Why then, when I open the books we have at home, paintings where women show their nakedness, at first I shake and then I shiver? Am I turning my spirit away from theirs? But of all humans and animals, it is those bodies and the minds within them that surprise and torment me the most: the men's bodies scare me; I see them as a necessary but ugly auxiliary to what is depicted in the paintings: *Adam and Eve, The Rape of the Sabine Women*, the *Venus of Urbino, Le Concert Champêtre...*

From the shapes we see as boys, and that we look at amongst ourselves, I infer from those I see on the women in the paintings, large hips, copious backsides, languor, thighs stacked one over the other, or reclining on their backs with their knees raised, pink flesh, fleshy lips, folds and tucks of nearly-red hips, that a mystery, a secret, lies around and at the bottom of this nakedness, good and licit since no one is afraid to show them to us children. Why are we allowed to see them naked in paintings and not in life?

Is there any reality to what has no name? What I do, the pleasure I take in the harshest cold, that effusion and the anxiety that follows, is that reality, since, beside the pleasure of it—they tell me I should refrain from pleasure, that it's evil in view of the misery of the world—I can say nothing about it, disclose no source, no matter, no goal?

Am I still even myself in the moment of pleasure, since all I see around me are shooting stars and blinding lights when I get up after it's done, and I must grasp the door handle with my hand that is still vibrating to push it open and fall back into the world that's been assigned to me?

In these colored images that I detach from their Ancient context and their luxurious draperies in order to have them all to myself, what is it that grows animate in this flesh? Is it the folds? The tucks? The lips? The eyes? The asses? Vaguely staring at the concrete of the muddy platform beneath my face, my eyes frowning from the tension of my calf muscles, I see those thighs that an adult hand, which I navigate through the painting, opens, parts over the draperies…

Now they are draped, veiled, crowned Virgins of the Seven Sorrows, Virgins in tears, with bluish eyelids, Virgins of the round belly, Virgins with the head and bearing of peasant women whose aprons seem to have been mislaid, serious, affable Virgins, faces as if bent over to unroll, measure, cut, and sell fabric, Virgins who've come perhaps from houses of ill-repute, but all of them veiled and draped up to the neck.

He and I turn the pages: a Virgin appears with an unlaced corset, her breast bare as she breastfeeds the Infant-God; later in the album there is Eve, standing beside Adam; they stand before us, a leaf hiding the center of their nakedness: is it my finger or his that forces the other to turn the page?

From his old man throat, above me, comes his humming: "That's quite a German Eve."

A stirring again between my thighs: but in what direction? Is the member retracting or protruding now?

What does that secret place contain? What deeper secret lies hidden there, a secret on which the fate of humanity depends? A German hand, only a few centuries distant from the monster issued of that same people, painted this image of Wisdom and Peace—and Justice: the apple she holds in her excessively upturned hand seems instead a weight on the balance of Justice, a miniature terrestrial sphere.

The noble nakedness of those three interlocking figures, head and neck, torso and stomach, legs, Evil is already unfolding above their ear from the shade of the Tree of Knowledge: my mother tells me these people tried to think the Truth, but they have just betrayed humanity; the Devil chose that ear, the German ear, to convince it of His Truth: murder, contempt, torture, rape, ruins, corpses.

Can I add this Eve to the different naked bodies that strike a pose in my young mind out of thin air? The Monster to come had already whispered in Eve's ear, our shared earthly mother, before she bit into the apple, before the Fall, when her nakedness was not yet guilty—before both she and Adam discovered themselves naked, and draped themselves in leaves and animal skins; I run the risk of spreading discord if I lead her, and keep her in my assembly of languid women who are all well intentioned toward Man.

With those two sentences, is he trying to distance me forever from women? Why me? No women, no future?

What will I fall into once I leave his room?

Or instead, will he lead me to the chapel with his hand on my shoulder, and consecrate me to God before the Blessed Sacrament that is illumined night and day?

So young, to be deprived of women?

But if his finger touches mine it means he's touching my body, and if he's touching my body, then he's touching that little member and its unnamed substance; his ordination as a priest so long ago confirms his knowledge and his reason, and the very fact that a single finger of such an adult has touched mine implies that he has learned everything about what happened in the latrines, and even more than I could ever understand of it. Can he read through my forehead, in that space between the eye and brain where gold, pink, and red bodies slowly stir?

If there is a link between this member that now lives another life, in the frost, other than simply evacuating piss, and the movements of these women whose nakedness I imagine is due to how hot it is around them, why does he want to sever it? Or are there other bodies I could be interested in? But which? The bodies of the Saints? Of the Virgin? Of Christ? Of God the Father? If feeling my "member" stir and transform before the images of these naked bodies means that I am interested in women, then how could I feel it stir and be transformed before the image of these sacred figures?

If my different strengths connect within me to believe in God, doesn't a clandestine one remain, my member's strength, that can't enlist? And are its new substance and the convulsion that evacuates it excluded from my prayer?

Can an omniscient God and Son exclude this force, this pleasure from my prayer—as well as the anxiety after the spasm?

But could he—at the time, I could not pronounce the word *he* outside his presence so strong is my love and veneration—obtain from me that I cease to pleasure myself? Even if he pulled me from the latrine at the moment of my act, and showed me off, like the half-naked Christ with spit running down his body, substance flowing from my member in the middle of my convulsing body, he wouldn't get me to renege: I have that pleasure, then that trial, and I keep them.

But is it really an act of what's called *love*? Are these women's bodies truly alone in my internal vision? Aren't other feelings, other objects hidden there, which the renewal of the act, season after season, could make me discover in myself?

What will this member and this substance become?

What hides behind the flies of adult pants? Is it this member, grown? Or is it some other shape?

Will there be change in the consistency of the substance, its color, smell, or use?

Is this what my languid women in the paintings contemplate without seeing it? Is this what they dream about—that they don't have? Is it a substance that must always be hidden? Is it corrosive? Nourishing? Is it something that you could make a living with, like milk from cows sold in *milk churns*?

If anxiety follows after pleasure, is it because the act itself is Evil? Is crime first joy then pain?

Am I both the assassin and the victim?

Knowing there exists a form of Evil worse than the evil done to others, and that is the revolt against God, or thinking against God, punishable as King Saül was punished, his body dismembered, exhibited in pieces on the city walls, I try to *hear*, as early as the first time, what speaks besides what moves, these women, in this place of thought, and especially in the moment when desire rises: there is nothing against God, against those whom I must love, nothing against my "human brothers," nothing against animals. But then against what? Against whom? For? Yes!

But for what? For whom? Is the fact of "speaking" to these women, to their nakedness, a sin against God who created them from the hand of the painter whom He created?

What can I say to these women resting inside my forehead—have I ever heard my voice lead it out from the interior to the frozen exterior? That I want to be in the painting with them, seated or standing in the drapes hanging behind their bed? Or in the service performed in the shadows, or behind the gallery: fruit baskets, trays of delicacies, vials of perfume; or on the floor with the dogs?

What to say, and in what language? Am I speaking, or are they, with their painted, smiling mouths, with their index— the index of the enigma—against their temples? Is a maid speaking to me from beneath her basket or her tray? Is it a manservant? A black man? Should I delay the spasm in the icy cold so that I can stay warm in thought? In these latrines, wearing these clothes that I very rarely change, far from her, my mother, can I stay in these luminous, velvet drapes under the vaporous but amused, even ironic gaze of this reclining woman who is staying awake to the sound of the flute in the bucolic corner of the painting—and be able to warm up by forcing my mind to feint, answer obliquely, and *discuss*?

With his wide, twitching nostrils, did he smell a hint of that substance still sticking to my thigh or to the tip of my member, and so opened this book of Virgins, in which a naked Eve stands alone on the page that he keeps open with his finger on mine? But does he know the smell of that substance, and even that substance itself? Was it because of a lingering vibration of my body, a lingering veil over my eyes that he opened that book for me?

For women to *interest* me, should I have known some, naked, and from up close? And—will I tell him this?—if women expose themselves in my brain, and gesture to me there, isn't that enough for him: I who am real, they who are imaginary?

To drop semen on the ground, or on myself, or even worse, into that pit of excrement, while these women, this nakedness, these beauties pull away from my brain and leave it nearly empty to be filled with distress; is that act too powerful for me? And should I learn all natural law to have the right to do it?

An act that must be done in pairs? With several people? With God's permission?

If he wants me to stop this practice, which I'm not even sure adults have found a word to designate, why discourage me from being interested in their imaginary protagonists?

Is he saying my imaginary women are inexistent, and therefore that they can't *interest* me? But on the first day of school, he was the one who told my father, who frowned at the news, that he'd develop my imagination while developing my will and freedom. How could he today want to deliver me from my imaginary creatures?

Flipping through several pages of clothed Virgins—doubly excluded from the flesh—and focusing my gaze on a sacred, but naked woman, Eve, is he trying to wake what he thinks sleeps within me: desire? But also provoke my "vocation": has he heard, since he is so close to me at other times, the call of what I know is calling me—to the poorest of priesthoods, to the most infinitesimal sanctity?

What is a virgin? Is she simply the one who gives birth to the Infant God, the Son of his Creator: and how, if she is the daughter of God the Father, can she be the Mother of his Son? And isn't this Son also God, one of the three figures of the Trinity? Father as well as Son, Son as well as Holy Spirit?

Fearfully continuing with this train of thought: his Son is also his Father, a mother gives birth to her own father, who is at least one-third a Father? And this Son exists for all Eternity like his Father—what woman does God the Father decide should give birth to this Son, whom He chooses to be reborn in the human Virgin—full of three gods?

From such a charged virginity, does the Father want me to understand that Eternity, along with the complexity of the thought that is associated to it, passes through the virginal? Eve, naked, is by contrast a clear figure, circumscribed in time and space: the infinite facing the finite?

During religious class, sometimes the word Eternity and its semblance of explanation make me grow pale, and my legs hang inert from the bench; it's only when I'm outside lying on my back in the field with my eyes lost in the blue of the sky that I find the strength to confront them.

The cult of the Immaculate Conception, which is celebrated December 8th in the Lyon diocese with lanterns placed in people's windows, lingers in my memory—the window of Miss Mignot, the professor of mathematics who'd died at the end of autumn, was the only one that stayed dark—and brings my thought back to simple Virginity, which is that man has not *bent over* woman to give her a child, but has only bent over her cheek, to kiss it, before the "first pains" begin.

Man has not pushed his shadow into woman, and woman makes the child alone.

In the same way, the nameless substance comes forth from me alone, and by myself, with my own hand and my *desire*.

For Her, the Virgin, does *desire* mean she wants to see that child arise in what my father calls "the waters," that child who will transform the World, like Moses arisen from the Nile who'll see his Law descend on the tribes of Israel?

And if the Virgin, Mother, is "without blemish," and the Child-God is conceived "without sin," it's because man is the blemish and the sin: man and his sharp shadow, his cutting-blade.

But if there are virgin women—aren't all mothers virgins, since only "whores" have stopped being so?—then there are also virgins in the animal kingdom: and in males as well, some of whom I know have a double sex, snails; in the human species, in very primitive, very isolated tribes, are there *virgin men* who could reproduce without sin, without bending over a woman or another man to conceive, carry, and give birth to off-spring—and raise them, or eat them, or sell them as food?

Because his ear is so close to my mouth above the book spread wide on a picture of a naked Eve, can he hear what I did in the latrines, and nonetheless continue to love me?

Or instead, a sob caught in his throat, should he take my hand and lead me to the chapel before God and the *real body* of His Son—but since Christ is also God, isn't is also the real body of his Father?—in the host, which was consecrated this morning and placed in the golden ciborium, and in the Church tabernacle, illumined day and night, which is suspended behind the altar in front of the brocade tent whose color changes with each liturgical season, so that I can admit to what I can't yet name, one word after another: neither the act, nor the member, nor the pleasure, nor the substance, nor the suffering.

Since he's a priest inspired and filled by God, I know that he is capable of seeing and hearing hidden acts and hidden things, even from far away, not as much as God who sees and hears everything clearly, but like someone who'd see and hear everything, even at the bottom of the ocean with it animal fights in the Great Depths, but only partly, confused by the excess and simultaneity of events he had not created, whereas God sees and hears everything that He continues to create.

Resisting confession, I am resisting a sacred person: but I want to keep my secret only because I know that he would understand my tenacity, having his own consecrated secrets, and that this is proof of the will he wants us to have.

In front of his old, happy countenance, in my throat and mouth I prepare what I won't tell him, and because I don't have the words to name the act and substance, from the deepest part of me up to my teeth I begin to describe, narrate, and animate what makes me know pleasure and disillusion: I take facts from reality, and from the French language that I am learning to write each day, and place them in order, give them color and even then, a movement, a drama, a rhythm.

From a clandestine act, "committed" over excrements in the latrines that lock from the inside, the only place of intimacy at the boarding-school, and where I also begin a mute conversation with my painted women that grows more and more direct, from what I can't, from not knowing, and mustn't, from morality, I extract an interior *word* parallel to the chatter of a child playing with others on the floor, or beside models and construction games, a word that ceased on the outside when I entered boarding school but continues on the inside—interior games—in a bath of melancholy and hope: interior water where words are born and disappear, where a discourse of self-defense arises, with arguments, objections, confessions, resolutions of compassion and universal fraternity, all of this contained in a permanent prayer to God the Father, to the Son, the great Saints, my patron Saint Pierre, in a perpetual offering of all that I do and think, the word of the latrines included.

Although, the smell—substance, sweat, excrement—is not as pleasant to the nostrils of the Creator than the odor of Abraham's animal sacrifices.

Is this act, which must be kept secret, His way of testing my faith in Him: the test of secrecy, the test of the distress that follows after pleasure, a distress that is sometimes longer than its brief three, five, seven second pleasure by three, five, seven days?

The Devil who is always by my side like a shadow, and here in the hole opening onto the excrement pit, and the Creator above in the pure sky must have an understanding about this double-faced act that is inflicted on me by my senses as a sacrifice—its secret—to my need to be transparent with the world?

It is because I don't know the words to this act, parallel to the current of words flowing through me like the circulation of my blood, that this *word* of secrecy develops inside me, in my brain set on learning the Latin language—its indirect discourse— periphrases where the constraints of modesty gradually produce more obscenities—greater than the crude, ignored words—and a semblance of social organization surrounding them.

I who have always delighted in writing *essays* for primary school, I believe that what is written, and what must be written, is the adult world, the facts, the sentiments of "grownups": can this minute pleasure, one that captures me entirely, be written, be read in books?

Little by little, from what I've heard of the minuteness of the atom and its recent explosive power, I deduce that the tickling I feel in my small member, as if coming from a seed that would germinate and become a tree, is *their* minute atom, that the pleasure that racks me is the explosion of the bomb, and that its devastating effects are the sadness and exclusion from the world that seize me, afterward, down to the bone.

In this small forty-seven-pupil boarding school, am I the only one to experience this pleasure and this torment?

The walls of the latrines are too thick for me to hear the sound of others defecating, and to look at their faces when they emerge would be undignified, as it would be for my gaze to follow one of us leavng our small multitude to isolate himself in a corner of the yard, or even to cross its borders, and disappear into the fields.

What do my friends see of my face and body when I emerge?

Most often, once I've gotten back on my feet, shaking my head to reestablish order there and jutting my chest out, I leave the latrines quickly as if to get back to the interrupted game at once; only when I'm inside, in class or study hall, does desolation rise from my heels to my heart, and chill me until I shiver—to the point of wishing I'd never been born.

Of all my friends, Roger is the closest, three years older than me, and part of our still rationed supplies come from his native village: we've sworn to move forward together in life, not to think of anything that the other doesn't think at the same time: a single heart, a single brain, in dissimilar bodies and under unequal social origins; I wish I had his body and his origins, and all of him, his charms stronger than mine, to submit and put to sleep all the dragons of life.

Endowed with such stately beauty, does he feel a need to call beauty to himself? Hasn't he already known women?

Hasn't he climbed into their beds already? Pulled the sheet over him and them? He has the ass for it.

Since he's as good as me in French class, maybe he could find the words I lack, but when I emerge from the latrines after doing nothing but defecate, his high piercing gaze filtered through very black eyelashes down slanting eyelids judges me for having withheld my body from his sight; can this gaze pierce the wood of the door like it pierces through my conscience?

Even if sometimes I speed up my desire during the time of defecation, its shaking and the necessity to recover from it and put on a good face keep me inside, and in the game circling around the yard, I listen for his voice, higher than the rest, and it's only when it rings out at the farthest corner that I exit.

Unless he already knows it—but then I'd hear it in his voice—how can I narrate what is becoming, week after week, a scene from which he is excluded? And if I describe my painted women to him, perhaps he'll want to take them from me? And would he want to climb into the latrine to scrutinize the remaining runoff of my substance in the twilight? Does he himself have a substance? With what laughter will he judge mine as he scrapes it with his hobnailed shoe?

Perhaps he's already lost his for a new one, ejected, heavy and white, from his red, wild body? Who does he show it to, on vacation, when he pulls it from his indifferent body without batting an eyelid, and spreads it on his red, odoriferous hand?

When he looks for me, from the game from which I've excused myself, as I sit dreaming on a rock on the pile of fallen granite that closes the school grounds along the Miserere valley, a spring audible there in the springtime, feeling my blood and breath accelerate, and my chest expand in preparation for my climb into the latrine and the crouching for the act, and finds me, he tips a laughing countenance over his shoulder, but when the game circles back and he no longer sees me, does he frown under his curly hair, and leave a game they've begged him to join, and knock on all the seven doors to detect, with his knowledge of sound—animals, even tiny, Elements, mechanisms, voices— my presence and my activity in one latrine or the other—which, by precaution, I switch every time?

If he found me, he wouldn't shake the door: nothing can resist him, and he knows, despite it all, what I must endure to hide this from him; but what can I hide of what I can't yet name? Only what can be named can be hidden.

Does he expect me to ask him the words he knows, and with which he could illuminate, order, and justify my act?

The more the scene grows laden with imaginary, the more the act recedes into the distance, and the secret deepens; do I want the pleasure of the act, or the pleasure of arousing it with speaking visions?

Do I resolve to do it for the pleasure of the spasm and the effusion of substance, or for the pleasure of reigniting my imaginary, despite the risk of desolation and exclusion that follows—and in this internal devastation, the women from the paintings, and the paintings themselves are rejected as inert and odious: the only thing that resists is the link to God, to whom I struggle to return?

Is it in order to return to Him more strongly in my interior sobs, a prodigal child prodded by the desire for the entire act with its imaginary and its convulsions, that I decide to complete the act, and endure its dreaded consequences: my exclusion from the living world, humans, animals, vegetables, minerals, water, sky, stars, Moon, Sun?

In the letter that I write weekly to our mother, can she read a sign of this distress in its still uncertain script, its words and sentences?

Since the drafting of that required letter happens on a set date, I arrange to feel a renewed desire then, and what she receives is written in a perky tone, with firm letters, and happy ascenders.

What could she know about my life here, about what more I've learned than what she knows of me—that as a young child looking up at the sky I'd wanted to live up there with her and had told her so in tears: to that feeling of exclusion from the place where God determined my earthly birth is now added the feeling of exclusion from the earthly world, after a kind of pleasure that she knows nothing about, she who germinated, carried, and fed me—how can she not know that a new substance is coming from this body that she made?

What little I know of love, and what propels me in the act toward the women in the paintings and animates my vacant arm toward them against the door, makes me imagine that the substance must seep from the embrace between two humans, and that pleasure comes from their caresses, and that they blend their disillusions there as well.

Another boy from school, Gouget, who is from the city and four years older than I, tries to drag me beyond the school grounds to do what he whispers—with his very red lips under very bright eyes that simulate a great knowledge of flesh and of the possible suffering to be inflicted upon it during pleasure—he knows about my clandestine act: is it because my wrist knocks against the door as I mime my embrace of the woman lying on the sheets that he places his ear on the wood as he passes by, and hears my breathing and my convulsing?

Several days, while Roger is defecating in the latrines, he takes me by the arm and drags me toward the edge of the pine woods along the utilitarian side of the school: kitchen, laundry room, woodshed, to the cellar window emitting the steam of mediocre cooking—never any meat, nor fresh vegetables—but whose smell reinforces my hunger and hardens my little member; I turn my eyes away from his as they fall to my belt, and hardened in my center, thrust myself away from him toward the yard, rush through, and climb into the latrine, to meet the golden, pink, and red women, and perfect the act with a member pre-prepared.

Gouget renews his charm on others apart from me, and Roger separates him from them with a stroke of the arm: he must think that I can resist him, and doesn't want to show that he might be prone to jealousy, a weakness he despises, by separating us.

Of these two powers, I understand that Gouget's desires pleasure, and wants to instill dependency on pleasure in the little human; my brother Roger's power is the power of knowledge and of the respect of the human heart.

And it makes no difference that Gouget, in front of everyone, climbs the wall of the farm that overlooks the yard, jumps into its small garden, and that all we see stirring above the wall is the top of his lacquered hair and the top of the blond hair of the young farmer's daughter.

Should I ask him to explain the meaning of his sentence as it settles over, beside, or under the uplifting or oppressing sentences my mother, my father, and my godmother have said to me—which remain with me—and between which I conduct my life under other sentences, sacred this time, from God to his people and especially from Christ to his own? I advance, negative sentences spreading away before me, as did the people between the two halves of the Red Sea curled to each side, led by the single voice of God toward the destiny that I know is mine.

Afraid that his explanation would only thicken the mystery and danger of what he'd said, and, afraid of placing him in a situation of confusion—could he avoid describing "women," and how one is "interested" in them?—I stay quiet, and let my reason charge this sentence with favorable depths…

…But, three, four years later, on that path in England, so close to that beauty whose fleshy extremities, those visible, the lips, and those non-visible, the tits, her *nature*, touched by the Red Sun, might inch toward my own, which might in turn separate from my body, that sentence still separates her from me, and reduces me, flooring me, into a *Saül* whose extremities, carved up by the enemy, bleed, hanging from stakes above the city walls.

A single gesture of my hand toward her, front or back, and my life is transformed. Should I collect and concentrate everything I feel about Nature, humans, History, even God, into my feeling for her? Into the single thrust of *sex*?

Or should I imagine—and charge all of the currents of my body with it—*sex* at work in the Nature where we find ourselves, and in this hour before nightfall, animals, large, small, infinitesimal, in burrows, under leaves, in tree trunks, on cow dung, on trash, prepare the necessary act, with her—but where does her imagination go? to where mine does? elsewhere?—and accomplish it?

Poetry holds my arm back, but there is no comfort there: how much madness, how many struggles and disasters weigh on that path? Especially madness: how much reason will I need to confront what poetry unveils—I know it through the text I am writing underneath: the monster?

Once out of the water, and rising in the silt along the shore—as if from a prehistoric dream—why didn't we take our pleasure when we reached the grass? Through the high trees, up to the path, near one of the houses with its music wafting down, did desire turn to hardship?

By reducing *sex*, am I reducing her? What secret or less secret act attracts her beyond *sex*, like me beyond licit poetry— for which I should feel guilty, already?

Is this secret material? Mental? Divine?

It is too late to make her confess. This act would strip us of what little clothes we have. Would it be easier fully dressed, one stripping what little the other is wearing, and uncovering the paler flesh, and at the center of each, the monster who is devouring our spirit? Here in free reality, how can we experience the power I give it in the slave darkness of my deep?

But why then does this image appear before my eyes, where I am stretched on top of her as she lays face up on the grass, our bodies extended, our arms outstretched in the shape of a cross, with blood from both of us trickling down to the river?

Did pleasure come to me too early, before my body and my gestures could adapt, and exult in the presence of girls and women?

At twelve, thirteen, away from the Joubert boys for the summer, my efforts toward girls and their secrets would have been much lighter if that pleasure were not set in my flesh like a permanent judgment!

These just barely tamed, why must I go back into our solitude!...

Now I know the drama of desire and pleasure in my body, and its results, and I am scared that this practice—with no other partners than the figures whom I don't yet know will occupy my life, and make my destiny—will exclude me through irreversible organic transformations from the normal exercise of human life: love, procreation, fatherhood.

I even know what has been made a *genre* in poetry: that repeated pleasure and "debauchery" damage bodies; I know what acts are committed by desire at its peak; and I see Nature, matter, and the most sacred History only in this form, through the movement of desire's rise and fall.

This beauty who is waiting at my side—like Eve, in one of Adam's ribs—would force me to go and live in another Time.

What I must accomplish will either be done alone, or with everyone.

Loving her is not enough, and it's still me, that me I must explore in order to subdue it—but under who, or what?— only for a collective cause can I remove part of the strength that is growing in me, so that I can level my being, thus reduced, on what I know of hers.

I've got physical strength, mostly long-term endurance; if I used it on a single body, would I forget everything else to which I could devote it: poetry, Sanctity, service to others, equality?

Because all the figures in the developing scene of slavery in the writing of my deep are beautiful, desirable, and because in my young experience as a creator of figures and acts, during the time of writing I start to become one or another of those as-yet-uncertain figures, my face and my body disappear to me. During the day and even a long time after the night's exercise, I don't know which is my face and which is my body among each of these faces and these bodies: I am only the one who no longer sees himself, and through which desire and its writing pass.

Standing up from the wall, with all of the Sun's heat beating on the contents of my laced-up swimsuit, I take the path with her toward the house where "Daybreak" has started playing again.

When we reach the middle of the facade, a young man calls us from behind the open stained-glass windowpanes: he saw me seated across the house listening to the music, and wants us to come upstairs where they are playing it.

But to enter an unknown house, maybe a dark one, half-naked and barefoot?…

And I, the soles of my feet wounded by the rocks of the path, down at the bottom of my body where the desire for reality dims before the desire for the ideal, and she, rearranging with her hand the hair behind her ears and on the nape of her neck as if her body had been disturbed by kisses or by sex, and settling her small and round feet on the rocks, their movement causing her to rub the top of her thighs together as if her *nature* had an itch…

Other, fresher voices echo from behind the stained-glass windows.

From that long, backward travel toward Notre Dame de Joubert and the book of Virgins, I'm afraid the Sun is already on the horizon, and that our friend on the banks of the River Aln with her children, our friends, are worried about us.

But to hear that music from up close, to dissipate what's left of what did not occur, through matter, to recover my certainty and pride in writing, and from inside the music to resist my father and his rejection of my poetry, of the music he refuses to see that I listen to, and of my body—which has failed here…

The front door, with its gothic frame, opens onto a blond boy, breathless from running down the steps of a sculpted wooden staircase partly illumined by tinted rays of Sun shining through the windowpanes. I see the Sun has only set halfway down the tall trees of the clump of alders.

He holds both our hands as we walk up the stairs and I see that his long hair hides an ear that's nearly flat around the concha, the pinna hardened by a burn; a chain hangs around his neck on his naked breast; a crêpe paper suit rustles around his hips; thighs, legs, and feet bare. On the first floor, a gallery-corridor of dark wood, decorated with bound books: we continue, feet bare, on light rugs, toward one side of the house, well lit, with several levels, filled with flowers in vases, in pots, in bowls; through the bow windows, light shines on a space that opens onto the rooms of an apartment; on the wood, tile, and marble floor, strewn with Chinese hats, loincloths, crowns, garlands, slippers, two other children. A small staircase leads to a large room, where Ravel's "Daybreak" plays repeatedly.

In a dark angle of the space, a large divan on which I can make out a woman lying under a cotton Indian throw; her eyes shine, her white arm stretches toward a small table covered with vials and tubes sparkling in the ending Sun; on both sides of a chimney, two adolescents are standing, one, a girl, the other, a boy, skirt, shorts, each holding a book; the young man across the room, closer to the window opening onto the path, lowers the volume of the music; the rustling of the paper on the naked body of the child with the burnt ear, who drops our hands now and backs up to the costumes, sends a thrill through my loins: how can I hide the huge hard-on under my suit? Nothing to put in front except my hands, but I have to walk up to that reclining woman to kiss her hand; will I keep my left hand on the expanding suit, and with my right, clasp the white hand rising in the darkness and kiss the top of it?

The rustling of the costume-paper on the child's hips, that's what I try to hear when I grab and pull my jizz cloth up between my thighs, once I've decided to wash the rag encrusted with a sharp caking of dried sperm, and after I've dried it in the strong warm wind, or in front of burning trash; the rustling of the fabric, heat-hardened on the member that thickens and grows rigid is the sign, in sound, that the "orgy" is beginning again in the deep, which for me becomes the real world again.

But what would the fate of a child or adolescent be, here, under the weight of that secret: that barely has desire risen in his ten-year-old body that he wants to be a "whore," unhooked from his human origin, delivered by the one who purchased him to the endless desire of others? Could he confide his infamy to his mother, his father, his brothers and sisters? Would they let him go to find a buyer, and even, work so that he could make what he was worth and offer it, along with his virginity, to the men or women who *buy* him?

But the sound of "Daybreak" rises and the desire for licit poetry, Saül, returns my breath to me. Forgetting what weighs down my bathing suit, I bow before this woman at whose side the two adolescents crouch as they sit down on the floor, and between their shoulders, I take the hand she proffers from a noble and weary body, and skim it with the lips that I've just peeled off the lips of debauchery.

Annick, seated on a sofa next to the young man, is already holding a glass of orangeade in her hand; one of her bikini straps has slipped over her shoulder and the top of her arm: from where I'm standing, I can see the breath moving part of her right sun-kissed breast; a movement to shift her cool buttocks on the rep uncovers her entire breast: instead of covering it, she lifts it with her hand cooled by the glass and looks at me.

Does the warmth of the man seated at her side make her hoist her beautiful feature through which she knows I could begin to take her?

I owe myself already to the figures of my deep: what engenders them comes from the middle of my body, it stops me here from bowing to that woman—I imagine none of these figures would dare to enter her mind—and touching her hand with mine, the hand that, in France if not yet here, writes those figures while the left beats off.

To bow and kiss that hand would add to the dissimulation that my father accuses me of: but the terms of the contrast are visible: my hand, stretching to perform an act typical of our class, and, in the middle of my body, the sign of illicit desire; what part of this erection do I feel for the friend uncovering her breast to me? Can I get a "boner" for domesticity, for couples?

But, above, music takes everything, ancestry, infamy, love, and leaves me starving only for Poetry—verses that are still obscure to me in the Book of Judges make me feel confusedly that I can maybe weave a few images, a few voices of the hidden text into the visible poem of my *Saül*.

A sharp pain, under the throw, contracts the woman's face—in my mind, I don't even dare to pronounce the word *woman* concerning her—her arm and hand pull back, the man, with the sound shut off, gets up, and with both adolescents who are standing, hides the divan where she suffers.

I sit down next to Annick: we blush, heads down, in our half-nakedness, to the sound of this pain that grows then ends.

This family has opened its heart to us, so we can't leave the room, but the day is waning, and the water of the River Aln will be cold.

I prepare a sentence in my mouth, to announce our departure and our goodbyes; but the music resumes from a shadow near the record player, and the adolescents sit back down on the wooden floor.

Were the children playing on the lower level born from that body that was already suffering at the time, and always lying down, or from a previous body running in the fields, jumping with horses, diving into the sea?

Do both adolescents hope to see her walk again between them, at their side, camp, discover paintings shoulder to shoulder in museums, and with a finger, cheek to cheek, search them for characters and for meaning?

The child with the *burnt* ear has stopped playing; he climbs the small staircase, and comes to sit and press himself against me.

How can I reduce the effect the rustling at his hips has on my member, when faced with such suffering, and when maybe all he wants is simply to invite me down to see his games?

How did he *burn* his ear? With it, can he hear the same sounds that we can? What more could he hear in the echo of the deep?

Would this mutilation be counted in his price, in the inventory of his charms?

I can see by his liquid eyes that he's listening, instrument on top of instrument.

Will he keep his hair long all his life to hide his mutilation?

Would I accept that mutilation if it would make me be his age again? And would I accept to figure in a real *deep* at that age?

As I sit between two sources of warmth, Annick on my left and the child on my right, as I hear the sentence that the child's nearly hoarse voice tosses into my ear and that I cannot translate on the spot, and as I watch the cool stare of his mother from the darkness I am reminded of an old sentence that our mother said to me as I was inventing a game for my youngest brother and his friends, invited for a snack, at the garden table: "What a great father you will be!"

But of what woman's children?

Hers, my mother from a more narrow embrace, a longer kiss, and there we would be, her hand in mine, leading our children between large petals, and bulbs higher than they were?

Hers, the wild one, manducated, hidden in our town of Almandet, France, who lives in a window-covered annex of the greenhouse nursery that she paces endlessly, and who sits at night on the threshold in the rags that are her clothes, constantly rubbing one of them between her thighs, her tongue sticking out, and the ends of her very long hair always covered in *robin-run-the-hedge* in springtime, and in winter, in dried sausage skins pulled from the trash heap from the next-door deli?

On Holy Thursday, the priest can wash and dry her bare feet covered in black grime; her face, so fresh, so beautiful, so quivering also under the grime, I can lick it with my tongue forming the words that I save from my stammering, along with the traces of her tears of rage and unshared vision: what beautiful, tender and wild children can be made from that solitude!

Here, I could fill a mobile home with what I could pull from her sides that are spreading on the rep, and from this flesh—*which is mine since I've seen it*—mine now, a visible continuation of my own flesh, which is no longer even my own flesh since the anti-procreative figures of my deep enter it in desire, and leave it in pain.

My flesh does not tell me what it will be, or if children will come from it: do I have enough flesh to craft new ones? But the figures of the illicit text who live so close reject this interior speech: revolt is not concerned about institutions; must the world continue living, and must men grow accustomed to inequality and cruelty?

To cut that endless string of sperm, to stop procreation, to live with what we have in the simple passion of the now.

To reject our human ancestry, guilty of having made us in its image, and to reject the progeny we'd weigh down with our own.

In my deep, no baby has yet been born from sex between workers and *girls*, or rather, no *little* one has *dropped*; but, since I can—fearfully—predict that both illicit and licit text will fuse once I become adult, the fate of those *dropped ones* will be settled by fiction.

But will I be able to hold out long without touching the flesh of my flesh, with my hand, one or the other, the one that beats off, or the one that writes, or the one that forms poetry?

Is the flesh that I make at night, the flesh of my erect member, that kind of flesh that counts so little at rest, and that my desire—like my desire to have children—causes to appear and rise before me like the rooting of generations?

As a young child, I turn one or the other of my sisters into the young mother of my children, according to their mood.

Here, what can I pull from Annick's clothed or naked flesh, to which I've grown accustomed in the last three days and nights, that would be worthy of both the licit and the illicit?

I am hungry for her, not for any other male or female; I have jaws for all the center of her body, to hold her in that way, and carry her, in secret or in broad daylight, to eat her with her consent: may her body be reborn so I can snatch her up again!

Should I whisper that in her ear as she clears away her hair, but I'd even eat that ear!

Hungry for the little ones who would come out of her!

Where does that hunger come from? From the stomach or the member? The stomach. The member has a social hunger; it is hungry to be done with my origins, and with the world that makes them possible and that maintains them; it wants to abolish it all in servitude, and deactivated procreation, and the ridicule of a new word, of semen, and of *juice*.

When the young man, the father of the family, clinks the neck of the bottle of orangeade against Annick's glass, my hunger grows with anger.

Will she move the hair away from her ear so that she can hear more clearly what he tells her—in English, very slowly, or hesitantly in French: if it's in French, it means that he must make an effort, and if he makes that effort, it means he wants to take Annick from me…

A while ago, back when I was sitting on the ruins of the wall and she was standing, did he place "Daybreak" on the record player and under the needle so that he could attract her by attracting me?

The mother has fallen asleep in the twilight. The two adolescents on the wood floor stretch out on their side and together slowly leaf through the large and heavy pages of an old atlas. The child to my right pulls my arm, trying to get me to stand up and join his game downstairs, or maybe lead me to his bedroom, to his books, and to his secret: a wad of clothes mixed with paper flattened under a mattress…

One day, a woman will kiss that mutilated ear with love.

Should I get up, follow that child and the rustling at his hips that would entice me, naked, to the end of the world, so that Annick can move beyond the man's warmth, and to the place where I will disappear?

Can I hide from my mother that this body that she has shaped from the project of the Creator, with all of its senses and with what remains prohibited in its mind, wants to be dehumanized, stripped bare, almost skinned of all its nobility, of all the spiritual beauty of its ancestry, of its divine skin, delivered to the passing instincts, and sacrificed to the needs of Evil, so as to reduce it? But if there is Evil, there must be those who perform it—is "sex" Evil? And since I need that Evil to be done to me, in me, am I not the most guilty before God?

Again, the "people" and their inferiority of spirit and custom, endlessly reviled in novels, poems, paintings, and theater, and that I'll burden with new drudgery and infamy, will help me satisfy a need that is so short when I do it at night, and that in life—can that be "life"?—I'll have to stretch out endlessly, with their help, with their numbers, with their desire of forced laborers, and using their forced labor to excite their forced desire.

In those moments when I feel closest to my own nature—but isn't it better not to be too much "oneself"—I wonder if she didn't give birth to me so that I'd want to sell this body off to anybody, a body that she carried, birthed and breastfed without any earthly profit.

Dizziness then sweeps over me like encrypted ideas to decipher: did she say "would" or "will"? The conditional would mean that what I do at night is Evil, an Evil at once social and metaphysical, an Evil that would definitely abolish my duty to procreate.

Straining to hear her voice, in that summer afternoon, between the woodshed where chopped, hundred-year-old timber exhales the previous century, and the disused garden outhouse where white worms crawl up from the unemptied pit during a heat wave, as I tend and clean my youngest brother and his little village friends who play and eat, the voice I hear fills me, not my own voice, which I don't know yet—neither is it the voice that I had as a child, or my voice today as it breaks—but hers, which is my interior voice, the one that speaks into my ear on the nights when I commit the act, and which grows desolate, and calls me, from farther and farther away, and as it mingles with the voices from the "brothel," disappears before the spasm, only to return when the time of desolation has passed.

This voice, which taught me the world, and through which I understand it today, with kindness and with hope, could it have stopped her younger brother's butchers in the camp of Sachsenhausen-Oranienburg?

In memory of the youth massacred before the age of procreation, should I prepare my body for the future act of procreation rather than risk to dry it out by extracting juice without producing anything else than phantom text, a body that I owe to the perpetuation of History—and of civilization against savagery?

Is my renunciation of Reason committed on part of her body—through "mine"?

For a few instants of pleasure and extreme text, the obscenity of which might sound like what her brother suffered from the voices and gestures of his butchers, I waste part of her hope—all of it—in the vanity of sacrificial debauchery.

Ten years after the liberation of the death camps, doesn't any act of life violate the violated?

The assassins misappropriated gestures, speech, words, desires, needs, anger, games, and all of human activity for their own profit. There are very few springs they did not poison.

To whom do we owe our comfort, the very fact that we are living and have grown past infancy, the hour of our acknowledgment by our father, this state of exception wherein living is more of a permission, a duty, than a right?

Since my first images of camps, and since the deportation of two among us, on my mother's and on my father's side, one of them deadly, all my thoughts, my gestures, despite my drive for life and the great numbers of those who are living around me, the movements of my senses are suspended as they wait for a divine resolution of memory, and the appeasement of His rage.

When "Sex" appears, it grows on that. The first distortion of the face and body in thrills and convulsions is not the beautiful languishing of satiated bodies in an ancient countryside as they turn around to the sound of flutes, but rather the tensing and shaking of torture, and of bodies in concentration camps.

Is pulling juice like the torturer forcing a confession from the tortured?

Like God the Father extracting the most he can from God the Son during his crucifixion?

A breeze coming from the river and the alder trees sweeps over our naked shoulders. If the father, now standing, plays the opening of *Daphnis* again, we'll be unable to leave this place where love comes out of nothingness: these harp chords, the birth of this world that is also music.

The mother has fallen asleep, and I can hear the small noise of her breath through her nostrils: is she too weak to breathe through her mouth? The music breathes so softly, bigger and bigger, stronger and stronger! We have to leave. And what do I know of this family—of its origins, the jobs of the men and women who shape it, its action during the war, even the name of each child, or the sound of their voice, except for the mother's small cry of pain, and the child's sentence as yet untranslated in my ear?

I should learn as much as possible before leaving! But by the time I've formed the English sentence in my mouth, free of stuttering, Annick has gotten up and the father is kissing her goodbye at the top of the small staircase where, with a sign of his index finger on his mouth, the children at the bottom of the stairs have stopped talking and are no longer touching their toys.

The two adolescents, sitting in front of their mother's body, just barely turn their pink and blond faces toward us.

The same child follows us back downstairs to the front door, where he pulls himself up on his toes and kisses my cheek that blushes from the father's kiss on Annick's cheek, he, the son, his father having gone back to his mother's side; I should at least take away precise sounds from this place: the detail of the crêpe paper rustling around his hips; what can I do to hear it again? And how can I make him repeat his sentence? With the fingers of both hands, I part the hair from his mutilated ear, and kiss him: would the sentence come back out of his ear?

The creaking door hinges drown out what I'd like to hear of the rustling at his hips, but I still hear it rise as the child quivers from my kiss.

Pulling my lips away from the mutilated ear, I see some grime on his skull between his hair. Is he really the child of that young man up there?

The two adolescents, and the other children whom I spotted on the way down the stairs are all dressed; they wear shoes and are well kept; this one is barefoot, barely washed—as a child, I wait for my mother to pull her fingers from my brother's soapy hair before she pushes them into mine and rubs my scalp—plays dress-up, and his mutilation is poorly tended—how recent must it be to have left a drop of blood on my lips?—he is responsible for opening the door to us and leading us out, and already in his mouth, and in a voice that's breaking a bit too early, comes this sentence whose rawness and cruelty I can sense even before translating it…

Did the young father, or stepfather abandon his wife's favorite child as she grew weaker—loosing even the strength to rub off a small spot of dirt on her child's face with spit on the tip of her finger—in favor of the others, who rejected him in turn and forced him to serve them?

But what strength and what secret lie behind the boy's high spirits? Which house has chosen him to be the adolescent that they want?

In a moment of vertigo, I turn my swimsuit with its laces loose again, the door frame, and Annick's flesh coveted by the insects in the dying day into nakedness, a ruined door-jamb, and the flesh of workers, and the re-rustling of the paper around the child's hips pulls my hips from the swim-suit to gird them with that crêpe paper: my whole body, tan, well-loved, gauche, too interior, disappears into that blond double who is unloved, confident, a body almost already public…

The rustling moves from table to table, from puddles of wine to deposits of sperm: it seems three years ago, before "sex" was structured in me, and in that bygone age where all the wisdom of childhood gathered in the saintly, disinterested body: where people come from all over to find and hear your intact wis-dom—your body…

To extract myself from the double, to feel the loose lace of my swimsuit on my hips, to tie it back, and turn with the Sun against my backbone toward the double whose left wrist has settled on his lifted left hip and whose eyes shine in the twi-light, blue, and whites: is this his last night?

How can I go back up there? Maybe through a sly excuse he could get his father and both adolescents to leave, and left alone with his mother at last, with a few words that only both of them would know, he could return her brief strength to her so that she'd tell him again that he was still her favorite?

We walk quickly side by side, toward the alder trees whose branches rustle in the heightened breeze; she sees I've pulled away from her into the double, and I remember the young man's kiss on her cheek in the small staircase.

Once past the tall trees, we walk down to the bank, crowded with white swans. In the silt, then in the water, we have to push them away so that we can begin to swim.

Behind her in the current that is cooler now, all I can see is her red bikini, and the foam before her as she swims like an effect of the breath of her anger, and through my ears that slowly gorge with water, recalling the memory of the sound of the child's voice, I try to retrieve, one by one, the words of the sentence that he whispered in my ear: I cry out the words I remember to Annick, who's now swimming beside me, and smiles at me again; and as we reach the diving board from which Anthony and Kenneth were diving earlier, with real, large birds flying overhead and cloaking us in shadow, I hurl out the entire sentence: "A dog ate my ear when I was a baby!"

Was it a single dog? Or two, fighting over it? And does he sleep on that mutilated ear?

Despite the lapping sound and flowing water, I have him pass from knee to knee, and through that crusty, cropped ear, between the flies enraged by human copulation, they whisper things that would make him disown his own mother. Do the dogs—one dog or several?—that ate his ear when he was a baby drag their loins along the threshold of the *locale*—the name I've given that dark place where the sperm flows in my secret text—and whimper for the other one?

Will I ever be finished with this tearing apart: thinking, organizing, and experiencing the worst—Evil?—at the heart of beauty, of progress and of the good—and here, at the heart of this nation that just conquered Evil!

Sometimes the sperm drinks away words. As I find them in my memory the following night, I inscribe them as fast as possible over the trace of the erasure, of the offense and its remorse, so that I don't miss what my rising desire emboldens me to dare to do in my mind, my throat, and then my hand. Maybe in the excesses of my interior sexual scene, and in the jerks of its nighttime transcription, I discover that I don't want sex, but that I reject it instead as unworthy of the body that both God and my mother made for me, and of the spirit whose progress I've enabled there.

Is that small itch in a hidden organ closest to the excremental cavity what leads my body to the edge of Evil, beyond the limits of the Good? Even if I despise its written result during the phase of desolation, when that whole side of me has crumbled inside and all around—in an excess of Conscience—life returns to me with time and through its new events, predominantly through what I write when I'm aroused—and mostly through what I've been *able* to write there.

I learn *will* there; and because sometimes I need to finish quickly, to pull incriminated facts from the obscurity of

Conscience, and place them in the light, like objects. For me, Conscience—what makes it so strong?—takes the place of Reason: it never misleads me with its calls, its visions, its torments, its prohibitions, or its madness—in the face of common sense—common reason admits, glorifies, and teaches principles and judgments that my Conscience rejects; in my Conscience I am not alone, the entire world is there.

We get close to the riverbank where our friends are: in the middle of the current, as it narrows and grows stronger before the bridge, the rhythm of my heart shoots up, but it's because I have to meet them although I am still heavy with new beings, with the poetry that makes me connect all things between themselves, and see in the minds and hearts that pass in front of me.

My hand reaches out to Annick's shoulder underwater: should I grab her hand in mine; should I do to her underwater what I wasn't able to do on earth, pull her under the bridge, pass beneath it, and find ourselves alone, beyond it, in the calmer waters, where the setting Sun lights and heats the depths...

And where does the River Aln flow into the ocean? Somewhere that would be far to swim to, in the sea in Alnmouth...

She lifts her arm heavy with water and touches my shoulder with her hand to turn me toward the bank; Douggie has already rushed into the silty river, and with his swimsuit at his ankles, he holds his member in his fist over the gray water.

Standing up to mid-ass in the water that has turned red under the Sun, facing the source of the river she splashes me; I see through the water, her right eye, the left side of her red face, Douggie's fist shining as he holds his member that we can't see in his fist, and with his little finger hoists up his testicles; he laughs, flips over into the silty water, and dunks his entire head until the silt closes in on it: but his fist on his member stays on the surface; the brain has disappeared, life and generation remain: is that me as well, when in the act my common reason is flipped over with my head, and all my senses are gathered in my fist—but where would the right hand be, the one that writes?

I watch the white of her eye between the fluttering of lashes; is her pupil staring at the fist above the water? Would it stay fixed on it if the fist opened around what it contains? The hand is so big I can't tell whether the member is erect or not. Is this the first male member—which she doesn't see—to which her eyes have turned? A naked member in a naked member?

Is that what girls dream about? The way that boys dream about *that* in girls? That precise stare, self-interested, oriented toward a single object of pleasure, detached from the rest of the body and its environment of beauty, makes me crouch and lower my member into the water.

If I isolate that member in her gaze, does that mean that I covet it for a special use, similar to what Kenneth's mother does to make a living?

Everything that I imagine of her spirit, protected in a head whose contours seem so soft, abruptly diminishes in that gluttony. But here at least, it is for a feral member, coming from a body whose origins are only partly known, possessed, to be tied down…

I take off my shirt on the grass, pick up my painting supplies, and walk to a thicket of willows in which I saw wild birds alight from the river.

Yesterday's storms have made the surface of the little pools rise. As I sit on a tree trunk sinking into the moss-laden water, I don't draw and paint what I see, but instead a single green and red reflection whose liquidity I sustain, as if to see my eyes reflected in it: from now on, I will paint what I am, bring to light those shadows whose voices I write in the nocturnal act.

But for myself—how could I imagine someone else reading such a text?—those shadows should only be handled with text, where they can move without being seen the way drawing would circumscribe and define them, whereas writing leaves them free?

Were I to extract them from the text in which they rest during the day and which I open at night, I would add stupor to those unfinished silhouettes that appear and disappear with a cross-fade or under a flash of detail: seated, shoulders down, hands clasped between open knees, raised faces, open and relaxed mouths, dreary eyes; or turned back, heads invisible but thighs spread wide, and laughter in their hanging heads; open groins where the sperm spreads and trembles; big hands on fresh breasts in which useless milk rots.

But where would I hide such drawings? For the gaze discovering a secret, writing is better: it takes longer to decipher and to read than the image that is immediate.

But if I were to trace the contours of bodies and members, of ragged clothes, of mouths, breasts, hips, groins, and the nape of necks caught in the grips of desire, I would reveal my *deep* too much; writing preserves that vagueness where the poetic hand moves to create, not to elucidate.

And can the right hand draw while the left wields the member? A crooked sentence scribbled on the page is still legible, but a drawing would be deformed in the urgency of beating off.

How can I continue to paint landscapes, when I torment myself already with God's judgment, in my poetry, through Saül, and even more when I move backward into the inside of myself to reach the deep that is my foundation?

What lies under those still waters, under those moraines, in those forests and houses that I paint so that beauty can emerge from my fresh, mute hand?

What I should try to paint is the origin of water, of rocks, the chemical depths of vegetable roots, working-class and farming populations, family violence, the open bed of concubines.

As for the sky, whether one thinks it is God's reign or space between the Earth and the other planets, how can I be content with painting clouds that are just passing gas?

The Ocean, the Sea, how can a trembling of foam, or a gradation of blue, figure the backwash and the waves, when the weight of that mass is unquantifiable? And to reduce the Moon and Sun, that are so remote in space-time, to a few rays that filter through the blinds during the summer, and to a whitish tablecloth on a mute garden!

The sounds of tea being prepared, a slamming door—is Norman, his job in Berwick finished for the day, dropping Dorothy off before going to his cricket game?—hasten the completion of my gouache: this same wrist, these same digits carve my shadows and their bursts of speech in the act of the deep, while those of the other hand slow down the rise of sperm around the member as long as the scene and its pre-meditated dialogue are not complete—so I attenuate the obscenity of the *picture*, choose more abstract, even noble words that come from good rhetoric to make the sperm inch back up to its source.

Suspend the dialogue, the voices that, more so than the description, stimulate and call forth the surging of the juice.

The same ones lull Saül's distress with alexandrines: but when I go back to school I'll show that poem to the friends who are already typing what I write for me; unless, through several enigmatic verses of Saül's history in the Book of Samuel, I can pull enough from my deep to add to the ruin of the King, or to God's anger: but how can I transport the "modern" twilight of that deep into the darkness of a house of ill repute at the heart of the light of Israel?

What then does my other hand do? It holds the notebook on which I write, where it beats the rhythm of the verse, it holds the drawing pad on which I copy the finished poem, sometimes with colored decorations.

It beats the rhythm of the verse, during vacation, in my room, above the table, to my left; at school, in study hall, this happens under the desk.

Across from me, on the other side of the three pools, Anthony and Kenneth are walking in bathing suits, the hand of one over the shoulder of the other: should I draw and paint their shared silhouette on the top of the page?

Will he make him sleep in his room tonight?

Will they both knock on my door downstairs, to demand my member?

Douggie, behind me, laces and unlaces his suit, pulls it up and down: let him take my gouaches and fling them in the water! I need to live on the side of the deep, with the child with the mutilated ear, and only for a short time only.

From the alcohol stove on which the tea is boiling, a cloud of smoke rises that dissipates in the high grass; Douggie's breath speeds up in his wet chest.

Annick's red body moves in the smoke to the high grass, I see the red of her bikini shift downward. Douggie's sisters are preparing tea and toasts, their mother and Dorothy wade into the darkened water; I hear the sounds of their first breast-strokes. The time it takes me to put my painting supplies away—should I rearrange the landscape with my hands, so that I leave it the way it was when I found it, before I painted it?—the two tall women are walking in the silt of the banks, and climbing up to the meadow. Their half-nakedness is red as well.

Anthony and Kenneth disappear behind the willows.

I catch the whiff of a smell from Douggie who is standing behind me, his back to me, and his shadow touching my back; it's the same smell, at night, after my final milking, and the last, often incomplete words—will I finish them during the next session or will I leave them aside for others that would make a mockery of them?—from which I turn my nostrils away to bury them in the pillow.

Not even the slightest shake in the curve of the nape of his neck at his shoulder, only his face that turns toward me in the red light, wrinkled by a smile; he has enough in his groin to pull from it without any damage or desolation, until far into the night, until the early morning.

What are the two tall, half-naked women doing, as they surround Annick who is standing and has left the tall grass in the smoke to tend the toasts?

Does the blood of abduction and rape still cling to her shoulders under the smoke?

From the pools beyond the ones that I've just painted, workers are pulling pipes over the grass to the bank of the River Aln: along the high grass, along the cropped grass; silt, mud, now up to the two tall women's feet, who, bent over slightly, pull Annick up to the top of the meadow with their hands on her shoulders.

More and more workers, their boots between the pipes, move down to the bank.

My shirt protects my shoulders from the hands of the tall women who might grab them to the bone. Clouds form and thicken, black around the Sun. Other workers cross the meadow toward the top, to a temporary modular structure made of wood and corrugated iron, abutting on a blockhouse. Girls in aprons, behind the smoke of grease, are frying donuts and sausages in lard, big chunks of which I see on the counter.

One of the girls' hair falls over the pan; she flips it back over her high, curved forehead under which very light eyes gaze out from their greasy orbits at the workers who bare their chests, sweating in the darkness of the coming storm.

What a good "client" Douggie is, with his endless juice!

Why are the two tall women leading Annick into the depths of the building?

The sound of a faraway dialogue, of two bodies walking toward us, reaches my ears where the sounds of Nature, birds, trees, water, have grown silent.

Faraway on the bank, beyond the high grass, two bodies walk toward us, one tall, the other short: is it the child with the mangled ear, and his mother who has gotten up from her sick bed?

As they draw near, I see him, naked but for the crown of crêpe paper around his hips, shuffling back and forth, but his mother's hand, still slightly shaky, holds his hand firmly. Has she prepared him, skin, hair, perfume, to garner the best price? Is she recapitulating in her mind all of his intimate weaknesses so that she can transmit them, as best she can, to those who are preparing the transaction in the back of the fortification?

What desire fills his slender chest, soon to be strengthened by thick hands used to stone, metal, mud, and hogs? What makes his stomach twitch above the crêpe?

"Mother, please, could we wait a day before delivering my body? One day more would make my desire stronger, and raise the price as well!"

"It has to be today, my child, because tomorrow I will be dead."

At the sound of the rustling around his hips, cleaning workers and the men leading against the bar turn their heads; those who are bare-chested, their chests.

Douggie inches backwards toward me, snorts, laughs, opens his underarms and scratches them, each with the opposite hand, then with the other hand. Why is he pushing his ass against my thigh? Where is he trying to lead me?

The smell of blood, warming within him, adds to the smell wafting from his juice.

Women for the boy, men for the girl.

Is Annick's blood already leaking on the pallet in the innermost depths of the fortification?

Are other workers heading there through another door?

Are other women preparing the pallet for the boy with the mangled ear, for other women that will come to lie with him, and on him?

But don't men come to join these women, and women come to join these men who are covering Annick with their shadows in the darkness?

The mother and son hunch as they walk on the path along the bank of the River Aln. Douggie lies face down in the soiled meadow: what is that shaking in his loins with which he probes the clods of grass that have been pulled out and flattened by the pipes?

Up there, behind the counter, the slattern's bare cleavage spreads; in that vast whiteness, the light of the storm brightens blue streaks of veins and vessels as the breasts curve toward the nipples: how many men's heads could roll on it? Is she naked under her apron, with its small cord unlaced at the bottom of her haunches? Eyes and mouth shine under the paper lanterns that are switched on in the growing darkness.

The bare-chested workers, donuts and sausages in their teeth, peel their stomachs from the counter, walk with their hands on their hair toward the hole where swarms of gnats grow dense.

In the curved and upturned face of his mother, the child's eye shines, his breaking voice now coating its childish bursts of sound:

"And what if men, my mother, climb into the bed, for the women…?"

"Let them love you, my child."

Fish, salamanders, plants flood out into the Aln from the pipes, along with muddy-colored water; Douggie's two sisters crouch, with a blanket on their heads, in front of the gas stove that has been turned off.

The woman and the child pass below, and once they are farther away, turn and walk up to the building: no other sound remains than the rustling of the crêpe, the buzzing of what flies are still awake, and, at my feet, Douggie's trepidation in the mud. The smell of the spreading bosom enters my nostrils: I reach lower, to the stench of that naked *nature*, which lessens as the bare-chested men retreat into the hole.

Should I remove my glasses and slide them in their case? But where should I keep the case? If I put them in the back pocket of my shorts, wouldn't I crush them if I had sex? With my eyes bare and my painting supplies thrown down near the stove, should I walk up to the counter, to that bosom, and that well-endowed nature and take it in my palm as the nipple vibrates near my shoulder, and my forehead butts against the girl's high, curved forehead…

The lard that she licks off the knife, once she's thrown the slice into the pan, makes her lips and the back of her nostrils shine.

Should I eat before or after? The member pulls its strength from the famished body. As I kiss her, should I suck the lard that she's storing in her cheeks?

The mother pulls the child by his full ear alongside the building, but the child re-claims his steps; flies get caught in the crêpe, vibrate there; he shakes his head, and pushes back his mother's fingers. He looks at me while my hand grabs the *nature's* flesh and hair, as I part the flesh under the hair to suction it to the base of my palm. Me, shirt, shorts, sandals, glasses in a case in my pocket, bourgeois hand on the sex of a girl of the people; he, my double, naked but for that rustling, which signals that he can be *taken*, a missing ear—his body is coveted so young!—his price and rates, mutilation included, already calculated in the mind of shrewd men and women buyers, many hands in the dark getting ready to make him grow hair through the incessant friction of their fingers on his tender parts; my double precedes me in infamy—for life.

Is my desire strong enough to wish, and to be able to follow him into the depths?

Does he garner the strength of his desire from his violated body?

His mother, who will soon die, serves as guarantor; when she will disappear, and the body that made him in its blood will lie rotting in the earth, to whom can she entrust him except the women or men who will profit from him?

What else can she leave on the surface of the earth but a hide, dragged from one desire to the next?

The great, light, flowered dress of the mother and the crown of pink crêpe disappear into the blackness of the entrance; the last of the bare-chested men turns his face to us, his left hand caught under his right armpit, then slicing down his right elbow, foams and disappears.

With the sound of thunder, wind flattens the reeds on the banks and on the ponds, flaps against the canvas of the building, flattens Douggie once again into the mud, hunches his sisters under the blanket, tips over the stove.

Large and small animals take shelter; vermin latches onto those who enter into the depths; does the vermin rise or fall over the hands that seize, grope, spread apart, lift, curl back, open the drawer and the wallet, slap down the bills, trace the new rate with chalk on the chalkboard?

Desire makes the worms come out; in the desiring and the desired; folds, plies, holes, slits, openings, toe cracks reveal their larvae; hair, body hair, eyebrows, eyelashes, fuzz itch.

Is the crown still fixed on the child's loins, or has it been thrown away? Or has it been put on his skull or on his neck?

Or has it slid from his loins down to his calves from so much grasping and trepidation, and lifting his right foot, does he throw it with his left beyond the women who push him toward others on the ground who snatch it up?

But is it still not used enough? Should they wait for it to have been worn thin by copulation, soiled by ejaculation, for fights of the flesh to have ripped it apart? For sucking to have discolored it?

Does a trace of wind outside shake the single light bulb on the ceiling of the building?

Among the cleaners and the bare-chested workers who pile their shadows and their mass on Annick's pallet in the back—

was she forced to take off her red bikini by the two tall women once they'd finished with the cashier, and is she holding it in her teeth?—do the least sated among them, their folds of clothing examined in the light, stand, move forward to the uncrowned child, his dirty shorn ear shaken between strands of blond hair—eye wide open—on the torn bolster under the shadows of the women?

Will the two tall women come back out into the day?

Is Annick there for life? As for my double, it is for life.

* * *

From my head protruding over the railing above the foam as I force myself to throw up, I see the gardenia flower on the ear of the tall woman, brownish-pink skin, shiny black hair, her back to the sea, leaning her tall hips against the staircase railing; and in the shaking of my head, the trepidation of the ferry and the stench of the sea, I smell the flower, its perfume of the adult world beyond *penetration*. With my two hands behind my ears, I press my earlobes against the arms of my Amor imitation glasses so that they don't fall.

We are on the right side of the ferry, the red Sun is already touching the cloudless horizon: on the high seas.

The little that I vomit frees my throat; she has turned back toward the sea, her hand touching my shoulders through my dark-blue cotton vest; my legs grow stronger in my knickers; I can finally talk to her, even with my vomit-muddled tongue.

Is she traveling alone? From America to England, and from England to France? Is she singing with those black musicians who are carrying their instruments up through the gangways and the staircases of the ship?

Her hand—what ancient hand, tied, bound, in shackles and chains, to be used for picking cotton?—slipped under my shirt, massages where the nape of my neck touches my shoulder; the gardenia flower is on the other side of her head above her right ear, and the overly strong wind spreads its smell backwards. But now I smell her skin, the skin of her wrist, of her arm behind my neck, of her elbow, where a bit of sweat kept there by the humid wind promises the *smell*—and later its consistency under my fingers and my tongue—the skin of her armpits.

Must I continue to make myself vomit so that a hand, a real hand at last, can continue to massage my neck, the fingers unfolding all the way to my left jaw, and maybe all the way to the left corner of my lips with their long violet nails?

That smell and the churning of the sea would make it so much easier for my right hand to climb along her left, over her wrist, along her arm, and cup her elbow and stay there.

And in that motion and that caress, if my mouth were to side up to hers, how could I clean my palate by then? With water? What if I grabbed the bag at my feet, took the bottle and drank?

The woman would pull her hand and arm away from my neck.

Speech, to reject the sanies of vomit, to produce a lot of saliva as I speak, and spit it out?

But a stronger wave of nausea makes me vomit again, and I'm afraid that the shifting wind will fling the vomit on her, on me; the woman's hand stays on my shaking neck.

Will I be vomiting all night? What more can I vomit than the last stew I ate, yesterday at my friend's house, in front of Mr. Praundlock rolling his little pea between his index and his old thumb?

What is the organ, the mucous membrane that could come undone from my interior body, which I imagine in the shape of a machine room, and be regurgitated for good?

Will I sleep tonight? Could the vomit surprise me as I sleep, dreaming of ingurgitation, and suffocate me to death?

Or stay awake, and, through the immobility of body and mind, keep watch over my interior body; reduce the power of feelings, the memory of my double, now motherless, the memory of the latest fight between my father and me, in a Jeep, on a shortcut down a rocky outcrop that shook both the car and our fight, and the memory of the "ball of orgy," out of reach of the Newhaven custom officer's hand because the bag was stretched taut by a 33 rpm record of a Schubert recital by Elisabeth Schwarzkopf and Edwin Fischer—I don't know much of her at the time, a member of the Nazi Party, sexually harassed—or worse?—by Hans Frank, the butcher of Poland, who degrades her voice in the Hitlerian spasm—which the record dealer just outside the City had slipped into a sleeve and jacket with the two boogie-woogie 78s that I was bringing back for our sisters' small parties?

But how can I quiet my heart whose beating I hear beneath the palpitations of the vomiting, in my clogged ears, next to the woman's fist who is now rubbing my back from top to bottom: a woman whom I don't know, who is not the ship's nurse, a beautiful woman who is just passing through, on an international route, and who touches my clothed skin, massages the bones and muscles of my shoulder, of my back, and knows them now…

Enough with vomiting, so that I can talk!

The foam revives the blood in my head, which was close to fainting; rather than food, I must be rejecting the accumulated matter of the text of the deep, which I've held back, unformed, for a month. Or maybe it is even the weight of what I might possibly create and write, beside my erect member, when I return to my room in France?

That brown hand, and that noble body in a suit tapered at the waist—all I've seen of her face is a touch of red on the left side of her bottom lip, and the profile of a bluish eye—descend from the bodies of ancient slaves; how could I transform them into the hand and body of a slave master in my locale and in the mechanics of my deep! I need white bodies, those who are still dominating the world, boys, girls, women, even workers, to enslave, to desire, to write most secretly.

Is that fist that roams my back, weakened by nausea, searching for the marks left on the curve of the spine by the act of arousal, writing, and ejaculation? What would such marks be, for her? For me, they are a burden on which I lay my back each time; but if I must go to that writing when the licit writing is exhausted, I must keep all its powers of exception, of mystery and sin, intact, in body, mind, and soul.

No black body will ever enter: those bodies, created by God in His Image, and for His use, that their Christian masters dared to buy and sell, and to haggle over, separating the children from the mothers and the mothers from the fathers, for the use of sugar, of cotton.

In the sound of turbines, foam, seagulls, and passengers preparing for the night, from my hanging head I can hear the stirrings of a small, muffled brass band, trumpet, and trombone.

Could I forget the life of my heart if I follow the music with my ear and mind…? Will they play all night? Will she sing?

If I enter the adult world, with no ties of blood or friendship, but through the smell of gardenia and this passenger's fist, with my fifteen years of age plainly laid down at the feet of someone twice that age, will I lose the images and words that drive me deeper and deeper into what has no end, and that must remain hidden because of it: that sex, desire, penetration, pleasure are acts of conquest, mastery and crushing of the other; and that the snickering of the pervert and the sobs of the victim do not resonate in my deep, but instead the silence of stupor, and the flash of cheekiness from the children of the people, girls and boys, in the rear courtyard of the worker's city, who pick up those sleeping men and women who desire them like they'd pick up garbage with their fathers?

What face, once the vomiting is done, will I pull up from the foamy void, to read her gaze, which will be shining, from left eye to right toward the gardenia flower pink from the setting sun: my long hair already dirty from the night of travel in the train, my dirty glasses and mouth, my still uncertain chin, maybe she carries on her or in a purse, a handkerchief, eau de toilette, pads to clean it and brighten its tan?

Won't she sweep me up, with me beneath her, into a swinging motion, a state of drunkenness signaled by the smell of the gardenia that is even stronger than the shaking of the sea and my nausea?

How much strength, how much time will I need before I can position myself on top of her? And where? Here, no private cabins with linens and polished wood: with the deck of the ship awash with seawater, how could I regain the advantage? Should I let my body go, as if it were naked, and more "advanced" than that head against which my father's anger strikes? Should I trust all those women who have pointed out my charm since my early childhood?

Should I allow pure speech to form at the source, which is in the chest, and to come out of the throat, the speech that I had to constrict, even in England, under the cover of language and the mistakes I make there—since I've been writing open poetry, my daily speech has changed along with my changing voice; but I feel that the writing of the deep pulls it toward its freedom, its cheekiness, and its lust, and, under domestic, familial language, that my stuttering often clutters with the clicking of my tongue, a *Word* swells with the smell of the "ball of orgy" as my voice sputters when it speaks of bodies, of feelings of desire, and of pleasure.

And if writing poetry, folding rhythms and rhymes in it, doesn't fill me with any superior certainty, I now know that my family's chatter, apart from my mother's speech, is below what culture, understood as social superiority and responsibility, should put there: against the visual and auditory background of my ongoing poetry, I hear the domestic speech of others, and in the darkness and din of my deep, despite myself, I hear myself speaking to and answering my father as best I can, or in dialogue with my mother.

These last few days, and nights, in the morning, or before we'd leave for Belford at noon, I would often swim to prepare for the three nights of train rides and ferry that I would have to take on my return trip, often looking at Annick's body and face above the reflective or dark water; is there still sand and seaweed in the folds, the hair, the holes of that only part of me I know, from which I milk the substance of my future, "sex"?

I don't see all the rest, the build, the curvature, the gait, the thickness and the form of my limbs and neck: what is the use of trying to see in the mirror what does not transform sensations into thoughts, into a future? And even in the deep, what emerges from the darkness are the folds of clothing, of worn rags near the genitals, the flashing of gazes: an ass, a thigh, a stomach, a torso would not be enough, the words must slowly grow voluptuous in my ear and under my fingers that trace the secret writing.

As she touches my spine, can she understand that the stronger beating of my heart is for her and not because of nausea?

What if I lifted my head and turned toward her, without a thought for the leftover vomit on my lips and in my mouth…?

A woman cannot help a boy vomit, or caress his spine as she would a man, without ending her care with a kiss; but if I turn my head toward her, instead of letting her kiss the nape of my neck or my cheek with my face to the sea, she'll understand that it's another kiss I want, at least as close to the mouth as possible.

She must know so much, being double my age, American, black, a singer, maybe, in a band of male musicians on tour— there are so many "experiences" to be had on intercontinental ocean liners… Children, already? Husbands, young or mature? Alcohol, madness, discrimination; a miserable or impoverished childhood; so many young children, hers or those of others from whom she grabs the excess of chewed and spit out food into her hand! So many men, from her father to her husbands, whose lips she kisses on alcohol—and vomit— saturated mouths? Lovers, clients perhaps, that she must push to drink and whose mouths she had to clean; her mouth, which singing has accustomed to regurgitating saliva, spit, sometimes blood, or undigested food. What can a fifteen year-old mouth, cluttered with picnic dregs and drained of blood by nausea, mean for her if she can't see, in my eyes tarnished by slightly foggy lenses, that I am starting an alexandrine in the trembling of my own resurrection and the rocking of the sea, an alexandrine about my *Saül's* respite in his struggle with his God, where he can finally rest in confidence—where does he get that lover's calm? From a witch that he's just visited in her perfumed, desert crevice? From a servant who has brought ointments back from her faraway native land, and is massaging them into his body taut with depression? From the princess of an exterminated, neighboring people, as he feels her belly move beneath his finger, adorned with a king's ring, the result of his member and his seed?

All of them brown-skinned as she is, belonging to the other people of the Bible, the captured, the deported, the enslaved people of America who free themselves through song and psalms.

Are the dregs still in my mouth, the leftovers of her anger, of her bitterness, and of their acidity that is extinguished there?

Greater than my emotion upon seeing her, now that we are face to face, is the emotion of the alexandrine, whose first words I've found, and the rest of which is still in my hand as I beat its rhythm closest to my ass, a ghostly development, but a sure ghost.

Will she strike down that small musical strain with a single gaze? Or can she see that in my ear and in my hand I still hesitate between the witch and the princess, and that, once the Alexandrine of abandon to reclaimed happiness is done, the other verses will depend on that choice, which I must make in front of her, almost eye to eye, our mouths just barely separate?

The abandon of the first verse is carried by the harp—the discontinuous—the plucked string; but if I yielded to the music coming from the band starting to play its melancholic prelude, level and continuous, of trumpets and trombones, it would be madness in tears again, then tension, and, of the three women, the servant would enter with her ointments and her spells.

Shouldn't I leave the deck, and find a corner in the tipping depths where I could write the stanza of the naïve but expert servant, with a flashlight?

But I've turned my back to the sea, and I have a woman in front of me, whose eyes, shining in the nearly setting Sun, are hooked on mine that don't look down: should we take it further?

But is my emotion enough? The one that comes from moving a woman: a woman who has explored my spine with her fist, and who knows my bone structure, my ability to thrust, my endurance, and my rectitude. There are other boys vomiting over the railing: did she see me as the passengers boarded the ferry in Newhaven, after the train? From the front? The side?

Did she hear me speak to the custom's officer, or to French people, during the transfer? Laugh?

Of all those young people bent over, in convulsions, their developing chests leaning against the railing, it was mine that she chose to rub? The weakest one perhaps? But which straightens under her fist.

In the self-portrait that I drew and colored before leaving, which is the only one I've ever made since I began to draw and paint, I know that my lips are fleshy when I daydream, because they curl back when I speak, or in surprise or rejection at what I see; if she is looking at my eyes, then she must like them, despite the lenses; I curl and press my lips forward because I want her to do the same. I must act as if I were daydreaming: allow the features and the organs of the face, even the hands, to act without restraint. But I need more than that emotion: shouldn't the member partake as well?

Nausea and vomit have relegated it to the mass of useless, mute, and absent organs.

As she turns the top of her body toward the musicians who are calling her, since the vest of her suit is unbuttoned and pulled taut, I catch the opening of her armpit under her pink sleeveless blouse beneath the brown strip of fabric near the top of the sleeve, and see a few very black hairs with gleaming tips: from the sunset? sweat? the song rising within?

More than the curvature of her spine, this crevice full of odors, tastes, solidity should make my member stir; it should move for the yawning, once the armpit has fully opened, that prefigures the stretching of her *nature*.

But even by thinking of that member and that armpit, am I repeating the desire and the expert gaze of the buyer who works for the plantation or the brothel? Am I profaning what even its Creator would not dare to use—but doesn't the same Creator create those who profane it?

Can the member stir and stiffen with an impulse toward another soul? Toward their thinking? Their past?

Does it harden for flesh alone: flesh to flesh? Soul to soul? Or is my member starved for what links one to the other, social *condition*? As if to make it disappear in its decrease; it wants enslavement, its images, its living representations, it craves to eat them as it hardens and to digest them with its substance; and if the girl is not enough, it will enslave and eat the boy.

Under the armpit the white strap of the bra stretches taut from the breast to the back and holds the cup with a snap: the tightness of the strap suggests a breast that is firm, always awake, always fresh, although it has seen much use: scars perhaps?

I feel my cheeks blush: because of an organ that I don't see, but onto which my infant eyes were opened. How can the same organ move and reassure us about the fate of humankind, through semi-public breastfeeding at the entrance of a house, in a city park, or a train car, when it can also awake and gather into a single impulse all the sanies of the voyeur when exposed under red-painted lips?

Between the two, it is also the organ of beauty of the girl or woman who keeps them hidden under her hands, because beauty must be hidden.

Except for my burning nipples, I can't feel my clothes. What am I wearing on the bottom? One layer, two? Nothing? I barely feel my feet, drained of blood earlier, covered in my walking shoes?

What does my member wake into, to harden, swell, expand? How can I hide my need to spit? Behind my hand, trembling along with my entire body? My member rises with the trembling.

She must appease me without appeasing my member; above us, the golden clouds have darkened; thunder next to the vanished English coast.

Is my member so hard, as if stuck at its greatest girth, only because of her, or because of all the women united in her? Is this what makes men penetrate women? What makes male animals do the same?

More than the brain and heart, this member is created by man: out of the small mass of glands and appendages that Nature has granted him, and the fluids and nerves which lead to it, his senses, his mind, and his pain form that real member.

And that member is ugly: or at least it is never painted, sculpted, molded, even adored as an image of beauty.

In art, testicles are meticulously made, and embellished with hair, but the expanded member is never shown: that's because it is inside the woman's organ, and so is the sperm, which is not shown either; but in intercourse, which we never see, sperm can overflow: blood, which is created life, flows everywhere with its straightforward color; sperm, which is the life to come, before its social use, has a fleeting color and consistency.

And what in man created that real member, man, the small creator of the cursed member, only barely controls it; for poetry, I must balance and harmonize all my other faculties on my desire to write it: mind, memory, knowledge, heart, the state of my body, my immediate future, simultaneous emotions, securing the body that will write, whereas for this I must communicate, in seconds, to my entire body, a forgetting of almost everything. To become an other who forms or takes shape around the sexual zone, or even who does not take shape there—so that the member can act freely.

I lift my eyes up to the sky, black under black: I always hide to draw or paint the night; sometimes I draw it in ink or very black pencil just before I enter the nocturnal act.

But regardless of what place or time I paint or draw it, a shape of prostitution always appears in the landscape, black but for a crescent moon, a window or a street light: a shape of prostitution, blank at first, then colored with red lipstick, red or black on her purse, red on the nipples of her abundant breasts, which I leave blank, red or green on her high-heeled shoes, then black, darker than the night, on the short dress and the long hair.

Then I must darken the face, darken the arms, darken the legs, with a black color that distinguishes them from the darkness.

Between the blackness that thickens as we get close to France, and the swinging deck that hangs over the luminous pit of the cabins where the youngest children are already asleep, as some adolescents still vomit over the railing, and men and women hold onto their hats and smoke long cigarettes in long conversations, my eyes latch onto a woman's gaze along the railing of the first class section, higher up; perhaps she sees in me what I no longer feel, and I wonder if she'll deliver me from always living in advance of myself; even as a child I would often turn around as I ran to catch a glimpse of my body trailing behind me?

And so now, with my eyes glued to the white strap of the bra below the still lustrous tuft of hair under the armpit, what swirling, what flash of lightning, what blast of a trumpet or ring of the bell announcing the first-class dinner service could interrupt this present that is my death, and return me to the future that is my life: down, down into that dark corner above the car hold to drive forth my poetry or draw a night in black where a single black strap, beneath a tuft of hair darker than night, remains uncolored.

I want that retreat: I will go down there despite the nausea, despite the stuttering that will catch hold of me as I search, asking steward after steward, for the calmest corner...

The ferry pitches and rolls over the swelling sea: just a slight inflection in the trombone music; she is used to singing over floating or rolling surfaces, that are often shaken, and answers the call with a fragment of melody without a falter in her breath; the din covers the name that the musicians call out, but I hear that it ends in an "a": is it "Stella"?

At the end of that fragment, her mouth settles on my cheek. Didn't I press my mouth toward her face as it turned away at the end of the melody? Did she push my mouth aside so she would only kiss my cheek? But it was with her mouth that she pushed it away, touching my mouth with the tip of her lips; why didn't I hold it back?

She must also have taken my hips in her hand, since I feel my hips again in a body that seems to have disappeared, just as I feel my cheek again, but how can I keep her mouth on my cheek?

I press my cheek forward, push it against her mouth, but the arm of my glasses catches in her eye socket; I move it back, and move myself back completely, in the deadly smell of gardenia. Did my chest inch up to hers, close to the heat that she exudes through her white blouse, lit up by a flash of lightning that also shines on the pink whites of her eyes?

Did she try to kiss my mouth, and afraid that I might become exalted, and since she knows me from the back, was worried that I might be sick, maybe she let her mouth slip over to my cheek?

My mouth? So it must be love, that's it! Even if short lived. If she'd only wanted to kiss my cheek it would have been maternal tenderness; but this is a new woman, who's come from far and who is going far, and whose maternity is covered over by the love of song and the necessities of the tour.

Even if I need still and forever need a mother's love, and I know that there is a part of that in all women in love, what I dream about is woman-man love, passion, pacification.

Now she's walking to the musicians, and I see the breadth of her shoulders across her back, and her strut that takes on a rhythm: what must I keep of her? Her voice? That strut? Or what her mouth left on my cheek?

Quick, write them down, but in what order? As I wait, should I put my hand over the ear, which, of both ears, has heard the most of her? Over my eyes, for the strut? Over my cheek, for what her mouth deposited there?

Should I wait on the deck for her to come back to me, or, as in the novels whose sentences I can feel drifting into my ears and starting to diminish the echo of her voice, should I turn my gaze away from her as she leaves me for another, or for others, and rush down the stairs with my impossible love?

On the pitching deck, I take my bag and go down to the cabins. Children are running down the passageways, covered, a few of them, with the same blanket; adults are playing cards on a blanket pulled over their knees, others are eating, reading, newspapers, books; others, alone, their pack between their legs, I see their throat swallowing their saliva—the anxiety of a new country and of uncertain hard labor?—blond girls in plaid skirts, watched over by a nun with a cornette, whose coral-hued crucifix beats against her gray scapular, above breasts whose aridness rings in my ears.

I go farther down, everything is full; farther down still, everything is full; I lean against a wall through which I can hear the vibration of machines; I'm going down to Saül's subterranean chamber, toward his body's walls of tears and filth, unwashed for so many days…

Why move like this, shift my digestive organs in this descent, three-quarters of the way against the current?

Since no one dies of vomiting, could I find a place where I might directly evacuate, through the floor, into the marine depths?

Should I open my poetry notebook, and, stomach on the floor, continue my *Saül*? Vomit, write, vomit, write…

But then, if that place closes, should I take out the "ball of orgy," pull on my jizz cloth, open the sheet of paper on which I haven't written for a month, and, back to the ground, hand on the member, begin the scene again that brings foam to my lips?

Write, jerk off, vomit? Where did I change from my knickers into my shorts?

A poorly lit passageway: I take it.

At the end, a heap of thick rope, thick chains with dust clinging to the grease; I step over the lowest part of the heaping mass: I can still walk and look without turning on the lamp in my shorts pocket; a metallic door slams shut in the choppy waters; on my right, under my palm, I feel the wide curve of thick sheet metal. A "new" Jonas, I walk to the door, grab it, crack it open: under the smell of grease, chipped paint, vomit, piss and excrement, a smell that I'd forgotten, Annick's smell on the low wall of the Anglican church above the butcher shop with its river of blood.

Is it because I've come down from the unattainable, a real woman, that my modest young girlfriend of this month of August returns to my nostrils? Why would sailors, the only inhabitants of these depths, carry around such a seasonal stench?

I enter; from the meager light of the wire mesh lamps in the passageway, I can make out a space about my size, with a wooden berth on the left.

To my right, part of the space is low, with thick metal or rubber tubing coming from below and rising upward, or flattening out, to the right, toward the back which is completely dark.

My chest swells at the sight of this berth, where I can sit and write; but couldn't that curved, slamming door close shut behind me with the choppy waters? And how would I open it? I look at the lock, identical on both sides, a latch without a bolt. I take out my lamp and reexamine the mechanism: what if there was a hidden locking device that no ray of light could detect?

I have to find a block to keep the door ajar; or, if I sat on the berth to write, could I, with my leg stretched, keep the door open with my foot? Since the door opens at the end of the passageway cluttered with ropes and chains, I cannot be seen, but I'd be facing the direction opposite the boat's movement, and risk a faster onslaught of nausea.

I have to write, I have to write soon.

I take out my poetry notebook, open it on my knees; of the three women, the Princess rises to my throat, a verse of hers, promising Saül a child to secure the dynasty and heal his madness with the sight of their son, posing, already standing at one year of age, on the rug of the small Israeli palace, baby teeth revealed in a smile, his small hands on the bars of his small, golden bed.

Will I have time to write how Saül emerges from his melancholy, and how long that takes?

My eyes grow used to the darkness, and I see my words progress on the page, square after square; a faint groan comes through the snapping, creaking, jingling, and grating: is it a rubber tube, in the darkness of the back of the room, as the ducts shift around? I take out my pocket lamp, shine it on the floor of the darkness in front of me, and I see a naked foot, with its woman's shoe laying beside it; the toes curl back like the toes of a child who is sleeping and dreaming.

If the foot is facing me, the leg and the rest of the body must be facing me as well: but how can I shine light on them without waking *her*? The heel is upright, in my direction, so *she* must be sleeping on her back; but since only one heel is visible, one leg must be folded over the other, or bent at the knee. From which angle should I illuminate her? First the ground around her foot; but if I bring the beam of light too close, its heat will touch her ankle; should I move the beam of light parallel to this leg as I begin to discover its beautiful, bluish knee, with no folds, in the darkness as I rise and move forward; farther up, the reclining thigh without the other leg; I move back and shift the light toward the left and see the other foot at the level of the knee; it must be that the leg is folded. I move the light along the ground toward what could be the bottom of the raised thigh; above the hem of very short shorts with brown hair curling out and wet folds, a bloody compress rolls with the pitching of the ship; my member, half-heartedly moved by the stanza to the pregnant Princess, thickens, and its sudden strength knocks me off balance.

Before falling asleep, did *she* take out the wad and throw it aside so she could dream more freely? Or, in a more brutal dream shaking through her entire body, did the dressing come out of her *nature* by itself, fall out of the shorts, and roll on the ground, drying in a ball?

If I shine the light along the folds of skin, it might warm up what they conceal: her *nature*, and wake the girl.

If I direct the light upward it will diffuse toward her closed eyes.

How can I illuminate the body from above?

I inch the light forward, but from farther away, along the folds of her skin then toward the inside: those aren't buttons on the shorts, but snaps that shine in the light; the shorts are wide open, and the fabric with the snaps upturned; the base of the shorts, slightly torn, reveals the top of her *nature*, its furry bulge, some blood stuck to the hair at the tear; and farther still, I light up the lower stomach, the high belly button, the splay of the right hip, the lift of the left thigh, the waist, a breast and, above it, the folds of a sleeveless light-colored blouse open on her chest; to the right, a large open armpit, a trail of hair, darker in the center; the arms are clasped at the nape of the neck; the light, on the side, shines behind the head that is resting on the left shoulder, and I can make out a black head of hair held back in a loose bun, and a symmetrical, fleshy profile; the inclination of the head, on the left side, reveals a beautiful artery on the right side of the neck—trust.

I lower the light over the curve of her breasts, and rotate it around the large pink nipples on the red tits. I search around the head, the back of the room, under the creaking tubes: no bag or satchel; the mouth protrudes toward the left armpit, the lips part, close, the eyelids flutter, the artery shines.

Why so few clothes? And why is she asleep here?

Did she open her shorts and pull up her blouse because she was too hot?

I look at her cheek: fresh, clean, no trace of tears.

Did she wander away from her group, lose her way in the depths, and fall asleep waiting for the day to come?

And in this retreat, safer than her own girl's bedroom or her sister's, did she uncover herself and stretch?

But why did she wander away from the group? Was it their endless rehashing of her beauty? And where else might she find real men to prove that to her, *bodily*, and in the intervals of their manual labor—but here, with the machines?

Does she also have a "ball of orgy," in her purse, up there?

I turn off my light, crouch down, and lie on the ground to her left.

With the backpack to the right of my head, I open my shirt and fold it out toward my armpits, open my shorts, unclasp my belt, unbutton my shorts over the bathing suit, spread them wide over my hips; in the feeble light that filters through the passageway—what did I use to keep the door ajar?—I see her *nature* breathe, the hair spreading open and shut; sitting up, I inch my hand toward her hair, my fingers above the furry bulge and the bloody tear: will I touch a *nature* finally; maybe I can softly peel the hair away from the fabric, push my hand in and grasp the entire *nature* in my palm, before it deploys its ostentatious butchery?

Is it what tethers her to the world?

If I place my hand on it, will she part from it and wake? My palm is over it now but doesn't touch it; all its heat rises along the lines of my hand: as a child, I'd keep my hand open above a nest of snakes, all my veins taut toward the hooked and venomous jaws below; if I could keep my cool in that seething heat, I could touch nests and scales. How many future male members—to be crushed by the Virgin's foot?— fill that *nature*?

A big jolt uncoils chains and ropes in the passageway. Have I prepared my crotch for women as she has prepared her *nature* for men?

She sleeps and dreams: better to sleep, and dream, in another world, one more powerful and more obstinate than ours, in order to experience, without fear but with new senti- ments, the men and women whom we each want for ourselves as they approach.

Let those men and women begin their labor on us both, sleeping, and dreaming!…

…On the wharf, in the fog of dawn, they push us forward through a hidden door, half-naked, already soiled with their substance and our own, to a sedan that brings us to some dis- affected auction as we sleep, a ruined, obscure place where boots crush fish heads and excrements under foot; as they search our cavities with torches, any laborer who yells out the highest price can grab the both of us, who've not been sepa- rated yet, and force us to have sex before we are allotted out.

Soon, no fragment of our body retains any memory of our old life; of the kisses, caresses, domestic touches of the past; now we only *descend* from those who seduce, capture, rape, rent, and sell us.

As the dregs of our clothes still garner a profit in the thrift stores of the foul suburbs, our orifices stretch back into suppurating buds, and our lungs struggle to emit the dregs of our ancient obscenity.

In my sleep, delivered from nausea, and from living, my hand stays above the cloth covering the chalice, and the large host, of the celebrant.

Christ, who was conceived without sin, emerged through that *nature*, breaking the hymen of His Mother, the Virgin. Are my hand and member forbidden there, as Christ's real body was forbidden in the chalice; what about my choirboy hand?

Upon waking, my wrist laced to the bag, and a sliver of day filtering through the passageway, I search with my eyes and nostrils for the girl whom I dreamed emerged from my side. The place is empty.

On all fours, I scour the depths of the room: my fist in the darkness hits against the tampon, its blood stained whiteness emerging in the dark, and a roll of the ship pushes it behind a pipe.

Above me, the sounds of cleaning, voices, calls, whistles, foghorns, grating noises; the ferry slows down and comes to a halt in jolts. What can I use to grab that tampon? My conscience keeps me from taking it, but if I sink behind my conscience, I can see it forcing me to take the tampon, even to grab it with my bare hand: my morals prohibit me from doing so, but the self of the deep, the one that will lead me furthest in life, makes it a *duty* to grab and take it. A greasy rag slides from the berth onto the ground: last night, the berth was empty.

The one who left it there saw me—and let me sleep: I feel around my crotch, grab the wad with its familial texture and crusts, throw it on the rolling tampon, close it over the cotton that I place and strap into one of the outside pockets of my bag.

Once my shirt is buttoned, my belt tightened around my shorts, I step over the heap of ropes and chains and climb back up. I take a washcloth, toothpaste, and a toothbrush from my bag, and enter the cabin toilets on the lower deck; in the rush before leaving the ship, should I take the time to wash, or should I use that time to search for the girl and the beautiful woman; but how could I speak to them if I found them, since my mouth is still closed on my mastication of the words of my dream?

After a quick wash, between two giants, I climb up to the level just below the main deck: I've kept an object from the girl, but what else could I keep from the woman than the gift I want to offer her of the page on which I have written *her* stanza?

Since I have an object from the girl, I'd better forego her, and find the woman as fast as possible.

Where do we disembark? Through how many doors?

I take out the notebook, flip through to the latest page, tear it out, fold it; will I have enough time to find the envelope at the bottom of my bag where I keep my papers and my correspondence pad, take an envelope and place the fragment in it—fragment that I'm trying to learn by heart: but wouldn't the gift be more beautiful if I were trying to forget it?

She can only come out with the other musicians; I follow the long exit lines one by one, ears alert, in a rush: in one of them, I detect some dancing movements toward the center, and hear the ringing of brass: is she there? But all the faces are pale; is there an exit reserved for blacks, for *colored people*?

If I let her go through a long ways ahead of me, a limousine will be waiting to bring them to a show in a casino near the coast, then in Paris, and how could I ever find them again? If only I knew her name, her stage name, the name of their group?

Should I join the line as if I were crossing it to reach another, mainly composed of children and adolescents, and stay there as if I were caught in the movement of the crowd?

I recognize her gardenia beneath a wide-rimmed hat, in the middle of the motions of a dance; then the trumpet on the mouth of a musician.

As she lifts her neck, I decide to slide the paper down her cleavage.

I choose the most debonair among the crowd to push aside to reach her, those with pink cheeks, and I move toward the smell of the gardenia that has been revived by the morning cool; holding the single sheet of paper against my hip, I rehearse the gesture I will make toward her cleavage with my arm and hand; but as I move nearer the opening to the dock, the fresh air makes her cover her bosom with a shawl. Between the packed bodies, I look toward her waist, hugged by the dark suit: where is her hand, where I could drop the folded paper over which she'd close her fist?

A small silver bag dangles from her elbow, but her arm is lifted toward her bra, toward her armpit; the bag is too close to the elbow for me to open it, as I sometimes used to do with my mother's bag, to find some change for the records I wanted.

With my bag in one fist, the slip of paper in the other, I walk between two giants; I see her, shoved around and her head flung to the side by a small suitcase that the two are throwing each other above the line of heads.

From what I've read about the treatment of women during raids, deportation convoys, and the selection process on the ramp of the camps, of the valid and the invalid, the women and the men, the children and the adolescents, from the images of the Virgin and the hymns that we sing to her, and from my mother, I've learned that a woman cannot be handled roughly, shoved around: women are the honor of humanity— although a number of them, of all social conditions, have helped and provoked dehumanization, the massacre of men, women, and children…

A sailor begins scouring the floor near the back of the cabin, and some lines I've read about Vienna after the

Anschluss come to mind, when the Nazis ordered Jewish women to wash the sidewalks with their underwear. For a time, I'd stopped taking out and strapping on my jizz cloth for the nocturnal act; and even here, that fragment from a girl in the pocket of my bag conjures up into reality that image of an atrocious epic logic.

The gangway is opened, and the passengers flow into it; I push against her softly with my shoulders, strengthened by bicycling and swimming, and open my hips against her lower back to feel her warmth; as I remember the figure-hugging suit in which my mother returned from Paris the previous winter, I lift my other hip toward where her right pocket might be.

But I won't be able to slip the paper into her pocket with my hip, I need my right hand to do so; but I'm holding my backpack with it, and, if I were to transfer the paper from my left hand into my right, I wouldn't be able to hoist up the bag with it toward the pocket.

To set the bag down at my feet would be to lose it in the onrush. And my left hand, expert as it is for beating off, is useless for writing, drawing, or any action: I can't take the risk of slipping the paper into the left pocket of her suit with that hand: if I were to lift the flap, spread the pocket, and push the paper in, my wrist would touch her left hip.

Should I transfer the bag to my left fist? And the slip of paper to the right? But in that exchange, I might skim her calves; and would she recognize me if she turned around? Would she talk to me? In the onrush, and in front of everyone, could she again touch her mouth to my cheeks? Wouldn't my hand shake too much in trying to find hers and sneak the stanza into it?

Here we are outside, on the gangway, then on the dock, still in the static shove before the customs.

By the way she pushes her hair back, adjusts the flower on her ear, slides her tongue and finger over her lips, I can foresee that she wants to open her bag and take out her makeup: I pass the fold of paper quickly to my right hand, and move my left hand back to the right.

She slips the small silver bag on her arm down to the wrist, opens it, takes out her makeup; I prepare my hand: will the little bag stay open as it slides back to the elbow, or will it close?

The paper, quick: have I folded and made it small enough to fit into the opening?

The silver mesh catches the Sun, refracts it into my eyes: I sneak the folded paper into what I take to be the opening of the bag, but feel it fall alongside my knee; I pick it up, and my head brushes against her right ass as it rises.

Her little mirror and lipstick in front of her face, she turns back toward my head, now upright; I have to lower my eyes to check whether the bag is still half open: but if I lower them, will she recognize me? I lower them: the bag is parted open on red padding, I reach my trembling hand above it and drop the slip.

Near the top of her face that has emerged from behind the mirror, her forehead gathers into bluish folds: does she think I've stolen an object or some money? Could she, a black woman among all these white faces, loudly denounce me as a thief, I who am white despite my tan?

From what she'd gathered about me the night before, wouldn't she think instead that I only reached my hand out to her bag to touch one of her handkerchiefs, and then to lift my fingers to my nostrils?

Her turn comes to pass through customs, men, women in uniforms; her companions have hand luggage; will the custom's officer ask her to open her small silver bag? Being a French woman, the custom's officer could unfold the slip of paper, read the stanza out loud and ask who wrote it for her. I blush till the roots of my hair burn: and what if the same woman ordered me to open my bag, the large pocket with the "ball of orgy" at the bottom, even if it's been dry for a month, and the small, exterior ball, with the bloody tampon freshly rolled in the greasy rag, how far would I have to defend one and the other, before what tribunal here in Dieppe, in Paris, then in Saint-Étienne, my father—as defense witness—by my side?

Because of the tampon, would they search for the girl? Would they push her to my side, before my judges, to testify to my theft, and confess her own abandon?

Then she'd have to confirm the state she was in when I found her, in the crawlspace near the machines.

As for the "ball of orgy," must I confess to five years of clandestine debauchery?

The custom's officer, gray hair under a cap, inspects the small bag, pulls out the paper, opens it: the lines of the stanza, written in the movement of the sea, and under very little light, seem so infantile to her that she smiles, folds the paper back without reading it; but her gray eyebrow stays raised: has she recognized that it's in French, and why would this American, what's more, this black American, have a child who writes in French, and poetry?

But the custom's officer behind her, behind the counter, a checkered handkerchief against his face, signals me to move forward; will I have time to turn around and see the woman's surprised face?

I have to open my bag: it's as if my heart were being sliced alive.

Where could I have dissimulated that *ball*? Impossible to burn it over there, or throw it in the trash, I'd have had to pull it back out with its added public defilement.

That "ball of orgy" is me. How could I separate myself from me? As he plunges his hand into the bag, will the man recognize the stench of a substance he makes his children with?

But he sneezes. Will his hand, which I've seen is thick and cracked, detect the "ball of orgy" at the bottom of the bag, beneath my extra clothes, my painting supplies and the Crampon Bible, and will his large red ear detect, amidst the commotion, the rustling of the paper, under his fist, curled around the jizz cloth at their heart?

Customs will only intercept objects of contraband or war: can a scribbled text spark their suspicion?

Have the spurs of sperm on the cloth flattened, or splintered off, during the trip, and the month-old smell somewhat dissipated? Could the jizz cloth pass for a swimsuit, wrung tightly in a defective washing machine, or in a wash that was too hot? But why would there be text around it, its letters imprinted on the soiled cloth? Perhaps he might take that mass for an effect of the rush to pack my bag before leaving?

The ball is so deeply buried at the bottom of the bag, he could not possibly think the hand of a stranger could have placed it there by mistake, or with ill intent; and what if, through one of his sons, yoked to the same act as I, he'd discovered, brought to light, and judged the secret? And so he might already be maneuvering his fingers around what he perhaps knows well, and that he's thrown into the fire like the idol that desiccates posterity in the testicles of his child.

But, upon discovering it, could he hold this ball in his open fist without incurring looks and judgment on himself? With the fingers of his other hand, could he open it, and spread it on his desk without blushing?

I could also face up to it: if I can go for a whole month—and even for several months during the school year—without indulging in the act that a momentary weakness makes me think of as an offense, it's because I master it, its frequency and its unfolding; it must then be an adult act that merits respect—or at least a proper inquiry, or a rationally articulated judgment—but whoever drafts the indictment becomes, through its words, an accomplice of my act and of the text that issues from it.

I must claim it as a right: it's from this extreme act of writing that I slowly cull the consciousness of my individual rights: that I abstract them from the Creator's surveillance—with His Son's clemency? But ten years after the liberation of the camps, can a child who is raised in the knowledge of what was perpetrated there claim his right to live, and even to exist, when only the survivors have acquired the right to any rights, on the condition that they have breath enough to demand it?

I see his face change: if he's touched and understood the *ball*, he will go no further, and will leave the pocket with the tampon strapped shut: with a feeling of relief, and with the reassurance and comfort that I find in his reason—so often disrupted by my own heart—when I think of those on which it will be brought to bear, I flash him a very wide smile, and share it in turn with the woman, who is now closing her small silver bag over my fragment of poetry.

But I who refused to be a good boy as a child, seductive, begin to twist my thoughts around the tampon and its greasy cloak, secreted in the pocket that I caress as I grab the bag— such little cloth between my fingers and this girl's blood, this blood of procreation—and my eyebrows knit above my smile: this morning, as I took up the stanza once again, should I have added a line containing that tiny bloodied cloth, that object of Biblical lust?

I see tiredness on her somewhat sunken traits: did she sleep and dream? And about what king, whose hymn, or whose dereliction she'd sung as a girl?

Will I see her reopen her bag, pull out the paper, and read it; and even if she does know snippets of our language, will she be able to restore its meaning, disrupted by poetry?

But because of my sisters' singing, and from recordings that some Fathers' have at school, I know that the gospel that she sings inside herself, all day, perhaps, is poetry, culled from the Bible.

Will I see her eyes lower onto my lines, her lips part and quiver at the proper nouns? Maybe I should have rhymed the rhymes more richly—the story of a king and of his captive who becomes his wife, and mother of their child?

Is the twelve-foot Alexandrine too long for a young girl whose breath races from her capture?

Whatever I cannot experience with her is contained in that fragment: but I want her to know that this is how I prolonged her life last night, how I invented her future life, and that she'll be rocking our child with her song, swaying the *blues* and the sea, the child of Saül, who shuts himself off from his God at times, and who goes underground to live in his own filth.

But here we are outside, in Dieppe, France, before the white cliff, the blinding wall. The wall of Babylon against which Robert Schumann pits the arpeggios of *Belsazar*!

Is that Sun, where a long flash of lightning brightens the green of the bosket over there under the black fog?

I follow the perfume of the one whose silver bag sparkles at her elbow; a black limousine driven by a chauffeur in white gloves slides toward the fence of the landing.

I am walking on my father's earth: what new arguments, what new force can I use to give form to that in my throat, my arm around his neck, to defend my rights?

I must finish my Saül and have him read it: that he may hear, and understand, why I pull away from his gaze, and how much I suffer from it.

He should open his heart to me rather than his Law!

Once past the enclosure, she climbs into the back of the limousine; luggage, instrument cases, drums arranged in the trunk; I see her through the slightly smoked glass, leaning toward her seated companions, pointing to me with her bag open as I walk to the shuttle.

Should I go up to the limousine, lean my body in, with its wrinkled clothes, its long, disheveled hair, maybe crusts on my eyes, my member disoriented by the border? I see her hand in front of the white gardenia signaling me to come; I walk up to the door that the chauffeur, who has gotten out of the car, opens before me: she backs her body away closer to her companions, and lays the back of her hand over the emptied seat; I see the spread of her pink palm, with, on one finger, a small precious stone on the inverted ring; should I set my ass there, an ass that hasn't been tightened by English food, and let the stone penetrate my *crack* a bit?

Where does she want to take me? To the casino? To see them rehearse? Her hand on mine, during a late lunch on the damask tablecloth? Or more simply to the train station where I want to walk, since I'm afraid I might be nauseous again in the shuttle. But if I climb in beside her, won't she kiss me, since it's still early in the morning?

On the cheek? Will I have the strength to offer my mouth to her instead? But all the gravity and passion I believe the fragment contains are dissipated in those gestures: the ordinary has no place in poetry.

Those big cars with their padded interiors, their silence, suppleness, and comfort mean immediate nausea for me, as if I were in a coffin, and extreme anxiety. And where would I vomit? In front of her again?

Would we both eventually believe that I'm vomiting because of her, because she is inaccessible?

I must also show that I don't obey.

I slip the top of my body into the car and extend my cheek toward her mouth; the musicians pass each other the unfolded slip of paper hand to hand; what if they had the lines translated and added to their repertoire?

I can already feel the nausea rising in my lungs; her hand on my shoulder, she kisses my cheek, but as I move the top of my body out toward the air, my mouth skims hers with its outward curl; her ringed hand tightens on my shoulder: how can one go toward an object of veneration, sexually, without degradation, without degrading the partner?

In the train, under the black, rainless storm, ceiling lights on, coal smoke flattened to the large windows of the corridor, with my backpack on my knees I try to find my place—without desire: all this landscape to look at, all this air to breathe through the lowered window of the corridor, all these passing beings to listen to and love…

But, beyond an armrest, a long leg, wrapped tight in a never-before-seen fabric, coarse and blue; a girl's leg, or a boy's? The folds of the fabric around the outstretched knee; I move up: beyond the lighter color of the thick, upturned hem, a thin, bare, muscular ankle; I lift my gaze above the armrest to the headrest; a profile sticks out that my member recognizes before I do; the head a bit forward toward the center of the car, the cheeks and forehead concentrated into a smile and a closing of the eyelids, it's her, the girl from last night, a navy sweater stretched taut around the breasts from the neck to the high and naked belly button.

A woman is seated across from her, her neck extended out to listen; brown-haired, mature, good clothes although some-what unkempt: is she her mother? But does a mother curl back her shining and humid lips before the lips of her big girl, and does she touch her naked foot with her shoe?

Standing in the corridor, from what little I can glimpse of both, and egged on by hunger, I feel my groin transported, my hair rise up. Skins and veins of my badly circumcised member stretch in the swimsuit which I've tightly laced up for the trip; the bare ankle in the woman's sandal rubs against the bare ankle of the girl, her blue sneakers in the luggage rack above her.

I move down the corridor and look through the side window with its raised shutters, over someone's head, asleep, his temple against the windowpane.

Now, I see her almost from the front, her chest tense, her eyelids half-shut, and above a smile where a hint of fresh foam gleams.

At the first stop, in the whistle of the locomotive, I hear the thunder, and see, through the large window of the compartment, a flash of lighting take the tree canopy in reverse, ripened fruit and the pink cheeks of the fruit harvesters.

In the darkened compartment—the ceiling lights are out, because of the lightning—all I see are her hips, held tight in the new fabric, the fly, closed with rivets, descending from the belly-button down past the bulb of her *nature*: the girl, her back pulling away from the seat, all shoulders forward, caresses and gropes the cool skin of the hips stretched between wool and cotton cloth, and the big belly button above a soft fuzz rising toward it from beneath the belt.

But her fingers continue downward, along the fuzz, under the top rivet, delve in past the first joints, the thumb remaining on the outside, hooked to the belt loop.

The foam swells on the corner of her lips. Her gaze, re-opened, settles now in the same direction as mine, but what can she see there in the darkness behind the panes?

What is she groping for, above her *nature*, on the flatness of her lower belly? With the tip of her ten fingers, in the fuzz turned into hair, is she searching for the tampon that I'm storing in the outside pocket of the backpack lying at my feet with its shoulder straps in my hand?

I can no longer see the face of the woman reclining behind the headrest, and the ankles are no longer touching.

Is her desire growing with the lack of that tampon—which I take to be unique—like mine from my member unsheathed for life? And will her eyes look down onto the panel against which my backpack is still propped? Is her *nature* itching for the tampon, as its blood continues to *live* in the greasy rag on the other side of the panel?

Won't she get up, and, eyes locked into mine, slide the door open, and lower her arm into my bag?

Or is it because of the framed picture, which I glimpsed in passing under the luggage rack above the head of the sleeping passenger across from her, and where, eyes closed, with all the strength of my shivering body, beyond the village washhouse represented there, I imagine a ground of sand and earth beneath the high and large awning of a shed; is it because of what I see there that she fondles her swelling *nature*, beneath her belt, its stretching top curled back? Is it because my desire grows with reminiscence—and with the desire to transform that memory into a scene spoken in my deep?

The train in motion again, what does she see in the frame as her hand sinks beneath her belt...?

...On the 14th of July, the month before, we are seated with some sisters, brothers, and cousins, in the dark end of the shed of our family home, among the flowering enclosures, on the side planks of the wine press; in front of us, large drops are falling beyond the awning onto a stretch of sand, earth, and sawdust, lifting pockets of ochre dust; behind us, the wall made of rammed earth and Rhône river rocks and, behind the wall, the sound of a brass band stifled in the heat; alongside the line of light coming from the lightning, and of the small ditch that deepens and fills with water between the gravel of the courtyard and the expanse of old earth, a boy and a girl begin to kiss, seated, wearing short clothes, on a large, hundred-year-old chopping block covered in gashes, he, from a farm, she, from the dairy, beneath the spider web extending down from the first floor of the barn.

They've left the party, found shelter from the storm whose electric charge they want for themselves. They haven't seen us.

As for us, in bathing suits, what are we dreaming of? Since that morning, an old man has been agonizing in the top of a nearby house, its louvers pried open with ivy, and around noon we hear his loud death rattle during a pause in the celebration.

In these depths, made soundproof by the piling of secular objects, and by the layer of powder at our feet, I hear the two panting, the boy's voice guttural already, the girl's softer and higher; from the back, I see her tip backward, and in profile, I see him bite her mouth and lick her face; I see his saliva dripping on her ear; seeing his elbow go back and forth, I can't tell what he's fondling of her, of himself. But how can one desire two bodies at once, which soon will perhaps make only one?

Two bodies of *opposite sexes*. Two bodies that desire each other. Should I stay by the wayside, simply with my desire?

And if I must split one from the other, it's myself that I split in two. Out of the two whom I see slide onto the bed in a cloud of rising dust, which am I, the most? Where could I be most desiring? That girl is me, that boy is me: but where am I most apt? In which body of the two, spewing dust beyond the line of large drops turning into rain, would I find myself at best to want what must be wanted?

She, her wail emerging from behind the dusty hair veiling her face, how can I be the body that intensifies her wail by its thrusts?

Has the rattle up there ceased? A few birds flutter in the ivy on the facade. Although books and films have taught me that women take pleasure *under* men—but is it good, following Faith, to know or give such pleasure?—my senses are repulsed to see me rise as dominator (or collapse as dominated): that is not the pleasure I want to satisfy others.

But my posterity would come from such moans!

I hold onto the plank: through small openings in the rammed earth, the lightning flashes above the jumble in the back: harrows, scythes, sickles, axes. If teeth and blades are sharpened, it must be that my member, out of the suit, is at its highest. But what good is it, if not to produce writing?

In the renewed rumble, in the gardens, courtyards, kitchens, public spaces, one of my sisters hears the cry of a newborn; here, beyond the limits of his practice, is our father delivering a new mother on her marriage bed?…

…looking at her as the train jumps, my eyes on her forehead and on her eyes, I try to locate a point in her thought, which I feel is of an extreme nature, and which would allow me to follow its unraveling until I hear her pronounce the sentence I've predicted: but does she speak? Through the sliding door, opening and closing with the motion of the train, I only hear her companion speak. Her eyes are now wide open and her mouth twitches with what she sees…

…of my member rising along the front of my hunched body, as if to shore it up?

Does she see the boy and the girl disembrace, rise, shake themselves and, in the slackening rain, go down to the washhouse below from which men from the town, in the morning before the parade, had pulled a bull who'd fallen in from wanting to look at himself, and who now, in the afternoon, snorts in the dry grass, penned in beside the spring flowing into the washhouse?

Does she see what my thoughts see? That they are both *washing their sins*, still in their embrace, in the water thick with fur and dung?

Who wouldn't want to be that tall, mute girl, so fresh, with her flesh of words impossible to say?

Girl or boy, beautiful and fresh, how I rush in! Their hand is mine, so is their mouth, their breast, their pelvis, and their hip.

Here, her hand grasps my genitals (like her) to hers, her hand mine beneath her clothing, which is my clothing; what is to be done with such a body, except to be it; to exult and pleasure in it from within? Desire doesn't stop with penetration: belaboring desire in twos until it becomes pleasure is just a preliminary step: beauty and desire are pain: what would lovers do at the apex of their desire: bite each other, decapitate each other with their teeth, eat each other's genitals with their teeth: erase each other from the surface of the Earth, leaving nothing behind but bone debris, vomit, and some excrement?

But once I'm her, what should I do? Devour myself from the inside?

Is it evil to want to be what is most beautiful? Is it a sickness? And as this beautiful girl, who would I want to lie on top of me? Who, and of what sex? What should I do?

All of me is good, without preparation, all is beautiful, desirable from all sides.

Open the thighs: but my member is in the way; isn't it attached at the root? Hair still remains around the extraction cavity. Is the hole deep enough? What does its conduit lead to?

Hands grope at my armpits under the wool, which loosens from my breasts: the joint of the thumb presses on the joint of the armpit.

Will the hole take in the member that yearns for it? Am I responsible for its hardness? Should I move my hands away, spread my arms as far as possible from my breasts so that the member can penetrate more deeply?

In the shadow of the body lying above me, is my mouth naturally red enough for that body's mouth to see, and take it?

Is the conduit smooth enough? Did I not leave something there that might obstruct it?

Can I move? Pull my back up the seat? Isn't part of my member...?

I close my eyes to feel the same, but as a boy who fucks me as a girl.

My testicles lie on the bottom edge of my *nature*. My boy's hand covers my girl's mouth and moaning.

Isn't the tampon soaked with my blood?

What will we do with our two breasts, freed from the sweater that she pulls up over her chest and back, as they thrust forward in the glow of a new flash of lightning and tremble as if from the thunder on the Seine?

Will she wait—and I with her—for the next train stop to rise, and all wrinkles, her cheek still swollen from sleep, cross the line of the doorway on the floor? I must stay inside her to experience some contours, movements even; how can I deduce what I am living, what I *am* without her? But neither are there contours to my thoughts: ideas, images, sensations, shooting thoughts, an infinite, nocturnal sky is sounding in my head, and even my hand above my skull cannot ascertain its reality.

And here she is, standing in the hallway, the curled-up sweater at her shining teeth, the flesh of the hip beneath the belt; and, from the splay of the hip crease, the *smell*, a reinforced or softened version of another, to which one must cede or be sacrificed: the smell of the Fall, of the serpent pulling out once its labor is done.

The same that rises from the *nature* of a fallen Eve, whom Adam will penetrate in ooze, at night, outside of Eden, both bodies on the ground, scraped by their nails, for the night.

Foam swells on the navy blue wool, below eyes slit into a permanent smile.

Her breasts, round and heavy, so close to my chest that I feel their root at the bottom of my torso, her hands that join over the belt to massage the stench, I haven't seen any of her back, or the top of her ass: if I touch them, am I still touching myself?

Does she see herself, feel herself, as me? Last night, why did she leave that tampon for me in the darkness, and why didn't she wake me up?

What did I feel upon waking? Did she touch my sleeping body? Slip her hand in my open shorts?

Did she play with my member? Or maybe lowered her uncovered *nature* over it?

Might she have heard me speak as I was dreaming? In what language? Anthony heard me, one night, asking for directions in English to the village where the rape had taken place.

Since I don't want to be seen next to her, with her breasts bare, I exit to the space between the cars: in the moving darkness, I see her coming toward me, backlit, but the lightning shines on her rounded tummy; she sets a bare foot on one platform, my feet are on the other.

The curve of the belt, its top rivet unhooked, seems made for my hand to slip in, and sidling my fingers inside, for me to pull the girl to me.

At the point indicators, electricity, coal, the lights blink, but her breasts, ours, don't need external light.

As I pull the curve toward me, I can feel that the rough and bluish cotton fabric—who will tell me its name?—is well-filled behind; she is now leaning against me, her loose bun tipping over her ear, her hardened nipples in my open shirt, I pull my hand out from the curve of her belt; arms loose, I move my mouth over her bare neck; my member very engaged under my shorts, I pull my stomach back; but she, her arms on my shoulders and hands partly linked against the nape of my neck, slips them down from my armpits to the top of my ass, which her fingers fondle: I must then have an ass? Contours?

Some stature? The movement of the platforms brings her stomach closer to mine, rubs them against each other, just as her mouth rubs against mine above.

Her hands pull up, and settle down, wrists trembling, on her hips.

The rotundity of the breasts keep the sweater pressed up along the throat; the growing smell of the *nature* rises toward the smell of the breasts, the mouth smells like mouth: never has a word passed through this throat and on that tongue, whose red I see between the open teeth in a yawn that stretches all the joints of this body that I wish were ours, a single body for both.

What is passing by beneath the platforms under our feet?

The ground of a planet close to ours, whose plates grow dislocated?

One of my hands leaves her hip, and covers one of hers, on mine, to intertwine with fingers unwashed since at least yesterday morning.

Scrape her *nature* with the fingers of that hand, past the curving of the belt, and touch that substance that incites to the unreason of the self in the great reason of the Universe.

Keep some of that fresh substance to coat the jizz cloth upon my return to my bedroom under the roof.

Has the woman in the compartment already kissed these lips that are now closing after a yawn? Has the girl renewed her saliva since then?

Does her new saliva, which my tongue begins to touch, come from her desire for me? And substance too?

Her smile remains unchanged; my tongue penetrates between the teeth, will her hand grab my member, entirely erect outside the suit, through the shorts? Re-individualize me, re-destine me to individual pleasure when I want it to be double, universal!

When we desire, everyone around must also desire; as for pleasure...

But if my tongue goes deeper into her mouth—the joy of knowing the inside of a desired body, of any body!—her hand will move toward my member; but if I pull it back, sidle it out from her lips, I sense beneath my fingers that her *nature* will quiver from it, and produce *substance*, beneath the thigh that lifts a bit and rubs against the furry mound.

But behind me, after I've extricated my tongue and turned my head, beyond the platforms, a ticket inspector speaks softly on the telephone in the service car behind a slamming door; my arm is behind her waist that dips backward slightly, again she yawns and stretches from her temples to her bare heels; my feet grip firmly to the platform: is the saliva in my mouth the saliva of a reasonable girl, or the foam of the *insane*?

Are the saliva, the foam, and drool of the figures of my deep sources of intoxication?

Is it the voice of the inspector in the receiver that turns her foam into drool?

Using her tongue, she dries her mouth and nostrils covered in the coal grit of a train ride before her trip to sea: is my saliva black already?

With my palm on her ass cheek squeezed into the unknown cloth, I could be hugging a poorly known Greek goddess, but a goddess nonetheless: not a clean and well-proportioned goddess, but an active one back from the depths of Hell, or, judging from the sweat soured into filth behind her ears, from the depths of the forests, or from the tiny hair my fingers fetch from under the curve of the belt, from the depths of the Beast?

Is she mute because it is impossible to speak from so far away, and from so long ago?

Or if a shock, some constraint, a blow, or a complete embrace forces her to speak, then she emits a cry, the natural sounds of springs, of the high canopy shuffled in the wind, grunts, whistling: will she answer the whistle of the locomotive entering the tunnel?

My member lies erect against the hollow of her groin: does she know what it is? In the thick darkness, her eyes, with whites that seem larger than usual, her lashes bat up against my lenses: should I take them off and slip them into my pocket as unworthy of an ancient embrace? Or should I keep them as an element of play for *later*?

Her stomach enters into mine, hollowed out by fasting, what do I have time to do to her in the tunnel?

I can already glimpse the chalky cliffs, white under the

lightning, and through part of the windowpane in the corridor, I see a river below, and the countryside gleaming under the black of the storm.

The ticket inspector looks at her as he passes us, wrinkling his forehead: those bare feet on the platform, that foam now gleaming over my face, those unknown clothes taut around rebel curves, that mute embrace, its small lapping grunts audible in the clanking between the cars, my backpack stirring at my feet, that feral stench rising in the stretch of the embrace, those human fleshed teeth jutting out a bit beneath the lip, now biting at my nostrils…

As the train slows down in the suburbs still partly ruined around Rouen, I see him walk forcefully toward the corridor of our compartment, along the line of people getting off; the shifting of the plates diminishes then stops: even before the travelers get off, three policemen in summer clothes climb into the train; did she see them?

Did she smell them with her sense of smell, which I sense is more powerful than ours? The nails of her hooked toes scratch my shoes and the underside of my bag, the nails of her fingers dig into my shoulders and along my spine; a tear, not transparent but white, then rose-colored, falls out of her left canaliculi toward the side of her profile that turns away from me.

Her cheek against my cheek, I feel her ear quiver against the arm of my glasses; from the compartment come voices, soft then strong, snippets of English, of French. Travelers have disembarked, others have climbed on, loaded with bags and suitcases, still others, who entered through the doorway behind us, fill the corridor: each voice of theirs lashes at the block of dreams where she and I devour each other.

From behind, a hand grasps my shoulder and pulls me from the platform, another grabs my bag, the hand at my shoulder separates my hand and arm from the body that tightens so strongly that the nipples could detach from the breasts; won't they crush her bare feet under the hard soles of their shoes, by mistake? But the arm whose hand unclasps mine from the *body* blocks me from lowering my chin to see. I tense up in turn, my teeth grind, my jaw itches above that powerful arm in its gallooned sleeve.

Her smell moves away: *nature*, substance, breasts, foam, sweat, filth, coal, hot hair...

The arm slides under my jaw, I shake the entire top of my body; with my bag in front of my chest I move toward the corridor; the woman is already on the station platform with their luggage, and "she," wrapped in a blanket, is restrained on a bench by other plainclothes policemen; her bare feet stick out from under the blanket, one of them curls over the other, a policeman bends down, tries to undo them, but the muscles hold firm; I want to get off but the door shuts and the train shudders away.

Such cold in front of my body, in the storm that breaks into rain! I dare not breathe, afraid that some breath of hers will be ejected from my mouth; our saliva dries on my face, on my throat, in my ears. With my bag under my feet, I sniff my fingers that moved from beneath the *nature* up toward... and my palm that got used to it. Overwhelmed by in her capture, does she remember me, my skin, my limbs, my mouth?

Is she spitting poisoned saliva at them?

I return to the compartment to sit in her friend's seat, across from hers with its rumpled fabric strewn with crumbs and buzzing flies: is it sweet or is it raw meat?

I scan for an imprint of part of her body, the dozing cheek, the space between the shoulder blades, the hip slumped to the side in sleep; a hair from her bun, loosened during our embrace, which her friend back there is maybe tying under the top of the blanket.

Will I be able to keep the mix of saliva, snot, and coal sticking to my face until my mother's kiss when I get home?

Is part of her tear on my cheek? Is what I am eating under my nails her substance mixed with viscous seawater from my last swim with Annick?

As I prop my shoulder against the headrest, I feel the imprint of her hand; rage—but, it was a hand from the brothel—intensifies the constant pain at my stomach, which only stops when I lie down.

Who is she? Her name? Her origins? The tampon that could provide her blood type, could it also provide the imprint of her *nature*, and what for?

Is she still cold? Are they giving her food? Have they separated her from her friend? Is she still biting their wrists? Will they wash her, bathe her? Will they put her friend in handcuffs?

Who is she? A relative? Her governess? A nurse from an institution for feral young deficients? Where are they from, and where are they going? From England to the south of France?

From some splashes of paint I remember seeing on her dress and blouse, I wonder if she is a painter, a potter, like the Australian woman we used to visit sometimes with my mother in the Drôme? Maybe they are Australian; she, the woman, the nurse, loved and raised her ward whose parents were killed in an air strike during the war? Did they lose her, or, after having fled the fire in their home, did she survive in the forest as a tiny girl, led to wild food by beasts, warmed by them in molting fur?

What animal does she cry like?

I place my bag on my knees, the outside pocket with the tampon against my member.

What I want is to lift it to my mouth, but can I, with all these eyes on me?

* * *

Outside the bus, with my heart beating, and my two youngest brothers fighting over my bag—will they open the inside and outside pockets as they rummage for their presents?—I look beyond the tall, sunlit chestnut tree, birds digging the earth under its shelter to sleep, toward the arch through which I can see if my father's car is in the courtyard.

I'd rather the car be there, and my father upstairs in the apartment counting bills between two house calls, than wait for his return; so that he doesn't have the time and leisure to prepare himself to see me, and have his grievances rise to the surface in the purring of his car!

All my strength falls from my shoulders, from my back: the poetry I'll write during the afternoon will give me back a good part of it!

We cross the *Nationale* and its bulging curve where the black tar melts during summer heat waves.

At the top of the dark, cool staircase, the light of the apartment, through the half-open door.

As I kiss my mother, I can tell she's been holding back tears, but not because of my return: before breakfast, in the light filtering through the shutters closed against due south, with trembling hands over the newspaper, she'd read about the El-Halia massacre, near Philippeville, Algeria.

Tens of working families, employees, Europeans and "Muslims," from a pyrite mine three kilometers away from the sea, were attacked and massacred at noon by an FLN commando joined by locals who had flipped in the frenzy of action: men, women, children, babies, their throats slit, disemboweled, eviscerated, castrated, decapitated, dismembered—some while still alive—with knives, axes, forks; girls and women were raped before their castrated brothers and husbands.

The words "slit throats" choke up the voice.

My mother retires to her room—she does so for each historic event. We have breakfast without her, with our father; then, in the afternoon, with my brothers, I accompany him on his calls to the north and south of our village.

As I rushed to leave, did I forget to take my dirty laundry out of my bag, which my mother, leaving her room somewhat appeased, and climbing up to mine, will take and wash in the sink downstairs; I feel her fingers at the end of my hand digging through the bottom of the bag and touching the "ball of orgy": will she refrain from opening my secret?

From opening the outside pocket in which I've stuffed the tampon to make it seem like a fold of the fabric?

Why didn't I throw that jizz cloth and that tampon on the rails, and let the train slice through them?

But what is that blood on the tampon, that dried sperm on the cloth, in regards to the bloodied child's mattress, or the shredded loins of the husbands and fathers of El-Halia?

That member that rises from my body during a session of writing for the *deep*, what a parody of those dismembered limbs.

I make that member rise from their bodies, for the pleasure of the text alone: I cut, and resew a jizz cloth from that mattress, impaled by axes and knives. Atrocity requires that we do not reboot the death-making machine: the body itself must be denied pleasure, used only for meditation, celebration, and faith.

If the killers are intoxicated by the blood they spill and where they plunge their furious hands, isn't the smell of drying sperm, once I've slipped on the jizz cloth, what makes me hard, and begin to write?

Not the smell of my own sperm, but the smell of brothel sperm, that of enslavement?

The good faces of the people of our "good land," as the city people call our southern slopes, judge me; my father's questioning as well, prodded by the interests of a tourist—he visited London before the war with his true friend, Jean P., a doctor *and poet*, killed on the road in 1939—but under which I detect a hint of irony and a menace. Only my two brothers bunch around me with their joyous bodies. The great purple digitalis, pricking up in their pine clearings, make my heart beat faster: their corolla harbor something to appease it: and forever: ever since my early childhood, they've been a storehouse, up there, with which I could change my life.

We enter the yard of a farmhouse whose latest born, out of thirteen children, has just been attacked and bitten by an asp viper. The red, decapitated snake lies on the windowsill of the main room, on a slab of granite with gleams of mica; the head is at the bottom of the wall, already visited, dragged, and rolled by vermin.

The fever has abated, the child is still moaning from the end of the room, underneath the comforter where he will fall asleep at the entrance of his simple, calm, and fruitful life.

What, in my body, kindles, transmits, and maintains desire—desire for the brothel?

Is it just its shameful parts? Shouldn't I rip out eyes, ears, nose, mouth, tongue, hands as well? Would my brain still lead me there without my five senses?

Should I slice off what circumcision has revealed forever, the head of the member—the head is to the male body what the *nature* is to the female one?

Without its exterior head, would the member still rise?

But once it's erect, wherever it is, Nature, night bed, the head runs the risk of being threatened, or cut, or ground to a pulp: the saw from a sawmill, below the grassy spot where I beat off and write, the tire of the truck squealing on the gravel of the turn above, the ax of the lumberjack, the shot of the hunter before he finishes off the wounded animal with a knife, the plane above, in the firmament, whose wing gleams like a blade!

Quickly, in my room when I get back I play the music that I could only hum, whistle, or beat with my teeth in England, but this time I play it for real, on the record player set in a sonorous wooden box that my older brother and I built.

Papillons, Toccata, Arabesque, Kreisleriana, Fantaisie; The Rite of Spring—my Christmas present from the year 1954; *Images* for piano: "Reflets dans l'eau," "Hommage à Rameau," "Mouvement"—that I stole from the street bin in front of a Saint-Étienne record store; for later in the night, the opening of *Manfred*, whose *fortissimo* I'll have to stifle under a blanket, since my mother worries that I should be so contemplative when I listen to this music, so ardent and endlessly reeling off an unspeakable secret.

The bag at the foot of my bed has not been touched; I bring my laundry down to the apartment; my mother is in the living room, and, I read in the paper that "many rebels were killed," and the "area pacified": what running, fires, rams against walls, searches, pistol-whips, spitting and killing by the tens, by the hundreds, perhaps by the thousands, hide beneath those ordinary words? Faced with a picture of the massacred lying in their own blood, in the blood of their children, the naked leg of a woman emerging from a mass of bloodied sheets on a bed, its headboard caved in by rape, my anger and my disgust are stronger than what I feel for the act that I commit in secret; I try to feel and think of myself as non-guilty: what in me, at fifteen, likens me to these assassins? What have I done, in a public life from which I'm still excluded, for my conscience to prohibit me from thinking of myself as pure, outraged as I watch impurity?

For that, must I have done the Good, realized an exploit, saved other human lives at the peril of my own? At that age, I've done nothing but defend my life, appease pain through my words, maintain my loyalties, and keep the secrets entrusted to me; but before those scorned, mutilated bodies in the nobility of their ordinary courage, as is always the case with the rotting or carbonized bodies of the death camps, and will always be, I try to *be* one of those killers, to feel the resentment and anger that they've felt since birth and that led them to crime.

When one reads the account of an extermination, or an action of radical murder, if one comes upon an executant who weakens, at a less cruel order, the strength of the account makes one feel, for a few seconds, that such is the world; since goodness reappears next to pity, I try to push my identification with the killer to its limits: knowing what I know of myself, of what others, including my father, think of me, of my weakness, my impetuosity, my madness, how far can I shoulder part of the criminal impulse?

How far can I, P.G., be the one whose action nauseates me by negating what I live by? That "one" is a human being like I am, even more "human" since he acts on the limits of morality, and beyond, *and can look at them from the outside.*

But doesn't he decide or execute his crime, whether individual, collective, or committed by the masses, based on my weakness?

I stop being a bit of him when he implements his will: I know where my will is, but it is not the one I am supposed to have. That very will is what the assassin possesses within, which he exerts and maintains on what is living; and which makes part of History.

A walk at the fall of day, my brothers and I come and go around our mother in the thorn bushes, broom thickets, tufts of blueberry; she prods me on and on, with a gesture or a word, in my descriptions of what I saw in the north of England. There are no constraints for Nature, the sea, cities; but for human portraits my voice often pauses at the edge of what her very sensitive ear could perceive as a confession: Anthony, the people from the circus, Kenneth, Annick, Douggie, the child with the mangled ear…

Only portraits of adults; I hesitate about the reclining woman in the house: I know that my mother, who was the eldest of nine children—one of whom died in infancy—who lost her mother at seventeen, and raised all her siblings with her father, in Poland, and who, despite the accepted constraints of her obligations as a wife and assistant, continuously dreams of the figures she used to know in Krakow, whom she has transformed into as many Mesdames de Mortsauf or Anna Kareninas, imagining herself as one or the other, will ask for more: hairstyle, dress, perfume, voice, shape of the couch: and why is she reclining?

The more I describe the woman, the more I know my mother will see herself in her: but maybe that mother is beginning her agony in this very hour, or is buried, so I search for anything to distract my mother from her questions; but why does she hold me so close, as we both shiver in the heat emanating from the tree trunks?

Once we've left the forest, and the myriad insects are surging back behind us, will I dare describe "Stella," the singer, my friend of the two kisses, who now knows, in translation, the meaning of the stanza that I slipped into her bag? I'd have to answer about her voice instead, one of those voices that I believe has saved humanity, and continues to save Blacks from dehumanization.

Descend into the ferry? Caught between my pleasure at showing that I could master my nausea by going down deep into the boat, and the fear of hearing the word *tampon* pass my lips out of an obligation to truth and because tampon and jizz cloth have now become one, I keep quiet in the sounds rising from the village where we prepare to dine.

If I make the girl appear, should I dress her in a small white blouse and a checkered skirt in order to justify my mention of her? Where is she lying now? On the ground? On a camp bed? Have they strapped her to an examination table? Is the blood flowing again from her *nature*? Did she escape, and is she running, nostrils to the ground, in the ruins of the suburbs? Is hunger driving her to suckle and eat the wool of her sweater? Or her own blood that her growing nails have scraped against the lips of her *nature*?

That blood, mixed with "substance," wafts up to my nostrils: to experience that smell, which is also the smell of massacre, so close to my mother! A mother only secretes her children!

The closer we get to town, the closer we are to blood. It is contained in what we can hear flowing under the town center— its cobblestones, sidewalks, buildings, covered markets, city hall—rarefied by drought, linens, wound dressings, tampons.

How will I find the compress—and its trail of darkened blood—that I have not looked at since I strapped it to an outside pocket of my backpack? Are the dogs already at the foot of our building, whining, fangs on the door?

Among the honking cars, and the trucks initiating the incline up to Saint-Étienne through our town, I try to detect my father's horn blowing on his way back from shopping, wanting us to shout down to him where he should go next; would the dogs follow him up the stairs to his office, and discover more dressings and blood there than upstairs in the outside pocket of my bag?

I hear him, so does my mother, and we walk faster; at the foot of the building, my father looks at us, walking hand in hand, with the impatience and reprobation of the working people for the leisurely.

Can he imagine that everything is working inside me, all the time?

And that most of all I refuse to designate myself as doted with an interior life that is superior to those of others.

I know he'll be appeased if I slip my hand out of my mother's hand; she only grasped it to help me and my brothers cross the street, which is very busy in the summertime—but he also wants my mother to assume part of the torment that he feels about me; yet I refuse that distribution: he is still my father, although I no longer feel like I'm his son, and it is from him that I expect *our* torments to end and the attainment of my freedom, a living made on my own, not by him with my mother's consent—as for her, impossible for me to touch her in any remotely evil way, even in my thoughts, since her body and her soul are also those of her young brother, deported and "massacred."

But if he grants me my emancipation, he will lose his father's power over his other children for a time.

Knowing that I harbor no ill will against him, and that I wish he were stronger—so that he could help me increase my strength with his, but away from him at the beginning—he senses that I will postpone my flight, and so he renews his fight with me, against me, with greater strength.

The confrontation having begun in the evening, after a very short sleep I am downstairs, in the night, wandering through the courtyard with its swooping owls, speaking the list of what I must take with me to flee; he comes downstairs, called out for a birth, and finds me rigid with anger: he places his trembling hand on my shoulder, it recoils. I refuse to be driven around as well. I no longer want to be seen at his side.

The car passes beneath the archway without me, behind it, on the square, the passenger-side door opens with the thrust of his fist, and, forgetting it's my father, I run toward the car and settle in as if I were hitching a ride in a stranger's car; once the door is closed, it's my father again, his smell of medicine— he stopped smoking since our mother is going to Lyon for a "treatment"—the warmth of the bed he has just left, of my mother, and of his dreams, which he interrupts to love her; I want to get out, but the car is rolling.

We climb, it's still night: a bit of fog in front of the headlights, a badger on the side; if I made a move, even the slightest, he would say something; as soon as we get up there, I will go back and run away! But as he turns into the farmyard, he warns me that it will be fast: the mother already has many children, this one will be easy.

I get out of the car, and steering clear of the stable where the cattle, mooing, could alert the family of my passage, I climb above the farmhouse where the smoke from the hearth, where a small pot of diapers is boiling, rises in the feeble glint of dawn.

I'm afraid that the cry of the newborn will weaken my anger; one of the house dogs has come up to me, without a bark, from the other side of the farm; wagging his tail, does he rejoice at the coming of this child, knowing he will dry its sanies and its mug, and later, catch the chestnut burs the child will throw to him in mid-air.

He licks my face and opens it. No cry, are the granite walls of the farm so thick that they cover it?

I hear noise in the yard below, the dog pulls my wrist, then my shorts, we go down: the child is born; its brothers and sisters escort my father to the car; I get in; his voice has softened:

"...I've delivered all of them. The mother should get a medal."

His right fist next to my left hip handles the gear stick, I see traces of thick soap and other matter that I cannot name, the light of dawn now shining on them: is that blood drying under the signet ring on his ring finger? His fingers also search through *natures*, but for the good of others. Is all that I do only for my own good?

As my fingers slipped out of the girl's *nature* on the platform between the cars, what else did they obtain than the pleasure to have touched the organ of childbirth? And I won't write anything about it, except in several months perhaps, a "crude" interjection in the text of the deep.

Whom can I tell about this lack of completion? Would an adult find in it a show of coherence and strength?

Because he is my protégé, our protégé, my brothers' and sisters' and mine, each gesture and sputter of his voice tears me apart—and why, so early, this inversion of feelings?

Is it because his mother preferred his younger brother?

Is it because of a hidden secret, a hidden evil?

Is it because of the war, seeing him face and hands against the wall along with other men from the area, rough-handled by the Gestapo and its French abettors?

Is it because I know that he is day and night, eye and hand on the misery of the world, and that sometimes he does not cure, and save?

We take the sunken lane on the way back: through the open sunroof I hear the loud commotion of the birds.

My face has become inscrutable, his face as well, and as we roll along the crest, with its view extending over the Alps, the downhill slope of the plateaus, the Rhône valley, our Dauphiné, and Italy, in the dazzle of the rising Sun, my lips part and from my throat comes the phrase: "The Great obstetrician before God!"

The car is now rolling on the tarmac, and in the thriving heather, I wonder if I should take back what I said.

He stops the car, but not the motor:

"What did you say?"

He, who can hear all interior sounds with a single ear to the chest, the stomach, or the back, wants me to repeat what must have touched him; with that sentence, I know that I am pushing my father away; I've said something about him and in his presence—although we were alone—something that should be reserved for an uncle, a small-town hero, and I've restricted him to a single specialty—judging its frequency—when he is *all* of medicine.

If I don't repeat my sentence, he'll blame my cowardice, and I'll be angry; if I repeat it, the sentence will touch him a second time, more harshly from being repeated in my mind, and he will be angry; I might as well repeat it and have our angers mix! I repeat it more distinctly, but without the tone.

Maybe it's because people used to call his beloved father, our grandfather, a doctor in the same countryside, "the Great seducer before God," but his face is pale in the pink light; before he orders me out, I leave: what can I use to bolster myself, to give myself strength, after three to five nights of very little sleep, to face him from the side of the road, on those granite outcrops, planted with juniper—what bone between their roots will what bird sweep away?—beside the radiant void?

My poetry, knowing that what I will write next will extinguish such illusory beauty? Those beautiful girls and women, yes, but whom I've just barely groped? The rolled-up jizz cloth with the secret writing? My mother's love for me—whom he loves so much he's always afraid that she will die?

How can I claim the right to live, in front of him, who is always saying that he's bleeding himself dry for the six of us?

A tree branch lies on the ground, carved into a thick stick, with dew still shining on it; the fragrance of milk rises from the misty valley; what love is our quarrel about?

The sky above becomes blue: not even a cloud behind which God could hide His face, and His voice, which might command my father to interpret my sentence in a positive light: doesn't my father deliver women who are pregnant through His will?

Nothing but this wooden stick between us, as we both shake in anger and fear, and each of us sees that the other has seen it.

Would you dare raise a stick against your father? Would you dare raise a stick against your son?

Is our mother, down below, rising from beside the form left by my father's body on the sheet, under the shining icon?

Is she walking, barefoot, wrapped in her long, ivory night-gown like in a haute couture dress, in the bright, twirling apartment?

Is she pushing open the door to my old room where our youngest brother sleeps, window open and shutters closed on the drumming of the torrent?

Once she has crossed that room, does she enter into what we call "the girls' room," where the youngest of our sisters is bedridden, with a large, suspended plaster around her hip and leg, fractured by the fall of a large keystone, dreaming, eyes wide open, before a James Dean poster on the opposite wall, the filtered Sun rolling over the sad mouth, and the crotch squeezed into the same cloth worn by the girl on the train— but what does her feverish stare see beneath it?

Is a kiss the only way to love? Will I tell her what I know is contained in that lighter *shape*, toward which all folds converge?

Walking on the red tiles down the corridor, does she open the front door? Does she put on her shoes to climb both flights of stairs, and on the landing, walk beside the coal stove, which is always full, and once she is past the maid's room with its sink with a trickle of running water, does she enter into the attic where some of last year's nuts, and the first mushrooms from the fields and forests are drying on a local newspapers?

Does she push the door to our room, which she has repainted for me, yellow walls, green beams, where my young brother now sleeps as well? Does she watch him sleep, in the mirror of the fine wood wardrobe, sculpted with flowers and fruit, a gift from the town cabinetmaker for their wedding, and that she's had moved into our room since she no longer wanted it in the apartment?

By the light coming in from the transom, does she also look at the large desk with its central drawer and side drawers, which we repainted together in green, and where I write my poetry? At my bed, not unmade but still showing the mark of my short, fitful sleep?

Have I slipped the *ball of orgy* deep enough between the mattress and the headboard? Why would she lean the top of her body toward the bottom of the high bed? Could she then see the *ball of orgy* sticking out from between the iron bars, jizz cloth and pad?

If she sees a fragment of written text, she'll lift the mattress to grab the *ball*, but my dreaming brother covers his head with his sheet and turns around; she pulls the sheet from under his head, buried face down on the bed, and positions him on his back.

Does she reach her arm and hand above the desk on which I've spread my notebook open on the torn sheet of the stanza for "Stella"? Why that torn sheet? For *whom*? I've given her, or made her read my first poems from last year: after all the poems of the year that I've kept for myself or for my friends, what is this hidden, torn-out poem?

As long as the poems have their origin in Nature, she approves them, when they depart from that, toward revolt, doubt about God, the desire to run away, and that she reads them without my knowledge, she tells me that they are not me, but I know that she is worried and glad that I'm affirming myself.

Does she hear me, as she flips through the pages, when she reads my interrupted *Saül*?

For the joyous adolescent who swims, runs, paints, who takes his bike apart and puts it together again, who asks for silence when music is playing, who still captures and raises many animals, and struggles and delays when it comes time to leave the ocean, why this despair, this God who turns away, this madness that dirties the body, this underground tunnel from which there is no escape?

What is that dream of quartered bodies, dismembered and nailed to the city gates?

And there he is, up there, fighting with his father: that torn sheet of paper?

What, in me, does he turn away from? From what I am becoming, in body?

With all the power of my imagination, and as I hope to become a father soon—it's either that or the monastery, and the exhilaration of the continuous celebration of God, or Sanctity in poverty—I feel his paternity over me, the way I've felt God's paternity over the world since I was a child.

His distress at the first steps of His creature, its first hiding places, lies, and pleasures; but would he later align himself with its tormentors?

I understand, and share, my father's distress about me; I twirl it among all the anxieties that I know are his.

But am I not the father of my poetry?

Concerned for every line, especially the weakest ones, and blaming myself for having created them.

Haven't I myself turned away from those I've written in a state of exaltation intensified by their being drafted in the study room, with my friends at my sides, in front of me, behind me, doing their homework?

The voice of two farmers comes from the misty slope, one, adolescent, the other, adult: a father and his son: laughter and ruggedness. Something about cattle, or mechanics, or maybe the son had fallen in love, and the father remembered the love that birthed the son?

I can almost hear the father's hand tapping and shaking his son's shoulder.

I know that if he speaks, my father will give me those two voices, as they move away one blending into the other, as proof of my infidelity, and as an example of how I might behave if I had a less "complicated" mind and a greater consciousness of the privilege of my birth. I can almost hear him, and my anger flares up.

Since last year, I've tried to find *physical* escapes to our confrontations: all language has proven impossible, and I know and practice another discourse, poetry, a coherent, precise, rhythmic and rhymed discourse of Law, and all he can retort to that power, and the new body that it gives me, are sentimental disorders and antiquated social customs. So in the rising heat, and the incipient sounds of labor, I am now calculating the time it would take to dash down, climb up to my room, grab my poetry notebooks, the prose I have already begun, my *ball* and the rest, and flee. But he'd be there before me, and in all legality, would threaten to have me locked up.

Now that I know how to travel, alone, and far away, and that, *among other things*—one day he'll learn that the adults in my *deep* make a profit from the body and voice of adolescents, boys *as well as girls!*—I could make a little money from my painting— alone at last, autonomous, *and* face-to-face with life, wouldn't I move forward faster in poetry?—and that my skills loosen his hold on me faster than his growing distance could have foretold, he'll keep me under surveillance for the rest of the summer.

If he sees me looking at the stick, it means I can defend myself: so he has a reason to contain me.

Know my rights: if I even have any. But how, and through whom? What adult would reveal the secret?

Rely only on myself: how can I make myself disappear, along with his paternity and his name? How can I let myself be discovered, far away, with no identity, free of the risk of ever being given a new one? To erase my name from my being, shouldn't I sacrifice a bit of my body?

Through the pressure of a heavy object, or long, regular abrasion, I could transform my face, make my nostrils curl, pull up my cheeks. Modify my eye color through instillation?

Dye my hair, and let it grow down to my shoulders? Transform myself into what I want to be, exclusively descendent from my mother and from God?

What liquid, what substance could I change in my voice? Weigh it down, slow it into a voice that observes, separates, weighs and judges; would poetry return my original voice to me? Isn't poetry the sound and the rhythm of the voice of the one who makes it?

How can I reach those tribes where scarification, face and body paint, sticks threaded through the nose would finally turn me into another, and would I only disappear completely by procreating seething and noisy litters in hammocks?

Two blond children come out of the woods and run, holding hands, boy and girl, along the line of the crest where rage—indifference?—petrifies the both of us like two casks of ashes. They are the two eldest children from the farm, going down to the valley to buy the medicine prescribed for their mother—the forester uncle who should have driven them was late.

My father tramples the stick with his feet, digs through the girl's very blond hair with his red fingers; the boy next to me pants in my place: anger should have freed up my throat, to let jumbled words spill out, but words are close to tears, and I will not cry.

On the backseat, the two children give off their natural smell: a shared bed, soap, milk, coffee, dung, pine; they speak to each other very softly, but in the fields or in the stables their voice is already very strong when they call dogs and cattle; in my distress, I make music of my immediate—that whisper—and imagined reality—the cry; and then what? The sound of my deep, and my throat starts working again: *"I wasn't responsible for being born!"*

We pass one of the last curves of the road at the bottom of the hill, and my anger—and my father's anger that tenses his hand on the steering wheel—reinforces my nausea; the car slows down on the gravel, I open the door and let myself fall into the small gully: back to the ground, stretched out in the pebbles, my eyes facing the sky, I slow down my breathing and expurgate my breath: have I grown weak? Am I not *also* responsible for being born? Does it devalue one's own crime to attribute its origin to someone else? Does it devalue the other person, and me as well? Does it devalue my father, since I'm his son, and we are One?

Whatever surrounds me, touches me, and speaks to me must be beautiful and good.

My father's shadow and those of the two children spread over me: as my eyes grow dark, I see above me the shadowy space between the boy's shorts and his thighs, and the pink, lacy bulge of the girl's crotch in the white, sun-drenched quivering of the flowered dress tightly hugging her wiry body: in the deep, they'll make sure to rip all that apart!

The bite that Douggie gave me on the right shoulder, near the River Aln in early August, and which was never bandaged, grew infected during the trip; and the night after my fall into the gully the wound festers, the fever rises and keeps me awake: now, three days after the Algerian massacre, as the anger still simmers, will I be able to continue my nocturnal act, after its interruption by my trip and by my stay in England.

While my brother sleeps, head under the sheet, I get up, take off my pajamas, slip the *ball of orgy* out from under the mattress—that ball is a symbol of life for me: text and sperm on the globe of the earth. I unfold the ball, the smell of month-old sperm mingles with the smoothing of the paper: my member is already up, and rises a few *notches*, as I call the phases of an erection: all I have are my testicles between my thighs, I'm free.

The words, the figures, and the locale reappear in the *ball*, unfolded on my open bed: I see them in English, and fill in the spaces that were blurred when I peeled off the paper with what I know of women's bodies now: but where can I put "Stella"?

Once I've loosened the jizz cloth from the text, I take it into my two hands and stretch it from one extremity to the other: sperm powder drops from it: should I smooth the cloth, or should I keep it the way it is, crumpled and in the shape of a hull, a cock shadowed by a testicular shape near the base?

At the back of the jizz cloth, the sperm deposits that are as thick as in the front seem less hard: because the sperm, when I ejaculate, runs quickly under the testicles, and the ass.

My brother turns on his side, then on his back, and as he folds the sheet back against his throat, he looks at me from the change in sleep and smiles.

I take the jizz cloth and papers and carry them to my desk, beside the poetry notebook, which is folded shut for the night.

My member hits against the front of the desk, its shadow in the Moonlight through the transom separates the notebook from the cloth with its sheets of paper.

Is my member the enemy of my poetry?

On the left side, poetry, art, the good, God; on the other, the unknown, abandon, the Devil with its contours lit by the Moon.

What good is this member, with its *unequalled* strength, for the act on the left: poetry, its thought and form—which I now know are inseparable?

Can the sex organs help, and intervene, in the composition of licit poetry? Later perhaps, the two sets that I'm touching with my fingers will be one.

But I now owe it to myself to experience those two opposites, and I also owe it to a stronger God than the one that I was taught. As for the Devil's part—how alluring he is tonight, filling my lungs and throat with crude words, fragments of narrative, and descriptions that my ear listens to and that my hand wants to transcribe right away!...

But I need more: pushing the chair away, I take the jizz cloth and, pull it on with my legs raised: the contact with the crusty canvas on the skin of my testicles, then on the bottom of my hard member, its top nearly flat now against my lower belly, adds to the sweat on my body from the fever: I am right; the memory of my latest crash, before my trip to England, turns the sweat cold; but if I arrange and rationalize the coming session, if I regulate the exchange between the rising of the sentences and of the substance in the *shameful parts*, I'll have at most an hour of pleasure beyond life; and desire will lead me where it will.

I'll be invulnerable, invisible if I want to; a new language will come from my throat, one that I've not learned; indifferent to the cold, to heat, stares, light, matter, garbage, vomit, blows. Nothing but desire, and the desire of the others for my figures—and my desire, who will have joined them! And desire for desire.

A breath of warm air passes through the open transom, over my shoulders and my back; truck tires squeal on the bulge of the *Nationale* below.

I lace the jizz cloth as tight as possible around my hips, and slide in my sheets of paper and the pencil. Rubbing the cloth against the edge of that desk, where for more than a year I've been writing, and then tracing the poems of my apprenticeship in careful calligraphy, with my dictionaries carefully aligned in front of the notebook, I leave the room and attic that conceals, during the length of the school year, the incriminating evidence of my accursed desire.

On the landing, as my left hip skims the door of the maid's room, my member rises even higher: is she sleeping, in her solitude? I am attracted by the blond hair and the breasts of my grandmother's maid on the other end of town, along the cobbled section where the *Nationale* grows narrow and which is named after my grandfather since he died this spring: can I reach it, half-naked as I am?

But I don't fold the top of my member back under the tightened jizz cloth, and I walk down the first steps; on the coal stove of the first glassed-in landing, I rub the jizz cloth, my member and my thigh against the sooty wood: the sounds of a falling body forced onto the rolling stones pull me from behind the frame of the landing.

I go down the second flight of stairs until I reach the landing of our family apartment; silence: on both sides, kitchen and bedrooms; the golden copper knobs of the two doors shine in the Moonlight coming through the top windowpane.

My mother is a light sleeper: during her adolescence she cared for her seven brothers and sisters as the eldest of her family, and now she is woken by frequent telephone calls; can she hear the rustling of the sheets of paper pressed into the jizz cloth, and the rubbing of that cloth against my *shameful parts*?

I can already feel vermin under my armpits: only worms can come from a body deliberately dedicated to debauchery, from the jizz cloth where the sperm, mingling with sweat, softens and sticks to my testicles.

I go down to the landing that opens onto my father's office; I catch a whiff of the smell of ether, of blood: the golden copper knobs on the door of his office, and on the waiting room door, that my father sometimes grabs with his fists when he scolds me.

In the basket full of bloodied waste, the blood changes, ferments: are there tampons there, like the girl's tampon that I have in a still unopened outside pocket of my backpack?

Blood is missing from the act, but I've seen it flow beneath me, between the elevated platform of the Turkish toilet of the school of Notre Dame de Joubert, and the first time that I masturbated again after my circumcision.

I rub my front parts against these doors: I can disperse the smell of my father and his voice throughout my deep, I can make his hands act there, but right now, it's through my body that he will live there.

My bare feet on the steps trample the footprints of his shoes, or of those of his working-class patients, that will be swept away in the morning.

Down below, between the doors to the courtyard, to the post office, to the printers and to the main entrance that opens onto the central square, I walk, member and papers in my fist.

I've already gone farther than where my episodes of sleep-walking have taken me, and I'm wearing my glasses on my eyes; if I were discovered, could I pass for a young poet, raving with his poem in his underwear?

I pull open the large front gate and stand on the sidewalk ledge. In the sky to my right, above the rounded mound of the pine trees, the Moon; to my left, at the bottom of the Côtaviol mound, the statue of Joan of Arc in its square; in front of me, the black and still smoking bulge of the curve of the *Nationale*.

A draft of warm breeze pulls in the effluvia from the large dumpster constructed behind our building to the right: a very high cast-iron Crucifix on a stone pedestal rises between that dumpster and the facade with the window of my mother and father's room, the room in which all of us were born, except for our eldest.

But first I must cross the square over to the large chestnut tree, toward the aromas of lemonade and wine wafting from the tree to the row of cafés-bars; then to the butcher shop where the flies stay late hanging on the beaded curtain at the entrance: maybe around there I'll discover the remains of a carcass, or large bones, beside which I can project the lunar shadow of my re-erect member.

Besides two of the three real alcoholics of the town, who are rolling on the melted tar, it's empty. A few illumined windows near the top of the dark houses: the sick, the impotent, there is no danger they'll come down for a breath of fresh air.

Lovers on the bench against the stone pedestal of the Crucifix? I can't see them, but if I veered to the right, and they saw me, what would I be in the giddiness of their embrace? Once their embrace was over, wouldn't they make me their accomplice, since we'd all be the same age? Unless the stench of the jizz cloth made them uneasy—but wouldn't the stench of sperm induce two lovers to finalize the act?

I count the minutes of my descent from my room, and of my station on the edge of the public square; it's already much longer than what I'd managed in my sessions before England.

But white headlights appear, far away in front of me in the narrowing of the *Nationale*, and blind me.

A vehicle, a red van with a yellow roof, slows down, then stops on the sidewalk behind the chestnut tree; the headlights turn off, the parking lights reveal the license plate: Germans.

Three, five people exit from the side door, all of them are young, blond and adults, except for a tall woman whose hair is gray. Two of the youngest ones, a boy and a girl, carry large transparent canisters to the public fountain on the other side of the road, which they fill in silence with cold water with the pump; others pore over large, spread out maps with flashlights; another one, my age, more wild, who is wearing leather shorts with suspenders, sulks against the chestnut tree; a young girl with long blond braids crouches next to the sidewalk above a sudden stream of water.

Where is the man?

Will I move up to those figures from the cursed nation? Once there, will I be able to control my nausea upon hearing their language? If the text must come to be, why not deliver myself to this Satan with five blond heads and a gray one, just as I am, soiled, shoulder festering, fever in my eyes?

Perfect my renunciation by giving myself over to the people who assassinated my mother's cherished brother? Let the tall, gray woman, once past the border, a large black wallet in her left hand growing thick with the wholesome rustling of good money, grab my shoulder, with its undressed wound, in her right fist!

After greed, another gray woman awaits me: Prostitution.

And later, in the darkness of its locales, one more: the German Language.

In the regions where the resistance is active, away from the safer, larger roads, *they* travel at night.

I hear spurts of German in the voices, the throats, and the heads of the children and adolescents, poor yet free, who answer each other from one window to the next, from one pavement to the next, from the tall, black courtyards leading to the locales of public debauchery where we are passed from knee to knee: is the mute girl from the ferry and the train on the ground, knees spread wide, her disheveled hair trampled by zealous feet, her tampon wet with fresh blood rolling on her stomach, which is gaunt between her hips as she breathes out?

Does the soiled, burnt door open onto a tall gray woman carrying the naked, sleeping body of the adolescent with the mangled ear in her white arms: will *sex* wake him up? In the back, is that Douggie's grunt among the sounds of big, milk-less breasts shaking, and the screams of bitten women?

Does Kenneth have the right curves to be purchased, and forced to lie down in the dive?

From English to German, morality emerges through the voice; flat against the ground, is Anthony's throat swelling with German? Will Annick's ancestry, her social circle, her goals at school, and the remote region where she lives save her from abduction and rape?

But the figures of my secret writing lining the sheets of paper that I've slipped into my tightly laced underwear are different than those doubles who are devouring my stomach: succinct, brutal yet with no clear contours, bound to fade away.

Each figure whom I bring onto the scene has a beginning and an end, an origin and death. Each figure whom I take from one locale to another later reappears in the narrative. There are no secondary figures, or they are taken up again in such a way as to become main figures; and the main ones, their importance temporarily reduced, will necessarily return onto the scene. My boner grows from what I haven't put there yet, those empty and obscure spaces between figures, between their movements, those words that are still only signaled by quotation marks that close on empty space, those voices described by a single code word; so I can have a boner whenever and wherever I want! With no real body or text in front of me!

The little girl, still crouching, far away, watches me, and bites her braid folded against her throat that shines in the effort to defecate.

The adolescent in the leather shorts turns around, his back to the tree trunk, his stomach jutting out, and his right leg over his left knee: do we both suffer from the same unspeakable torment? But with his blond hair and young, supple body, no need to groom him for the brothel!

The two others walk back to the van, their canisters full. In the short time left before they leave, can I *really* transform the tall woman into a procuress, the adolescents and children into bait, simply through an action of my will?

If they are exposed to me, with my rags, my stench, my mouth with its protruding tongue, can I transform their heart, their ancestry, and their destination?

Even here, as they triumph with their mechanics, their objects, and their stature, they are defeated, cast out by the Universe; they will obey the will that rises under my forehead: even as Procurers of debauchery, I am reinstating them into a society without Blame.

All of them have climbed back in the van—when and where will they sleep?—the tall woman in the front turns on the vehicle; on the bulging curve of the road, the blond faces blink through the back windows: did their father die at war? From what weapon? War or massacre?

The tall woman's gesture on the gear stick is the movement of her solitary will.

Up near the free schools, the low motor at the back of the vehicle purrs and rattles. Cold has solidified like a block in front of me, I cross through it under the chestnut tree still full of the day's warmth; I can hear a few birds who have been woken by the firing of the motor, as they huddling close against each other, making small cries; I walk along the far end of the sidewalk, where I know that the gutter water carries the child's excrement, and maybe a hair from her braid.

Is the carefree nudism of Germans, which everyone adds to their infamy, compatible with my debauchery, the dive I live in, my rags, and my spilt wine?

Can their order, and their method, cohabit with the stupor, the erring and squandering of bodies in the deep?

In my constant projection of thought, I forget that I am half-naked, and have already reached the end of the row of businesses: only in the stench of the butcher shop rising from the gutter where part of the animal blood is poured do I slip my hand back into the jizz cloth, below the exposed head of my very tall member and the top third of the sheets of paper.

A bit farther, at the bottom of the alley that runs down from the mound, I know that another, smaller dumpster is always full, and also that dogs go there day and night, but I turn back: the two drunks have wandered into the town center on the solidifying tar. They might see me, shout, and lights would go on in the windows, with heads appearing on the windowsills.

The large blue and red eyes of one of the drunks, stare, low to the black bulge of the ground, toward the darkness through which I walk.

From the side of the dumpster that projects past the angle of the butcher shop, shoes emerge from the trash, some women's high heels; my toes curl against the sidewalk on which I've climbed; I inch backward toward the marble storefront, place my ass against it, barely covered by the very tight jizz cloth that rises up the crack of my ass. Am I not, along with my figures, meat to desire, to slice, to spread out, to pound and vomit after use?

But before that, we must find a place, expose ourselves, extend our front parts forward—asses are for girls and women—until the passersby can brush against them as they go; we must spread our thighs, attract to our well-endowed *spreads* the most women possible—men are for women, but, in the caresses, the pursuits and coercions of the brothel, workers could touch us, help the gray women and the other women count our earnings, tame us, teach us pleasure, and pull us away from the scene after use.

Could I sit here, my back and the nape of my neck leaning against the white, red-veined marble, my legs spread out on the sidewalk, and pull the papers from the jizz cloth, push, force my straight, hard member under the small piece of taut fabric, open the paper on the concrete and start to write with my right hand, while the left one starts to fiddle with the member, arched and compressed into the cotton triangle caked with old sperm?

Why squeeze it so tight? Is it more attractive, more desirable? Does that constrict its strength, increase it through constriction, increase its power and the extent of its desire for the text that is being written to the right? The more the member is constricted, almost negated, the more action it can endure, and the more it acts where it must not, and the text along with it.

But do I run the risk of breaking my member in half with such wear and tear, and losing not only its natural use, but the desire that helps me write onward, more deeply, and in a more adult way than my poetry which is visible to all?

Here, above the animal blood that flows toward the gutter, could I spill my sperm in transparent clots, add a few nouns, some interjections, some empty quotation marks? Wouldn't the butchers, man and wife, hear my breath, and the tensing of the muscles of my calves through their open window above the storefront?

The ringing of the quarter-hour on the church tower bounds the space that separates me from my room, its transom hidden by the leaves of the chestnut tree.

Go back already? Walk beneath the chestnut tree, along the shops and terraces with their chairs flipped over on the tables? Take the alleyway that climbs and turns along the slope of the mound? But maybe there are old people, sitting, awake, at the narrow windows of their houses in that remnant of the medieval quarter?

Across from me, beyond the tree and the square, the blackest black of the arch under which my father's vehicle, Jeep or Fiat, shuttles back and forth, during the day and in the night.

Up there, in our apartment—but is it really still mine?— there is no light behind the shutters: he must be asleep. I walk under the tree, my bare feet between the torn chestnut husks. As I shift to the edge of the bulging curve in the road, I see that the bench is empty beneath the Crucifix; but to reach the large dumpster, how can I bridge the space in front of the post office, under its bright lights?

Should I wait for a truck to pass, and run along with it, at the same speed, in its shadow as it rumbles? But won't the trucker, and especially his co-pilot, see me running along the vehicle as if I wanted to climb in? And, with the heat, my fatigue, and my desire to be satisfied far away beyond the pass, in a truck stop in the mining suburbs of Saint-Étienne, half-naked, with my jizz cloth pulled so tight that it gives me female *genitals*, will they take me for an adolescent girl to invite into the cab?

Can speed cancel out presence? The faster I run, the less visible I am? But can I run very fast with my member erect? My shaking testicles rubbing against each other could make me ejaculate as I run.

Or I could play the adolescent running away from the desire of women, from the brothel where he's been locked up.

But is *playing* really necessary, as the jizz cloth squeezes me tight, as my wound festers, as my glasses hug my eyes, and as the text lies against my stomach where I *realize* the brothel with all my heart, and all my knowledge; am I not enclosed there for life?

Is this flight only to a more desirable, more sacrilegious brothel?

I run in the light; the insects that could veil the bulbs grow rare in this late August; I slow down near the bench; I lift my eyes to the crucified body. Feet, legs, knees, thighs, loincloth, hips, sunken stomach, ribs turned outward by asphyxiation, armpits, neck, face, crown of thorns, all in yellow copper on the black cross: with His eyes lifted toward His Father in heaven, can he not see me?

The stench of the large dumpster is stronger in my nostrils than the rumbling of the torrent in my ears.

During the spring of 1942, some Germans had parked their vehicles against this dumpster, and called to each other in the night; I felt my mother's palm tense up against my forehead at the grumbling of these voices carrying the burden of extermination.

Would they have made me confess my secret act?

Barks break out in what remains of that memory, while the sounds of the motor from the silent family's van peter off, up there, in the first curves of the road.

I sift through the stench, with my nostrils, for the smell of rotting flesh: what if, in that smell, a stronger desire against death could pull wilder, more feral text from me?

Where can I sit and support my back and the nape of my neck, or, better yet, lean the way I do against a pillow, with my heart appeased, to masturbate and write? Against the dumpster? But the dogs are leaning their front legs against it? Should I lay my neck on one of the pillars of the cast-iron railing of the embankment, and let foam splash against my lower back as the torrent crashes against the rocks on its way down into the ravine and into the tunnel?

No water, too purifying for the "impure" act!

Rats nesting in the walls climb up to the dumpster, fight the dogs for waste; will the text still come into my throat and hand, or is this too much? Should I shut my eyes when I begin the act, once I'm seating or lying down?

At the base of the high wall of the drugstore, under the shop window where I glimpse large jars of fish, I sit with my jizz cloth slightly loosened and my member freed, paper in my fist, between two clumps of grass dried by human and animal urine.

Up across from me, the parted shutters of my sisters' room, the shutters of our youngest brother's room, and at the top of the facade where the large Crucifix casts its shadow, the parted shutters of our mother and father's room.

I stretch my legs on the tar of the embankment; the tails of the dogs wag as they rummage; the more they eat, the more they fart. What are they eating?

One of them turns to me, his muzzle closed on a large bone with two bloodied joints: I'll give his vague stare to one of my adolescent or adult figures; the same stare is brewing in my own eyes.

Under the streetlight, I examine the lines that I wrote last month on the dried sperm-embossed paper: some words have dissolved in its juice. Should I search for them, rewrite them, but then desire would be dulled by the excavation of memory?

Write new things, all that I have learned, all those real figures that I was close to, and that I touched during the month of August?

The member will decide; and to lead it, I quietly mouth both paths: old or new?

I put the member back into the loosened cloth, as if, after the orgy, it had been pulled, taken off, slipped on again, laced up, tugged at, stretched out; I churn the member in it and pull the testicles in that had been lying on the loose gravel.

The scene from July comes back to me, before I went to England, and hardens my member a bit more, but I hold it back under the cloth; it is not my hand; *it is never my hand* that churns the member under the cloth; it is the hand of the females and males who enter into my deep, who feel, weigh, evaluate, and maybe try?

And whose body is this, seated, lying at an angle?

Whose are those legs tensing at the calves? Whose armpit is this, open on the right, and whose young hand releases back onto the paper that lies directly, with nothing underneath, on the street along the embankment? Whose is this fist that smooths the member now completely bare, its circumcised head shining in the smell of the sweaty fur of dogs?

The heart that moves the spirit, and that spirit, are *mine*; they were at least desired by that God whose Son hangs above me, and on whom I try to see what hides under His martyr's loincloth, from the side, through my glasses.

The roar of the torrent covers the yelping of the dogs and the cries of rats: how can I single out the voices of my adolescents, and those who use them, in that roar?

If I stuffed my ears with wet clay or goat droppings, I'd have the beating of my heart as background noise; in the void, how could I work on that beating, which could cease at any time according to the will of He Who *is* beyond Time?

To the right in front of me, vehicles coming upslope from the south—from the Rhône and the Ardèche—would shine their light on me when entering the bulging curve, and would scrutinize me with their headlights, others, more rare, coming from the east, the mountains—farmers taking their production to market—would drive alongside me.

If I hear a telephone ring up there, my parents' lights will turn on: if the call is for a delivery to the east, in the mountains, my father will take the shortcut and drive his car on the road along the embankment; if it's in the Noyers neighborhood, he'll certainly pass this way; if it's to the north, toward

Saint-Étienne, his right high beam will shine on the entrance of the embankment where I'm sitting.

If it's to the north west, south west, the Haut Vivarais, once he has crossed the *Nationale*, he'll take the cobbled alley that runs along the covered marked toward the church and the road to the Haute-Loire, and he could see me in his rear-view mirror.

Our canton is one of the most fertile in France, especially in the eastern and northern mountains; up there, at the end of the crest where we fought last night, I know that at least one family is complete for more than nine months; but in the intervals of the torrent's roar, I can hear the moans of women on the edge of childbirth; I can see its stream grow tinted with their waters.

But once I trigger the text on the paper, I must fold the member back under the cloth; text takes precedence over pleasure: if I allowed the member to discharge freely, I would isolate it, imbue it with a power that it does not have, and become used to looking at it as an idol.

The member is the servant, barely the aid-purveyor of the text; in the text itself, the member is just a necessity.

To describe it there would even indicate a moral, spiritual, and artistic weakness. It's what surrounds it, groin, thighs, pelvis, that acts on the desire of women; it can only be used there when it is grabbed, like the shoulder, neck, or hair as purveyors, buyers or madams rope in their prey or their goods.

An emergency in the town, a delivery, a fainting fit, madness, murder, would light up the bay windows above me, and the high sidewalk of the pharmacy as well.

I stiffen against the wall; some text emerges against the faded squares; I must go at it harder; as the hand churns the member in the soiled cloth, is that enough for the text produced to scandalize me, and make that livid martyr agonizing up there blush?

One of the dogs pulls out the long carcass of a dog, a bitch, from behind the heap of kitchen scraps, bathroom trash, cooked meat trimmings, and waste from the saddler, the hairdresser, and the pharmacy—I see its nipples on what remains of a skinned underside—jumps to the foot of the dumpster, drags the carcass. Who ate its insides? Who killed this bitch, its fur gray but scattered in small tufts, its skin gleaming in shards in the dog's slobber as it snaps at its back.

Black or rust, the fur wouldn't be suitable for a jizz cloth cut from that carcass; too exotic, even if the skin is neither panther nor tiger: what my member, my heart, my entire spirit now, and my right hand desire, to the point of moaning, is another kind of savagery.

Who killed the bitch? Dogs? A couple of rats? Children, by stoning?

What did it die of? Under the tire of a truck? Of illness, during labor?

Which death does my desire most avidly crave?

Is its eye intact? Would my desire end at its dead stare?

How can I pull the dog off the carcass?

If, spreading my legs and churning my member until it juices, *I* discharge, would the dog turn his ears, his muzzle and his head toward my moans and toward what my hand is churning? Would he drop the carcass to come lick the sperm disseminated at the center of my shaking body?

Lick the top of the jizz cloth through which the hot sperm sticks to my hand? Probe my groin and under my testicles to lick the clots from the hair under the fabric, and rising along my stomach and my chest, lick my mouth with my juice on his tongue?

Bring his muzzle back down between my nipples to my belly button, and probe under my thighs and testicles up to my crack? Climb back, wrap the mass of fabric and flesh in his warm breath, snap at it...?

But if I discharged before I'd written a sufficient amount of text, that would mean that I wanted neither that carcass, nor that text.

But couldn't the lapping of the dog's tongue make my desire live again, stronger? But then why not experience that desire wrapped around the dog, with my right hand free to write?

His cheek rubbing against mine, his tongue smacking mine, our drools mingling, his own member protruding from his squat hindquarters, rummaging through the jizz cloth heap, and spreading his own slimy substance there as my member stiffens.

But what should I do with the carcass, whose force of desire I must not lose?

Pull it with my heel, my curled toes, toward our embrace, but shouldn't I first whisper the question in his ear—and would I have the time, and a stable enough hand, to write it on the paper to my right? And maybe he'd lick them, snap at them, stop me from writing?

And once I'd dragged the carcass between my legs and his, should I pull it up from beneath his stomach onto my triangle, pointed and still shaking from the last jolts of the new discharge?

Will the dog let me get up, crouch down, walk on all fours toward the carcass? Are my wrists and hands strong enough to rip another jizz cloth from it, that I would slip over mine?

Shouldn't I instead get up, leave this place, return to our building, climb up to the apartment, open the landing door onto the kitchen, enter the dining room, walk to the tall, narrow, diamond point armoire where my mother keeps her samples, scraps of fabric, patterns, sewing kit, and take the large scissors whose snapping stops, much to our dismay, when our father returns? But what if she decided, in the intervals of sleep rarefied by the more and more frequent radiation she receives in Lyon, to get up to finish a dress forfeited by one of my sisters, where would she look for the scissors that I often borrow to cut the paper for my drawings and gouaches, or for my notebooks of calligraphed poetry? In my room? Upstairs, where my bed is unmade and empty?

Where would she look for her scissors? Would she open the poetry notebook on my desk? Would she forget that, in a fit of sleepwalking, I could be outside, my pajamas rolled in a ball on the unmade bed, naked in the late summer night?

Are the scissor blades sharp enough and the pivot robust enough to carve into the skin of the carrion, even if it is softened by rot?

And once I'd carved the carcass, what disinfectant would work for such a job? And would the mirror of the blade retain some images? But the sacrilege that my growing desire wants to perform would be accomplished: in desire, everything must be besmirched if not killed.

And penetrated.

Although using scissors is a pleasure, all I know about using a scalpel is what I see and hear when my father manipulates one; but does carving by incision take longer than cutting? As much for my desire as for the text, should I draw out my carving of the carcass?

Let's go down through the circular staircase that leads from the kitchen to the waiting room, let's open the two doors separated by a small cubby-hole where my father keeps his X-rays; let's enter into his office with its shutters closed for the night, walk up to the examination table against the window; between the bed and the sink with its shelves of vials: the instruments, their blades shining under the filtered Moon, on the white wood table.

Does he flip the girls, and the women who lie naked on the gray leather against which their breasts roll and press up?

With their back against the leather, what hand, what finger, what heart does he use to probe their *nature*?

My hair was flattened against my forehead as I walked

down the stairs. The silence of this haunted office is so material that I don't dare jerk my head and flip it back against my skull: he would see it, he would still hear it in the morning.

My hand grazes the row of instruments: which one should I use to slice into the carcass, which has been rid of its flies for the night? Shall I take the newest one, or, among the most ancient, the one that he no longer uses? My member presses up against the encrusted fabric of my jizz cloth: where shall I carve the bitch? It would tell me.

Where they are serviced, mounted by dogs? I should cover my cloth with that part, the hole against the head of my member.

If it were the carcass of a male dog, could I lay the part with testicles flush against my own, wrapped tightly beneath the cloth?

The noise of the torrent would cover the sound of the incision; but would the incision let out a stronger, fresher stench, and make the dog tussle with me over the gash?

Vermin circulates, jumps, gnaws at that skin, dotted with gray tufts, like it does in the back-end of my deep, where acts are accomplished that I don't yet know: are human bodies transformed into the bodies of beasts?

Exit the office, scalpel flat against paper under cloth, what is missing from my equipment? Climb the circular staircase, the two flights of stairs up to my room, and there, finally, extract the tampon from my pocket; but in the ferry, I wrapped it in an oily cloth, cut from a sailor's ragged clothes; if necessary, I will slide the tampon inside my jizz cloth and the rag against the scrap of carcass skin.

But why would I put the scrap of the animal carcass under the torn shred of the human rag transformed into a scourer for my mechanics? What should the correct order be?

If I warmed it, would the three-night-old tampon still make blood?

And she, a girl from out of Time, of whom, for the last three days, I've avoided washing the finger that oh-so-slightly entered her *nature*, does she take part in this desire?

Can I get her to drag herself, rub her fabric against the gravel of the embankment, her young hair undone beside the fur of the vermin-ridden bitch, roll her hips, her haunches, inside, full of a luminous flesh, along this carcass emptied of its entrails?

As her endless smile narrows her eyes into slits beside the dead-eyed muffle of the rotting bitch, its jaw racked by vermin?

A case of lipstick shines in the dust, among what the dog had dragged up: to rush headlong into desire, I must reinforce the color red, perfume, active parts, and *charms*; since these should not be used by boys, it's as a quasi-girl that I must seduce, and push through my deep with some chance of being seen and desired there; the high heels from the dumpster downstairs could have done the trick; and, now, I have that red which the dog is rolling around with his jaw at the base of the Great dumpster.

If I pick it up, the dust and sanies will rise to my arms and face, and cover them: turning against the wall, leaning against the heat that lingers there, will I be able to slather my lips against the dirt as one, and bring red back onto my mouth, between two rough embraces on the ground?

But I need writing, quick, before a single smell of breeze from the new water of the torrent tips my member, now at its maximum, and forces it to discharge, and bring part of this urgent desire down with it!

With the lapping of the dog—what liquid is that at the center of the trash?—I hear the swish of sperm discharged into the jizz cloth.

The greatest possible amount of writing must be done before that sound, which echoes in my deep from front to back.

On the opposite river bank, in the row of yews bordering our garden, cats and owls spy on each other.

Farther away, higher, in the tall cedar, what sleepless eastern birds prepared their songs, and their enigmas, long ago?

Beyond the city center, from the narrowing of the *Nationale*, the sputter of heavy voices: are the two drunks dragging themselves along the asphalt? If a truck thundered through, its cab at the level of the bedrooms where couples, young and old, are fighting in their nightclothes, would its headlights shine on their red faces? Wouldn't its tires crush their parodies of love songs?

The impact of a wooden leg on the sidewalk in front of city hall: a volunteer at seventeen, his leg swept away at Verdun, he walks his insomnia.

I smooth my member, unsheathed from its cloth, from bottom to top with my fist: make it firmly erect, and return to the center of town to risk its rectitude and firmness, its head gleaming, in that space that will be filled with bodies, work, hands, and voices, with the arrival of dawn?

But writing is stronger than life: I press the member back under the jizz cloth, bend it, submit it to writing; and I beat off with it bent, its head under the cloth touching the testicles; juice must also be bent to circulate.

The page is already a third full; some gallicized English, story and dialogue, English from up there, slow and melodious, phonetized into heartbeats, which I try to appease by matching them to the slower beats of the torrent; the writing of this desire, of this scene, cannot be done in the language taught at school: seduction, prostitutional appeal, the usage of the prostitutional body by the free body; why write, and sound, these prohibited acts in that model language that removes sound from the written?

The more sound fills this calling—how can I write the language of pleasure fulfilled, if desire disappears with pleasure, and with it, language?—the more bodies congregate, and the more the text can do without the member—whose strength I must keep for later: the night will have to be filled.

But as the quarter-hour rings on the nearby bell tower, to my right beyond the *Nationale*, rushing footsteps under the cement covered-market: maybe a father from the working-class suburb of Leygat, whose wife "is coming into the pains of childbirth," and who is rushing to fetch my father?

Let him cross the *Nationale*, run to the front door, ring the doorbell below the metal plaque.

Lights go on behind my parents' shutters, at the level of the head of Christ crowned with thorns; the dogs scatter, leaving the carcass on the ground: is animal hunger less furious than human desire? I stay put: the rise of desire, and the swell of its writing can't be interrupted; a ray of light—maybe my mother passing in front of the lamp, and flipping on another, stronger lamp—reaches my face, thick with a bad sweat from beating off: what could I write that would be more *orgiastic*, more sacrilegious, while that light, which comes to me through her, unveils my face, and the effort, so apparent on it, of a will that is condemned by all?

In the time it will take my father to dress, to reach his office downstairs, to pack his case with all its necessary instruments, to meet the man waiting for him below, his cap wrung by hands used to working with leather or lime, I'll have written what should allow me to believe in myself—since I've overstepped the bounds, by a few lines at least, but through what mental operation, what upheaval of the heart!—and to confront him, if ever he were to catch me at it.

I write, I beat off—but all I milk is desire, and certainly not juice.

I hear the small car, which we use to drive around town and the close suburbs, start in the courtyard, drive under the arch, and catch on the small gravel of the courtyard; I hear the front door open before the man, close behind him; I hear the pause before the rounded mound of the road, and then I see it: since the man will be on my father's right, he will have to look up the incline to check on downward traffic, toward the embankment where I'm sprawling, half-naked; what if a vehicle ran over my outstretched legs, would I feel it crush them?

Will he see me? Will he recognize me? "Doctor, is that your boy next to the dumpster?"

But my father, uncertain, will also look that way.

What shadow could I project from the wall to hide myself from him? What could I use of myself to make it?

What I write, my spirit and heart that darken as I retreat from the human community?

I should at least pull my face away from the light shining down from the bedroom; but won't my mother turn it off, and go back to bed?

Or should I drag myself, with my legs folded under me, behind the largest tuft of urine-drenched wild grass?

Call the dogs back, so they can rise, with their shadows, before me, between him and me?

The sky is pure, and the Moon is full and pure: should I command the clouds?

Would I confront him better if I were standing up, my member erect out of the cloth, rather than sprawled out with juice already lapping in the fabric?

In intact, or in diminished desire?

Sprawled out to calm my heart, or standing, with my heart threatening to break?

Two trucks cross paths on the mound of the road, their tires in the melted tar: what arms, what hands drive, pull, and push the brakes: add this to the writing, quick!

Once the smoke from their exhaust has dissipated, the car moves onto the mound: where have I gotten with my world, with its members, its wads, its cloth, its wine and shadows?

Whose turn is it to speak, to be exposed, to push his or her pelvis forward, with his *parts* or her *nature* wrapped tightly in rags?

Has the child there, at the foot of the great slope of black pines, emerged from his mother's stomach, whose pink veers to red?

Later, when it grows into an adolescent girl or boy—but will I then be done with this writing?—what price will it fetch?

The car slows down in the alley, along the covered-market where tomorrow's stalls have been set up.

With the car now farther in the suburbs, I hear the swifts beating against the angles of the cement quadrilateral.

In the deep, hunted adolescents beat their *parts* and *natures* against the angles where women and men have cornered them.

But aren't their rags and tattered clothes now the skin of dead bitches, and women and men now wait outside, like dogs, to fulfill their desire there? Juice no longer laps inside rags made of cotton or wool, but inside shreds of the ventral or rectal skin of bitches; it's from that skin that the Great gray Woman cuts the jizz cloth—fur inside or out?—that the adolescent girl, or boy will slip over her *nature*, his *parts*, once they have been seduced, captured, forced, sold, once the shirt they wore during their capture has been stripped of its fibers; the adolescent boy or girl will keep it, on their flowering, ripening, souring body, till their death.

The pure flesh is so close, up there, out of which a newborn comes in these early years of the War, and I, now below, an impure body whose desire is to be clothed in animals rot!

Gravel squeaks under my ass, one third of the page is written in a pencil, found—for this use—in a Paris gutter, chewed by unknown teeth: the pages, already scribbled on, and soiled by food scraps, I pulled from a public dump—a devilish fire was burning there!—beautiful paper and new pencils are for poetry and painting.

To match the maximum of the scene—necessarily voice, and dialogue—to the maximum of the member's erection in the cloth, should I wait for my father, back from the delivery, to enter the paved alley, and for his car lights to sweep across the curved back of the *Nationale* and light up the top of the pharmacy, at the foot of which I lie, and for the car, as it drives down from the mound onto the square, to swing in: then, running the risk of having the headlights flash against the bottom, and shine on me, simultaneously eject from my throat and on the paper the most lustful exclamation, and the thickest, hottest clots of cum into the cloth, and as the filament runs through the conduit, have the adolescent girl or boy answer to the man or woman who wants some!

And if the headlights, even as low beams, light up the lover's bench, the base of the Great Crucifix, the Great dumpster and the bitch's carcass, and me, as I lie legs retracted by the spasms, the text will discover by itself the words that I am missing for the *absoluteness* of the sacrilege, and pleasure; and if, once he's parked his car on the square, he climbs out and comes to me, his face white with horror and fury, I will continue, sperm dripping through the fabric over my ass, to make my figures speak, and it will be from procuress to procured, and I myself, their hand clasping my shoulder, will pass from one whorehouse to another, in a beautiful sound of wads of cash!

But once the brunt of my want is satisfied, I must exhaust all its subterranean passages, and have it come back with increased strength: retrace the description of the place and gestures in the text, and even better, return to the origins of the enslaved figures, to their ancestry, their parents' living quarters, describe the movements of maternal protection—and maybe make them speak—and of the father's warnings against the dangers the child faces in the street; describe how seducers and seductresses pluck the adolescents, girls or boys, in their first flowering, their first lover's torment; how the procuresses receive them, clothes already in tatters, skins, members, and voices vibrating, and milk them of their first insult, their first juice.

And so, up to seven times, till the last session, and the last spasm, with the last word irradiating my entire body up to my hair that stands on end against the wall.

Quick, what can I do to stop my body from cooling as I crash, and to stop my mind and heart from dampening into depression?

Who, what can raise the shadow of want in me? Where, what can I rub? What text can I trace on the wall? On the cement of the dumpster? On the empty stomach of the bitch's carcass? On the stomach of the dog standing upright with the length of its back and legs against the trash?

What can I use to trace my price on my neck?

My rate on my chest? The chalk of the butcher's blackboard? From my exposure, ass leaning against the dumpster, can I cull enough to re-expose one of my enslaved figures on the page: from a dog barking far off in the suburbs, and my answer as I stand by the dumpster near the horny, rummaging dogs, can I make the enslaved girl or boy on the page answer the procuress who is on the lookout for choice bodies?

Make a couple of apprentices appear on the bench, she, working at the ribbon factory, he, at the tannery, he, in workers overalls and bare-chested, she, already in a short dress, chains and medals at their necks, interlacing and clanking as they kiss; is the girl leading, as they say of bitches in heat leading males? Is he a "cummer," as they call those who deposit their seed whenever they want, and where she wants? Or have they known each other since childhood, here, under the droplets of the blood of Christ?

If I beat off again, I'll bleed.

Separate those two heads, one blond, the other brown-haired, have them taken to two opposed procuresses, curb their neck and backs, break their ties: draw out from them the

peasant dialect of their ancestry, pervert it through the *show* of
bare bodies; sold, they will themselves milk and pervert the
language of the factory and of the tannery for the brothel.

The member comes back to life, bucks up in the cloth: is it
enough to re-suscitate the need to write that language?

I ingurgitate, I repress what would make it rise into my
throat, but how can I erase the premises from my mind in this
warm night, and in the stench of trash and its dogs? The two
drunks over there are real, living beings: creatures of the deep;
their hands and lips touch, their feet walk, their nostrils smell,
their throats speak, their ears hear, their eyes see, their heart
still desires, their mind still calculates.

But how can I attract them to the Great Crucifix, to the
Great dumpster, and would their racket make the lights turn
on, and the windows open?

I rub my tightly wound *parts* once more against the cement
frame; almost naked, I walk through the light of the street-
lamp, across the paved passageway, and the square, cross under
the large chestnut tree with its population of normal birds,
and follow the shops until I reach the small dumpster built
into the base of the alley; there they are, lying on their sides
around the mouth of the gutter; bare-chested and red, head
and stomach, from the day's Sun.

I turn my head away: how, what can I use to hide my face?
If they recognize me, my father will pay the price of my
debauchery.

My hair is long and thick enough to cover my face, black enough to hide my features, and that's most often how my enslaved figures expose themselves and let themselves be hounded.

If I could wrap my eyes with a woman's pantyhose pulled from the dumpster, part of my identity would be hidden, and maybe they'd want to play some kind of blind man's bluff? Would they get up and chase me through the sloping alley, or across the narrowing of the *Nationale*, under porches, in the recesses of the houses?

Would they touch me, on the shoulder, the hips, the chest, without grabbing? But if one of them touches my erect *sex* in the cloth, he'll grab it in his wine-stained hand, and will pull me to his raging body.

But all they're looking at, forehead to forehead, is the gutter through the grate.

How can I use my newly-hardened member, to attract men?

With one of the drunk's gray hair, I turn him into a woman.

The wound on my shoulder aches, as do my eyes.

Two procuresses who'd wager me on a roll of the dice?

Should I pull out my thickened member from the cloth, to raise my price, pulling them from their game?

From a red breast, which one drunk's prone position crushes against the other, I transform the other drunk into a buyer, a mistress of the deep.

Now that my member is out, with its filaments, should I churn, and smooth it before their liquid eyes?

But they must continue being the women I've made them into: I must stare, at them, at their red heaving breasts as they ingurgitate their wine, the bottle shining between their tanned faces on the thick pavement strewn with trash that the dogs are pulling from the dumpster.

If they go back to being men, how can they use this member, which I hold inside my fist, with the testicles out as well, dangling against the slimy cloth?

What would a man want from a boy?

I hear the tiny sound of suction and dejection of thinking in their brain, while they scratch its box.

Are these men, these women, calculating a price, a rate? What can a man do with me, whether drunk or not, as I advance, still in full public light, my member free, that thick member now over their flanks, its shadow advancing above them?

But I feel the writing rising in my chest, and I must go back there, at the bottom of the wall, in front of the Great dumpster, under the closed shutters of the bedroom where I was born, and under the Great Crucifix—its shadow tracing a path to follow—to write on the white checkered space left on the paper; from what I'll write there, my member rises high enough to hit against my stomach.

I walk along the traces of my bare feet, where the sweat of fever settled. A vehicle, up where the black streak of the *Nationale* disappears, is shining its brights against the entrance and the long wall of the primary school, the Brothers of the

Christian Schools, which I entered after the war, already knowing how to read, to write, and count.

Leaning back against the wall, my legs spread wide again, I place my member back inside the cloth, but, since I've unlaced it slightly on the side, the member points up, straight.

The dogs now have heavy paunches; a vehicle ran over the carcass, flattening it.

From the grunting of the drunks as my member advanced above them, I must reclaim the voices of the deep in my throat and hands.

I banish the entrance and the wall up there from my gaze; I shut out from my heart that late, rainy afternoon in early autumn 1947, when, after the chaotic rush out of math class, the Older children re-organize themselves around me—I am three, four, five years younger—grab me, lift me, and throw me into the large paper container.

Three of them, the hardiest among them, step over the container, rub me with paper, stuff me under: tall V. and tall G., their red mouths at each of my ears, in husky voices: "The prettiest common denominator…!" The sentence, carried by their breath, crosses through my brain while their members come out of their unbuttoned shorts, and they beat-off.

They ejaculate on me, as they kneel at the back of the container, their bare fists holding my stomach down against the floor; I get up from under the paper, and the three of them, bite their forearms: a hot substance rolls along my bare flank; I bite farther down, near the wrist: what makes the firm, soft flesh so salty? What makes my *bubuze*—as we call the tube for piss—rise against my thigh? My tongue—my teeth clenching on the wrist—licks V.'s skin: is that wrist now beating off, or is it holding down my bare shoulder?

Through the torn, crumpled papers, I see the gray light penetrated now with flashes of lighting: where am I? The high edge of the container blocks out our long slope of black pine, and, against it, the gray church from which no sound comes.

Where are our friends? Their black shirts with red piping, their gray shirts with no piping?

Because I lick between bites, tall V. ejaculates again; but what is tall G.'s hand doing on my thigh where my *bubuze* has risen?

Has a new member been born to me? Simply through my will?

Will they slip their member into this one, as it grows, to ejaculate again?

I don't see their member, but from where else could their substance seep?

And what if it came out of mine as well? Their hands turn into fists on my hips; they push them and flip me over. Tall G.'s other fist grabs by member so hard I'm scared he'll tear it off: along with the little testicles?

What would be left of me, once their desire, and their hunger was satisfied?

Will I have to live disabled, mutilated, reduced to my mind, and heart?

V.'s fist grows slack, while G.'s sinks into my hips, that have been flipped around; my right hand is already on my mouth to defend it; where should I put my left?

Under my palm, I spit out the saltiness from V.'s wrist.

Under the crumpled paper, where splashes of substance drink the ink of algebra formulas, my eyes grow rimmed with black: the voices, even the crumpling of the paper reach me as if from very far away; who takes my free hand into both of theirs, and rubs it?

Am I now flipped on my stomach, and is my stomach being lifted up? What can I feel since everything is reaching me from so far?

I feel nothing of G.'s stomach lowering down over my buttocks, and rising up again, nothing of his member searching for *me* beneath his fists that spread my hips apart, all I feel is V.'s wrist shaking its bracelet toward G.'s stomach that he pushes back.

My face is now against the bottom of the container, I close my eyes: did I defend myself enough? And against what?

Perhaps what they are doing is a game, a right that Older children have over younger ones? The way we young ones take our rights over animals?

But what did I do for them to settle on me?

Do I have a taste, a smell that is attracting them?

Didn't I lick V.'s wrist, and feel the hardening of my little member as a surge of power?

Are they taking their revenge on me because they didn't understand *the smallest common denominator*, when I'm still struggling with *division*—since I always want things to be more difficult and mysterious than they are?

Is it because I am the *Doctor's son* that they grasp and defile the flesh of his flesh of he who brought them into this world?

Is my flesh socially superior because of that?

Do they degrade me under what they are, sons of workers—using, *abusing* me, the grandson, on my mother's side, of Nobles of the Robe—with their hands, their member, and their voice of future workers?

But does my guilt come from long before that? And is that what attracts them to me?

Should I hate or love them?

Who, above the bed of papers, will hear me die?

At the top of my body that shakes with G.'s rocking back and forth, hot substance, fragrant, bursts on the nape of my neck: a yoke they've placed around my shoulders.

The dog, the head of the pack, standing on his hind legs against the dumpster and tossing his paunch against it, turns his muzzle to me, looks at me: have I *advanced*, since my assault in the container? Shouldn't I throw myself in the dumpster? Soiled with all its festering, should I wait, entice the customer, as the tall gray woman stands on the corner, the top of her body leaning toward the clientele, her long black pocketbook at her flank?

Is this member, swelling at the thought of that "infamy," connected to my heart, and to my mind? Is it linked to them? If so, what kind of monster am I, even if it's weak?

But the hand traces and fills the rest of the page.

Before these dogs, and this trash, am I the Saül of my poem that is unfinished but readable by all?

Quick, I must turn the page, and begin to fill the other one, before two, three new spurts bring me back to ordinary morality!

Does Job not cry out against his God, ass in the trash? It would be better for God to see me in my desire for the forbidden, rather than have him turn away from me when I crash!

For His gaze to stay on me, His son, brother of He who guarantees my salvation from up there, should I draw out the thought of infamy, and the writing that perpetuates it?

With some desire and juice still in my member, some want for words still in my throat and hand, I stand up: I'll exhaust the rest up there.

Climbing the stairs, as my member palpitates near a last discharge, in the slimy fabric, I wonder why this divine filiation, still! I am my own creation: I must accept all of myself; it's from my own desire, from the desire that I've created for myself that I pull what needs to be transformed into the power that terrifies and tortures my double.

Strong is how I must accept myself, not compliant: strength is always scandalous.

Saül, Job, and so many others, prophets, artists, each is tormented by an unprecedented Destiny—madness, sanctity, oeuvre.

Up there, in the bedroom, with my sleeping brother flipping over on the sheet, and smiling, I reach into my bag, at the foot of the bed, open the outside pocket, pull out the rag ball, open it on my desk; the tampon is there with its blackened streak of blood and its red margins, open under the ray of Moonlight from the transom open to the southern sky, which the east now colors with pink.

In the cloth, what runoff seeps from my member without an orgasm?

Under my fingers: blood.

Is this punishment—for nine ejaculations, by my own hand, and with the sole desire for a world that only exists through words?

But, since I still have some desire, enough for a third of a sheet of paper, two, three acute ejaculations, where is the punishment?

And even after I crash, will I feel at fault: no? But to turn the Creator's gaze away from me, yes.

But for Him, the Creator of all and of death that conflates all, human, beast, freshness and rot, beauty and filth, Good and Evil, what is this desire for filth within me, for the human through the beast, freedom through enslavement?

I must raise myself to that level: think as He does.

Over time, could I die from the blood running on my palm? Can I stop it with a new erection, and a new ejaculation, but I mustn't: I must keep what's left for the day, for tomorrow night, when I will return to the street, with accrued desire, and this time, do more.

How much more *charming* would I be, more considerate and joyful during the day, if I were full of renewable desire and juice!

A slight breeze, before the Sunrise, through the open transom, pushes the tampon onto the pages that I've pulled, cum-caked, from the cloth. The girl's odor rises to my nostrils, lights up my heart and lungs.

Could I have pulled this bloody compress from my body? And from what *nature*, at the root of my member, under my shameful parts?

To be the girl is more than to love and desire her: to be possessed is more than to possess: one blood already circulates and warms the one body that we are.

The blood that rose up to my member, instead of seed, was accidental blood; I need willed blood.

With my unsoiled hand, the one that writes, I rummage through the backpack which I've pulled along the tiles to the desk, take out the razor and the pack of blades my father gave me at the beginning of summer, and which I've never used; I set them on the page next to the tampon, I must be quick: I unscrew the head, take out the blade, and place the back of my wrist on the open tampon; tightening my fist as I've seen my father's patients do, I slash a vein, from the hairless side, blue in the pink light; blood swells and gushes, red—like wanted blood, extracted from an enemy—over the trace of darkened blood, and spreads on the red margins.

The blood on my member's head has tarried. On my wrist, should I stanch it or let it flow? And even if I stanched it, would it continue to flow, and my heart to drain?

Should I take the stairs, go down to my father's office, and look for something to cauterize it with, to close the vein?

Desire returns into my member, at the center of my body that vibrates in the pink air.

Is it from the blood pact with my double, between my two natures?

Is it from the empty two-thirds of the page, its whiteness in the Sun blinding my eyes, which become ringed again with black?

Will I have the strength to walk, to lie down on the bed, and wait, tampon at my wrist, for the transformation?

I dictated this text to my friend, the painter Aïda Kébadian, five mornings a week, from March to September 2009. I thank her for her silence and her patience.

Pierre Guyotat (born in 1940) has been a source of French literary scandal since the 1967 publication of *Tomb for 500,000 Soldiers*. The French government banned his novel *Eden Eden Eden* from being publicized, advertised on posters, or sold to anyone under the age of 18 from the time of its publication in 1970 until 1981.

204